Salera's Storm
AT THE THRESHOLD OF DARKNESS

J.R. Marro

COPYRIGHT

This is a work of fiction. Any resemblance to any person, living or dead, place, or thing, including names, organizations, events, and locales is completely coincidental. This work is not intended to offend but only to entertain and although some of the content is gross by my standards, I wrote it anyway because that's what the characters demanded. A good story shouldn't be based on how much blood is spilled but how much it keeps you wanting more. With that said, let's begin.

Acknowledgements

I'd like to first thank my family for their encouragement and support to go on even when I wanted to stop. A special mention goes to my precious grandchildren who loved everything I wrote even when it stunk.

I would like to also thank all those individuals at the United States Geological Survey: Gertrude, Brian, David, and Marie. They were patient, kind and answered all my questions without making me feel stupid.

An important thank you goes to the people who invented the internet. Words cannot express my gratitude. I humbly bow to them.

Last but definitely not least, a very huge thanks goes to my editor, Summer, who practically whipped the words out of me. Her continued support and toughness are what kept me going and I can't thank her enough.

J.R. Marro

*"Something of vengeance I had tasted for the first time;
as aromatic wine it seemed, on swallowing,
warm and racy: its after flavor, metallic and corroding,
gave me a sensation as if I had been
poisoned."*

Quote from Charlotte Bronte, 1847

TABLE OF CONTENTS

Copyright
Acknowledgements
Quote from Charlotte Bronte
Prologue

PROLOGUE

"How many aboard?" asked Captain Haron.

"There are a total of six," said Lieutenant Ruce, his pure white skin, fanged teeth and with a crown of sharp spikes on his head made the Teven-human a fearful sight. "Shall I order the Envil to power down their weapons?"

"Negative," said Haron. "It's just Awler and his friends trying to let off steam again. Just make sure we're out of his scanner range."

Haron carefully studied the small vessel on the screen. Awler was in a Messer-craft, the kind put together with leftover junk. Every imaginable color spotted the hand-made ship. Life was hard on the poorer planets, especially on Wecton B, where these kids were from. However, the Ripton and its crew had been assigned by the Federation to monitor this quadrant of the galaxy and Awler was at it again. The kid never gave up.

Another beam vaporized an asteroid. The vessel had only enough power to blast small asteroids lingering outside the field, so no major damage could be done. However, teroid blasting was forbidden under Federation law and for good reason; over sixty million lives were at stake on Aven III, the only populated world within the five-planet star system. Aven's blue-green waters and patches of green and brown land were beautiful, but the Aven-humans were primitive when it came to technology. They had no idea their small planet and two moons were surrounded by an asteroid field so thick it took days to maneuver through it. Unfortunately, Awler had ignored the previous six warnings, so now a short stay in a Federation jail was in order. He sighed. There was no choice.

"Let them have their fun for a little while then we'll bust them," said Haron. "Just watch for drifting asteroids."

"Aye, sir," said Ruce, adjusting the controls in front of him.

Haron sat back and rubbed his chin, feeling his long canines. He wondered if his green skin and three eyes were just as intimidating as Ruce's spikes.

Nah, he thought to himself.

"Captain," said Ruce, "I'm detecting an unknown ore within an asteroid close to the Envil."

"Is it volatile?" asked Haron.

"I do not know, sir," replied Ruce. "I've never seen properties like this. There is approximately six ounces of pebble size stones. It's located in the center of a half-mile asteroid."

"What's the proximity to Awler's ship?" asked Haron.

"It is coming within the Envil's firing range."

"Inform base we're taking the Envil," said Haron.

"Aye, sir."

"Ahead slow," said Haron. "Prepare to send out a probe. I want to know what that stuff is."

"Aye, captain."

Haron felt the ship move forward. "What's our ETA?"

"Fifteen min—Sir! They've fired on the asteroid."

The asteroid exploded with an enormous flash of light. The screen turned white and Haron grunted, covering his eyes to the blinding light. When he opened them, speeding their way was a giant bubbling cloud of fire and gas.

"Shields!" he shouted.

The wave hit the ship with a loud boom, sending it tumbling. Haron and his crew were thrown to the floor. Sparks and mini-fires burst throughout the bridge as the vessel rumbled and shook. Breathing was arduous as the pressure on his chest was squeezing the air from his lungs. Haron glanced at the screen. The stars were streams of light. They were speeding through the cosmos. Loud creaks and groans resonated throughout the ship.

"We are in a spin!" shouted Ruce, who was already on his knees working the controls.

"Steady her!" shouted Haron, gripping the leg of his seat to keep himself from rolling. They had to get control or the Ripton would be torn apart.

"Aye, sir!"

The vessel gradually leveled off, but they were still moving backwards at a tremendous rate.

"What's our speed?" yelled Haron, struggling to breathe from the crushing force.

"I cannot read it," shouted Ruce. "The instruments are faltering."

Within moments, the ship slowed down and grumbled to a stop. Haron strained to pull himself into the seat. "Damage report," he said, coughing from the smoke.

"Levels ten through thirteen have minimal damage," said Ruce. "Forty-six have been injured and no deaths have been reported. All weapons and engines are fully capable."

"Take us to those kids," he said.

"Aye, sir," said Ruce. "ETA is twenty minutes."

"What? Why so long?"

"The explosion pushed us over a light year away, captain."

Haron sat up, shocked. "Are you sure? Nothing has that kind of power."

"Yes, sir," said Ruce.

*If it pushed us that far away...*Haron's breath caught in his chest. "Find those kids. Warp three."

As they approached the area, the center of the screen displayed a white gaseous ball.

"What is that?" asked Haron, staring.

"That is our destination," said Ruce.

Instantly the screen switched to where the Envil lay. Nothing was there. The thick asteroid field was gone.

"What you see are the remains of the young ones, the asteroid field, and the five-planet star system," said Ruce, his eyes studying the data before him. He turned to Haron. "Captain, they have all been vaporized and there are no survivors."

Haron felt his muscles go limp as he stared at the screen.

"How?" he asked in disbelief. "It was only six ounces."

CHAPTER 1
Kalin

Intergalactic starship: the *Quasar*
Location: Orbiting Nisor II in the Titan Galaxy

"No life at all?" asked Kalin.

"No, captain," answered Marante, his First Officer. "All communications with Nisor II stopped three hours after the discovery of the alien mechanism."

Kalin squirmed in the captain's chair, his stare anxiously fixed on the forty-by-sixty-foot, three-dimensional wall screen. The blue and green planet was perfect for sustaining human life, *so where are the colonists?* he thought. *Who or what could take out five hundred people and leave nothing behind?* He recalled the mission to Cetion 4, the remote planet near the galactic axis. An uncomfortable feeling rose up within him. *Are these creatures also invisible? Undetectable by scans?* He hoped not. The Uly creatures had slaughtered ten men, setting their bodies on fire with just a touch. He and Marante had barely made it out alive. "Are there any signs of a battle?"

Marante waved his hand through a three-dimensional hologram emitting from a yellow recessed orb.

"No, sir," he replied, his clipped accent smooth and eloquent. "All their ships are intact. There are no bodily remains. I cannot detect any traces of Ondor-human blood. It is as if they were never there."

Kalin ran his fingers through his thick black hair. It was happening again. Something inside telling him not to teleport to the surface, but what choice did he have? The continuous Ancis signal had stopped three days ago, a sure sign of an enemy attack. The Federation was concerned.

"Inform Baskka and Muab we're going down," he said.

Marante swiveled in his seat. He was considered handsome by Chaslean-human standards. Skin-tight black tunic and pants covered his boney angular frame and along with his oversized round head, he looked like a giant popsicle. Taking up most of his face were almond-shaped eyes pointing inward to a coin-sized nose, which at present was white and marble-size.

"Perhaps a probe would be more suitable?" said Marante. "We could monitor its findings from here."

Marante was a scientist at heart and frowned on dangerous assignments. However, in over four hundred years he had never let fear stop him from going on the missions Kalin accepted from the Galactic Federation. Of course, being on the *Quasar*, the largest and most advanced ship in the fifteen explored galaxies, helped.

"No," Kalin replied. "I'm not going to rely on a probe to find out what happened to them. Let's go." He turned to the Chaslean helmsman. "Tolba, monitor us and ready the teleport in case of trouble."

"Aye, sir."

The four men stood in the center of the Market Square beside a dry fountain. A thick forest pressed against the Ondor village where only thin rays of sunlight peeked through the canvas of lush foliage, sprinkling the town with radiant pearls of light. Temporary homes made of a durable gray plastic called Solfrit, lined the streets stretching out in all directions.

Kalin caught sight of his reflection in an arched window. His Saleran bone structure made him tall and thick with muscle, a trait noticeable beneath his clothes: a black vest, long-sleeved white shirt and tight stretch black pants. There was a loud snap of a branch and he swung his Barra around, ready to fire. Keeping the black rifle aimed down a side street, he noticed hundreds of green and red vines had spread across the roadway. He glanced down all the streets. The vines covered the roads, even the alleys, and some had made their way up the walls and into the houses.

The strangeness increased his discomfort. A gentle breeze rustled the leaves and he felt his stomach knot up. Something was very wrong.

"I am not registering any life," said Marante, studying the small holo on the scanner. "Not even animal or insect. Only vegetation."

"It looks as if they've been gone for months," said Baskka, his red eyes glowing against the shimmer of his light green skin. "I'm sure the Preconts cleaned up the roads before allowing the colony to move in. So what gives?"

Muab was shaking his massive blue head, the four antennae on each of his ears waving side-to-side. "Evil here. Must hurry."

"I agree," said Kalin. "Keep alert and—"

Suddenly, the ground began to rumble and move. The men struggled to stay on their feet. Muab shouted something, but Kalin's attention was on Marante, who had a look of horror on his face. He followed Marante's gaze.

"Back up! Back up!" shouted Kalin, waving his arm.

On the other side of the fountain, an enormous black vine in the shape of a hand was creeping out of an open fissure. It pulsated as if breathing, and although the plant appeared to be eyeless, Kalin sensed they were being watched. Without warning, it rose into the air and slammed down on the fountain, smashing it to pieces.

"This is a new species," said Marante, studying the scanner. "There is no record of this life form. It—"

From within the crevice, a bellowing roar vibrated the air and the tentacle rose higher. It shrieked and vaulted towards them.

"Run!" yelled Kalin.

They dashed into a small nearby house, where a couch, a soft chair, and an overturned dining table were the only visible furniture. Stacked on both sides of a large window were blue boxes. Some had tumbled off and broken open, scattering long nails and screws on the Solfrit floor.

"Block the doorway!" shouted Kalin.

Muab grabbed the cushioned chair and flung it against the door.

"They come from under the ground," said Kalin. "Ready your Barras. Set to disintegrate." He was grateful their weapons could laser blast through six inches of solid steel.

Pounding and deep growls vibrated the metal door. Kalin's grip tightened around his Barra. The floor beneath them started to shake. A deep crack began splitting the ground.

"Jump!" shouted Kalin.

All leapt to safety, except Marante. Kalin could see the tips of his eight-inch fingers desperately trying to hold onto the loose dirt as he dangled in the crevasse. The snarls of angry monsters began echoing from within.

"Kalin!" shouted Marante.

Kalin jumped to his feet and ran, but he tripped on a box and fell face down. The growls were getting louder.

"Kalin, this is no time to be slow!" said Marante.

"Hang on! I'm coming!"

Ready to spring to his feet, he shifted his weight and felt the skin on his chest rip. His body quivered with excruciating pain. He lifted himself to his knees. Through his bloodied white shirt protruded the end of a hefty screw.

"They are coming!" said Marante. "You must hurry!"

The soft earth beneath Marante's fingers started crumbling. Kalin yanked out the two-inch bolt and dove with outstretched arms as the cliff gave way. Kalin hit the ground with a thud, sending up a cloud of dirt. The floating grit blocked his vision as both arms dangled over the ledge. To his relief, he felt Marante's fingers in his hand. After pulling him out, they both crawled behind the overturned dining table.

"I cannot believe you took so long," said Marante, making adjustments on the scanner. "Were you deliberately trying to give me a heart attack?"

"Actually, I wanted to see if your nose could get as big as your head." He glanced at Marante, whose nose instantly went from marble-size white with worry, to orange-size and angry red. "Almost."

"You are pathetic," said Marante. "Where are Baskka and Muab?"

"There." He nudged his head. "Behind the couch."

The whining sound of a fast-moving object was getting louder when suddenly another vine flew out of the chasm and lunged towards the men.

"Shoot it!" yelled Kalin.

Laser fire bombarded the creature. The vine flailed in the air, shrieking to the laser blasts tearing through its membrane.

"They feed off the nutrients of the planet, but they can be carnivorous," said Marante.

"Duh…I guess that's why there are no colonists."

Marante was always a scientist even in the face of the obvious.

"Your sarcasm is not appreciated," said Marante, juggling the scanner in one hand and firing his Barra with the other. "And why must you always get us into these predicaments?"

"Because you need to keep the blood moving in that big head of yours."

"Stop making fun of my head you oversized fur ball and—oh my!"

Out of the pit vaulted a creature standing over eleven feet tall. Protruding from its hip, the damaged vine was healing at a remarkable rate. The pitted dark green skin of the monster sparkled as it moved. Its slender body was hunched over as if straining to hold up its long arms and oversized hands. Curved spiked nails tipped each three-toed foot. One large red eye glared menacingly down at the men while its slightly elongated maw repeatedly opened and shut, exposing its serrated teeth in an obvious threat.

"What is it?" whispered Kalin, noticing an uneven bulge moving in its stomach.

"It is definitely not human," said Marante.

"Really? How did you figure that out?"

It quickly turned towards the table where it heard the sounds. A high-pitched squeal came from its mouth.

Kalin kept his aim as he slowly stood up. "Marante, set the scanner to translate."

Marante waved his hand over an orb and a strange gentle music began to play. It silenced the creature.

As Kalin spoke, his words became soft melodious tones. "We come in peace. Who are you?"

The voice of the beast was deep and scratchy. "Thuron. Invaders must die."

"The people that were here before us meant you no harm. If you had told them to leave, they would have. The colonists, where are they?"

"All dead!" roared the creature.

The Thuron grabbed the couch and flung it against the wall where it shattered. With lightning speed, its hands gripped the necks of Muab and Baskka and lifted them off the floor. Static bolts ripped through their bodies as the mended vine sent offshoots into their open crevices.

"Blast it!" yelled Kalin.

Muab and Baskka screamed, trying to loosen the creature's grip.

"There is a static shield surrounding the Thuron," said Marante. "It is deflecting all laser fire. Penetration is impossible."

Kalin shuddered at the morbid sounds of popping joints and cracking bones. The creature's teary eye was wide open as if in a trance. A steady flow of red drool streamed out from its gaping mouth. Kalin began pulling the trigger so fast the laser pulses became a stream of light. He had to save his men.

"They are dead, captain," said Marante, standing up. Kalin kept firing the Barra, unable to accept their deaths.

Marante put his hand on his shoulder. "They are gone, Kalin. It is over."

Kalin shivered with anger as he lowered his laser. *They were eaten alive.*

The creature dropped Muab and Baskka to the floor. Their hollow bodies lay flat. All their organs, muscles, and skeletal structures had been devoured. The beast quickly took their empty bodies and lifted a slice of skin over its stomach, then stuffed them in its pouch. Immediately, its stomach undulated to the added items. Kalin heard Marante's telepathy loud and clear.

It is digesting their remains.

The monster glared at Kalin and Marante and began moving towards them, claws ready and fangs snapping. The two backed up.

The window, Marante, thought Kalin.

Got it, answered Marante.

The two dove through the glass to the outside. They rolled on the ground, got to their feet, and began running. The crunching sound of the Thuron's spiked nails digging into the dirt was closing in. The vine latched onto Marante's arm and slammed him to the ground.

Kalin skidded to a halt and lifted a Norin Blade from his boot. Marante was on the ground, fighting off the shoots of vine trying to enter his body. Kalin leapt towards the vine, flipping in the air and slicing it in half as he came down on his feet. An ear-piercing shriek came from the creature as black liquid spurted out. The vine on Marante shriveled. Kalin rammed the knife into the monster's back. A gut-wrenching shrill vibrated the air and the creature fell dead.

"We must leave," said Marante, panting as he picked up the scanner. "There must be more."

"Yeah," said Kalin. A heavy wind began blowing through the trees. He tapped the small Comlink on his vest. "Tolba…."

Crackling sounds split the air as if it were electrically charged. Kalin felt the hair on his head rise.

"What's happening?" he asked.

"They have cut off communication with the *Quasar*."

The ground in front of them rumbled once again. Numerous fissures burst open and out leapt ten more of the same creatures.

"Run!" they yelled together.

They dashed into the forest. Kalin glanced back. The Thurons were shrewd and fast, spreading out as they took chase. Dark clouds formed in the sky, turning the day to night. The ground tremors intensified. A vicious wind howled through the trees, sending thick branches down, just missing them.

"They control the weather!" shouted Marante.

"I know! Watch out!"

A small tree dropped down into their path, then another, and another. They strained to leap over plant life deliberately falling in front of them. High-pitched screeches emanated from the violently shaking trees and bushes.

The plants are sentient, said Marante in Kalin's mind. *We may not make it through this, my friend.*

Suddenly, it was quiet. Everything was still. The creatures had disappeared. The sun was peeking through the fast-moving clouds. Kalin pulled Marante to a stop. Out of breath, they surveyed the area.

"Where are they?" he asked, suddenly aware of the thin air. It was getting harder to breathe. "The oxygen level is dropping."

Marante studied the scanner. "Yes, it is. I cannot find thei…we must go now!"

Five trees in front of them reshaped themselves into the creatures, along with five behind. Within moments, ten angry beasts surrounded them. One Thuron leapt into the air towards them. Kalin blasted the creature. The other Thurons charged, and the two men stood back to back in a shooting frenzy.

A beast latched onto Marante's neck. Kalin turned to fire when teleporter beams ignited and they were on the *Quasar*. The startled Thuron dropped Marante and froze. Kalin grabbed Marante's arm and quickly jumped off the teleporter deck.

Kalin shouted, "Tolba, return teleport, now!"

The Thuron disappeared in a flash of light. Without warning, the ship lurched, throwing them to the floor.

"Tolba, report!" yelled Kalin.

"An energy beam is emitting from the alien device, captain. We are being pulled into the atmosphere."

"Full reverse!" shouted Kalin. "We're on our way!"

The sounds of the powerful engines whining and scraping filled the ship. The vessel trembled and bucked, fighting to stay in space. Kalin and Marante stumbled down the hallways and into the lift.

"Bridge," said Kalin, clutching a wall bar.

The lift zoomed off sideways, lateral pale blue lights showing the passing facilities. The upward shift was barely felt. A loud boom sent them to the floor. The doors slid open and they leapt to their feet, staggering onto the bridge, grabbing anything that would steady them. Marante hurried to sit beside Tolba at the main controls.

"The creatures are part of the root stock of the planet," said Marante, carefully maneuvering the colorful holo in front of him. "This is a living world, captain. Every plant is alive, conscious of their surroundings and able to communicate with each other. This is the first discovery of its kind."

"What's the energy source of that device?" asked Kalin sitting forty feet from the large wall screen.

"It is one grain of Pril," said Marante. "How did these creatures know about Pril?"

"I don't know, but we have to stop this or we're all dead."

"Tolba, engage light speed at my command," said Kalin. "Marante, ready a Ronar Pulse and fire at my command. Three-two-one-fire!"

On screen, they watched a white pulse race down the middle of the energy beam. A large explosion erupted within the planet.

"Now, Tolba!"

Kalin was slammed back into the seat as the *Quasar* zoomed away. He sat straight, feeling his muscles tense up from anger inside him.

"The whole colony is gone!" shouted Kalin, bashing the armrests with his fists. "I lost two friends down there! Why weren't those things detected in the earlier scans?"

Marante worked the holo. "According to the original study of the planet, they searched twenty miles into the crust for any sign of life or volatile activity. However, the Thuron City is forty miles beneath the surface therefore they were not detected. I have scanned their city, and there is no human life. Baskka and Muab did not stand a chance, captain. The energy output that engulfed them was ten thousand times that of normal."

Kalin sat back and sighed. There was nothing worse than losing human lives, especially good friends, due to human error.

When is the Federation going to listen? he said to Marante in his mind. *I've told them many times to search deep down, right to the core of planets. Now a whole colony is gone and I've lost two friends.*

I agree, said Marante. *This catastrophe could have been avoided.*

It has to stop, said Kalin. *We're losing people to stupidity.*

Yes, I agree.

Kalin said aloud, "I'll speak to the families of Baskka and Muab personally."

He felt the sorrow of having to inform their wives and children who lived with them on the *Quasar*. He had to prepare himself for the onslaught of tears, something he was never ready for.

"Inform the Federation of the loss of the colony and recommend they put this star system under quarantine," he said. "We don't want the Thurons to have our technology so find the access codes to the Ancis device and set the village to self-destruct. Let's leave these beings to themselves."

"Aye, captain," said Marante, waving his hand through the holo where a twinkle of light appeared, then vanished. A small burst of fire appeared on the planet surface.

"Captain," said Tolba. "I have an incoming message from King Altor."

"Put it on screen," said Kalin, welcoming the change of subject.

The death of good friends was becoming a habit due to the Federation's idiocy. However, speaking with his father always ended in another argument and right now, he just wasn't in the mood. He'd have to cut him off again and take it in the Overview, which would anger his father even more.

The tall broad figure of a graying man appeared. His square chin and well-defined features gave him the look of authority. Although over three thousand years old, Altor still had the strength and appeal of a man much younger in age. Kalin just wished his own black hair wouldn't gray; only nine hundred years more and it would begin. He sighed.

That's way too soon, he thought.

"Ah, my son, finally," said Altor, his deep voice carrying throughout the bridge. "I've been trying to reach you for over a week. How are you?"

"I'm fine, thank you. Deep space is hard on communications. How's Mother? Disa?"

"They are fine. I wanted you here for the historic event, but alas, it has already started."

"What event?"

"Two days ago your cousin, Vorkis, began testing his new weather system. I wanted you to see it first-hand."

"What?" said Kalin, rising to his feet. "You allowed him free access to Salera's atmosphere? Dad, have you lost your mind? When are you going to believe me about Vorkis? He's dangerous. You should banish him from the planet like you did Vurro."

"Vurro tried to steal information from our data banks and we caught him, however, Vorkis has always shown the proper respect."

"I've told you many times, Vorkis has left the planet repeatedly. His reputation on the outside is not good."

"Nonsense, I will never believe the accusations. Vorkis is family, and besides, he has never lied to me."

"And I have?" asked Kalin, recalling his anger over previous conversations. "Just because I chose a different path doesn't make me the enemy. You're allowing an evil man to use Saleran technolo—"

Altor raised his hand. "Enough! Just come and see his greatness. You will be impressed."

"Yeah, I'm coming," said Kalin. "Somebody has to watch over him because you're not."

"We look forward to your arrival," said Altor. "End transmission."

Kalin dropped down into his seat not believing what just happened. How could his father have done this? Altor trusted Vorkis more than his own son. Although they were the same age, of the same blood, Vorkis was Kalin's opposite, a power-hungry liar and a thief, which Kalin had yet to prove. As a teenager, Vorkis had formed a secret gang that repeatedly stole from Salera's citizens, selling the items to outsiders for a profit. When Kalin told Altor about it, he refused to believe his nephew would do such a thing and dismissed the idea. Therefore, Kalin took it upon himself to punish Vorkis, accusing him in public several times, besting him in fights, and each time calling him a coward knowing how much it angered him. Vorkis had long ago sworn to kill him. And now Altor had simply handed him all life on Salera.

Vorkis has long been working on your father's trust, said Marante in his mind. *I fear something dreadful is going to happen.*

"Set a course for Salera," said Kalin. "Warp 12."

Kalin stood on the balcony of the Krystal Palace overlooking the City of Light, home to thirty million, and the capital of his home world, Salera. The light of the three suns sparkled against the colorful odd-shaped buildings spread across the city, where giant Gebin Trees shadowed the streets and homes with their red, yellow and blue foliage. To his right was the Great Hall of Knowledge with the tops of its forty towering buildings passing the clouds, some rising thirty miles into the atmosphere. There was no doubt in his mind: He was proud of Salera and his people.

He tugged at his collar. The gem-encrusted white tunic fit but it was heavy and tight around the neck. The mirror in the *Quasar* had reflected a tall, broad, snobby-looking guy with a red sash and gold sword. He hated royal attire. Give him everyday normal clothes and he was happy. Royal life was irritating at times and there was nothing he could do to change it.

"Kalin!" shouted a mousy voice.

He turned just in time to catch Disa who jumped into his arms.

"My beautiful little princess!" he said, squeezing her tight.

Her long black hair, rosy cheeks, and bright blue eyes made her the most beautiful four-year-old Kalin had ever seen. His father, King Altor, was standing behind her with a smile.

"Daddy, this is my time with Kalin," said Disa. "Your time is later." She began hugging and kissing Kalin.

"Did you hear her?" said Altor. "I get more respect from Offi the dog."

"What can I say?" said Kalin. "She loves me." He turned to Disa. "Booger kiss."

Disa giggled and rubbed noses with him.

"I brought you something," he said, putting her down and sensing her excitement over the gift. He pulled from his black pants pocket a gold locket on a chain and slipped it over Disa's head. "Open it," he said, squatting beside her.

When Disa opened the pendant, a three-dimensional hologram of Kalin rose up from its center. The vibrant image said, "Hi, Disa. I had this made for you so you'll always remember how much I love you." Disa's smile could not have been any wider.

Altor crouched down, studying the locket. "It is magnificent," he said. "The holo is perfect in every dimension. What's the energy source?"

"Marante and I rescued the daughter of King Renar of Kern," said Kalin. "He was so grateful he offered to make me this locket. The sliver of Pril taken from a grain will power the locket for at least a thousand years."

"He truly was grateful," said Altor, standing up. "Only a handful of civilizations have been honored with a few grains for study, yet Renar wasted a precious slice on something so trivial. How foolish."

"It's not foolish, Daddy," said Disa with an attitude. "It's mine and it's beautiful."

"Yes, of course," said Altor, smiling as he patted her head. "My apologies. Now I must discuss something with your brother. Can you spare the time from him? It is very important and after all, I am King."

"Okay," said Disa. "But you be nice to him."

"I'm always nice to my son," said Altor solemnly as Disa skipped away.

"No, you're not," she said from the steps where she sat, her back to them. "And don't make fun of Offi."

"She is showing signs of rebelliousness like you," said Altor. "But alas, she is the light of my heart."

Kalin smiled. "Mine too. Now why in the world did you allow Vorkis to tamper with our atmosphere?"

"Because this will allow us to control the weather, a remarkable achievement that I am most proud of."

"Dad, I know for a fact the Federation has assigned him to search for more Pril and...."

There was a tug on Kalin's leg.

"Kalin, help me!" cried Disa.

Disa's skin was cracking open, blood was oozing from the open cuts. He caught her before she hit the floor. Altor doubled over with a deep groan and fell. His eyes rolled back in his head and he began convulsing. He looked back at Disa, her bright blue eyes were now blood red. White foam bubbled from her mouth. Her long black hair was falling out in clumps.

She was decaying before his eyes.

"Help!" cried Kalin, not knowing what to do.

Altor began coughing and spurting blood from his mouth. His skin had turned a brownish-red with wide bleeding splits opening in numerous places.

"Kalin, make it stop, please!" cried Disa.

"Disa," he whimpered, her small body now listless in his arms. "Help me!" he screamed.

She reached for his face and gently touched his cheek. Kalin took her small hand and it detached from her arm, spattering blood across his face. Kalin froze, staring at her in horror. She closed her eyes and stopped breathing. Realizing she was gone, he clutched her close to his chest, sobbing. There was a popping sound and her left arm thumped on the floor. His stomach roiled and he gently set her down.

"I'm sorry, Disa," he whispered through tears, not knowing where to touch her. "I'm so sorry."

She was unrecognizable. His father lay still facing him, one eye wide open, the other on the floor. It was then he heard the screams.

All strength had left him, and on weak legs he used the wall of the balcony to pull himself up to standing. Overlooking the City of Light he heard millions of agonizing cries, the sound was so loud it vibrated his body. Helpless and overwhelmed, he wept like never before.

His world was dying.

CHAPTER 2
Kalin

Six Months Later…

She was four years old and frightened, running down the hill whimpering, trying not to fall. Behind her, the dark shadow raced along the grass, a malefic black hand hurrying to capture its prey.

"Run, Disa!" shouted Kalin, dashing up the hill, stumbling and sliding on the wet grass.

"It's too fast!" cried Disa, her black bangs soaked with sweat.

"Don't stop running!" he yelled.

He couldn't let it get her. She was helpless against the beast. His heart nearly stopped when he saw her trip and fall facedown. She sat up crying, a stream of blood running down her forehead. The slithering black hand rose in the air above Disa's head. She screamed as its clawed fingers swooped down, engulfing her small body. Its slimy tendrils were forcing their way into her open orifices. He could hear her gurgling and choking as they pushed downward into her throat.

Kalin dove into the air and onto the two and rolled, tearing off chunks of the creature, desperate to save his little sister. As he flung the black slime, it shrilled and scurried back to her, digging into her skin, sucking out what life she had left. He ripped off the piece burrowing into her left arm and froze. He was holding her detached appendage….

"No!" screamed Kalin.

He was sitting in his bed trembling and covered in a cold sweat. After taking several deep breaths to slow his heartbeat, he darted a glance around the room. It was dark and quiet, lit only by the panel lights on the ebony desk around the corner from his bed. Nothing had changed in the multi-level cabin. He was on his ship, the *Quasar*.

Another nightmare, he thought. *The fourth one this week.*

He threw the covers aside and sat on the edge of the bed. At the far end of the room, a walk-in domed window extended into space. A blanket of stars twinkled outside, but they were no comfort tonight. He shivered as he recalled the cold slimy feel of Disa's skin, something he'd been trying to forget. He swung his legs off the bed and got up with a groan. The dreams were always exhausting. He made his way across the open room, passing the lower levels filled with couches, tables, and assorted artifacts from the planets he'd visited. He entered the bathroom and winced when the lights automatically came on. A stark unbroken white covered three walls from floor to ceiling where a flowing mural of alien sea life offered some relief. The fourth wall was mirrored with a small stainless steel basin and several clear shelves containing towels and assorted bath items. It was to this one that he went, planting his hands on either side of the basin.

"Water. Seventy degrees."

The spewing faucet was barely audible. Kalin splashed the cool water on his face, running it through his hair. He glanced over at the Sarvin light in the corner. Normally he would stand under it to clean his body and regenerate cellular growth, but with the way he felt, living forever with his pain was not something he wanted. He leaned forward and peered into the mirror.

Swollen red skin surrounded his eyes; he'd been crying in his sleep again. He blinked a few times to clear his vision then stared at himself in disbelief. Before him was a sickly-looking man. His face was pale and drawn. His black hair stood on end. His eyes were so bloodshot they no longer looked green.

This is killing me, he thought, pulling down his bottom eyelid with his finger. *I have to find him.*

He ran his hands down his chest and felt the jutting of his ribs from the forty pounds of lost flesh. No wonder his women friends felt sorry for him, there was nothing left of his Saleran-human traits. His emotions had been replaced by a giant black void, which his physical body now reflected.

I look like the walking dead.

The doorbell sounded.

"Come in, Marante," he said, grateful for his telepathy. It had saved him in the past; now, he thought, he needed it more than ever.

Marante walked in with a clear tubular glass in each of his eight-fingered hands. Eyeing him from the bathroom, Kalin felt a little better about his weight loss. Marante's nose was white and twice its normal size.

Great, thought Kalin. *Something's up.*

He snatched a towel and went to the steps leading down to the sofa and chairs. His loose black pants were damp with sweat, so he sank onto one of the steps.

"I'm getting tired of them," he said as he dried his face and hair.

"Yes, I know," said Marante in his smooth accent.

After flinging the towel over his bare shoulders, Marante handed him a glass. Kalin took it, no longer noticing the large intrusive hands.

"Lyu?" Kalin asked, eyeing the green liquor. Lyu was the best drink in the galaxy, and the most expensive.

"I thought you could use it." Marante turned and walked down the three steps to the lower level then sat on the white couch.

Kalin said, "I could have used Ilya tonight but she's at one of her Nentran Rituals."

Marante frowned. "There is something about her I cannot place. She has a way of blocking my telepathy."

Kalin sipped the sweet drink, savoring the cool mint. "Good thing. I don't want you seeing what we do."

Marante's nose instantly turned green and shrank to pea-size. Kalin couldn't help but smile watching it change.

"Wonderful." Marante scrunched up his face and set his drink on the glass table in front of him. "Thank you for making me sick. How could you sleep with a woman who enjoys the company of an Emuugor animal? They are hideous and are foul-smelling."

Kalin drained his glass. Marante always knew how to calm him.

"It's what her kind does. The absorption of the Henual cells from the animal's sperm is necessary for their lungs to function properly. To them, it's natural. To you, repulsive. It doesn't bother me as long as she does a cleansing bioscan, which by the way, is also part of the ritual. She isn't infectious."

"I can deal with your variety of self-absorbed women, but a Tàtress is difficult to accept."

"Wimp."

"At least she is more intelligent than the flighty doughballs you usually associate with - BBs – Brainless Beauties. As the crowned Prince of Salera, you could have women of higher stature."

Kalin sneered. Loose women, or "Kelfins," were his preference, though his father had disapproved.

"I'm attracted to women who are less fortunate," he said, ending the discussion. They'd had it many times and it always culminated in yelling. He didn't have the strength for it this early in the morning. "The point is I can't keep living this way. Any news on Vorkis?"

Marante hesitated.

Here it comes, thought Kalin.

"We intercepted another message from the Federation. Apparently Vorkis managed to conceal a large quantity of Pril from the Federation."

"I knew it! The Federation wouldn't believe me about Vorkis either. If only my father had listened, he would be alive today."

"I blame Salera's Code of Ethilia," said Marante. "Those laws have been strictly upheld for over five thousand years, and it was the primary code of forbidding association or activity outside the planet that destroyed Salera. Saleran-humans were unable to develop the antibodies necessary to fight the virus Vorkis sprayed into the atmosphere. Your body fought it and won. You are living proof that Code should never have been followed."

Kalin leaned his head back and closed his eyes. He could still hear Disa's pleas. Tears welled in his eyes. There seemed to be no end to the crying.

In time, coping with your sorrow will become easier, said

Marante.

"No, it won't," Kalin said aloud. "This is forever." He held his breath for a second, reorganizing his thoughts. "What else did you find?"

"The Federation discovered Vorkis' base on a planet called Draka in the Nebis System. He was not there but ten Xeon Diffusers were being assembled by Zorcons."

"Xeon Diffusers? That's ancient technology. He must have stolen them from a Ritan freighter."

"I agree, but there is something else." Marante leaned forward in his seat. "Kalin, Vorkis is on Earth."

Kalin couldn't believe his ears. He jumped to his feet and threw up his arms, sending his glass flying across the room. "Finally!" Then he paused. "Wait, did you say Earth? In the Stargas System?"

Marante nodded. "Yes, the one whose theater you enjoy so much. Its core has an extremely high concentration of Pril."

Kalin tossed his towel on the couch next to Marante. "Set a course for Earth. It's time for Vorkis to pay."

Marante didn't rise. "Captain Vurro has been assigned to the mission; he is on his way there now."

"Vurro, that thief?"

"You were not to be told. The Federation is concerned for your safety and for the future of Salera."

"Now they're concerned?" scoffed Kalin. "They knew Vorkis had a secret lab and did nothing. They knew he was collecting pathogens and did nothing. If they had told my father in time, he and thirty billion people would still be alive. Now they're sending a moron who was banished from my planet for thievery to find the man who murdered my people. Next to Vorkis, they're to blame for the extermination of my race. No, they've lost my trust forever."

"Your logic is correct, but unfortunately Ilya was the last to use the Comscan and she mistakenly left the Ruode Wave setting too high. The Federation detected our intrusion. Councilman Lozari was not at all surprised and considering the circumstances, he assured me no criminal action would be taken. However, he did insist you stay clear of Vurro's mission. They are firm in their decision."

Kalin remembered the first time he left Salera to assist the Federation. It was over five hundred years ago; he'd been a mere ninety-two, young in Saleran society. His father had insisted he remain on the planet, but Kalin's desire to help people was stronger than his father's will. With the *Quasar*, Kalin had successfully completed hundreds of missions for the Federation, yet they hadn't cared enough to save his world. He became so enraged with the discovery of their knowledge of Vorkis' secret laboratory that he personally went to the Ravion System, forced his way into their Council Chamber and angrily withdrew Salera from the Federation, swearing never again to help them.

"I'm done with them," said Kalin.

Silence fell over the room. Kalin sensed Marante couldn't accept the possibility of his friend dying. He had to make him understand.

"I want him dead," he said. "I want to see the last ounce of life leave his eyes and feel his last breath on my face." He gritted his teeth. "I want him to beg for his life."

Marante sat forward, his elbows on his knees. "I know what you want. I would want the same, however, I would have to consider the lives of my people. Salera is depending on you for survival. It is your responsibility to bring her back to life."

"It's too late. My race became extinct when he killed the last female."

"I do not agree." Marante's tone went up an octave. "This universe is enormous, filled with millions of assorted life forms we have not yet contacted. We will eventually encounter a species capable of gestating a Saleran-human. This is a certainty."

Kalin shook his head in disgust and turned away. He walked to the bubble window and stood in the glass dome where twinkling stars surrounded him.

"Remember our last encounter with Vurro?" he asked, staring at a distant comet. "I had to beat him unconscious to stop him from killing a small Rajan just because the man wouldn't pick up Vurro's garbage. The Rajans put him in jail for seven weeks. I embarrassed him in front of his fiancée, and he swore to get even." He turned back to Marante. "And this is the guy they sent to catch my enemy? Something's not right."

"You must understand; your safety comes first."

"I'm the only one who can fight Vorkis on equal ground," Kalin insisted. "It's going to be my way. Period."

Marante came and sat on the white cushioned bench in front of him. "Revenge is similar to a caliginous pit filled with dead bones, and you are standing at its threshold of darkness. There is no life there, no happiness. Your sorrow will remain until you learn to live for the people that loved you."

Marante didn't understand. How could he? Not even an empath could feel his emptiness, his deep-rooted pain. He turned back to the stars. "I gave an order. Set a course for the Stargas System."

"I will not be a part of Salera's destruction."

"You will do it or be relieved of your duties."

The reflection on the glass revealed Marante's bright red nose. He was angry again, but this was no time to be weak.

"You would actually relieve me of my duties?"

Kalin faced him. "If I have to."

Marante vaulted from the bench. "My concern is for your well-being and your future, but like always, you are being stubborn and obnoxious. I will set a course for the Stargas System and when you fall flat on your face, I hope I am there to see it."

Marante stormed out of the room. Kalin dropped down on the bench, bent forward and rubbed his face with both hands.

A dark pit filled with dead bones…how right he is.

The hatred was so overpowering at times all Kalin could do was think of different ways to kill Vorkis. He'd decided the most satisfying would be to cut out his heart while he was still alive and let him watch it stop pumping as he bled to death.

He went to the desk beside his bed and tapped the surface. Several colorful orbs revealed themselves, and he pulled up the gray cushion hovering in front of the desk. As he sat, the padding grew around his body, forming a high back and armrests. He waved his hand over a blue orb and it displayed a three-dimensional holo star map. A red blinking light moved slowly through it. The *Quasar* was adjusting her course. Even when Marante was angry, he obeyed orders.

Doubt trickled through him. *Am I allowing hatred to consume me?* If he allowed Vorkis to live, billions more would suffer Salera's fate. Vorkis had to die at any cost and he would make sure it happened.

He waved his hand through the holo. "Tolba."

A Chaslean-human helmsman appeared in the display. Chaslean-humans were differentiated by the size and shape of their eyes. Tolba's eyes bent slightly upward before meeting at the wrinkled bridge of his nose, which made him appear angry, but beneath the rigid features, Tolba was compassionate. As Marante's cousin, he'd become one of the few Kalin could trust with the *Quasar*. He also followed orders explicitly.

"Yes, captain?"

"Cloak us and set the scanners to locate Vurro's ship, the *Arliss*."

"Aye, sir."

Kalin sat back and noticed the white jewel-encrusted handle of his Norin Blade levitating vertically on the corner of the desk. The organic weapon never laid flat, but always upended; why, he didn't know. He took the bladeless handle and felt it widen in his palm, a perfect fit. Carved into the handle along the edge were the words of a language not even Salera's high tech could figure out. As he concentrated, small green branches and offshoots began climbing out of the handle, twining and solidifying into a perfect twenty-two-inch razor-sharp silver blade. The double edge made it perfect for battle, especially since it would begin cutting three inches away from its target. Nothing like this had ever been invented.

He was fourteen years old the day he'd found it in his home on Salera, in a secret chamber he'd discovered in the dungeon of the Krystal Palace. Fearing it would be taken away from him, he never told his father. He called it Norin, meaning "stealth killer," and it had saved his life many times. He wished it could save him now. There was a small flash of light and the blade swiftly liquefied into the white handle. He returned it to the desk and waved his hand over a yellow orb. The captured message from the Federation appeared.

Vorkis' private army is composed of Zorcons, he thought. *The most despicable race in the galaxy.*

Their disgusting habit of cannibalism turned his stomach. The fact that they enjoyed terrorizing their victims before eating them alive made them worse than animals. In the past, he had stopped countless rebel Zorcon ships from kidnapping humans.

He rested back in the gray chair, feeling the warm cushion adjust to the shift of his body. His muscles relaxed and he snuggled in. This was home.

The *Quasar* was over ten miles in diameter, a masterpiece of technology yet to be duplicated, and Salera's pride. The silver sphere was biogenic, able to repair itself instantly. It could alter its shape for battle and speed and came equipped with a REM IV, one of the few Saleran creations released to the Federation. The REM, short for ReFormer, could alter inanimate matter at the molecular level. On ships, it could cloak and shield; on planets, it altered the shape of rock and liquid, producing pressurized tunnels for mining. Many of the *Quasar's* weapons had never been used, because against such a ship fear overwhelmed all.

Since human nature was to misuse power, only a handful of the *Quasar's* secrets had been revealed, a command ordered by Kalin's father, King Altor, and one of the few Kalin agreed with. Unlike Salera, the *Quasar* was home to a variety of life forms who adhered to Salera's peaceful laws. These close friends volunteered to assist with the *Quasar's* operation and maintenance.

Within the Federation's message was a revolving holo of Earth; a beautiful blue ball with brown terrain and puffy white clouds. It was one of his favorite planets he had visited hundreds of times. Their slang of Tislun, or what Earth-humans call English, was easy to use.

But most important, Earth-human females were voluptuous and very accommodating.

Little did the small planet of primitives know how valuable they'd become to the Federation. They carried within their world the rarest and most powerful source of energy the universe had ever known. Never before had this quantity of Pril been found, and he was sure the Federation was elated with its discovery. They just hadn't planned on Vorkis betraying them. Nevertheless, they would excavate all the Pril without telling the Earth-humans. To put it simply, they were planning to steal the Pril like common thieves.

The Federation only accepted into their membership societies with a high level of peace, integrating their knowledge and military capabilities into the larger whole. They'd become so powerful that many worlds had changed their ways just to come under their protection.

Were Earth's inhabitants ever given the chance to change?

Earth-humans didn't know of the Federation's existence. Because of their ignorance and volatility, they went ignored and unassisted, yet now their world would be raped. That was why his father felt as he had about the Federation, and why he'd allowed them only limited access to Saleran technology. Kalin felt a stab of guilt.

Am I any better than the Federation? Will I allow Earth to be destroyed just to kill Vorkis?

The loss of Earth-human lives would be inconsequential compared to the number of lives saved. He was justified in his reasoning. He tapped the orb and stood up. It was time to dress and head to the bridge.

Kalin sat in the captain's chair on the main level of the bridge, where twenty crewmembers monitored the ship using holos at their assigned stations. Before him was the giant viewing screen and to his left was the main console, where Marante and Tolba were carefully manipulating their holos.

"Captain, the *Arliss* is less than twenty clicks away," said Tolba.

"Stop all engines and hail Vurro. I'll take it in the Overview."

"Aye, sir."

As Kalin walked across the bridge, he could feel Marante's gaze on him. He was careful not to reveal any thoughts or emotions; Marante's empathic abilities were powerful.

At the far side of the bridge two silver-colored sliding doors opened, and he entered a beige oval room. Several revolving holo pictures of his family rotated on the walls. He sat on the black cushion behind the desk. Off to the side and slowly spinning on a thin beam of yellow light was a rare blue Credite stone, the hardest ore known to man. Twenty years ago, it had plowed through Salera's planetary shield and gouged a hole in an orbiting platform. His father had tossed him the stone and told him his head was harder than Credite.

He tapped the desk and eight pastel orbs rose up. He waved his hand over the blue one and a holo appeared, displaying a dark oblong vessel motionless in space. The holo flickered and the upper half of a Setrellan-human appeared.

Vurro was a lizard-like creature with massive muscles and blue skin pebbled with thousands of white heads. He enjoyed flaunting his abrasive appearance and consequently exposed as much skin as possible. Today he was wearing only two wide brown leather straps crisscrossed over his tightly packed torso.

This pimple needs popping, thought Kalin.

He recalled with a smile, the many instances he'd punched Vurro's elongated snout and knocked out a few teeth each time. Unfortunately, they always grew back. Why the Federation picked such a wart to be Captain of the Galactic Guard was one of the true mysteries of the universe.

"Vurro, it's good to see you," he lied.

"I'm happy not to say the same," replied Vurro in his grating voice.

Kalin grinned. "How's your jaw? Did your new wife divorce you yet?"

Vurro growled like an animal and dug his hefty four-inch claws into the armrests of his seat. Strings of saliva dangled from his quivering lips, a sure sign he was furious. His glowing yellow eyes squeezed into bright slits and his blue skin began to darken. Kalin's grin widened.

"I haven't forgotten your insolence," said Vurro. "The Rajan prison was filthy and because of you I've been banned from their airspace. This mission is mine, Saleran. I've been given it because you are weak."

Kalin slyly waved his hand over the pale green orb. "Let's lay this out. Vorkis is the most powerful criminal in the galaxy. You and I both know if you confront him, you won't survive. His Xevniors could fry you in a heartbeat. You have some good people on your ship. If you value their lives, you'll leave now and let me handle this."

Vurro let out a deep, raspy laugh. "Give up, Saleran. You should have died with your people."

Kalin's smile left his face. How many times he wished he'd had! If not for Marante's empathic abilities pulling him back from the brink of suicide, he might have done it. Vurro had not one ounce of compassion. Kalin longed to punch that snout again.

With strict control of his emotions, his tone remained the same. "Has your relationship with the Rajans improved any?"

Vurro eyed him strangely. "They're little specks of dung."

Kalin nodded, cautiously waving his hand over the same orb again. "Well, Vurro, I hope you enjoy the ride. Try not to let the little specks hurt you too much. Good-bye."

A holo rose up from the green orb displaying the *Arliss*. Kalin watched a cloud of twinkling blue dust burst from the *Quasar* and zoom towards the other ship.

"What are you doing—shields up!" yelled Vurro.

Instantly, the blue particles surrounded the vessel. Vurro's glowing yellow eyes widened to saucer size. Kalin couldn't help a wicked smile. Static filled the holo, overcoming Vurro's obscenities. With a booming suction sound and a flash of light, the *Arliss* was gone.

Marante came running into the room. "How could you?" he said, his red nose the size of an orange.

Kalin adjusted himself in his seat. "Don't worry. They'll be in Rajan space soon. Their chances of surviving Vorkis were next to nothing."

"He was on a Federation mission," Marante said firmly. "You will be court-martialed and imprisoned."

"I said no one was going to stop me. Especially not him. When are you going to understand I don't give a crap what the Federation says!"

"This is not just about you. Why can you not see this? You will have destroyed the peace your people have worked so hard to achieve. Your race was a beacon in this galaxy, a tribute to humankind. In doing this you desecrate everything Salera represented. You have become an uncontrollable storm that may finalize Salera's destruction."

After a pause, Kalin said, "I'm not killing Salera. She did that herself. Because of her trust, a vicious criminal was allowed access to her inner secrets and created the most lethal biological weapon in history. Anyway, it's done. Vurro is out of the way."

He tapped a yellow orb. Ignoring Marante's obvious disapproval, Kalin silently read the Federation message scrolling in the holo. After a moment, he looked up.

"Vorkis used REMs to form a planet tunnel and created an elaborate complex in Earth's core," he said. "Can you imagine Pril in the hands of a psychopathic killer?"

"Not a good thought," Marante said reluctantly. "Do you think he is capable of breaking through Salera's planet shield?"

"Yes, but he'll need time and he won't have that with me alive. Before I left Salera, I had a cranial implant of all the new technology. During the download, I discovered he stole the plans to make a Borit Reactor. Apparently, he did this while the virus was killing everyone. He must have had inside help."

"What is a Borit Reactor?"

"It's a machine about the size of this desk and with only three ounces of Pril, it can annihilate a planet."

Marante's black eyes opened wide. "What are you saying?"

Kalin clasped his hands together on the desk and fixed his gaze on Marante. "With me out of the way, who would be able to stop him from taking over the Federation? When he escaped, I changed the Quaren attributes of Salera's planet shield, but he will eventually find a way through. Add together Salera's science, unlimited amounts of Pril, the most evil man in history, and you have the end of peace with billions dead."

Marante's nose turned white with worry. "I hope you are wrong."

Kalin sat back. "I hope I am too. But I don't think so."

"All the more reason you should leave this assignment to someone else," said Marante. "We need you alive to defend Salera."

Kalin banged his fist on the desk. "When are you going to get it? Vorkis dies by my hand and no one else's! This is something I have to do!"

Marante folded his arms across his chest. "Now you listen to me you stubborn jackass. Aside from the enormous strength you both possess, Vorkis is a Master of Uru. He has no conscience. I have calculated there is a seventy-five percent chance he will kill you. This is unacceptable."

"Unacceptable or not, I'm the only one who can withstand his attacks. Including the Uru."

Marante stood and slammed his hands on the desk, hovering in front of Kalin. "Really? And how will you fight him when your head is sitting on the floor beside you? Uru fighters are vicious and inhuman. Their aim is to maim and mutilate. The trauma has sapped your strength, my friend; you have weakened considerably. You are not your former self."

Kalin pushed himself out of the chair, grabbed the Credite stone and squeezed. The stone began to crack and splinter, chunks falling to the table.

"Just because I look sickly doesn't mean I don't have strength."

Marante's mouth dropped open as he slowly straightened up. Kalin glanced down at the holo, trying to ignore the excruciating pain in his hand.

"Earth is experiencing atmospheric and geological turmoil. The end has begun. We'll need to set up Deltrons. Twelve of them should stabilize the core."

Marante sat down to study the holo. Kalin sensed his apprehension.

"Do you honestly think Vurro's first task would be to save the Earth-humans?" he asked. "They're primitives. His main mission is to capture Vorkis. If Earth blows up, so be it. He has no compassion."

"I suppose you are right," Marante said finally. His long arm easily stretched across the desk and tapped the green orb. A list of data appeared in the risen holo. "There is something else you must know. Rumor has it Vorkis may have a child."

Kalin held his breath, shocked by the words. "What? How? Who told you that?"

"Science Officer Gildrad on the *Arliss*."

"It's probably a lie to deceive us, and I'm not going to concern myself with idiocy. What's our ETA to the Stargas Sector?"

"Eighty-six hours, captain. At Warp 12, we will reach Earth two months into their future. Approximately ten hours will remain until implosion after we arrive. Not a long time I might add. What are your orders?"

Kalin walked around the desk and sat on its edge, facing Marante. "I want all families off the ship. Ask for volunteers and inform them the Federation is going to come after me full force. There'll be no turning back so they must be certain of their decision."

Marante nodded and rose out of his chair. Halfway to the door, he paused. "Perhaps your life-mate awaits you on Earth."

"I doubt it," Kalin said. "Besides, I'm not interested in a life-mate. I just want Vorkis."

"Still selfish. How sad."

Kalin watched Marante leave through the sliding doors,

wondering if that had been a joke.

Am I letting vengeance get the best of me? Could I live a somewhat normal life if I didn't pursue Vorkis? Disa's violent death flashed through his mind. *There's no choice.*

Kalin picked up a piece of the Credite and moved it between his fingers, feeling its hard surface and admiring the shiny brilliance of the blue stone. The Federation was like Credite, beautiful on the outside but deadly in its determination.

Will they salvage every ounce of Pril and possibly put the planet in jeopardy? If so, will they safely relocate its people to another world? Or will they let them all perish, saying a rogue asteroid destroyed the planet?

Their laws of segregation suggested the asteroid story was more likely. He sighed, feeling the heavy sadness of guilt because only one thing was certain; nothing would get in the way of his killing Vorkis.

Not even Earth.

CHAPTER 3

Jiro, Rina

July 1, 2043: Earth—the Indian Ocean
Sunda Trench: Maximum Depth 25,440 Ft.

Captain Jiro of the fishing boat, *Toki*, was a fourth-generation Sundanese angler who took pride in his family's heritage. The *Toki* was named after his father, a humble man honored throughout the fishing community for his generosity and skill.

Today, the Sunda Trench was proving fertile. Already twenty thousand pounds of fish had been secured. His five men were working hard with the recent catch. He would be sure to give them good bonuses.

High above he eyed the lookout perch set on the sturdy mast supported by six steel cables. A stiff ocean breeze grazed the dark weathered skin of his face, and he quickly inhaled the fresh air. The sea was where he found a peace surpassed only by the thought of his family. He took their picture from his tan shirt pocket. His wife and two small children were his most prized possessions, his reason for living.

"Captain!" yelled a frightened crewman, pointing to the east.

Less than a mile away, the water churned and bubbled as if something were coming up from below. Jiro quickly manned his binoculars and studied the phenomenon. Suddenly, a deafening explosion shook the *Toki*. The force slammed Jiro back against the mainmast. He watched thousands of smoldering boulders blast from the turbulent seas; meteors with tails of steam and water that rose so high they seemed to touch the clouds. His mouth gaped when the glow of ash and fire transformed the clear blue sky into a burnt-orange flame. Hundreds of fireballs were screeching down towards them like missiles.

"Take cover!" he shouted.

The crew scattered, looking for places to hide. A boulder the size of a basketball hit the mainmast, shattering it to pieces. The steel cables snapped and sliced through the air like knives, cutting three crewmen in half. Jiro dove towards the bridge just missing the onslaught of wooden shards shooting into the deck. He heard the terrified shouts of his men and used the window rim of the bridge to pull himself up. What he saw stopped his breath. The wall of the trench had risen, creating a huge waterfall as far as the eye could see. Millions of gallons of water ran into the open sea floor. Jiro's knees began to knock. His body trembled. He stood in a puddle of urine. There was nowhere to run.

The trench wall dropped with a thunderous boom causing a tremendous vacuum, pulling the remaining two men off the ship to their deaths. Jiro desperately held onto the broken window rim, his face pinched tight to the pain in his head, hoping his eardrums wouldn't burst. When he opened his eyes, a three-hundred-foot tsunami was coming his way. He had maybe two minutes.

Jiro ran into the bridge and spun the wheel, steering the *Toki* into the wave. As he fought to hold the wheel in place, his thoughts turned to his men. All had perished, yet there was no time to mourn. The engines grumbled and choked as the propellers bobbed in and out of the raging sea. No matter how hard the bilge pumps worked, Jiro knew his ship was sinking.

The wave reached the *Toki* with a roar, sending the bow of the vessel surging upward. The engines whined and bucked, straining to climb the enormous wave. His gaze went up the towering black wall of water.

This is the devil, he thought.

The curl of the furious wave smothered the small boat, tumbling it over backwards. Water rushed into the bridge, bashing Jiro's body against the rear wall. Within seconds, the bridge filled with water. Jiro held his breath, and his thoughts.

The *Toki* was foundering bottom side up when its bow slowly began tilting downward, toward the abyss. It squealed and moaned like a dying animal. Jiro peered into the dark water below and saw a fiery light. He was directly over the Sunda Trench. Another round of missiles was coming his way. There was no escape.

Plucked from his pocket, the photo of his wife and children drifted in front of him. Grabbing it, he swam to the helm. With one arm hooked through the wheel, he palmed the picture. There was no doubt in his mind he would be with them forever. He tenderly kissed the photograph and held it to his chest, then closed his eyes and pushed the air from his lungs until there was no more.

Oceanic Seismic Research Institute (OSRI)
Indialantic, Florida

Dr. Rina Young kept tapping the "Enter" key, wondering why her computer monitor just went black.

Another glitch, she thought.

She'd give it two minutes then restart. Resting back in her brown leather chair, she swiveled around studying the MCC, the Main Control Center of OSRI. The totally black room was cool, comfortable and lighted only by the four giant 30K Ultra High Def screens set into the far wall. Her station was on the bottom floor with the five other working terminals and next to the stairs leading up to the only exit.

Her stare stopped at the station behind her. She rolled her chair to the black reflective monitor. The new glass was like looking into a mirror and she began inspecting herself. She ran her fingers through her long black hair draping over her shoulders, checking for knots. Her double-thick black lashes exemplified her big aqua-blue eyes; the only thing on her she liked. Everything else spelled "ugly." She remembered what her mother had told her since she was a little girl.

True beauty is in the heart, not anywhere on the body…and my body sucks, she added. She pushed off the station and rolled back to her terminal.

The room was empty except for her; most of the scientists were at lunch. Her father said she was a workaholic, but it wasn't that at all.

She just loved geology. This was her favorite place away from home and she spent many nights working here. Her gaze went around the room. They had power because the lights were still on.

Did the servers crash again? The blinking red dot at the bottom left of the black screen told her they were rebooting.

Relieved that's all it was, her thoughts went back to California in 2039 when the San Andreas fault erupted. It nearly leveled the entire West Coast, including their headquarters. Broken seismographs, caved-in ceilings, and so many scattered papers it was weeks before they found the floor. She had suggested to her father, the Administrator of OSRI, that with all the advancements in telecommunications, it wasn't necessary for any main base to be within a seismic zone. So they moved to Florida, a virtually non-active area. OSRI was the first five-story building built in the small town of Indialantic on the east coast, and supposedly able to withstand a category 5 hurricane by incorporating a design similar to earthquake-resistant structures.

It's never been tested, and I hope it never will.

This recent 7.8 earthquake she was trying to get the information on was in the Pacific Ocean, south of Guam, and in the Mariana Trench. Carved within this dark crevasse lay the deepest crack in the planet, the Challenger Deep. At over thirty-five thousand feet deep, it rivaled Mt. Everest by a mile. She had to examine its dynamics. Depending on the kind of shift, the quake could generate tsunamis.

The four displays on the far wall blinked on. Different satellite views of the eastern side of the Indian Ocean appeared. She sat up straight.

The Sunda Trench?

The same picture came up on her computer monitor. The satellite imagery showed a tsunami overtake a small ship and continue forward without losing momentum.

"Tsunamis don't happen over open water," she said aloud, perplexed at the sight. "What is that?"

She leaned closer to the monitor. Visible above the area was a thick cloud of smoke. *Could there be some type of military testing going on?* Rows of data scrolled on the left side of the screen.

"11.8? A mega-quake?"

The reading had to be wrong. According to the most recent studies, the Earth's crust was divided into slabs of rock called tectonic plates that floated over a thick river of plastic-like magma. The Sunda Trench was a result of the Indo-Australian plate pushing itself under the Burma plate. The door at the top of the steps was flung open and her father, Justin, came running down the forty black-carpeted steps.

"Get me the info on the Sunda." He was still breathing evenly. The man was a true fitness freak.

"According to this," said Rina, whisking back her long black hair, "the India plate rammed itself under the Burma plate like a bullet bursting from a gun. A vast amount of energy was released and the computer says there's an eighty-three percent chance this shift will cause a reaction in the other plates."

"That's impossible," he said, leaning over her. "One subduction zone can't do this. In order for a quake to affect all the other plates a crack would have to surround the whole planet, and that doesn't exist. The reading must be wrong."

"I agree, but that's what the data is saying." She took a deep breath and said the worst words her father could hear. "I need to get into a satellite."

Justin shook his head. "Absolutely not. You know the repercussions."

A few months ago, hacking into satellites and downloading the information she needed was simple, but now with the threat of jail time, she stopped. If it weren't for her father being the Administrator of OSRI and having friends in high circles, the Secretary of Defense, General Theodore Bauman, would have made sure she remained in a dark prison for the rest of her life.

Part of the release agreement was that she hand over her hacking program she called "Jordy." He was among the elite of programs, something she developed only for the satellites. But his basic commands could be easily altered to add or remove items from a victim's computer, an invisible worm whose presence could not be detected, at least not by anyone else. To prevent anyone from having him, she'd given them a placebo, the failed prototype of Jordy. It would take them years to figure out he wasn't working right. She never told her father. He had to remain out of the loop, for his own sake.

"If you want me to find out how this is going to impact the other plates, I need to access the SDL over the Sunda," she said. "It's the only way, Dad."

Her father didn't answer. The SDL or Seismic Depth Locator was his invention, a monumental stride in technology with an amazing eighty percent success rate in predicting earthquakes. Every ocean trench had one floating above it. She needed the data off Gemstar II, the orbiting satellite, to get the information concerning the Sunda.

Her desk phone rang. Rina recognized the number and grunted. It was General Bauman. Justin tapped the speaker button.

"Mr. Secretary," he said, his concentration still on the monitor. "I'll have to get back to you. Right now we have an emergency."

"Don't bother," said Bauman, his voice raspy and loud. "You will not allow your daughter access to any, I repeat, any of the satellites. You got that, Young?"

A heated anger rose up in Rina. "Lis—"

Justin covered her mouth and shook his head. "So you know about the quake?"

"I know everything that's happening."

"This shift may affect the other plates. We're going to check all angles."

"Just keep your daughter out of the satellites." A click ended the conversion.

Justin released her mouth. "Can you not irritate him now? We have more important things to do."

"He's a snake and you know it," said Rina. "Why was he so quick to make the call? The quake isn't even five minutes old. He's got eyes on us."

"I'm sure he does but right now, I don't care. My concern is for what just happened, so let's stay focused."

She faced the monitor again, trying to push the creep out of her mind. Bauman was a devious, malicious man who enjoyed flaunting his power over everyone, always trying to make others feel small.

Four weeks ago, she was sitting at this very computer when someone hacked in, and before she could turn off her system, they'd stolen the real Jordy. Bauman had an entourage of hacking goons at his command, and unfortunately, she wasn't on to him until then.

Sadly, two weeks later, four senators who'd repeatedly opposed Bauman's issues were indicted for downloading child pornography. Eventually, they would be cleared of all charges, but the stain would remain, ruining their lives and careers. Her own investigation revealed the hacks had all the traces of Jordy. So, like any good citizen, she took care of the matter. She waited until Bauman broke into her system again, then sent him a virus that spread to all the computers containing Jordy's program, blowing their hard drives to smithereens. There was no way any of them survived.

She glanced down at the new mini iPad resting beside the keyboard. Apple had miniaturized the iPad to the size of a large cell phone, thus making it more portable. As soon as Jordy was stolen, she downloaded all the programs she had created onto the thin red device, and this time it was unhackable. The encryption couldn't be broken, and if anyone tried, they would only get her lethal virus, nothing else. A wide smile crossed her face. Bauman had lost. She stuffed the iPad into the Velcro pocket of her khaki-colored shorts.

Suddenly, seismic alarms began blaring. She hurriedly typed on the keyboard. Hundreds of earthquakes were rumbling across the planet. Africa, Chile, Japan, California, every continent was being affected by the anomaly.

The OSRI building began to shake. A deep rumble grew louder. Rina was momentarily stunned.

This doesn't happen in Florida, she thought. *This place is all sand. We're going to sink.* She felt Justin grab her arm and lift her off the seat.

"We have to go now!" he shouted.

They ran up the stairs into the windowed hallway. There was a sharp jerk and the building seemed to bounce. Rina lost her balance and fell into Justin. There was a loud snap and the windows shattered. Flying shards raced towards them and they hit the floor for cover. Her father kept his face pressed against the floor. He was shouting to her, but the deafening roar blocked any sound. The two got to their feet and rushed to the back wall, trying to stay clear of the chunks of ceiling crashing down.

From the third floor they had a clear view of the outside world. Rina watched the Atlantic Ocean drive powerful waves inland, smothering everything. Down on the streets, cars swerved off the road. Buildings collapsed like paper cards. Water lines ruptured. Gas mains exploded into plumes of fire.

Just then, the ground movement ceased. All was quiet. They waited motionless with their arms out sideways, ready to run again. Nothing happened, so they relaxed. Gray dust clouds floated in the hallway.

"Are you hurt?" asked Justin, gently touching her face.

She reached up and wiped a trickle of blood off his forehead before it reached his eye. "I'm okay," she said. "At least the building held."

"Yeah, but the town didn't."

Indialantic had been leveled. The ocean claimed four blocks, stopping less than fifty yards from OSRI. Palm trees, boats, and broken homes bobbed in the dark water, remnants of a once beautiful beach town. People were wandering about dazed. Power was out everywhere.

"Shiro!" she said anxiously. She hadn't seen her friend of over seven years since breakfast.

"I just talked to him," said Justin. "He was down at the generators."

A crackle came from her cell phone and she unclipped it from her shorts.

"It's him," she said. "I can't believe AT&T is still working. Shiro," she said into the phone, "are you all right?"

"Yeah…wet my pants…fine…okay." The phone went dead.

"No service," she said and returned the phone to its holder. She glanced out across the demolished town. "We need to find out what happened."

"Let's go," said Justin.

They walked back into the MCC. The walls had rippled and cracked open, exposing bunches of banded wires. Scraps of sheetrock lay scattered on the floor. A few chairs were lying on their sides beneath the wall screens, which remained intact. A low hum sounded throughout the building and the lights flickered then came on.

"Shiro must have started the generators," said Justin.

They carefully went down the stairs, stepping over broken ceiling tiles. The five computers came to life. The four giant screens lit up the far wall. She picked up her chair and sat at her terminal.

"It was a jolt from what just happened," she said. Her fingers zipped across the keyboard. "Every single plate is feeling the effect. So far over five hundred earthquakes have registered at over 7.5." She spun her chair around and faced Justin. "Why and how did this happen?"

Justin said nothing as he stood with his arms folded across his chest, staring at the wall screens. The door at the top of the steps banged open and Shiro came stomping down, out of shape and winded.

"It was a quake," he said, dusting off his black jeans and white tailored shirt in quick motions. Sheetrock dust covered his round face and straight black hair. "Is everyone okay?" he asked, shaking the gray powder from his hair.

"We're fine," said Justin, sitting down at the computer next to Rina. "Shiro, get on a terminal. I want a full spectrum analysis of the Sunda and I want to know about aftershocks. Rina, I'm punching in my code so you'll have access to Gemstar II. Tell me exactly what happened."

They nodded and their computers whizzed into action.

"I've got the news from Orlando," said Rina. "I'll put it on screen four."

A red-haired woman with sharp delicate features came into view. The broadcast had already begun.

"...from WFRT in Orlando. To the best of our knowledge, Orlando has experienced its first real earthquake. We don't know the size of it yet, but we do know there is substantial damage throughout the city. We've contacted our traffic helicopter flying over International Drive. What you'll see is live. Take it, Frank."

The picture changed to a young spike-haired man in a white shirt and red tie. He was strapped in and sitting beside the windy open door of a helicopter, pressing his earpiece to his head.

"This is Frank Belco reporting live from the WFRT helicopter flying over International Drive in Orlando. We were up here giving a traffic report when the earth below began shaking. And folks, what's happened is unbelievable. It seems the ground below the new Wet 'n Wild has turned to sand."

The camera shifted to the surface. Rina slowly stood up, horrified at the sight. Many of the twisting water slides—the Blue Niagara, the Black Hole, the Storm—had either toppled over or were leaning at forty-five-degree angles. Both the Surf Lagoon and the Wake Zone, a half-mile-long lake, were empty of water. Thousands of gallons had just disappeared, their hard beds now a sandy brown color and simmering like a pot of oatmeal.

In the center of the park, the camera zoomed in on a building-size mound of sand boiling up like a volcano. Rina judged it to be over five hundred feet in diameter and growing in height. The camera panned to numerous smaller mounds popping up throughout the softened ground, stewing like a thick sauce.

"I'm not sure what's happened," said Frank, "but I know the park was near capacity. So where are all the people?"

Not a single person was seen.

"It's liquefaction," said Rina.

There was silence.

"Get me the mayor of Orlando," said Justin. "Everyone within fifteen miles of that park has to be evacuated."

Shiro picked up the phone and began dialing.

"What's happening now?" asked Rina, unable to stop staring at the screen, her stomach in a knot.

The soil beneath the park began to shudder violently. Although the engines of the helicopter drowned out any sounds, something similar to a sonic boom vibrated the air, shaking the flying craft.

"Whoa!" yelled Frank, who clutched a handle on the sidewall. "I sure don't want to do that again. Jack," he said, looking beyond the cameraman. "Can we get a little lower? I want to show the folks here what real quicksand looks like."

The helicopter flew down and hovered a couple hundred feet above the volcano of sand, its wide-angle lens capturing the rapid deterioration as the giant mound dispersed itself over most of the park, a thick sludge unable to sustain any weight. The earthen floor was altering its state again.

"Somebody tell that idiot to get out of there!" shouted Justin.

There was a high-pitched swoosh and within moments, everything sank into a thin liquid like rocks in a glass of water. The helicopter began spinning out of control. Terrified screams from Frank and his crew came through the speakers while the craft swirled about wildly, distorting the picture. The static sound of a lost image along with a snowy picture filled the wall. The screens flickered a few times before the female reporter came back on, her face pale and her eyes teary.

"We don't know what just happened, but we can only hope everyone at Wet 'n Wild got out safely and Frank"—she sniffed back her tears—"and his crew are still alive...I can't—" She broke down crying, covering her face.

The OSRI building trembled for a few seconds, the wall screens wavering as the three held onto their desks. Rina sank down into her seat, her hands shaking as she tapped the keys again. The view on wall screen three changed to encompass all of the United States.

The entire west coast was under water.

CHAPTER 4
Tanya

Please give this letter to my mother, Brenda Jensen, who lives at the address below.

5943 Laurel Ave.
Houston, TX 77011

Dear Mom,

Whenever we argued, you made me write letters to "express my feelings." That always ticked me off, so I wrote hateful words. I wanted to make you cry, and it worked. I was such an idiot. As much as those letters hurt you, you never once belittled me. So I'm writing this now, Mom, my last letter. I wish I could make everything up to you, but if you're reading this, I'm already dead.

I'm sorry for all the bad things I said to you. I'm sorry for hurting you and I'm sorry I'm not with you now. I wish I'd stopped for one moment and seen how much you love me. When I ran away, I thought I knew more about life than you. But all I really know is what you taught me. Never panic in a bad situation. Take what life gives you and deal with it. Well, part of me wants to scream, but I know that'll do no good. No one will hear me.

Kenny and I are hiding in a small cave on the side of Mt. Charleston near Las Vegas, Nevada. Kenny's unconscious on the ground next to me. I think he has second- and third-degree burns. I'm not sure, because I can't remember the burn pictures they showed us in Health Class. They were disgusting and, like a jerk, I skipped class most of the time. Is Kenny going to die because I can't help him? He doesn't deserve that. He's wild and often thinks only of himself, but deep down he's a good man, and he loves me.

After we ran off together, we got married in Las Vegas. Yes, Mom, you have a son-in-law. Like idiots, we used most of our money on a fake ID for me, so we lived in his truck for the first two months, but I won't complain. It was my decision.

Kenny finally got a job as a ditch digger. The pay wasn't great, but the first check was enough to buy a tent and a few camping supplies. He works real hard and comes home exhausted. How did you know he drinks a lot?

Anyway, this weekend we decided to pack up the house and hike up to the highest point in southern Nevada, Mt. Charleston. I love hiking. I love nature. But I hate rain, at least when I'm stuck in it. Kenny wanted to try the roughest trail, even though he was the one carrying all the big stuff in his enormous backpack. He's an adventurer, a mountaineer. I guess that's what attracted me to him. He has a zest for life I couldn't find in younger men.

On the other hand, you taught me to be safe and I guess that's why I'm this chronic complainer. Kenny insists grumbling is my favorite pastime. Looking over at him stretched out on the ground, it's hard to believe this is all happening. He's twenty-four years old and too young to die, and looking at the cracks in the stone ceiling, I guess I'll be next. I'm scared and I can't stop shaking, but somehow writing this letter to you makes me feel better. Even if you don't get it, I still feel better talking to you. I always have.

Mom, you would have been proud of me when I reached the peak of Mt. Charleston. It's over eleven thousand feet high and the view was breathtaking. Kenny said we were seeing over 100 miles away. It was awesome!

The beauty entranced us so much we didn't notice the sky behind us until a clap of thunder almost made my heart stop. It was so loud the whole mountain shook and we almost fell to the ground. My body still aches from the vibration. I've never seen such thick black clouds before. The worst thunderclouds in Houston are babies compared to these. A strange purplish tinge around the edges made them look like something out of the *X-Files*. But Kenny was elated! As a native-born Lveg (Las Vegas person), he was hoping the storm would hit the city. With a rain average of two inches a year, people would be thrilled to have a rainstorm. Only not this one.

It started as a gentle rain; nothing more than soft drops on our heads. I ran screaming like a maniac, holding my backpack over my head because I didn't want my hair to frizz. You know how our red hair works, Mom, one ounce of water or any kind of humidity and it sticks out everywhere. I found this small cave and huddled inside. Kenny tried to coax me out but there was no way. He asked me if I would mind if he went exploring a little more and of course, I gave him my blessing.

The cave I'm sitting in is about the size of a small walk-in closet, close to four feet high and a good eight feet back, just enough for me, my frizzing hair, and Kenny. The black dirt has a strong earthy odor that's actually kind of refreshing. The cave floor slants downward facing a patch of tall pine trees and past them is a view of Las Vegas.

I remember looking out at the pine trees with their dark green spindles moving gently in the rain, when suddenly it started pouring. Water droplets had formed around the ceiling cracks and that's when it all began.

I crawled to the entrance and sat, worried about Kenny. He's always daring and I swear he fears nothing. As I brushed my hair, a flash of light and a thunderous boom scared the wits out of me. Within moments, a gust of wind slammed me back into the cave wall. I was shaken and stunned. My head hurt. I can recall lying on the ground, trying to focus my eyes because I couldn't believe what I was seeing.

The pine trees were literally melting away and smoking! Some were on fire! The rain was harder and (you're not going to believe this), DEADLY!!! Each drop of rain was hitting the ground and hissing, sending up small plumes of smoke. I saw it but I couldn't believe it. I crawled back to the entrance and could feel the heat. One drop hit my left hand and I screamed in pain as a burn blister bubbled up.

I remember the horror that swept through me as I thought of Kenny. I kept shouting his name until my throat was raw. I couldn't stop crying because I was sure he was dead. I finally saw him running towards me. He was holding his backpack over his head and yelled for me to move away from the entrance, then dove in and bashed against the back wall. I went to help him but my fingers got burned when I touched his drenched body. He told me to stay clear of him. After ripping the sleeping blanket out of its hold he threw the rest of his pack outside. It sizzled under the pouring rain.

Kenny fell flat on his back and that's when I noticed the burns. We were wearing shorts and T-shirts and all his clothes had huge ragged, smoldering holes. He had a lot of puffy burn blisters, and black skin was peeling off his arms and legs. It looked like someone had cooked him in an oven. I'm not sure whether he was shivering or convulsing. I covered him with the sleeping bag and it began to sizzle. I don't know what to do. I laid down next to him and watched him fall asleep. I can't stop crying.

It's been over six hours and the rain hasn't let up. My watch reads 7 p.m. and it should be daylight, but it looks like nighttime outside. Kenny hasn't moved. I know he's still alive because I can see the vein in his neck pulsing, but his breathing is shallow.

This hurts so bad, Mom, and I wish so much we were with you right now.

With the trees gone, I have a clear view of Las Vegas. What should be bright lights are now hundreds of fires. Violent explosions are bursting the city apart. Most of the casinos and hotels are in flames. The clouds blanketing the city have an eerie amber glow, reminding me of an inferno. Everyone must be dead. This rain eats everything. I just counted nine, no; make it fifteen, heavy billows of steam burst from the ground in and around the city. They're huge, almost eye-level with me, which makes them at least ten thousand feet high. It reminds me of that super volcano special they had on the Discovery Channel, but Las Vegas doesn't sit over a volcano so it must be something else. Kenny had told me Las Vegas has aquifers way down under the ground, could it be these? I don't know, but the ground beneath me is shaking and—

The city sank! It sank into the valley floor! The earth beneath it crumbled, cracked in all directions, then everything caved inward and slipped into a massive hole. This is unbelievable! Las Vegas is gone. The beautiful city is gone. All those people are dead.

From the far corners of the cave, streams of water are running down from the ceiling and out the entrance of the cave. The cracks in the stone are getting wider. The rain is eating its way through. I'm going to wrap this note pad in several plastic bags and between several layers of clothes, then I'm going to stuff everything inside my sleeping blanket and roll it up. Hopefully, this will all fit in my backpa

Kenn de! it tok Ke

I don't know how long I was in hysterics and my heart hurts so bad it feels as if it were torn out. I'm all alone now and the pain is almost unbearable. A huge piece of stone caved in and I dove away. The water rushed in so fast I couldn't get to Kenny in time and it took him out of the cave. He was dead the moment the rain touched his face. I won't tell you what he looked like when he floated away, but it's a memory I'll never forget.

I'm crunched up in the far corner trying to stay away from the river of acid that's getting closer. My notepad is sitting on the top of my knees, which are pressed against my chest. The acid river is so close that if I straighten my feet, it'll eat off the tips of my sneakers. It's hard to write like this so I'm going to have to end this letter.

Please forgive me for all the times I hurt you. I was stupid and selfish.

I'm only fifteen, Mommy, I'm not supposed to die this young.
Goodbye and I'll love you forever.

Your daughter,
Tanya Jensen-Baxter

CHAPTER 5
Rina

Two months after the Sunda Trench mega-quake:

Amt.		Cataclysmic Event
9,210	—	Hail storms - 7,452 softball size
406	—	Earthquakes - 208 over 9.0
202	—	Tsunamis over 80 feet in height
25	—	Acid rain - total devastation of 6 major cities worldwide, including Beijing, Rome, and Sydney
12	—	Category 5 hurricanes/typhoons within three weeks

"Look at those numbers on your screen," typed Rina, tired of arguing with Shiro on his laptop. "Every day that list gets bigger. How could the effects of one earthquake, in one trench, cause the whole planet to self-destruct?"

"I repeat," answered Shiro, "the Sunda is where it started and that's where we'll find the answers. Quit arguing with the scientific community. You'll just get yourself in trouble again."

Rina grunted. No one saw the problems like she did.

Another angle, she thought.

"The epicenter was over one thousand miles in circumference," she typed, "that's an enormous area for one event, so why didn't the SDL pick up any seismic activity in the Sunda before the initial quake? The SDL has never failed us, yet for months prior to the mega-quake, the Sunda's activity was only minimal, not showing any signs of a mega-quake. In fact, none of the SDLs over any ocean trench reflected the kind of stress needed to warrant such a tremendous shift in the plates."

"Okay, I can't explain that," replied Shiro, "but I'm sure, in time, we'll find the answer. There's a first time for everything and this phenomenon is definitely a first."

Rina made a loud sigh. He was right. She hated when he was

right.

"Look," said Shiro, "President Larson ordered OSRI to assist the USGS in solving the Sunda problem and he sent the Secretary of Defense, Rina," he reiterated, "the Secretary of Defense, here, to help us and although he's basically taken over the place, he is doing his job. The only thing I don't like is that your father is helpless, and the last thing he needs is for you to be a brat, so just go with it. Everyone else is obeying orders. Don't be so difficult...."

Rina stared at the screen. Shiro's words echoed in her ears, far away and distant. The answer given for the Sunda shift was lame. They said the plate zone at the trench had somehow weakened, causing an enormous uplift in the crust, offsetting all the tectonic plates, and disrupting the magnetic field of the planet. The amount of energy released in the mega-quake was close to one hundred sixty trillion tons of TNT. The thought sent chills down her spine.

So much power lay within the planet, yet its inhabitants are so frail and sometimes stupid.

"...I think deep down inside Bauman likes you," continued Shiro. "Maybe he knows you're a virgin and wants your body."

Her eyes popped wide open. "Don't start with me, butthead, I know where you live," she typed.

She was grateful her parents had instilled a strong set of morals; it kept her alive and safe from the mutant form of AIDS that killed two of her friends, Vera and Callie. "If they had sent Uncle Payton to help us, I would be okay. He's an admiral in the Navy and he has more heart. But no, they sent Godzilla with an attitude."

"Yo, dingbat," said Shiro, "Bauman's the SecDef, he makes the call. Right now, he's giving me the evil eye. I think he knows I'm talking to you. Bye."

She sat back in her brown leather chair and looked around the MCC. The place was empty. Everyone was at a meeting she wasn't invited to, and for that she was glad. Bauman finally got the hint she hated his meetings after she disrupted them with questions he couldn't answer.

She recalled the day he arrived. A barrage of soldiers forced their way into the building, taking positions at every exit on every floor, hoisting their rifles and pistols in clear sight, upsetting many of the staff. Her father, Justin, tried to convince Bauman they were on the same side and military tactics weren't necessary, but Bauman refused to listen, insisting OSRI was now under military control.

Dad had no choice but to relinquish his authority, thought Rina.

At their initial meeting, Bauman told everyone he expected conduct like that of the military, standing at attention and saluting him when he entered a room. She raised her hand and told him she'd salute him the day he was elected President of the United States, but until then, forget it. The comment sent invisible daggers out of Bauman's eyes. From then on, he did everything in his power to annoy her, like installing a special three-inch-thick sliding security door in the MCC, where she worked ninety-eight percent of the time. It was bad enough the place felt like a dungeon; now it was a tomb.

The only good that came with him was now she had limited access to the satellites, something the President approved against Bauman's wishes. She shifted in her seat, feeling the rectangular shape of her iPad in her shorts pocket. It never left her side, especially since Bauman's arrival. She checked her watch.

Four p.m. and I still haven't eaten breakfast.

She tapped a key on her keyboard. "Access Error" was blinking in bright yellow on her screen. The satellite, Telstar VI, was malfunctioning and not relaying information from the probe over the Mariana Trench. Bauman's response had been: "You'll get it when the satellite's fixed, so can it." He was always in a bad mood.

A dark green sleeve came from behind and plopped an eight-inch-thick computer printout on her desk. Her heart nearly stopped beating from fright. The nasty old-man cologne told her it was Bauman. She turned to see a tight-lipped man with beady steel-gray eyes trying to bore a hole through her head. His wide stiff jaw and cratered skin gave him a raw I-could-kill-you look. He demanded perfection from everyone he worked with, a personality flaw she loved to irritate.

"I told you I would deliver." With his hands clasped behind his back, Bauman rocked back and forth on his feet. Perfectly placed medals sparkled on his dark green jacket.

"And not a moment too soon," she said dryly. She'd been waiting almost two weeks for the data.

"We got this from Telstar twenty minutes ago. I hope you're satisfied."

"The satellite's repaired?" she asked, flipping through the pages.

"No, not yet. The satellite's programming is difficult and Rick only managed this data by chance. You're fortunate he got it."

"Why not let me try?" She gazed up at him. On the top of his head a few strands of salt and pepper hair were flipped to the side. *He should just go bald.* "Rick could sit next to me and watch everything I do. I could have it fixed in no time."

"Not a chance. We don't allow traitors to access our satellites."

His remark sent ripples of anger from her head down to her toes. She stood up and glared into his eyes, wanting to smack the smirk off his stupid face.

"At least I only used the satellites to study geology," she said. "You're using them to spy on people."

His expression went from a smile to a solid glare. If hate could physically attack from someone's eyes, she would have been mutilated.

"I have no idea what you're talking about."

Her grin widened. "Yes you do, General," she purred, taking a step closer to him. "You've been a bad boy. How many drives did my virus burn up? It was fun imagining you and your creep squad running around the place with fire extinguishers."

Bauman's teeth dug into his bottom lip so hard she was sure it would bleed. He yanked the brown leather chair out from behind her and kicked it hard. It flew across the room, crashing beneath the wall screens. She didn't flinch.

Another temper tantrum. This was a common occurrence with Bauman. Yesterday, a computer monitor sprouted wings after she told him he was a pathetic little worm. She knew it was dangerous to provoke him, but it was almost impossible not to.

She glanced at the helpless chair lying on its side. "I see you didn't take your pills. Maybe they should make them chewable."

Bauman's face went bright red. "If you weren't his daughter, I'd …."

"You'd what?" Her voice stone cold.

"This isn't over," he ground out, then stormed out of the room.

Another day's work, she thought, grinning wide. She pulled another chair over and sat down.

The phone rang and she tapped the speaker button. "Speak."

"It's me, Dad. I'm on my way to the International Peace Conference. Behave yourself and don't aggravate the General."

"No problem," she said, eyeing the chair. "Tell me something, why did they pick Memphis to hold the most important conference of the century? It's the first time in history every leader of every country will be gathered together in one place, and they pick the center of hick town?"

"Beats me," answered Justin. "Bauman picked the site. He said it was the safest and easiest to protect because of its location. Anyway, your father will be rubbing elbows with the high and mighty."

Rina heard a clinking sound.

"Oh crap," said Justin.

"What happened?"

"I dropped my keys and the cover broke off my pocketknife, the one your mother gave me."

"First of all, twenty keys are too much," she said. "You need to lighten your load."

"I need every one of these keys," he said firmly. "I just don't remember what each one is for. I can't believe I broke it." There was sadness in his voice.

"You still have your ring," she said. "We can fix the knife when you get back."

Rina squeezed the necklace beneath her red T-shirt. Five years ago, after the violent eruption of Mt. Vesuvius, her mother, Mary, a famous geologist, found pieces of a lustrous black stone she concluded was a form of Obsidian but with a slight iridescent shine. Mary loved it so much she designed a pendant for Rina and a ring for Justin and made them swear to wear them forever. Her mother was very sentimental. Rina could feel the shapes of diamonds and gems surrounding the beautiful stone, which was over two inches in height and oval shaped. The necklace was too exquisite for cut-off jean shorts and a red T-shirt, so, as always, it remained hidden.

She changed the subject. "You're going to have a grand time."

"Yeah, right," he answered sardonically. "I'll call you when I get there. Love you."

"Bye, dad."

Wall screen four displayed a satellite view of a cloudless United States. Memphis sat over the New Madrid Fault Zone, not a straight-lined fault like the San Andreas but rather a rift in the North American plate, a seismically active area running under five states. Back in the years 1811-1812, numerous earthquakes jolted the region, the biggest over 8.0 on the Richter Scale. The Mississippi River changed its course for seven hours, whole islands disappeared, and even the sand along the Mississippi boiled. The earthquake and aftershocks altered the land so much maps had to be redone. She typed on her keyboard and checked the Richter. Nothing.

She heard the door slide open and turned around. Shiro came stomping down the stairs of the MCC, his paunch bouncing with each step. He loved Italian food and it showed. A pair of thick black-rimmed glasses glinted beneath unruly strands of straight black hair. No matter how much gel he used, they waved like blades of wheat in the wind.

"Hey," he said. That was his formal hello.

His oversized front teeth created a slight overbite and a slurpy lisp in his speech. He grabbed a chair from across the aisle, wiped it off with his handkerchief and sat next to her. His Obsessive-Compulsive Disorder had gotten much better since the meds.

"I'll bet you thought I was Burt Callaghan," he said with a smirk.

His relentless poking about her ex-boyfriend made her want to bash him sometimes.

"Burt's a low-life idiot who thinks with his pants, so why do you bring him up all the time?"

"Because it irritates you. Why else?"

Rina rolled her eyes and grunted. Burt was her third and last mistake. The walks on the beach, the flowers, the exquisite dates, were all fabricated to get her in bed. For her to trust any man again, he would have to prove himself big time.

"What's this?" Shiro asked, picking up the readout.

"It's the latest data on the Mariana," she said, typing and keeping her focus on the monitor. "Bauman just brought it in. I still can't get into Telstar VI."

Shiro spoke as he skimmed through the pages. "The meeting was the usual 'get it done or you're fired' stuff."

His words seemed to bubble from the sides of his mouth. He needed braces but was too stubborn to see a dentist.

"Ugh…Rina…this is an old readout from the Mariana."

She turned and looked at him strangely.

"I downloaded this before the mega-quake," he said, pointing to a barely noticeable adjustment of the number six. "I remember writing this alteration. This data is at least eight weeks old."

Her attention went back to the computer screen. "If he lied about this data, he's lying about the satellites."

To break into Telstar VI would end her career. She would be thrown off the project. But if Bauman was tampering with the satellites, it could only mean he was up to no good. Her gut told her to stay out of it.

"I'm going in," she said.

"How? I thought you gave up Jordy."

"I did…sort of."

"I knew you didn't," said Shiro. "I can't believe you, woman. You ask for trouble."

"You know I don't handle authority well. Besides, I haven't used him until now."

"Wait," said Shiro, gripping her hands to halt her typing. "If you do this, your life in geology is over."

"I know," she said, "but I don't trust Bauman and if something bad happens, I'll never forgive myself for not trying to stop him."

The overhead speaker clicked on.

"This is General Bauman. We, your government, personally appreciate the effort everyone has put forth on this project. Most of you have been working eighteen-hour days and sleeping here at the facility. As a reward, a room is reserved at the *Pirate's Chophouse* for all to enjoy dinner on us. Your buses leave in five minutes. We expect all employees to attend, so drop what you're doing and join us. Thank you for your time and patience and, of course, your loyalty and hard work."

"Great!" said Shiro, rubbing his hands together. "Let's go eat. I'm starving."

"I'm in," said Rina. "What the—" Her typing sped up. "I'm detecting homing signals in the Mariana Trench."

"It's probably the SDL. Let's go."

"No. These are coming from within the trench." She continued typing. "Oh crap." Her mouth dropped open. The info had to be wrong.

"What is it?" asked Shiro.

"Who would do this?" she said concerned.

"Do what?" he demanded.

"Three hundred and fifty nuclear warheads have been anchored to the walls of the Mariana Trench in the Challenger Deep."

"What?" he shrieked.

"Oh crap."

"Tell me!" he said desperately.

"You were right. The readings Bauman gave me were wrong. The Mariana's width and length has almost doubled. It's over twenty-five hundred miles long, seventy-eight miles wide, and its depth is near fifty thousand feet." She sat back, astonished. "Someone is going to blow open the biggest crack in the world."

A raspy voice came from the top of the stairs. "I knew it was just a matter of time before you hacked into the satellite."

It was Bauman.

Rina and Shiro jumped to their feet. Two soldiers dressed in black and white camouflage suits guarded the exit door. Another four came tromping down the steps in front of Bauman, hoisting XL-20s, automatic rifles equipped with laser pulses that could burn four-inch deep holes through solid steel from three hundred feet. Attached to their wide black belts were the latest in military small arms, the S-8, a medium sized laser-guided automatic pistol with quadruple the power of a Magnum .600. The guards took positions beside her and Shiro.

"What's this?" asked Rina, eyeing the silencers on the guards' weapons.

Bauman sat on the computer desk in front of them leisurely swinging his legs. Small froths of spit cornered his ugly smile.

"You mean you really don't know? I'll show you."

Bauman nodded at a soldier who immediately bashed the butt of his rifle into Shiro's head. Shiro fell to his knees.

"No!" shouted Rina.

The guards held her back. Shiro struggled to his feet, his hand to his temple, blood oozing between his fingers. A soldier put a gun to Shiro's bleeding temple.

Unable to control her emotions, she blurted out, "You worthl—"

"Wrong words," Bauman chuckled.

One of the soldiers grabbed her hair and pulled her head back while the other guard rammed his fist into her stomach. Pain exploded through her torso as air burst from her lungs.

"That's enough!" yelled Shiro.

Bauman nodded. "I hate her name calling."

"Why?" asked Rina, the air barely escaping her throat.

"Because you're meddling is blocking the way of progress."

"Progress?" asked Shiro.

"You want it this way," said Rina, ignoring the fire in her stomach. "You want half the population dead, don't you?"

Bauman's thin lips formed an evil grin. "I knew you wouldn't obey the rules, and I couldn't wait until you broke them. By the way, Doctor, the building is empty of all civilians. No one will hear your screams."

"What are you saying?" asked Shiro anxiously.

"You're the one tampering with the satellites," said Rina.

"Affirmative," said Bauman. "I couldn't let you discover the Mariana's deterioration. We figure the whole ordeal will take less than one hour. It's the quickest and most reliable plan ever conceived."

"Who's we?" asked Shiro.

"We are the New Continuum," Bauman said proudly. "An organization determined to unite this world, something those useless world leaders could never accomplish."

Rina's heart sank. "You're taking out the Peace Conference."

"It's the perfect plan," said Bauman. "No one will suspect a hundred and fifty nukes are planted within the fault zone near Memphis. A minisub will be our detonation device in the Mariana. When it ignites, so will the nukes in the New Madrid."

Rina squirmed to get free. "No, please, you'd be killing—"

Bauman interrupted, "This discussion is over."

He jumped off the desk and straightened his moss green tie. One of the guards swung the skeletal butt of his rifle and Shiro hit the floor, unconscious.

"No!" cried Rina.

She elbowed the stomach of the soldier on her right then back-fisted the other in the face. She lunged for Bauman but something hard bashed the back of her head and she hit the floor with a grunt. A soldier grabbed her arm and yanked her up to standing. The room was spinning as she wobbled on her feet, trying to gather her senses.

Bauman approached with a malevolent smile. "This one's mine."

The last thing Rina saw was Bauman's wide fist heading for her face.

CHAPTER 6
Rina

Mariana Trench: Challenger Deep

The air was stale and smelled of mold. Rina's eyelids felt heavy, weighed down by the relentless pounding in her head. She was scrunched up in a ball on her left side, every bone and muscle hurting as if it had been beaten with a hammer.

A low moan came from beside her and she slowly opened her eyes. It was dark. She wiggled her nose, feeling her damp hair strewn across her face. *Where am I?* The last thing she remembered was…Bauman's fist. Her jaw was throbbing. Droning sounds were coming from the floor.

She lifted her arm to roll on her back but a searing pain on the right side of her torso snatched her breath. She slid her fingertips gently over a bulbous bruise over her ribs. It had to be the size of a plate. Her right thigh hurt just as much. Bauman had used more than his fist.

Angry and frustrated, she used her weight to thrust herself onto her back. The pain shot through her and she stifled a scream as tears formed in her eyes. Shaking and barely able to breathe, she went limp, her thoughts fading.

The unexpected memory of Bauman's fist burst into her mind and she woke up abruptly. She wanted so much to rip off his head. Moving her leg slightly she sensed her iPad was still inside her pocket. Her cell phone was gone, but the idiot was too stupid to take the iPad. Above her, lines of light were surrounding two rectangular panels. She took the iPad from her pocket and felt for the button near the upper righthand corner. A cloud of light illuminated the area.

A floor compartment.

She pressed the button again and the device shut off. *When did I last charge it?* There was another moan. *Shiro.*

"Wake up," she said, her throat scratchy from thirst. *How long have we been unconscious?* "I think we're in the minisub going down into the trench."

"What?" Shiro thrust himself up to a sitting position, banging his head on the door panel in the process. "Ow! I bit my tongue!"

"Shh. Listen."

The whirring of engines and propellers filled the silence.

"Crap!" said Shiro. "He put us in the sub going down into the trench."

"Really?" she said.

"My tongue is bleeding."

"Quit being a baby, Einstein. We have to stop the countdown."

"How?" he asked, his lisp worse from his cut tongue. "He probably removed the override switch."

"This is no time to be negative, retard. Let's just see what we can do," she added, tamping down her frustration.

"I'm not negative, lizard lips, I'm realistic."

"You're realism is negative. Now help me open this door."

With their legs and arms, they heaved and pushed until the lock snapped open. *Too easy,* she thought. A rush of light flared into their enclosed space and she turned her head away, blinking several times. When her vision adjusted; they were staring at the wheel of a yellow hatch on the ceiling.

Shiro got on his knees and stuck his head out of the compartment. "Wow, it's an *X-38*. And I thought he was a cheap guy."

The *X-38* was the pride of Vector Industries, a subsidiary of Steinmann Conglomerate. Only two existed in the world; one was owned by the military and the other by Vector itself. A year ago, she had the rare privilege of exploring the Puerto Rican Trench with an *X-38*. The systems were state-of-the-art, controlled and monitored with computers inset into the two-foot thick walls. Anchored to its bottom were the ballast tanks and batter pods. It was designed to withstand over nine tons per square inch of pressure for more than ninety-six hours, a remarkable accomplishment hailed as a victory over the seas.

"Of course it's the best," she said, lifting herself out of the compartment and sitting on the floor. "He couldn't tell the President he was going to send an old sub into the Mariana."

Rina swung her legs onto the indigo carpet padded with soft rubber to ease the strain on the physical joints. Next to them on the wall, three rows of green lights above two black metal doors signified the readiness of the main systems. As she crawled to the front, the dark gray interior of the minisub was perfect for revealing the four wall terminals with keyboards—two in front, two in back. She passed several sets of ceiling, floor, and wall straps scattered throughout the crawl-only vessel and hoped they wouldn't have to use them. Stopping in front of a three-foot-wide porthole she stared at total blackness. She shook off a chill and kept going.

Upon reaching the main controls, she sat on the two-foot ledge and watched the charcoal-gray joystick move on its own between her legs. The forepart of the sub was transparent Titanium, a ten-inch thick domed window allowing a full view of the outside. The only light came from luminescent marine life. This was the darkest area on the planet; it was as if they were encased in solid rock. As her nerves began to tighten, she forced herself to change her thoughts.

Behind and to her left was the main systems station with its slide-out keyboard. Scrolling rows of yellow data lit up the black display. Sitting on her knees and facing the terminal, she tapped the upper left-hand corner of the screen, *Mechanics and System Flow.*

"He's removed the manipulator arms," she said. "We've got eight minutes until detonation."

"Crap!" said Shiro, crawling to her with pounding thumps. "Do something!"

She lifted the iPad from her pocket. An open crack ran diagonally along the back of the red case right down to the cord compartment. *The jerk busted my baby.*

"Hurry up, woman!" Shiro plopped himself beside her.

"Knock it off with the 'woman' stuff."

"You are a woman, right?"

She rolled her eyes and tapped the screen on the iPad. The visual display flickered then turned on. The low battery light was blinking. *There's maybe fifteen minutes of power left.* She quickly flipped the unit over and opened the cable compartment. A thin flat USB cord unfolded and she hooked it into the port just beneath the monitor. She began typing on the keyboard. The exterior lights came on. A deep raspy laugh echoed through the sub.

"I wanted you to be awake when you die," he said. "How are you feeling, Rina? A little sore? I can't begin to describe how much fun it was to beat you."

One good punch was all she would need to loosen those gold caps. Tearing out his remaining hair would be good too. *No.* He wanted her to lose control.

"Never felt better, Bauman. You're a kitten. So where are your New Continuum friends?"

"What the heck," he cleared his throat. "North Dakota, far away from the New Madrid and listening to our conversation. You've caused monumental problems for us and we all wanted to hear your last words."

As he spoke, she carefully scanned the sub. On the ceiling, hidden between the relay switches was a small blue light. *A miniature camera.* She laid on her back and kicked it until it cracked.

"It doesn't matter," said Bauman. "We'll hear your scream."

She began searching for the hacking programs in the iPad.

"Soon the New Continuum will unite our great world, and you will be gone forever."

She wanted to shut him up so bad. "You could've thought of a better name. Psychopathic Killers-R-Us is more appropriate. By the way, did you tell your little worm buddies, the one hundred and fifty nukes planted in the rift are going to kill them too? When the New Madrid ignites, the central half of the country is going to sink into a river of boiling magma, and that includes North Dakota. You're all going to burn, thanks to your best friend."

She heard men yelling in the background.

"Yeah, guys," she said loudly, gratified by the commotion. "The big maggot wants you dead." The mic clicked off.

She began mumbling to herself, angry she didn't see this coming. "Crap!"

"What happened?" asked Shiro.

"The sim card is damaged," she kept typing, "the original hacks aren't working…but…the duplicates are in subfiles. Got them!"

Shiro was hovering over her shoulder. "You rule!"

"This is my game," she said, keeping focused on the screen as she typed.

"You're the Queen."

The lights went out and the engines whined to a halt. "Oops," said Rina.

"We're going to be vaporized and all you can say is oops? I take it back. You're not the Queen."

"I liked it better when you called me 'woman.'" Her fingers didn't pause. "Get on a terminal and sound off the countdown."

No more mistakes, Rina.

The power came back on. Shiro crawled to the station across from her.

"Six minutes," he said.

"I have to find Alfalfa."

"Who's he?"

"Alfalfa is Jordy's base code. Once he's inside a computer, he starts tearing apart the hard drive, literally causing a meltdown."

"Wow. Is he the one you sent to Bauman?"

"Yep! Did you know Bauman was spying on the President of the United States?"

"The President?" asked Shiro. "Holy cow. Why didn't you tell anyone?"

"Who would believe a hacker? So I did the next best thing—I sent him Alfalfa. This little guy is the perfect weapon."

Three programs popped up on the display, each one containing twenty lines of code.

"Blue tail, is it you?" she said, typing. "No. Mariana?" The lights flickered. "Oops."

"Knock it off with the oops," said Shiro. "This is freaky enough."

She didn't answer. Flower lily was next.

"Four minutes," said Shiro.

She tapped the enter key and a three rows of data appeared.

"Got him!"

"Cancel the detonation!" said Shiro, his eyes wide.

The screen wavered and the lights shut off again. An insidious laugh came over the speakers. Bauman had turned her own virus against her. Four Alfalfas were chasing her through the system. Her fingers were beginning to cramp.

"What's wrong, Rina?" said Bauman, sarcasm heavy in his voice. "Can't outrun the zippers? I wanted you to think we couldn't hack your iPad, but we did and I'm overjoyed. You gave us programs that will help us in our quest. And you're wrong about the New Madrid. We've done an extensive study on the rift and you're foolish to think you can outsmart us. Oh look, one of those zippers is getting real close."

He's connected, she thought. *He can see everything I'm doing.*

"She can beat you anytime, Bauman," said Shiro. He leaned towards Rina and whispered from the corner of his mouth, "What's a zipper?"

"Yes, explain it to him," said Bauman. "After all, they're your creation. We just made them better."

She wished so much for him to shut up. Using Shiro to distract her was making her angrier, and more determined.

"If an attacker goes after Alfalfa," she said, "he creates subfiles that hunt and shut down the enemy's program, forcing them to restart. Zip up, zip down. Shoot!"

The screen fluctuated again.

"You can't beat them," said Bauman.

"You shouldn't put anything past me," she said, turning and hastily crawling to the back of the sub; grateful she wore jean-shorts, nothing hindered her legs. "So, how'd it go when I told your lame-o friends you were going to kill them?"

She signaled Shiro to bring the recessed flashlight in the wall. She yanked open the gray metal doors to the main circuitry. Over fifty circuit boards sat vertically in the narrow chamber. Colored wires and relay switches crowded the small space. Above the boards were the abbreviated names of each system.

"It's been proven one man cannot rule this world," said Bauman. "We've already formed a High Council to oversee Earth's affairs. Your feeble attempts to disband us are foolish. They only exemplify your stupidity."

"Really?" She slid out three circuit boards. Rearranging the wires was tedious but if done wrong, she could force the detonation. She kept glancing at the inset wall monitor displaying the countdown in bright yellow numbers.

"Two-minute warning," said Bauman. "First you'll see a bright flash of light. Unfortunately, you won't feel the heat melt the skin off your bones. But it will be satisfying to hear your blood-curdling scream." His laugh echoed through the sub again.

"You're a monster," she said, eyeing Shiro, who had sweat rolling down his face. He was terrified.

"And just where are you, Bauman?" she asked.

"I'm in a jet over the Antarctic. I'm rather excited about your death. I've been waiting a long time for this."

"You're a coward," she said, "and an idiot. You put me, the enemy, the one who created Alfalfa, smack in the middle of the most critical stage of your plan, the detonation sub. How's that for exemplification of stupidity?" She gripped a set of wires on a circuit board and said, "Eat this, moron."

She ripped out the connection to the surface and angrily threw it across the sub. The mic went dead. She shoved the three boards into Shiro's arms.

"Slide these back in."

She rushed back to the main computer up front. Snaps and beeps told her the boards were in.

"One minute!" yelled Shiro. "If you're going to do something, do it now!"

"I'm hurrying," she said. "Let me concentrate."

The lights flicked on. An alarm began to blare. Overhead, twirling red lights signaled the oncoming blast that would end their lives.

"Thirty seconds," said Shiro, "and we're toast. Rina—"

"Don't talk," she said, her fingers flying across the keyboard. "I can do this."

Suddenly, the screen went black. All the data disappeared. Rina sat back and stared at the monitor. Her gut was in one big knot and her jaw was still hurting.

"Did you do it?" asked Shiro, his brow scrunched in worry.

"I used the sub's programming to kill the Alfalfas but I'm not sure I stopped the detonation."

"We'll know in eight seconds," he said. "You did all you could."

Although his OCD was at times annoying, he was always consoling, but right now his calmness wouldn't help. She sighed and wondered if it were her last breath. Her heart began to pump hard and fast, pounding in her chest like a jackhammer. She started trembling and cupped her hands over her ears, squeezing her eyes shut. The rush of panic was strong and she wanted to scream, but she knew it would do no good.

Don't let Bauman win, she thought. *Don't let Bauman win.* She repeated the words over and over, trying to slow her breathing.

The memory of the F-5 tornado in Oklahoma was nothing compared to this, although she'd felt bad about Shiro getting forty-two stitches in his leg from a flying fence plank. There is no escape from this. The Mariana would be their grave. She watched Shiro as he silently stared out into the cold darkness. If she'd just listened to him and not hacked into the satellite, things would be different, but here they were, waiting for the flash of light. Waiting to die. Nothing could be worse.

A deep rumbling vibrated the small vessel. The ship began

violently rocking from side-to-side.

Shiro yelled, "This is it!"

CHAPTER 7
Rina

The *X-38* lurched to one side. Rina grabbed the wall handle beside her with both hands. The force swung her to the left and she smashed into the wall beside the keyboard, just missing the monitor. Shiro side-slammed into the terminal next to him and the screen shattered.

"Earthquake!" shouted Rina, grabbing a wall handle. "Strap yourself in!"

Shiro quickly unfurled a safety belt from within the wall and buckled it around his waist. Through the glass domed front, Rina watched house-size chunks of rock crack off the wall face and plummet down the trench. With a loud boom, the back end of the vessel crashed downward. Rina's hand slipped and she went sliding down the sub headfirst.

"Shiro!" she cried out, reaching for him.

He stretched out his arm, but she had already passed him.

"Grab a strap!" he yelled.

Her arms flailed in the air desperate to snatch anything. A black foot strap was ahead and she caught it with her fingers. She snapped around feet first, bashing into two portholes before jerking to a stop. The minisub was nearly vertical and she struggled to keep her grip. Another bang on the ship and the nose went down hard. Rina managed to get one foot into a floor strap and held herself in place. The vessel finally leveled off but the heavy rumbles continued their vibrations.

The bruise on her side had gone from a dull throb to a piercing pain. Through a porthole she saw a thirty-foot gray dome attached to the wall. In its center, two red and green lights were alternately flashing. The sounds of cracking rock echoed through the sub and she watched several falling boulders crash onto the dome and tumble off. Running along both walls of the trench, rows of ashen domes with blinking lights faded into the darkness.

The nukes, she thought. A wave of fear overcame her. *We're dead.*

Another strike on the sub and her foot popped out of the restraint. Before she could secure it, a succession of hits bounced her on the floor, her legs thrashing in all directions. Just above her, an explosion blew open the metal doors on the wall. Fiery sparks bulleted through the electrical boards then followed the wires in the wall, bursting like a strip of firecrackers. She scrunched her face against the floor, hoping the sparks wouldn't ignite her hair or clothes. Then everything stopped. It was quiet.

The rumbling outside had ceased abruptly but the frenzied water kept jostling the ship. Finally, the movement came to a halt. There was silence except for the fans working at full speed, clearing the smoke from the air.

Rina lay on her stomach exhausted with her face to the side, not wanting to move her stiff and aching body. The coolness of the indigo carpet was refreshing, and a nap was coming on fast. She felt Shiro's finger touch her bottom lip and she opened her eyes. Blood covered his thumb.

"You stopped the countdown," he said, grinning with his big teeth. He helped her sit up. "Are you okay?"

"Yeah," she said, pushing the black hair off her face. "That hurt."

"Yep," he said, still smiling, "but we're alive."

"We need to get topside." She crawled past him, her ribs aching but her muscles were finally starting to loosen. "If we can get close enough to the surface, I can break into a satellite and inform my dad, that is, if Bauman doesn't blow us up first."

"Oh good," said Shiro, "fun time with Rina isn't over."

"I keep your life exciting," she said, kneeling in front of the main systems monitor. Without me, your life would be dull."

"Unfortunately, excitement with you always means a near death experience."

She winked at him and tapped the screen. "We're at twenty-eight thousand feet. We have enough oxygen for eight hours and…no."

Dread threatened to overwhelm her. "We lost ballast."

Without the ballast tanks, we can't reach the surface.

Kneeling in the center of the sub Shiro held up a smoldering circuit board. "I think I found the ballast."

Equations and theories raced through Rina's mind as she searched for an answer. There had to be a way out. *No problem is unsolvable.* She willed herself to persevere, to keep searching for a plausible escape, but nothing sufficed. As her hope waned, she sat back on her calves and looked at Shiro who was checking the circuit boards.

Did I just kill him? The thought was agonizing.

She turned and dangled her legs over the ledge, watching the control stick wobble between them. She glanced back at the data. The ballast tanks could only be repaired from the outside but without the manipulator arms, it was impossible. The realization of certain death began to set in. Bauman had won.

"Shiro," she said with a heavy heart. "I can't get us out of here. It's over." Her eyes flooded with tears. "I'm so sorry. I wish you weren't here." She banged the floor with the side of her fist, then swiped the moisture off her face. "I can't believe this. We're really going to die."

Shiro rushed to her side. "Die? As in forever?"

"Yeah," she said, watching his face pinch tight with fear.

"Can't you do something? I don't like death. I'm only twenty-nine years old; I'm not supposed to die this young."

"I'm only twenty-one," she said, taking his hand. "I'm sorry."

The panicked look on Shiro's face told her she had to forget her frustration and calm him down once again. On their last field study of an active volcano, Mt. Etna, Shiro couldn't stay still, always checking everyone's work, yelling at people, rushing the study so they could get off the mountain. He made the team so nervous they wanted to throw him into the volcano. Right now, he looked like he was going to scream in a frenzied panic.

"There's got to be something you can do," he said, his lips trembling.

She sighed heavily. "There's no way out of this. All the repairs have to be done from the outside. Just try to relax."

His face whitened; his breathing sped up.

He's going to hyperventilate, thought Rina. *Again.*

"Cup your hands over your nose and mouth," she told him, helping him position his hands and recalling the many times in the past she had done this. "It's all right, Shiro. We're heroes, even if no one knows it."

Shiro's words came out between his breaths. "I-don't-want-to-die." His eyes were teary; his forehead was dripping sweat.

"I don't either," she said, noticing twinkles of light outside the sub. "Look, chances are someone knows about Bauman and a rescue attempt is in progress. Keep your hopes high and everything will be fine."

Bauman's too smart, she thought. *No one knows.*

"Can you imagine what Bauman is doing right now?" she said, trying to lighten the mood. "Picture a fat hippo in a tutu lying on the floor kicking, screaming, and crying for his mommy because he didn't get his way."

Shiro let out a chuckle and lowered his hands. His breathing was returning to normal.

"I guess you're right," he said. "Someone is probably trying to save us right now."

"Exactly. And look where we are. We're in the most unexplored region of the planet, the place we love the most. So let's use this time before our rescue to study the trench."

With her hand she turned Shiro's head towards the clear dome. Outside, the lights revealed a swarm of alien-shaped macro plankton jetting about, lighting up the dark water like diamonds. Their sizes varied from one inch to over eight inches and some were close enough to view their transparent bodies, which simulated turbine engines with flywheels. They truly were a wonder of nature to survive in the immense pressure. Two years ago, Vector Industries who was working with the military, announced they were going to do a long-term study of the Challenger Deep using an *X-38*.

They weren't studying for science, she thought, *they were accessing the best place to plant the nukes. Bauman and Steinmann are working together.*

A fit of anger gave her the urge to punch something but the vessel was too fragile at this point, and she didn't want to have to explain it to Shiro. It would just panic him again. She gazed out the front of the vessel. The exterior lights of the craft caught the ominous shape of a dome, one of the nukes with its lights off. It would have made her day to have seen Bauman's expression when his bombs didn't ignite. The control stick tapped the inner side of her leg. It would be useless to drive. There was nowhere to go except down.

"I hate this blood on my shirt," said Shiro, pinching the white material from his chest. "You wouldn't by any chance have a bleach stick?"

She shook her head and laughed. "No, and at least it's your own. Remember the time I accidentally got pushed down a crowded stairs and hit my head, bloodying your shorts?"

Shiro grunted. "Yeah, it made me sick. I wasn't on meds then."

"And you freaked out," she said, "tearing off your shorts in the middle of main street Las Vegas. The pain in my head was really bad but I couldn't stop laughing."

"That was kind of funny," he admitted with a smile. "If it wasn't for your dad I would've been arrested for indecent exposure."

For the first time, she noticed desiccated blood above his right temple. She delicately fingered through his black hair and found congealed blood covering a half-inch cut.

"That grunt hit you pretty hard with the butt of his rifle," she said.

"I'm fine, but this shirt is ruined." He released the spotted cloth and wiped his fingers on the leg of Rina's jean-shorts.

"Hey, think back to Colorado," she said, ignoring what he'd just done to her shorts. "That was my favorite place in the whole world."

"The air is too thin at twelve thousand feet, and the headaches were atrocious."

"Yeah, but the air is so clean. I loved the fact we were the only people for miles. If you had the chance again, would you climb the big oak tree by the lake?"

"No way. I was scared to death. The first time it took me two hours to climb fifty feet. Your mom had to bribe me with her chocolate chip cookies." They laughed and he continued, "I can't believe I climbed it at least ten times, just for the cookies and to hear her space stories about a planet called Verlea. I could swear she put an addictive chemical in those cookies because I still crave the stupid things."

"Yeah," said Rina, patting his hand.

Shiro loved her mother, especially since his parents died in a plane crash five years ago, leaving him alone. Her parents, Mary and Justin, immediately treated him like a son, seeing to his care. Shiro became family. Rina gazed up through the domed glass. The swarm of plankton had vanished. Not a visible ray of light shone through the black water.

"Mom loved astronomy," she said, closing her eyes. *Soon it'll be over.* "That's why we built the house up so high; she wanted to be near the stars. She made Verlea seem so real."

"She was the best," he said. "Hey, is it getting lighter outside?"

"Whoa," she said, taken by surprise. It had brightened at least forty percent.

There was a loud thump and the vessel shifted. The sonar began to ping. A high-pitched scrape against the ship's metal hull sent quivers down her spine.

She gripped the control stick. "Get on the terminal beside me and tell me what's out there."

"Aye, sir." Shiro swung his legs around and knelt behind her. "I don't get it. Nothing is registering on sonar."

Rina's mouth dropped open at a massive translucent bubble rising up in front of the glass window. It was the size of a truck. She dipped forward, not wanting to lose sight of the strange phenomenon bobbling through the dark water.

"What is it?" she asked.

"I don't know."

"The volcanic vents are over a hundred miles from here," she said. "Could one be forming below us?"

"I certainly hope not. Look!" he pointed, "there's more."

Hundreds of bubbles were clearly visible. The *X-38* lurched as a half-bubble slid up the glass, squealing like fingernails on a chalkboard.

"We have to go!" said Rina, tightening her fingers around control stick. "I'm going to—"

There was a hard shudder, then a jerk, and the sub moved forward. Rina tried to steer the craft, but the stick wouldn't budge.

"We'd better belt up," said Shiro.

She thought she heard him say something, but the phenomenon was fascinating. The minisub creaked and trembled, moving faster and faster, until the large bubbles became streams of light. The roar of the moving water thundered through the ship.

"What's happening?" yelled Shiro.

"Hold on!" she shouted, barely able to hear him.

She released the control stick and grabbed a wall strap. The vessel raced downward with the spiraling water.

"The Gs are at fifteen," she shouted. "We should be unconscious." She touched the screen to view the sub's velocity. "One hundred feet a second," she yelled, unsure if he could hear her. "This can't be right!"

She tapped the screen a few more times trying to make adjustments, but the reading remained. The external lamps revealed the swirling water, which reminded her of the F-5 tornado, however, they were in a whirlpool going down into the deepest crack in the Earth.

The sounds of bending metal echoed through the minisub. Red lights flashed on the monitor. Their depth was over thirty-four thousand feet and growing fast. The rushing water was so fierce she swore every cell in her body was vibrating. There was a loud pop in the rear of the vessel and seawater came gushing in. Rina tapped the computer screen and the valve shut. How long would the ship last? *At this rate, maybe a minute.* Her thoughts returned to Bauman. It would just be a matter of time before he sent the other sub for detonation. A voice came from the speaker above. It was him.

"If this message activated, you're below thirty-six thousand feet. I've won, Rina. Your father is dead. I killed him. He died a sniveling coward and you're going to join him soon. May you rot in your cold grave."

Rina froze at the statement. Her heart pounded and she swallowed hard, her hysteria quickly rising.

"That's a prerecorded message," said Shiro, reassuring her. "The detonation of the New Madrid fault never happened, so your dad is safe."

"You're right," she said and pushed the thought from her mind.

Perimeter alarms began blaring. One thousand feet to the bottom. She touched the monitor and the alarms stopped.

"Less than a minute," she said.

Shiro offered his hand. "We go together."

Rina nodded and clutched his hand tight. They could see the cold gray mud approaching fast. Shiro clamped his eyes shut and squeezed her hand. She refused to close her eyes.

Bauman's the sniveling coward.

Blinking in bold red was "IMPACT 200FT." She held her breath and scrunched her face. This was the end.

Without warning, the vessel made a sharp turn into a cave. Rina went flying into Shiro and they bashed into the sidewall. He quickly shoved her back to a sitting position.

"I told you to belt yourself in!" he shouted.

"Look!" she said excitedly, pointing outside. "The rock face is…it's…moving."

The grizzled stone glistened with moisture and seemed to shift in place, squirming and bending shape. She blinked several times, wondering if her vision would steady itself because what she was seeing didn't appear real. The roar of the water was gone. Bubbles streamed backwards over the domed glass of the sub. She reached up and touched the metal ceiling where water droplets had formed.

"Are we in air?" she asked.

"Got me," Shiro answered softly.

"This has got to be the Moho," she said, not taking her focus off the moving stone.

"The Moho?" he asked nervously. "How could that be? We should be dead."

"Yeah, but we're not." He was getting paler by the second. She had to get his mind off the danger. "Tell me about the Mohorovicic discontinuity." He didn't answer so she slapped his arm. "Wake up! What's the Mohorovicic discontinuity?"

Startled, he began talking. "The Moho is the chemical change in the rock separating the earth's crust from the upper mantle—wait a minute...." He cleared his throat. "Why are you asking me stupid questions?"

"To keep you from puking," she said, grateful he'd come to his senses. "Keep it together, bro. I need you."

At the end of the tunnel, a bright light was approaching fast. The control stick was shifting on its own with perfect direction.

"Someone's controlling the ship," she said.

"How can that be? No one can survive down here. This is nuts! We must be dreaming."

She pinched his forearm hard and a high-pitched cry nearly shattered her eardrums.

"What the heck is wrong with you?" he shouted, rubbing his arm. "You gave me a bruise."

"This isn't a dream. I don't know what's happening but I need you to get a grip. I mean it, Shiro, something strange is going on and I need you with all your senses. Don't make me hurt you again."

"You're a psycho," he said, still kneading his arm.

"You're right," she said. "We should be dead. This has to be off-world technology."

"Little green men? Get real."

"You have a better explanation, Tarzan?"

Shiro glanced at her and didn't answer, skeptical as always. Questions were running rampant through Rina's mind. *Who are they? Why are they here? What are they doing to the planet?* The white light changed to a pale yellow then broke into three separate lights. Rina stared in amazement. Within moments, their heads snapped around to a dark brown vessel zooming passed them. Colorful lights outlined its oblong shape.

"I don't believe it," said Shiro. "Was that a—"

"Spaceship!" said Rina, thrilled at the revelation. "There are people down here!"

"Do you think they're British?"

"A spaceship from another world just flew by us and you think it's the British?"

"Hey, they use their cute accents to distract your thinking so they can empty your bank account. I don't trust them."

Suddenly, the light went from pitch black to sun-fire yellow. They screamed and leaned back, cupping their faces.

"What the heck?" said Rina, blinking and waiting for her vision to adjust.

"We're in another tunnel," said Shiro.

The minisub spiraled in the air, tearing through the tunnel at incredible speed. The quick turns and gyrations jolted them side-to-side and Rina was sure her head was going to snap off; it was all she could do to hold onto the wall strap. The sub whipped around a bend, then slowed and gradually came to a stop.

Giant glowing boulders were gingerly floating through the magma, resembling magnificent chunks of gold. Rina was so anxious to absorb the wonders it became difficult to control her breathing.

"This must be the mantle," said Shiro. He put his hand on the domed window. "It's not even warm."

Rina palmed the glass. "This technology is way beyond us."

Hundreds of various size boulders surrounded the small ship. A large one was passing overhead and she couldn't take her eyes off it, leaning forward and almost falling off the ledge.

"Do you think it's iron?" she asked.

Before Shiro could answer, the sub bolted into high speed again. Rina went tumbling back and Shiro snatched her hand just in time.

"What the heck is wrong with you?" he said. "Keep a grip on a strap at all times!"

He pulled her back and she grabbed a wall strap.

"Sorry," she said. "The science is incredible."

A section of sepia-colored stone was closing in.

"What do you think it is?" asked Shiro.

"The second Moho," she said, "between the outer core and inner core." Her voice softened with the fascinating realization. "We're actually inside the planet, Shiro. No one has ever seen its interior. This is so awesome."

"Yeah," he said softly. "It feels surreal."

The vessel raced through the light brown cave. When it rounded a corner, the light flared to a blinding white. They yelled and shielded their eyes with their hands, but it wasn't enough. The light was so strong the outlines of their bones and veins were visible through their hands. It was like staring at the sun.

"This must be the liquid outer core," Rina said, her voice straining.

"Yeah, and it's killing me."

The *X-38* cruised downward with an unusual smoothness. She squeezed a peek through her fingers. There was a dark spot in the distance. She took two thick wads of her long black hair and wrapped her hands, then cupped them over her eyes. The dark spot was...*spinning!* She poked Shiro with her elbow.

"Look! It's the solid inner core," she said, unable to curb her enthusiasm. *The science was incredible!* "We were right. It spins opposite the outer core, creating our magnetic poles. This is great!"

Shiro used her hair and did the same thing.

"What's that revolving black spot?" he asked.

"I don't know. There's no texture on its surface. Maybe an

entrance to a cave?"

"A cave to what? How is this happening? We should be dead."

Rina was busy timing the spinning cave. They had to hit it precisely or they would crash into the core. The closer they got, the faster the core was spinning. She carefully counted the revolutions.

No more than twenty seconds.

As they neared the opening, the solid rock was still there.

"Not this way!" she shouted.

Just then, the hole reappeared and the vessel entered the cave. The ship swung around and went into a horizontal spin. Shiro banged his head against the sidewall and lost consciousness. Rina screamed as her body rolled backwards down the sub and bashed into the back wall. Everything went black.

CHAPTER 8
Kalin

Kalin and Marante stood in the heart of Earth. Many times the missions from the Federation had sent Kalin into the core of a planet and each time he got the same feeling.

Humans shouldn't be here.

The black jagged stone of the cavern contained deep slits every twenty feet traveling up its sides and across the ceiling. *The tell tale signs of a REM alignment.* At the top of the hundred-foot high cavern, a thin cloud of dust and moisture drifted silently in its confined space, diffusing the artificial light created by the sprayed-on Vitra Crystals. Numerous boot imprints embedded the earthen floor and in front of the walls, foot-high mounds of dirt littered the ground. *Could Vorkis' REM be malfunctioning?* He could only hope. Four large tunnels led out of the cave.

"Why do the bad guys always pick these kinds of places?" he asked. "It feels like a crypt."

"Because they know you are afraid of the dark," said Marante, keeping his focus on the scanner.

The small black rectangular device was tiny in his hands, yet he worked the holos with ease.

"Ha, ha," sneered Kalin. "Bonehead."

In the center of the open cave, a massive white platform lay anchored to the floor. Tall columns marked the four corners, each having three sets of red, yellow, and green lights. Marante placed his foot on the edge of the platform; the width of his leg almost matched his arm.

"This is the main teleporter pad," he said. "The Quilia particles date back two months. The majority of the tunnels in this complex are approximately eighty feet in height. Large enough for Xeon Diffusers."

Kalin fixed his glare on several slate-blue boxes resting on the floor near the far wall. Stamped horizontally across their centers were white letters: *SalTech*.

Saleran Technology, thought Kalin, *stolen from Salera.*

Unknowingly, he squeezed the handle of his gun, bending the black metal. He immediately let go. His Barra was his protection, an extremely lightweight rifle able to laser a target from over three thousand feet. Kalin slid the strapped Barra off his shoulder and raised the rifle, aiming at the containers. He could never allow Vorkis to retain any Saleran technology.

Marante grabbed his arm. "If you fire your weapon it will reveal our presence. You do want the element of surprise?"

Catching Vorkis off-guard was the only way. He had to be patient so he nodded and lowered his weapon.

"How far to the Xeon Diffusers?"

"Ten clicks," said Marante, "and I'm afraid he's altered their systems. If we tamper with the Xeons, it will initiate a destruct sequence in their reactors." He glanced at Kalin. "Enough energy will be released to incinerate the core."

"Let me get this straight," said Kalin. "If we mess with the Xeons, they'll destroy Earth. Yet if we don't, the dredging will destroy Earth." He shrugged. "This is a no-win situation. Earth is doomed."

Marante pointed up. "Tell that to the millions of men, women, and children who will be eradicated. Give me time, my friend. I will find a way."

"Time is what I don't have," said Kalin. "Vorkis first, then Earth. He has to be stopped."

"And what if the implosion becomes critical?" Marante stepped closer. Kalin felt his telepathy digging into his mind. "Will the crowned Prince of Salera allow the slaughter of so many?"

A rush of fury soared through Kalin. "How could you think I'd let Vorkis kill again? How long have we been working together?" He shook his head in disappointment. "I've never failed a mission to save lives and I'm insulted you're doubting me now."

Marante's eyes pressed into dark slits. "I want to hear you say you will do everything possible to save them and not forfeit their lives to satisfy your vengeance."

Marante's nose had grown to two inches in diameter and shined red as an apple. He was livid.

"I will do whatever is necessary to save them," Kalin said, frustrated. "Satisfied?"

The stringent hold of Marante's telepathy was powerful, but Kalin worried more about his empathic abilities. When his family and people had died, Marante helped to control the varying emotions determined to bring him down, and he'd succeeded. But over time, Kalin learned how to manipulate Marante's powers, occasionally permitting small spurts of anguish and torment to break through, just enough to pacify him. Never would he allow his friend to sense the explosive emotions intensifying each day Vorkis lived. He would soon lose his mind if nothing was done. Seeing him die was the only way to stop the misery.

He's dead, no matter who's involved, thought Kalin, hiding his words from Marante.

A breeze of putrid air howled its way in from a tunnel.

"What is that nasty smell?" he asked, scrunching his nose and looking around the cave.

Marante's cathectic probing ceased and he took up studying the scanner. "This core is home to a variety of large creatures. Some are carnivores. We must be cautious."

"Shh," said Kalin, raising his hand. "Listen."

From the tunnel behind them, a high-pitched whining sound was getting louder.

"Incoming!" he shouted and pushed Marante hard, slamming him into the far wall.

A yellow ship zoomed out of a tunnel spinning in the air. Kalin dove behind the blue boxes watching a whirlwind of dust rise up from the ground like a tornado. The vessel stopped turning in mid-air then slowly leveled off on the platform. Kalin stood and saw Marante walking towards the rear of the craft.

"What is it?" asked Kalin.

"It is an Earth-human submersible," Marante said, reading the small holo. "Two Earth-humans are inside and alive, a male and female."

"I wasn't aware Earth-humans had the technology to travel through their planet." He noticed the bold black letters scrolled across the vessel's side: *US ARMY – X38*.

"They do not," said Marante. "I have detected REM particles on its metallic surface. Apparently, Vorkis escorted this vessel through his planetary REM tunnel. He deliberately brought them down here."

"Why would he want Earth-humans? They're a primitive species with nothing of value."

"I agree," said Marante, standing beside him, "but Vorkis will be sending a troop of Zorcons. I suggest we take the Earth-humans with us and leave this area."

"Right," said Kalin. He handed his Barra to Marante. "Now, where's the door?"

CHAPTER 9
Rina

Rina slowly opened her eyes to the sounds of water droplets echoing in her head. Everything was white and blurry. A tiny blue light gradually came into focus. She was lying on her side facing a dangling electrical panel. Her body felt heavy and stiff; she was sure riger mortis had set in. She swung her right arm around to get up and instantly stopped; her bruised ribs reminded her of Bauman.

With one hard push, she sat up and groaned, aggravated at the pain radiating through her torso. Shiro was sitting up front, slumped over unconscious. She looked out the glass dome and her mouth dropped open in shock. *We're in a cave.* Shiro began moving.

"Wake up!" she said, straining to crawl towards him; her muscles were fighting her.

"Where are we?" he asked, rubbing the side of his head.

She tended the main systems monitor. "According to the readings we're in an oxygen atmosphere." She tapped the screen. "The air outside is breathable. I think we're in Earth's core."

"Wait a minute," said Shiro, unbuckling himself. "You're not making sense. Start at the beginning."

She hurried to the center of the vessel, got on her knees and spun the wheel to the top hatch.

"We need to leave," she told him, using her shoulder to shove the hatch. "I'll explain on the way. Man, this is heavy. Help me."

Shiro joined her and they both pushed. The hatch popped open with a suction sound.

"The sub was being controlled, and—wait!" Her voice sank to a whisper as she quietly shut the hatch. "I heard talking. It's two men. They're coming for us."

"Crap," Shiro said. "We have no weapons to defend ourselves."

"Hand me the flashlight," she said.

He gave it to her and said, "What are you going to do?"

"Remember the spaceship? Hopefully, the aliens won't know what this is."

"That isn't going to work," said Shiro. "Didn't you ever watch Star Trek? They all have Tricorders."

Rina rolled her eyes. "You're pathetic. Now listen," she said, testing the flashlight, "we have to do this fast and catch them off-guard. Are you ready?"

"I guess," he said. "But, wait. What if all this is a hoax? What if someone is playing with our minds? This can't be real, Rina. No one can survive in the core."

She got in his face, annoyed at his repeated doubtfulness. "Do I have to pinch you again?" He quickly moved his arm away. "This is real, Shiro, and you'd better accept it. Now quit being asinine and let's go."

"Fine," he said sternly.

The insult worked.

"And I'm not asinine, retard."

"Help me," she said, ignoring his words. "We're going to push this open as fast as we can, then make a run for it."

He positioned his shoulder across from hers. "One-two-three!"

They rammed the hatch open and it banged into something that grunted. There was a low whir and then a dull thud. They eyed each other suspiciously.

"I think we just knocked one of them off the sub," she whispered. "Let's go."

Shiro pulled her arm back. "What if they're friendly? Maybe we should talk to them first."

"They're not friendly. They're destroying our planet. Now let's stay low and quiet."

Shiro nodded. They crawled out and peeked over the side. A man with black hair was lying on the ground incoherent. Rina pointed to a tunnel facing them, their exit. After carefully climbing down behind the sub, they tiptoed around the vessel and stopped, frozen in their tracks.

A tall thin alien dressed in black skin-tight clothes was kneeling beside the man and fiddling with a small device in his hands. His bony fingers were at least eight inches in length, and he resembled one of the tall round-headed aliens from the Cantina band in the old movie classic *Star Wars*.

This is a real alien, she thought as an uncomfortable feeling settled within her. *Beings from another world are trying to kill us.*

The big-headed thing turned to them.

"Hello!" he shouted.

Rina grabbed Shiro's arm and began running to the tunnel.

"Wait!" yelled the alien.

She ground the dirt under her sneakers and stopped, then swung around pointing the yellow flashlight at them in a menacing way. It wasn't on.

"Don't come any closer," she demanded, waving the flashlight at them. "I'll shoot and you'll both be dead!"

The big head tapped the device in his hand and a miniature image rose up.

A hologram?

"That is a light emitter," he said. "Not a weapon. We mean you no harm, my lady."

The big head has a British accent!

Shiro spoke from the corner of his mouth. "Told you."

"The British are not aliens," she said quietly.

"Thank you for nearly killing me," said the dark-haired man, who was on his feet and brushing off his black vest. "We don't have time for this. Now come quietly or we'll force you."

Rina flung the flashlight at them. The two aliens jumped to the side, allowing it to hit the ground between them. She backed into the passage, pulling Shiro with her. His trembling hand was cold and sweaty.

"We have to run, Shiro," she said quietly.

Keeping his stare ahead, he nodded. His breathing was erratic.

He's going to hyperventilate, she thought. *I just hope he can run.*

"Your escape will only put you in danger," said the big-headed alien.

How could he have heard me?

The big head continued, "There are carnivorous creatures throughout these caves. Stay with us and we can protect you."

"Run, Shiro!" she shouted.

Rina and Shiro vaulted down the lit tunnel. A phosphorescent ore was glowing on the ceiling. *Artificial light.* They ran for what seemed forever through different passages, hoping the alien pair wasn't following.

"Hold it!" She pulled Shiro to a stop. "I hear footsteps coming this way. Hide!"

They ducked behind an outcrop of brown rock. The thumping sounds got closer and louder until finally three beings jogged passed them. She hunched down further and felt her stomach contents rise into her throat. Their light gray uniforms hid every part of their extremities except their heads. Clear gel covered their transparent skin. Red and blue veins pulsed within the sheer pink muscles stretching over their skulls. Round crimson glowing eyeballs rested in ebony sockets, giving them the eyes of a "Terminator." They were like skinned humans sheathed in plastic wrap. She shivered at the thought of what they looked like beneath their uniforms. The three creatures jogged out of sight. Shiro was pale white.

"Show some backbone," she said, getting to her feet. "I need you to be strong."

"Those-guys-are-nightmares," he said between the panting as she helped him up.

He was trembling so badly his legs could barely hold him. She was about to tell him to cup his hands over his mouth when blood-curdling screams came from down the passageway. The sounds of hacking flesh echoed through the tunnel.

Shiro screamed and ran to her. "Something touched me!"

Behind where Shiro once stood, the ominous shape of a clawed hand seemed to be moving within the stone.

"What is that?" she asked, stepping back. *This can't be good.*

"I don't know!" he said, rabidly brushing his shoulder. "I have to get it off!"

He kept sweeping at the white cloth of his shirt, visibly repulsed and shaking, trying to remove something that wasn't there. Just then, from out of the russet colored wall, a massive animal stepped onto the ground. She grabbed Shiro's arm and pulled him to her, backing them both away.

Surrounded by a thin cloud of swirling brown dust, the monster shook its body, creating a small mound of dirt. The animal stood hunched like an ape with thick long arms dangling below its bent knees. Its scabrous dim gray skin trickled a blackish fluid. Two rows of sharp spikes lined its shoulders and arms, ending with platter-size hands where four long fingers boasted five-inch talons. Standing hunched, it was over six feet tall. The creature's white glowing eyes tightened in anger as it glared at them. The beast opened its giant maw and roared with quivering lips, revealing blackened gums and rows of serrated dagger-like teeth. Rina squeezed Shiro's arm.

"Run!" she shouted.

They dashed down the tunnel with the monster chasing them on all fours. It was scampering up and down the walls at an incredible speed.

"I can't keep up!" Shiro grunted through heavy breaths.

"Yes, you can!" shouted Rina. "You go, I go, so run faster!"

The animal's claw latched onto Shiro's shoulder and he hit the ground rolling. The creature leapt onto him and Shiro screamed in terror as it snapped at his face. With all her might, Rina swung her leg and kicked the beast in the head, knocking it off him. She quickly grabbed Shiro's outstretched hands and yanked him up straight. The monster jumped to its feet with a growl. Another animal stepped out from the wall, hissing as it hobbled towards them, its hefty claws ready to sever their flesh. Rina and Shiro turned and bolted down a darker tunnel with the creatures in pursuit.

CHAPTER 10
Kalin

The Caves

Three spiked creatures jumped out of the wall, roaring and waving knife-like claws. Kalin leapt backwards and fired his Barra. A blue beam struck the nearest animal in the chest. It shrieked and stumbled backwards, falling to the ground in convulsions. The two other beasts charged. Two laser shots from Marante and the monsters went down. Gaping holes opened their torsos, their bodies twitching with what life remained. The high-pitched whining of their Barras settled into a low hum. Kalin stared at the creatures whose skin was darkening as death rolled in.

A painful way to die, he thought.

He pressed a blue button on the side of the weapon and a tiny door slid open. Two small orbs appeared and he gently tapped the yellow one. A rotating holo displayed the three-dimensional specs on the weapon. He waved his hand through the holo and the settings readjusted.

"What are they?" he asked, noticing the foot-high mounds of dirt where the animals had manifested.

"There is no record of this life form," said Marante, kneeling beside a beast. Its body was still and black in color. "They have minimal intelligence and are indigenous to this world."

"Set your Barra to incinerate." Kalin watched the door on the weapon slide shut. "We have to find those Earth-humans. I need to know why Vorkis wants them."

Marante was busily studying the scanner. His telepathy hadn't picked up Kalin's thought of using the two Earth-humans as bait. It would force Vorkis to come to him—an ideal scenario. If Earth's implosion became eminent, he would be sure to save the Earth-human pair for species regeneration. It was better odds than what he had.

"Let's go," he said.

They hadn't jogged far through the tunnel when they heard voices up ahead. Quietly they crept along the tunnel wall, listening to what sounded like snapping bones. Around a bend in a cavern, six Zorcon guards were sitting in a circle voraciously devouring their meal, their Barras resting alongside them on the earthen floor. In the center of the group lay the waste pile, a steaming mound of blackish-red human bones and raw viscera. Kalin's stomach twisted. The smell was putrid, the blatant disregard for human life repulsive. Marante gagged loudly and quickly turned away, holding his mouth. Two Zorcons glowered in their direction; human entrails dangled from their engorged cheeks. Kalin grabbed Marante by the arm and pulled him behind an outcrop.

"What's wrong with you?" he whispered. "You almost got us killed."

"I will never get used to Zorcons," said Marante, whose nose was leaf-green and marble-sized. "They are disgusting creatures."

"Yeah, well, we have to pass those disgusting creatures and I need you to get a grip."

"All right," answered Marante, flaccidly waving his hand in acceptance.

Kalin peeked over the boulders. The Zorcons had resumed their eating. He signaled Marante to follow. Just as they were ready to pass the feeding guards, six of the same spiked animals that had previously attacked them leapt out of the walls, snarling at the Zorcons.

"Oridians!" shouted one of the guards.

The Zorcons went for their Barras but it was too late. The monsters lunged at them with flailing arms. They ripped and slashed at the guards, who screamed and fought to stay alive. The sharp talons of the beasts easily tore through the soft flesh, severing appendages. Within moments, all the Zorcons were dead. Pools of white blood and shredded limbs lay scattered on the ground.

A gray Oridian with a spike-ridden body picked up a detached head and began sucking an eyeball. A brown one tried to swipe the head away but the spiked one shoved him hard and he stumbled back.

The brown animal roared and swung its claw, slicing open the spiked one's shoulder. The creature yelped and dropped the skull, clutching its bloodied wound. It growled at its enemy, exposing two-inch-long serrated teeth. Without warning, the spiked creature bent its massive legs and jumped with such power it seemed to fly in the air before pouncing on its opponent. The two began fighting, swiping with their claws and biting each other. The other Oridians anxiously gathered around the pair, hooting and whooping as they wildly jumped about waving their arms.

It's like an Uru death match, thought Kalin.

He signaled Marante. They cautiously moved past the boisterous crowd then ran down the tunnel until the sounds of the monsters were gone.

Marante checked his scanner. "Apparently, the Oridians are only capable of detecting all heat signatures and odors but cannot perceive sound. The Zorcons were wearing Neth Blockers able to mask their heat and scent, but they malfunctioned due to the increasing electromagnetic field of the planet. I can create NBs to work around this, but we must secure a location for this purpose."

"We need to hurry," said Kalin. "Those Earth-humans need our help."

What could Vorkis want from two Earth-humans? he wondered. *Why didn't he just teleport them?* He couldn't wait to talk to the two.

Using the scanner, Marante led them to a narrow entrance. He easily slipped through the slivered opening, but Kalin had to suck in his chest and ram himself in. After heaving and huffing his way for fifty feet, Kalin emerged behind Marante into a small cavern with several flat knee-high boulders scattered about. Marante sat on one and sifted through his belted waist pouch, extracting the essentials to build the NBs. Kalin leaned against the wall, trying to catch his breath.

"You could've picked a better place to get into," said Kalin between heavy pants. "My lungs are almost crushed."

Marante tossed him the scanner and he fumbled to catch it.

"Stop being a baby and check our location."

"Baby?" said Kalin, annoyed at the put-down. "You have no lungs. You breathe through your skin. And don't call me a baby, pencil-neck. I'm surprised your head fit."

"Baby," said Marante, never looking up.

A loud rumble shook the cavern. Clumps of loose dirt and stone cracked off the ceiling and walls as waves oscillated through the stone. Marante swooped up the equipment in his arms and huddled by the wall with Kalin. The shaking stopped abruptly. Clouds of dust particles flittered down like rain, settling on the ground.

"That was nasty," said Kalin, eyeing their surroundings suspiciously. He placed the scanner on a boulder and hoisted his Barra.

This is not going to be easy, thought Kalin. *Those creatures come out of the walls. Another surprise attack is inevitable.*

"I have also created NBs for this chamber to make it a safe base," said Marante.

Kalin had yet to meet someone that could equal Marante's intellect and speed with electronics. He always carried the basic devices already half-built in case of emergencies, and there were many times his ingenuity had saved their lives.

Marante went around the cavern pressing six silver coin-size devices onto the stone walls. When he finished, he took the scanner, stepped to the middle of the cavern, and waved his hand over an orb. In the center of each flat disc, six tiny red lights blinked on. He tossed Kalin his NB.

"She was a perfect replica of a Saleran female," said Marante, attaching the silver NB to his own black tunic.

"Not really," said Kalin. "She was too short and she smelled different."

Saleran women had been special; their Lasgera Gland secreted an alluring scent which they controlled, and it was difficult for a human male to resist it, including himself.

It's just something else I have to forget, Kalin thought, frustrated at never again being able to take in the sensual aroma. Suddenly a morbid thought entered his mind. *What if the rumor of Vorkis was that he'd located a female to have his child? Maybe an Earth-human female?*

Just then, terrified screams of people exploded through the cavern. Kalin tapped the NB to his black vest and hurriedly slid through the crevice, mumbling obscenities all the way. He stopped at the main tunnel and peeked out. The two Earth-humans sped by him with snarling Oridians in pursuit.

"Come on!" he said.

They dashed after them.

"A tunnel up ahead will loop around and take us in front of them," said Marante, reading the scanner.

"Lead the way!"

Marante took him into another tunnel and soon they came to the crossway. Stomping footsteps were closing in. Kalin raised his Barra to his cheek, ready to fire. When the pounding feet were almost upon him, he stepped into the passageway, blocking the oncoming Earth-humans.

"Hit the dirt!" he shouted.

The two dove onto the ground and rolled. Laser blasts sent high-pitched reverberations through the tunnel, disintegrating the two creatures into balls of yellow dust. Kalin stood behind the Earth-humans whose attention was on the ashes.

"They're called Oridians," he said.

The girl turned around and Kalin's heart sank. He had never seen such big aqua-blue eyes and thick long black lashes with skin so soft and clear, he doubted if she'd ever had a pimple. A slender nose upended just above a set of moist lips. Her blue shorts and red shirt covered a body any man would die for. Marante appeared beside Kalin. The jaws of the two Earth-humans dropped open. He always had this effect on primitives, especially up close.

"Are you all right?" asked Kalin, staring at the female. She was focused on his friend. "He's harmless," he added, thumbing Marante. "Except for his nose. It can jump start a cruiser when full blown."

"You, shut it. My name is Marante of Chaslea, and this thing—" he pointed at Kalin, "is my captain and comrade of many years, Kalin of Salera. It is good to meet you, Rina and Shiro of Earth."

"How…how do you know our names?" asked Shiro.

This guy has a strange lisp, thought Kalin, *probably from his deformed teeth.*

I agree, answered Marante.

"Chasleans and Salerans are telepathic," Marante said aloud.

"How do you know our English language?" said Shiro.

Marante said, "English is a common language throughout the cosmos, and one that was planted here many millennia ago—"

A bellowing boom split the air followed by a thunderous roar. The tunnel rocked and swayed. Fractures raced up the walls and across the ceiling bursting the stone apart.

"It's at least a niner!" yelled Rina.

"Let's go!" shouted Kalin.

He ran through a haze of black dust with the others close behind, keeping his senses in touch with theirs, making sure they were alive.

They need NBs, said Marante in his mind. *We must make skin contact in order for our NBs to work on them.*

We stop and we die, said Kalin, swerving and jumping over tumbling rubble.

The quaking ceased unexpectedly. Aside from the sprinkling sound of falling pebbles, an eerie silence hovered within the tunnel. Kalin studied their area. Behind them down the passageway, black boulders covered the place they'd been. *A cave-in.* Plumes of steam rose out of six wide cracks that arced across the tunnel.

Earth does not have much time, said Marante.

Yeah, said Kalin, watching Marante brush off his dusty head.

The Earth-human called Shiro was bent over, resting his hands on his knees and gasping for air. The doll-face named Rina was coughing and leaning on the tunnel wall. Kalin saw fingers creep out of the stone behind her. He yanked her away and shot the beast. The blast echoed through the tunnel along with the shrill of the dying animal.

"Thanks," she said, eyeing the ashes on the ground. "Who are you?"

"We will answer your questions when we reach our safe base," said Marante, approaching them. "To shield you from the sensory glands of the Oridians, you must wear what we call Neth Blockers, or NBs." He pointed to the silver pin on his black tunic.

Kalin noticed Shiro examining the cave wall where hundreds of egg-sized crimson balls protruded.

"What are these?" asked Shiro, gently touching a bulb. "I've never seen this type of rock before."

"I don't know," said Kalin, feeling its smoothness. "Marante, do a scan."

An animal roar echoed in the tunnel.

Marante took Rina's hand. "We must make skin contact for our NBs to work on you. Our safe base is not far from here. Come!"

He ran off with Rina. Kalin eyed Shiro.

"I'm not holding your hand," said Kalin.

He grasped the nape of Shiro's neck and they began their jog. Kalin noticed the girl didn't have a problem keeping up the pace. She was firm and tight, her long silky hair bouncing to the trots.

The resemblance is uncanny, thought Kalin.

"In here," said Marante, waving at them.

Shiro stopped at the narrow entrance and stared. "I'll never fit."

"Yes, you will," said Marante, clutching his arm. "Your torso is soft. Come."

Marante and Shiro went in first, then Rina and Kalin. Shiro's grunts got louder as he squeezed further into the crevice.

"You are doing fine, Shiro," said Marante. "We are almost there."

Rina was sliding through unrestricted and pushing Shiro from behind. Kalin hoped Shiro didn't get stuck; using his strength might hurt him. Shiro exited the tunnel and fell to his knees, gasping for air. Rina knelt beside him and patted his back.

"See," she said with a smile. "You made it."

"Barely."

She helped him to stand. "Sit over here and relax."

One of the wall NBs was on the ground. Kalin put it back up while Marante began working.

"Now tell me," said Rina with her arm around Shiro, "what's happening to our world?"

"The most vicious criminal in history is here within your planet and we are here to capture him," answered Marante, his focus on the scanner. The six wall NBs lit up. "His name is Vorkis. He has been sentenced to death for the genocide of his own race of Salerans, he and Kalin's people."

"His own people?" Shiro said in surprise.

"All of them, except me," Kalin said, irritated he may have to explain the whole matter. "He slaughtered everyone with a lethal virus and I'm here to execute him."

"You're the last of your race?" asked Rina curiously.

"Sort of," he said, turning away ashamed. "Vorkis is my soon-to-be-dead cousin."

"What kind of a man would do that?" said Shiro, disbelief in his voice. His breathing was almost normal now.

"A cold-blooded murderer," said Kalin, "and I don't want to talk about it." The acrid revelation was torturous, a twisting dagger forever in his side.

"So," said Rina, "how are we standing in a place where the pressure is over fifty million pounds per square inch? We should be flatter than paper."

Marante went on to explain how Vorkis used REMs to penetrate the planet and create the vast complex. He told them about the Borit Reactor and according to the scans, Vorkis had two ounces of Pril; three was all he needed to destroy any world. Kalin watched Rina closely. She was intrigued with his friend, studying his physique.

A brainer, he thought, *too smart to know what's good for her*.

He lifted one foot onto the boulder next to Rina and raised the Barra to his cheek, checking the alignment, hoping to get her attention. It worked.

"Why did you bring us down here?" she asked.

"We didn't," said Kalin. Her aqua-blue eyes were mesmerizing. "Vorkis did, so tell me why you're here."

"Maybe he's horny," said Shiro. Everyone turned their heads to him. "She's pretty," he said, shrugging his shoulders.

Rina slapped his arm. "Maybe he wants you, hero."

Kalin sat next to Rina. "Vorkis is not into men. He prefers women, but that's not the issue. You must have something he wants."

The two Earth-humans glanced at each other.

"We're geophysicists," said Rina. "The only thing we have is knowledge of Earth."

"What you call knowledge most children are learning at the age of two," scoffed Kalin. "Your race is primitive when it comes to planetary sciences. No, it has to be something you physically possess."

Rina's expression changed from curious to angry. She stood up and raised her arms, gesturing down her body. The dirt from the dive onto the earthen floor couldn't hide the shapely legs and curvy figure.

"This is it," she said. "We don't possess anything of value."

"Maybe it is your looks," said Kalin, ogling her.

"You're sick," she said. "Keep the leers to yourself. I mean it."

"Don't tell me what to do," he said sternly. He had to set the boundaries with this fireball. "Keeping secrets is not going to save your world."

"What secrets?" said Shiro. "We have none. Go ahead. Strip-search her. I dare you."

Rina's eyelids shrank to menacing slits. "Touch me and you're dead. I said I have nothing. Whether you believe it or not, it's the truth."

He got up and stepped closer to her. She didn't budge. *She's not afraid of me.* "You're lying," he said, "and I will get it out of you."

"I tell you what," she said, pushing up on her toes to get closer to his face. He sensed her frustration at being only five feet tall. "When you find out what it is I have, you can tell me about it. But until then, don't call me a liar."

A snorting laugh came from Marante. *She is taking you on*, he said to Kalin in his mind.

She won't win, Kalin answered.

Maybe. Marante sprang to his feet. "We are ready, captain. Rina, Shiro, press these to your clothing."

He tossed a silver NB to Shiro, who attached it to the collar of his white shirt. Marante walked to Rina and handed her the other.

"With this, the Oridians will be unable to detect your heat signature nor scent. Guard it, my lady."

"What's that?" she asked, pointing to his left upper sleeve.

"It is my Comlink," he replied, rubbing his finger over the gold, triangular pin, "a communication device. We cannot use it here for fear of detection. Which reminds me." He turned to Kalin. "With all the shooting, Vorkis is certain to know we are in the vicinity."

"Good," said Kalin. "Bring it." He walked to the narrow exit tunnel and stood, waving his hand forward. "This way, your Short Highness."

A lethal glare from Rina told him she didn't appreciate the appellation.

"Where are we going?" said Shiro, rubbing his forehead in exasperation. "Can't we stay here?"

"Our primary goal is to destroy Vorkis' Command Center," said Marante, "thus saving your planet. Come, you will be fine." He went into the crevasse first, pulling Shiro behind him.

Kalin scrutinized Rina as she pressed the NB to her red shirt. There was something deep within her mind, out of reach, hidden. He would have to continue his probes. She resembled Kara, one of his former girlfriends he'd left behind and one of the most beautiful women on Salera. After he'd left to work with the Federation, Kara took up with Vorkis. There was a distinct change in her personality. When he'd last spoken with her from the *Quasar*, she had kept her head low and never made eye contact. The conversation was short and to the point, a remarkable difference from the old self-involved Kara.

Three months later she died in a mysterious fire. Vorkis was cleared of all charges concerning her death and soon after began his assignment for the Federation searching for Pril.

Rina's beauty surpasses Kara's, he mused. Then he sucked in his breath, shocked at the notion. *Could she be working for Vorkis? Did he place Rina here as a distraction? Possibly as a spy?* Her consciousness harbored high levels of cautiousness and concern for someone else besides Shiro.

As far back as he could remember, Vorkis had always had a beautiful woman on his arm doing his dirty work, and this one was by far the prettiest. But where did Shiro come in? The chubby Earth-human's uncertainty and confusion were innocent—typical emotions sustained by someone unfamiliar with life outside their world. The female was the connection. He was sure of it. Hot anger began building up inside him.

Steady, Kalin, he said to himself. *Don't lose it now.*

His hatred was like a bubble that threatened to burst. Here, in front of him, was someone who may be working for Vorkis and he had to wait. Time would expose her plan, and patience would justify his killing her, but self-control was nearly impossible. The need to choke it out of her was getting stronger. The only way to press her into revealing Vorkis' plan was to make her predicament difficult, make her suffer.

You have no proof, said Marante in Kalin's mind.

She's hiding something and Vorkis is involved, said Kalin. *I swear, Marante, if she's working for him, I'll bleed her until there's nothing left.*

Your hatred is consuming you, my friend. Allow your conscience to guide you, not your heart.

If I could do that, I wouldn't be here, said Kalin.

"Darn," Rina said, wadding her hair into a bun. "I knew I should have clipped it up this morning."

"Sometime today, doll," said Kalin, hoping to irritate her with the cutesy name.

"Must you be so childish?" she said before slipping into the passage.

I'll give you child, he thought. *Time in a Telvor Beam would fix you.*

He slid into the crevice behind Rina, thinking of different ways to torture her. The Telvor Beam was used for medicinal purposes but could be altered to create unimaginable pain. A whiff of perfume floated his way.

It would be a shame to kill her. What attracted beautiful women to Vorkis' hideous personality?

It had to be something Vorkis had concocted, some kind of biochemical, after all, that was his specialty. He was startled to bump into Rina who had stopped just before the exit. She was pushing Shiro.

"It's not working," said Shiro, his voice squeaking from his constriction. "I can't move."

"He is truly wedged," said Marante, who was outside the crevice in the main tunnel, pulling Shiro's arm.

"Hurry up," said Shiro. "I can't breathe."

Kalin reached over Rina's head and pressed his hand against Shiro's upper arm. "Suck it in on my count. One, two, three."

Shiro yelped and flew out of the crevice. He bashed sideways into the far wall with a thud, then moaned as he slumped to the ground.

Rina rushed to Shiro. "Did you have to push so hard, King Kong?"

"I'm sorry," said Kalin, exiting the tunnel. "I thought I was gentle."

"What is a King Kong?" asked Marante, kneeling beside Shiro and checking his vitals with the scanner.

"It's an old Earth-human movie about a big ape," said Kalin smirking, aware of Marante's hatred for Earth-human thrillers. "The insects were great."

Marante's eyes formed into dark slits. A loud groan came from Shiro as Rina helped him off the floor. Ragged tears opened both sides of his white shirt.

"Sorry," said Kalin. Pink splotches covered Shiro's puffy face, a sign of high compression. "Are you all right?"

Shiro squeaked out his words. "I'll live, thanks."

A low rumble grew louder.

"Another quake?" asked Shiro, suddenly totally awake.

"No," said Rina. "The feel is different. It sounds like thumping. Listen."

Kalin ground the soles of his black boots into the dirt. She was right. *Impact tremors.*

"Scorpion!" yelled Shiro, pointing down the tunnel.

A fifty-foot-tall arachnid was charging at full speed.

CHAPTER 11
Justin

OSRI

Justin sat in his office reading the article for the fourth time. Tanya Jensen-Baxter's account was the only existing description of what had happened to Las Vegas. Not even satellite imagery could break through the metallic clouds above the city. The military was helpless against the acid rain and the scientists hadn't had enough time to figure out how to combat it. The destruction took less than seven hours. When the rain ate its way through the hard dirt it hit the aquifer, causing a rapid vaporization and resulting in a monstrous sinkhole. The whole city dropped into the valley floor. Over eleven million people were dead, swallowed forever.

They'd found Tanya with her arms tightly clamped around the sleeping bag, her face buried in the cloth, everything below her waist eaten away. Brenda Jensen gave permission to print the letter in its entirety in an effort to help save the planet. Justin couldn't help feeling the mother's pain. To lose a child was the worst tragedy of all, but to lose one that way, had to be devastating. His heart pounded, and he rubbed his chest through his white shirt, crinkling his paisley blue tie.

I have to stop reading this article, he thought. *It's killing me.*

He put the paper down on his maple desk and noticed Mary's ring wasn't on his finger. He remembered leaving it at Rina's terminal in the MCC after he'd washed his hands. He gazed at a marine tapestry on the wall; its vibrant colors lashed out like fireworks, a reminder of how much Mary had loved the sea.

She had decorated his office with every kind of nautical and sea ornament ever made on Earth. Every week she'd come in with something new to either hang on the wall or place on a desk or table. Every piece of wood was carved into some form of aquatic life, including his desk where a multitude of sculptured dolphins, whales, and assorted marine creatures sat beneath the clear glass top. Even the legs and the ends of the padded armrests of the two maroon-colored chairs in front of his desk were chiseled into the heads and bodies of Beluga Whales.

A solemn emptiness crept up inside him. The three years she'd been dead had felt like a century. When she died, he decided to leave the office just the way it was; a memoriam to a beautiful person. He missed her so much.

He glanced at his left hand again. If Rina discovered the ring was missing from his finger, she'd be upset. She never removed her pendant, not even for showers and pools. The cell phone clipped to his belt showed no messages from Rina. *She must have had some night.* The chiming of the white phone startled him. The caller ID said it was his old friend Admiral Payton Williams.

"How's it going, Payt?" asked Justin, clearing his throat.

"I'm fine," he said. "I can't believe you left me here with these irritants. Some friend you are. How did you convince the President to let you go?"

"I showed him the letter of the young girl who died in Las Vegas. Did you get the gift I sent to your room?"

"Yes, I did," answered Payton happily, "and I called to say thank you. It's the best gift I've ever gotten. Pickles and ice cream."

Justin made a loud chuckle. "Are you sure you're not pregnant?"

"Yes, I'm quite sure," said Payton. "My wife says the same thing and you'd better not tell anyone. Only you and she are privy to that secret."

The office door opened abruptly and General Bauman marched in. Refusing to knock was typical of him. He stood at attention between the two chairs. Justin wondered if Bauman ever lightened up; he was always stiff as a board.

He probably sleeps standing up, he thought.

"I have to go," said Justin. "Something just came up." Bauman glared at him. "I'll talk to you later, Payt." He hung up the phone.

"The President released you?" asked Bauman.

"Yes," answered Justin, holding back a laugh. "I was released from captivity after I pointed out if there was no world to save, why the Peace Conference?"

Bauman nodded and eased into a leather chair. His demeanor was calm, relaxed, yet beads of moisture glistened from between his thinning hair, and the few strands across the top of his head had frizzed. His facial wrinkles were deeper, more carved, and his steel-gray eyes were bloodshot. Something was wrong.

"We need to talk," said Bauman.

There was another knock on the door and Justin's secretary, Barbara, poked her head in. Her bleached blonde hair and heavy blue eye make-up belied her age of thirty-five. She was a wife and mother of two and had an unshakable commitment to her job. Although better offers had come along, she refused to leave claiming OSRI was her home.

"I'm sorry to interrupt," she said, furtively glancing back into the hallway, "but I'm going to dinner. I'll see you in an hour."

"Enjoy yourself," said Justin, noting Bauman hadn't turned his head to acknowledge her.

"Darn right I will," she said. "It's the second time in three days the military is picking up the tab and I'm taking advantage of it. I'll bring you back something."

"Thank you," said Justin.

Barbara left, shutting the door. Bauman walked to the window and peeked through the putty-colored verticals at the parking lot below. He was a firm bulky man whose silhouette filled half the height of a single floor-to-ceiling window.

"What can I help you with, General?" asked Justin, hearing the faint sounds of car doors slamming.

"The world wants answers, Doctor," said Bauman, strolling back to his seat. He straightened his jacket and ran his hand over the wiry threads on his head before sitting down. "I have a way to save the human race, and I believe a man of your stature is needed." He took a deep breath and relaxed back in the seat, leaning his elbows on the armrests and clasping his hands in front of him. He continued, "Due to the world's apparent lack of leadership, we've formed an organization that will ensure the eternity of mankind. The New Continuum will provide a perfect government for all remaining survivors of our new found world."

"Survivors?" asked Justin, scratching his head. "New Continuum? What are you talking about?"

Bauman suspired then continued, "The New Continuum has been founded by a handful of respectable men taken from high-levels of society who in some way, have contributed to the greatness of our race. These men, including myself, have formulated a plan to rid the world of the unwanted, those who give nothing to our way of life such as the hundreds of worthless beings set around the ring of fire—"

"Wait a minute," said Justin, confused, trying to understand. "Are you talking about killing people?"

"Kill is such an ugly word," said Bauman. "Let's just say we're going to clean house. In order for the perfect society to flourish, all refuse must be discarded. Blacks, Orientals, Asians, Latins, and the list goes on, every race, excluding the whites, have to be eliminated. This is an important step to perfection that must be carried out."

Justin sat up horrified, his words stuck in his throat. He caught his breath and spoke. "This is lunacy! Have you lost your mind? You sound like Hitler. You just can't—"

"Hitler had the right idea," interrupted Bauman, "but he did it wrong. There won't be any need for us to build gas chambers or concentration camps, you see, the Earth is going to do the work for us. Three hundred and fifty nuclear warheads at fifty megatons each have been placed within the Challenger Deep. When they ignite, so will half the world's ground faults, henceforth, taking care of most of our problems. It's a perfect plan developed by resourceful minds and whoever doesn't die in the initial blast will be used to serve the greater. We're hoping you'll join us in our crusade to save mankind from itself and birth a new civilization where only peace will rule."

Justin jumped to his feet. "This is an outrage! How can you turn on your world?"

"I haven't," said Bauman, snorting a breath. "We're trying to save it."

"Killing innocent people is manslaughter in any book."

"It's a shame there's no changing your mind," said Bauman. "Your knowledge of the planet would have been useful."

He squeezed his wristwatch and two guards entered the office carrying XL-20 rifles on their shoulders, and S-8 pistols on their belts. They closed the door behind them.

"I'll ask you this last time," he said. "Will you join us?"

"Absolutely not. My daughter was right when she said you're a selfish pathetic man who hides behind a uniform. You really are a coward."

"She said that?" said Bauman, grinning. "Do you know where your daughter is, Doctor?"

Justin stood there motionless. *Could he actually have Rina? It can't be. Not my baby.*

Suddenly, the two soldiers rushed him, grabbed his arms and held him in place. The one to Justin's left was young with blonde buzzed hair, the name "Rick" stitched above the pocket of his gray and white camouflage uniform. The other guard, "Joe," was on his right and older in years with brown hair and silver stubs at the temples. A jagged scar crossed his left cheek. Bauman was shutting the vertical blinds.

"What's going on?" asked Justin, struggling to free himself. "Where's Rina?"

"I gave you your chance," said Bauman, returning to his seat. "The world is going to be ours with or without you. Your time has ended."

"Where's my daughter?"

Bauman made a slight nod at his soldiers. Rick yanked the chair away and Joe punched Justin in the face, sending him reeling into the wall where Rick rammed a fist into his stomach. For a moment, Justin had no idea of his surroundings. The shock of the incident had him doubled over in pain and disoriented. It took several breaths before he gathered his thoughts.

"Why?" asked Justin, slowly standing straight. He used the top of his hand to wipe the blood from his sliced bottom lip.

Bauman nodded his head again. Rick kicked the chair back and Joe shoved him into the seat. The nauseating puke was getting closer to his throat. Bauman was smirking.

"The President will hear about this," said Justin.

Bauman didn't flinch. He nodded and the two soldiers hurried to his side, standing at attention.

"Ever since your daughter broke into our system it hasn't been the same," said Bauman. "Her virus destroyed all the main hard drives, including those of the back-up computers. We'd be fools to allow her to run loose in the system. She's a danger to our way of life."

"My daughter sent that virus because you came back to steal more of her programs."

"Indeed, I did," said Bauman. "We needed more, and she would have refused us. Our actions were justified."

"You've lost your mind," scoffed Justin. "You want to murder the majority of the human race and you think you're rational? Where's my daughter?"

"In good time, Doctor," said Bauman.

Justin knew he had to settle down. Perhaps reasoning with the monster would work. "Let's see," he said, doing a quick mental calculation. "Three hundred and fifty nukes at fifty-megatons each and you'll be releasing the equivalent of over two hundred million tons of TNT into the deepest crack in the world. What makes you think anyone on this planet will survive?"

"We've estimated an eighth of the world's current population would remain," said Bauman. "This works to our advantage. With so few left, we won't have any problem assuming command and we can start anew."

There was a sense of dedication and determination in Bauman's voice that turned Justin's blood cold. He'd actually convinced himself it would work.

"You'll be exterminating whole races of people, whole families, and our heritage." Justin turned to Joe. "Do you have any children? A mother? Father?"

Bauman promptly interjected. "These fine soldiers are loyal to their General. Innocent lives are always lost when peace is attempted. This plan will guarantee humanity's survival."

Justin vaulted out of his chair and bashed his fist on the desk. "Who are you to play God? You and your colleagues will go down in history as the men who massacred the human race! You're worse than Hitler!"

Bauman sprang from his seat. "Enough of this bullcrap!" He slammed his hands on the desk, the wiry strands of hair whisking across his pinched forehead as he scowled at Justin.

"Its people like you, scientists, that created bombs and bio-weapons for our unjust society and if any of your kind survives, I'll have them slaughtered first!"

Bauman's tanned skin changed to a purplish-red color. Rapid breaths shot spittle through his clenched teeth. Bloodshot eyes bulged from their sockets, anxious and ready to kill. His right eye began twitching feverishly, but he kept his glare on Justin as he panted with nostrils flaring. Almost instantly, his eye stopped its spasm, his skin lightened in color, and his shoulders relaxed. His familiar callous expression returned. He straightened up and gently tugged at the ends of his sleeves.

Two personalities?

"Have you seen your daughter lately?" asked Bauman. "I know exactly where she is, Young."

Justin didn't recall seeing Rina at all today, not even last night. It was common for her to stay all night working on the project and he wasn't used to keeping tabs on her. An uncontrollable hate began simmering within.

"Where is she?" he asked in a hardened voice.

Bauman bellowed an insidious laugh. "At the bottom of the

Mariana Trench with Shiro."

Justin leapt across the desk and swung his fist straight into Bauman's nose. The blunt force was so strong Bauman tumbled back onto the floor. A second later, Justin was peering inside the dark barrel of an S-8 pistol.

"Wait!" said Bauman, waving off Joe while Rick helped him off the floor.

Joe immediately backed away from the desk, keeping the gun aimed at Justin and signaling him to sit in his chair. Justin slid off the desk and sat, his stare riveted on Bauman.

"You're a liar," said Justin. "I don't believe you."

"No matter," said Bauman calmly, using his handkerchief to pat the blood draining from his nose. "It's over for you. Gentlemen, complete Phase II."

Rick unshouldered his XL-20, attached a black suppressor to his rifle, and pointed it at Justin. Joe walked around the desk and stood at Justin's left side, facing the entry door, his back to the window. He reached into a Velcro flap on his pants, screwed the silencer onto the gun, and held it to Justin's head.

This is happening too fast, thought Justin.

Justin asked the two men. "What's his promise? Money? Safety? If it's safety, forget it. If every nuclear bomb were set off simultaneously, they wouldn't touch the amount of energy this planet will release. You won't survive even in a jet flying thirty-five thousand feet up. Debris will saturate the atmosphere. The very dirt beneath us will boil. The magma under the crust will burst through the hundreds of fault zones and—"

Justin shut up when the cold metal of the gun barrel pressed into his temple.

"We've taken everything into account, Doctor," said Bauman. "During the initial rupture of the planet, we'll be flying in a jet at a safe distance from the failing fault zones. From there, we'll assess the damage and remaining life. When the planet settles, we'll land and continue our quest. The plan is simple—"

There was a knock on the door.

"Come in!" yelled Justin, not giving Bauman and his men a chance to stop him.

Rick quickly lowered his rifle, pointing it to the floor. Joe moved his gun down into Justin's side near his armpit. Barbara and six people entered the office.

"I hope we're not interrupting anything important," she said. "We felt bad you couldn't come, Dr. Young, so we brought our food back to eat with you."

"You have perfect timing," said Justin as the gun jammed into his upper ribs. "Come in," he said, ignoring the pain. "The General was just leaving."

"Excuse the doctor," said Bauman, "but we're having a private conversation."

"Nonsense," said Justin. "There's nothing these people can't hear."

Joe rammed the gun into Justin's side and twisted the barrel, wrenching his skin. He dared not flinch. Barbara was looking at him strangely.

"Is your lip bleeding?" she asked.

"Yes," said Justin. He turned to Bauman. "It's over, General."

"So it seems," said Bauman, who nodded at his men.

Rick stepped in front of Bauman and Joe moved to the side of the desk. Both aimed their weapons at the group near the doorway.

"What's going on?" Barbara asked.

Justin lunged in front of Barbara just as the two soldiers began firing into the crowd.

CHAPTER 12
Vorkis

The Earth-human male was forty-two years old with thinning brown hair and a rounded gut. Splotches of dried caked food crusted his upper sleeves and the front of his shirt. Two faded brown elastic bands stretched over his soft shoulders and clipped to his torn blue pants, apparently to hold them up.

Another vagrant, thought Vorkis. *He will not be missed.*

Two Zorcons dragged him to the round yellow floor pad of the Telvor Beam that sat to the side of a full-sized standing mirror. This room was specifically designed for Zorcon enjoyment. Mirrors were placed throughout the room to supply extra visual gratification, and they loved it. The frightened man kicked and screamed, fighting to free himself. They held him on top of the pad while an Eivor transparent beam swirled up from the mat and encircled him, holding him in place. The two released the man and stepped back. Vorkis watched the Zorcons in the mirror, They were eagerly observing him, anxious to slurp up his fear, their frothing mouths craving for human meat.

Unable to move his arms and legs, he began pleading for his life, crying pitifully, begging for mercy. The two Zorcons raised their claws and moved closer, snarling and hissing, their white serrated teeth in stark contrast against the blood-red color of their mouths. With lightning speed, they swung their claws and ripped open his torso. The man wailed in horror as they tore out his organs.

Off in the corner, Vorkis stood in silent amusement. The physical form of Zorcons was despicable but their habits were entertaining. He clasped his hands behind his back, content his plan was working. Soon he would have enough Pril to demand anything from the Federation, even the Federation itself.

His eye caught the mirror on the wall beside him. He ran his fingers through his thick black hair, the waves settling perfectly into place, a Saleran trait he appreciated.

I will never see baldness.

He slid his fingers along his trimmed beard and thin mustache surrounding his mouth, feeling the strength of his square jaw, a duly notable vainglorious attribute, and one exemplifying his authority. Puffing out his chest, he tugged on the hem of his dark gray tunic, feeling it straighten around his broad shoulders. He was proud of the nobility he radiated. Only his cousin could match his tall menacing physique, and soon he would be gone.

Kalin was like an infected wound, an unending torment usurping his dreams. He had almost rid himself of the House of Altor and all those who followed him, but the one Saleran gnawing away at his soul was still alive.

Patience, he thought. *I will smell his blood soon.*

He heard the approaching footsteps of Taru, his Captain of the Guard. The tall thin Zorcon stopped at his side and began whispering into his ear. Zorcons had a body temperature of 68.4 degrees, and Vorkis loathed the feel of the cold gel covering their skin, killing any Zorcon who dared touch him. He quickly turned his head and Taru gasped, immediately pulling back.

Vorkis sneered, "Lead on."

They left the feeding Zorcons and headed for his Avec, a lustrous black domed-shaped vehicle. Taru touched a dulled square on the outside and instantly yellow static flared, dissolving into a six-foot wide entrance into the vehicle. The scent of perfumed air rushed into Vorkis' nostrils and he inhaled the rich aroma. There was no need for everything to smell of Zorcons. The plush white seats faced each other and Vorkis sat in the rear. Taru took a seat across from him. The Avec lifted then zoomed down the tunnel.

"Are we ready?" asked Vorkis, keeping his expression stiff. The skeletal guise of Zorcons was never pleasing to look at.

"Yes, my lord," said Taru, his voice clear and robotic. "All is complete."

Taru's glowing eyes were a fierce red, like a monster of nightmares. With the star charts stolen from Salera, he knew which planets contained the best eating humans, and these rebels were obedient, provided he fed them live meat. Earth-humans were an easy capture and he would be sure to take enough of them to keep up the supply.

"Excellent," said Vorkis. "And how is our spy doing?"

"Your servant is gathering the information as we speak," said Taru. "The *Quasar* will soon be yours."

Vorkis nodded. His first plan failed with the survival of Kalin but this one would enunciate his superiority. It was flawless.

Red lights blinked passed him. To fend off Oridian attacks, the interior of the complex was inlaid with NBs, but the closer the planet came to implosion, the more difficult it was to control the magnetism. Many were faltering.

The Avec drove into a large spacious cavern and stopped. The room was empty of furniture except for an ebony desk, a small disposal and his Sarvin light, the latest means of healing and cleansing oneself; a must for survival amongst Zorcons. Hundreds of NBs netted the walls and ceiling. He stepped out of the vehicle and the ground shuddered beneath his feet. A cloud of dust drifted down.

"The implosion is on schedule, my lord," said Taru.

"Good," said Vorkis, restraightening his tunic.

He sat behind the shiny desk, a replica of Kalin's on the *Quasar*. Several recessed orbs emerged and a holo displayed the rotating planet Earth. He grinned at the thought of what the Earth-human General was devising for his world. Vorkis' original plan to destroy the planet began with an experiment. Several REMs were used to uplift the Earth's crust in one of the deep trenches, and the results were more than what he'd expected—they were fantastic. But this Earth-human General was going to blow up his own world. Vorkis smiled wider. All he had to do was sit back and savor the show.

Ten Zorcons marched into the cavern escorting a handcuffed Zorcon. They stopped and the guards surrounded Commander Yan who was visibly shaking, his knees knocking. Vorkis approached him, exhilarated at the man's terror.

"How did a helpless Earth-human female escape you?" asked Vorkis, keeping his stare fixed on the Zorcon's grotesque eyes.

"We did all we could, highness," implored Yan. Pink beads of sweat sprinkled his transparent forehead. "Our NBs failed in the tunnel. The Oridians attacked and I barely escaped. The vicious animals slaughtered two of your loyal servants, sire."

"Your stupidity is what killed those men," said Vorkis, "and you allowed the largest piece of Pril ever discovered to slip through your fingers. This is treason."

Yan fell to his knees pleading. "My lord, she is in the complex. Please allow me to find her. I will not fail you again."

Vorkis swung his arm and backhanded Yan in the face, knocking him to the floor.

"No one defies me!" he said through gritted teeth.

With one hand, he lifted Yan by his gray tunic and threw him across the room. He smashed into the wall; the sounds of cracking bones resonated through the chamber. Yan went limp and slid to the ground on his side. Vorkis kicked him onto his back and stood, straddling him. Yan's eyes were wide open in terror.

"You're right," said Vorkis in a calm voice. "You will not fail me again."

He grabbed Yan's neck and squeezed, compressing his airway, watching as the guard's transparent skin changed to an opaque purple. Vorkis reeled his other arm back and plunged his fist into Yan's chest. He held it inside, moving it about, tearing at his innards as he watched the crimson eyes slowly whiten. When he extracted his hand, Yan's pumping heart was in it. White blood sprayed everywhere, drenching Vorkis' black pants and gray tunic.

He stepped to the side of the corpse and flung the still-beating heart at the guards. The soldiers jumped back, terrified, huddling together for safety.

They're cowards who can only serve, thought Vorkis. "This is what happens to those who fail me! Make sure everyone knows this."

He glanced at Taru, who snapped his fingers. Two guards rushed over to the mutilated corpse and dragged it off with the other soldiers following them out the door. Taru remained. Vorkis picked up the fluttering heart and tossed it into the small green can beside the desk where it disintegrated in a puff of smoke.

Another day's work, he thought, delighted.

His gaze went down his body to his black boots. He hated Zorcon filth. In the corner of the cavern, shining down from the ceiling was the hazy amber glow of his Sarvin light. He stood under it and raised his arms horizontally. The light turned a deep orange, the warm soothing sensation caused tingles to dance on his skin throughout his whole body. Of all Saleran creations, this one was his favorite because of its ability to regenerate cellular growth, thereby healing wounds and, of course, purging any filth. A satchel filled with Sarvin Crystals always remained in his pocket.

A ping sounded and a holo rose up from his desk. It was Maruke, Taru's cousin. Vorkis nodded at Taru to take the message.

"Speak, Maruke," said Taru, standing behind the desk.

"Sir, Kalin and Marante are in the complex. What are your orders?"

"Do nothing," said Vorkis loudly, approaching the desk. He placed his hands on the table and leaned in closer to the holo. Maruke was just as grotesque as Taru. "Do not kill Kalin. I repeat, do not kill Kalin. Keep strict watch of his movements, but do not kill him. Do you understand?"

Repeating his orders was a necessary habit; sometimes they just didn't get it.

"Yes, Your Highness," said Maruke. "I will obey."

The holo disappeared and Vorkis sat in his chair.

"Finally, to be rid of my enemy at last," he said. He lifted his feet on the desk. "Soon I will be the King of Salera, and all that knowledge will be mine. Taru, you're looking at the man who will destroy the Federation. Does this please you?"

Taru bowed to Vorkis. "Yes, my lord. The destruction of the Federation indeed pleases me. May I ask a question?"

Taru knows his place, thought Vorkis. "Yes."

"How, my lord, can you access the codes to Salera's planetary shield? Kalin has altered its configuration; if he is terminated, the changes will die with him."

"Salera's defenses can be broken, but time is what I need. With Kalin dead, I will have this. Have you located the girl?"

"No, highness," answered Taru. "She and her companion continue to elude us. I believe the concentration of Pril she is wearing is interfering with our signal, but we will find her. She is the only female loose in this complex."

"Indeed," said Vorkis, sitting forward, "but we must find her before Kalin does. I don't want them to meet. Do you understand?"

"Yes, my lord," said Taru. "I will obey."

"Now fetch me the General. I must have a word with him."

"Yes, my lord." Taru bowed and left the room.

Vorkis rested back in his chair. He tapped a pink orb on the desk and a holo appeared. He'd been studying this Oridian nest for over two months. The Zorcon word meant "twisted, dangerous one", an appropriate name. The malformed creatures were accustomed to a lightless world, their eyes glowing white as they shuffled about the vast chamber. A moving river split their domicile in two. On one side, the female cows cared for the eggs and newborn calves. The other side was the dwelling of the male bull Oridians.

A female Oridian standing ten feet tall hobbled over to a section of wall, her red crest of softened flab showing her distinction, the egg layer. Vorkis named her One, for she was the strongest and largest, the Alpha-cow. The hunched creature turned around and glanced across the water. No females dared to pass into the domain of the bulls for fear of their voracious appetites. She shifted her gaze to the young hatchlings far from the water's edge and near the back wall where older cows tended the calves, their small bodies full of energy and bouncing about.

Instinct is what leads her, yet she is shrewd and cautious, thought Vorkis. *Qualities that have kept her alive.*

Six weeks ago, this female assumed her high position by butchering the previous cow while she slept. After tearing out her heart, she held it up for all to see, displaying her claim as their new leader. Afterwards, she methodically went around the cavern slashing open the red bulbs partially embedded in the rock face, killing the unborn fetuses of her predecessor. Of the live nest, only those who did obeisance survived; the others were slaughtered and eaten. A meal she readily shared thereby strengthening her authority.

A display of power with outstanding results, thought Vorkis, remembering his gratification with Yan.

One turned around and faced the wall where her eggs lay. Her long black tongue carefully slid over the ovules, coating them with a thick slime containing all the necessary nutrients. A juvenile female, a fourth of One's height, hopped over to her excited and squealing. One was extremely unpredictable. Sometimes she was the loving mother with her calves, tenderly playing with them, however, other times he'd seen her tear them to pieces without provocation. She growled at the young one, her lips quivering over dagger-like teeth that snapped at the calf. It yelped and stumbled back frightened, then ran off to the nest.

Again, One suspiciously eyed the males. Vorkis had seen her slay many of her bull companions after mating. Towering over them, it was an easy victory. She hobbled to the river's edge, her long arms dragging on the ground. Four males were feasting on a mutilated Zorcon; their bodies glistened with moisture, a sign of hunger. Normally they would eat large insects but lately Zorcons had become their favorite food. Bones and torn appendages lay scattered on the earthen floor. They ate briskly, while keeping their stare on One.

They would love to kill her, he thought.

One turned about and made her way to another section of wall at the far end of the cavern. She resumed her egg feeding. Vorkis noticed a male hatchling no more than three weeks old, hiding behind an outcrop. He sat up anxiously and watched the youngster cautiously crawl towards the waterway, his body sweating with hunger. The fledgling stood up and quietly slipped into the water up to his neck. From the far nest, a guardian female called with several loud whoops. One yelped and dashed to the riverbank, knuckle-running at a tremendous speed, desperate to save her calf. On the water's edge, she stood straight up, her hump protruding like a giant swell in her back, a massive animal calling for her infant with howls and yawps. Other cows assembled beside her squawking, but the calf was defiant and dipped under the water. Vorkis saw it quietly crawl out on the opposite side, hiding behind a boulder close to the feeding bulls.

The baby reached out and snatched a severed hand, pulling it back to him, caressing it to his chest like a gifted prize, nervously looking about.

One stopped her calls and slowly backed away; the other females followed.

A male Oridian was squatting on the boulder staring down at the little one. He leapt onto the calf and dug his teeth into the soft skin of its shoulder. The youngling screamed and dropped the hand, wildly writhing in fits of pain, trying to free itself. The bull wrapped its large hand around the calf's head and with one pull, ripped it off the body. He held it high in the air, waving it about and screeching, proud of his victory, then angrily flung it across the river. It bounced, landing near the feet of One. She growled at the male and kicked the head into the water. As it floated away, the other bulls joined in on the kill, tearing at the decapitated body. One hopped away, squawking at the other cows, who immediately returned to their work. Vorkis tapped the orb and the holo disappeared.

He always enjoyed a good laugh.

CHAPTER 13

Marante

"Run!" yelled Marante.

The frightening taps of the scorpion's feet made him want to sprint faster, but that would mean passing up Rina and Shiro and leaving them behind. He glanced back. The insect was zigzagging up and down the walls, avoiding boulders, speeding through the tunnel with remarkable agility. It banged one of its massive claws on the stone ceiling and the tunnel shook, almost making them fall.

"Follow me!" shouted Marante, taking the lead and studying the scanner.

Without warning, the scanner shut off.

A malfunction? thought Marante. *I had just calibrated it.*

He tapped each of the tiny orbs, hoping one of them would revive the picture but none responded. Without the map they were lost. They passed another tunnel and Marante wondered if that was their escape. The beast was catching up. Just then, Marante skidded to a stop. The tunnel ended in an open cavern scattered with dark brown boulders.

"Where are we?" she asked, frantically looking about.

"I do not know," he said.

The scorpion stood at the cave entrance with its two large pincers raised in the air. Five pairs of red eyes were staring at them from beneath a lateritious hard shell. Directly next to its perpendicular mouth, two smaller claws clicked away, ready to reel in its prey. The four scurried to the back wall.

From there Marante caught sight of the segmented tail. The caudal appendage looped high over its body and ended with a three-foot long curved stinger.

A formidable weapon, thought Marante.

Kalin fired a shot. The monster jumped in the air and bashed into a bulge of protruding rock. Its body flipped and crashed to the floor upside down. The creature whined and screeched, wildly thrashing its legs attempting to right itself.

"What happened to the scanner?" asked Kalin, keeping his Barra pointed at the beast. "Did she touch it?"

Another shriek pierced the air. The upright tail of a black scorpion was visible behind the red one.

"I'm done!" said Kalin.

With one push of his legs, he jumped onto an eight-foot high boulder and took aim. Two blasts punctured the outer shell of the red scorpion. High-pitched squeals flooded the cavern as blood spurted in all directions. Marante saw the tail of the other insect backing away. The red scorpion staggered, then crumpled to the ground dead.

"Where did the other one go?" asked Rina.

"Who knows and who cares," said Shiro. "I just want out of here."

The scanner blinked on and Marante quickly did a calibration.

"Were you implying I had something to do with the scanner breaking?" asked Rina.

"Yes, I was," said Kalin blatantly. "I don't trust liars."

"What reason would I have to lie to you?" she said. "We don't know why we were brought down here. Why can't you understand that?"

"I tell you what, doll, you tell me who you're working for and I'll let up."

Rina's mouth dropped open in shock. "You think I'm working for Vorkis?" Marante sensed her overwhelming anger. "Why would I be working for the man who's trying to destroy my world? He's killed millions; whole generations of people are gone and you think I want to support him? What is wrong with you?"

"There's always a skank," Kalin said calmly, "and you stink of her."

"Think what you want," she said. "Obviously, you've made up your mind and won't listen to reason. But hear this," she pointed her finger in his face, "I am not working for Vorkis. I did not touch the scanner. But I will do everything possible to save this planet with or without you. Can you understand that? Or should I spell it out?"

"My lady," Marante interjected, "please, ignore him. We must remain calm if we are to save your world."

"Tell that to the annoying tongue blister," she said, pointing at Kalin.

"You're the one hindering this mission," said Kalin, "and you need to come straight if you want to save your world."

It is enough, Kalin. *Your suspicions are impeding the mission.*

Will you relax? She's going to break soon.

Marante dismissed Kalin's thought. "An outside power source is interfering with the scanner's operation, and I cannot decipher the source."

"Like I said, I'll save my world with or without you," she said. "I think you need to reevaluate your objectives. Are you here to save us? Or yourself?"

He shook his head. "This isn't about me, doll. It's about you not telling the truth."

Rina made a heavy sigh. "You're the most unreasonable, immature man I've ever met. You wouldn't know the truth if it bit you in the nates."

"All you have to do is be honest, Rina," he said, slinging his Barra over his back, "and you just might survive this."

"I'm not stupid. Anyone connected with Vorkis is dead in your eyes. Obviously, you care more about yourself th—"

"We don't have time for this!" Kalin interrupted. "Marante, fix the scanner."

"If I could, I would have by now," said Marante, sensing Kalin's urgency to find the answers and his disappointment in losing the battle with Rina. He did not appreciate her perceptiveness.

"Are you saying there's nothing in that fat head of yours to fix the scanner?"

Marante saw his own nose balloon out glowing like a red sun. "Now you listen to me, you oversized fur ball. It is interference, not physical damage. And why," he added, pointing to the scorpion, "do you always attract the ones with legs?"

Kalin's lips pressed into a coy smile and he addressed Shiro, turning his back on Rina. "Marante's afraid of pheladons, or what you Earth-humans call spiders. When we were on Earth some years ago, we decided to sleep under the stars. In the middle of the night, he woke up with a big hairy one crawling across his forehead. He made a girly scream and jumped around smacking his head trying to get it off. To this day, it's still the funniest thing I've ever seen him do."

"The incident was not funny," said Marante, recalling the loathsome experience. "I was panicked, and you should be more sympathetic."

"Yeah, cute. I hate spiders too," said Shiro. "But can we get out of here? I don't want to be trapped again if the other one comes back."

Shiro was visibly shaking. Streams of sweat lined his brow and his dark hair was wet with perspiration. He began pacing, rubbing his brow, unable to control his fear. Marante knew this type of terror. The Hake beast on Arna was his most dreadful experience ever. He would never forget being in the creature's mouth, watching Kalin battle it. A shiver overcame him. Unfortunately, because of the Ison glands just beneath his skin, he could still feel the slimy warm saliva of the monster although it had been over ten years.

"Be still, my friend," said Marante. "Kalin and I have Barras and we will protect you. Everything will be fine."

Shiro gazed at Rina, his lips trembling over his large teeth. "You know how much I hate this."

"I know," she replied. "I hate this too but Marante's right. Just try to stay calm."

Shiro nodded and sat on a boulder with his hands on his knees, struggling to control his breathing. Rina sat with him and held his hand, consoling him. Marante observed the two. She was Shiro's strength, though he did not realize how strong he could be. His condition was deceiving him.

"Are the scorpions indigenous too?" asked Kalin.

"Yes and no," said Marante. "According to the previous scans, when the upper continents separated, a large mass of crust, approximately six hundred miles square, broke off and sank into the planet."

"Pangea," said Rina.

Marante eyed her strangely. "What?"

"Pangea is the single continent that separated into the world we know today."

Marante regarded her knowledge of the planet, though some facts were inaccurate, she truly loved her profession. He continued, "Yes, the insects on this descending island took refuge in the deep caves. Over time, they adjusted to the pressure and, as all life does, they survived because according to the data, there is a vast area abundant in water and plant life not too far from here. Phosphorus crystals have allowed the plants to exist. The prodigious land mass eventually became a part of this core, and we are standing in that piece."

"Why didn't you tell me this before?" asked Kalin.

"Because, we were running, berk."

"I'm not a moron, bubble head."

"Yes, you are, twit."

"Are there any dinosaurs?" asked Rina. She seemed excited. "They're large animals who once lived on the surface."

"I have only detected their petrified remains," said Marante, "nothing else."

"That's just great," said Shiro, shaking his head in disgust. "Now all we have to worry about is giant man-eating bugs."

"Can we move on," asked Rina, "before someone has a coronary?" Her eyes flicked to Shiro.

"We're leaving," said Kalin. "Shiro, stay close. Marante, can you at least guess the way to the Command Center?"

Marante wanted to knock the patronizing tone right out of his mouth. At times, Kalin was like an irritating skin rash and he wished he had brought Vecton glue to seal his lips shut. The wavering screen on the scanner made it difficult to assess the images.

"I believe we must go right at the next tunnel, then take a left. The signals are intermittent. If we die, it was the scanner's fault and not mine."

Rina walked to Marante and took his arm in hers.

"I'm not worried," she said.

Her warmth was inviting, and her hypnotic eyes subdued any disappointment.

"You're the smartest, coolest alien dude I've ever met," she said. "Let's go."

Marante felt Kalin's stare on Rina. Being a telepathic empath had its downfalls. There were many times the thoughts of people made him nauseous and he would cast them from his mind. The best example was Ilya. His stomach knotted up recollecting her foul memory. Kalin was inspecting Rina in his usual disgusting way.

Watch what you think, he said in his mind. *She is a lady and does not deserve your disrespect.*

Stay out of my head, replied Kalin.

This mission calls for us to remain connected telepathically and I do not want to see your vile pictures in my mind. Besides, I thought you were angry with her? You are so feeble when it comes to women.

Kalin didn't retort; he just grinned and slid into the space between the beast and the rock face. It was no more than two feet wide. Rina was next, then Shiro, and he took up the rear guard. He watched Kalin for any signs, not wanting to enter his mind. Kalin was being the naughty little boy craving the new toy.

As they passed the dead insect, icy chills sent shivers through Marante. Several appendages were twitching as he backed along the wall. He hoped the sharp black bristles jetting from the legs would not render him in two. And how he wished only his nose was his olfactory organ! What these humans smelled with their tiny noses was nothing compared to a whole-body receptor. The smooth Seerdon cloth allowed his Ison glands to assimilate the touch of others, absorb oxygen and, unfortunately, odors, many of which he was able to filter out. But the overpowering ones such as this dreadful stink of feces was making both his stomachs nauseous.

"Hurry up, Rina," said Shiro.

"Quit pushing me," she said. "I can only go as fast as Kalin."

Kalin deliberately slowed and Shiro repeatedly tapped her shoulder, desiring a faster pace.

You are not being nice, Marante said to Kalin.

This is no time for nice, said Kalin. *I want answers now and I'm doing all I can to not choke her, so leave me alone.*

Kalin's hatred was clogging his reasoning. He would undoubtedly kill her at the least provocation, and then regret his action for eternity. He had to protect Rina from Kalin and protect Kalin from himself—a difficult task requiring shrewd thinking. They stepped into the tunnel and Rina turned to Shiro.

"You can relax now," she said, glancing at Kalin. "We're good."

Behind them, lying flat on the earthen floor across the tunnel was the scorpion's segmented tail and stinger. The thought of the three-foot long umber-colored stinger penetrating a man was unnerving. Marante took a few steps back, adding more distance from the creature. Too many times, he'd seen unconscious monsters come to life and scare the wits out of him. A soft whistle echoed. It was Kalin signaling them to follow. They cautiously inched along the wall of the shadowy tunnel.

"Why is this place so dark?" asked Shiro, his voice quivering.

"Perhaps Vorkis was limited in his supply of Vitra Crystals," said Marante, sensing Shiro's anxiety. "This complex is enormous."

Shiro's illness kept him from showing his true worth. Marante decided to use his empathic abilities to help him, just as he had helped Kalin with accepting the deaths of his family and people. Shiro would need all his strength to endure this mission.

"Shiro," he said quietly. "Would you mind if I kept my hand on your shoulder? It will help me to not lose track of you."

"Yeah, no problem, thanks."

Marante placed his hand on Shiro's shoulder and began the slow healing.

"What the—" said Rina. "Is it raining in here?"

"I have been feeling it too," said Marante. "It must be condensation."

The quiet trickles of water droplets surrounded them.

"Why is it warm?" she asked.

"The rock surrounding this place is hotter than the sun's surface," said Shiro. "I would think the water here is warm."

"No, this is sticky—"

A shrill split the air. The four leapt out of the way just as the black scorpion jumped down from the ceiling, snapping its claws and hissing. Shiro froze in horror. Marante clutched his arm and pulled him to a run; Rina and Kalin were close behind.

"This one is faster!" yelled Marante.

Shiro would not be able to keep up the speed.

Do something, Kalin!

"Take them!" shouted Kalin.

The three ran down the tunnel, then Marante yanked Rina and Shiro to a stop. He would not leave his friend in danger.

"What's he doing?" asked Rina.

"Observe," said Marante proudly. "A Saleran male has the strength of five hundred men."

With one swift kick, Kalin sent an embedded boulder flying out of the ground towards the creature. It jumped to the side and the stone hit the dirt with a boom, crashing into the cave wall. The scorpion banged its tail on the ceiling several times. Jagged stones tumbled from above, missing Kalin, who bolted down the passageway. The monster raced after him. Marante readied his Barra. He noticed a whitish membrane covering the entire beast. It was beginning to molt.

"Run, Kalin!" yelled Rina.

He winked and threw her a kiss, then flipped his body forward in mid-air and shot several laser blasts from upside down before landing on his feet again. The insect shrieked and stumbled to the ground. Three legs were missing. A smoldering hole opened its thorax.

Just then, the tunnel started to shake. Rocks and debris began falling. Marante pulled Shiro to the wall and they huddled. Kalin dove towards them through clouds of dust. The rumbling ceased.

A pile of stones covered the scorpion except for its face and a bent claw. Marante and Shiro stood up, dusting themselves off. Several smaller boulders tumbled away and Marante watched Kalin lift himself off Rina. He rechecked the scanner. It was still malfunctioning. Kalin hauled Rina to her feet.

"Thanks, Kalin," she said, brushing off her red shirt.

"No, problem," he said, ogling her with a smile. "And thank you."

"Pig," was all she said before walking away. Kalin frowned.

This one will be your challenge, said Marante, laughing in his mind and sending the telepathic impulse to Kalin.

I'm not interested in her, replied Kalin. *I just want her body.*

Hmm..., said Marante. *You really are swine.*

Kalin scowled at him.

"See, you had nothing to worry about," she said to Shiro, straightening his glasses. The left lens had cracked. "I'll bet your OCD is kicking in big time."

"OCD?" asked Marante.

"Obsessive-Compulsive Disorder," she said. "Shiro hates anything out of place, although he's gotten better with medicine."

"Ah, yes," said Marante. "So that is the name of your condition."

"Shut up, Rina," Shiro said, annoyed. "Those were the ugliest bugs I've ever seen."

Marante noticed Shiro repeatedly brushing off his clothes. The psychological stress of not being clean was agonizing to him. Rina, on the other hand, didn't care. She accepted their situation with grace. Shiro cleared his throat and swiped at the sweat rolling down his face. Marante patted Shiro on the back. A light was coming from a nearby tunnel.

"You will be all right, my friend," said Marante, keeping focused on the light. "You are braver than you think."

"Shiro, come here," Rina said, studying the scorpion's mouth. "The carapace has to be at least eight inches thick."

Kalin was checking his Barra. "Is she always a scientist?" he asked glancing at Shiro.

Marante peered into Rina's mind and realized how intelligent she was for an Earth-human. Then her hostility surprised him. In the past, women literally threw themselves at this masculine Prince of Salera, giving him whatever he pleased, yet this Earth-human from a primitive world harbored such an indignant animosity towards him, she was contemplating assorted ways to clip off his manliness.

Oh dear, thought Marante. *My lady*, he said in her mind, *please continue your patience with Kalin. He can be very pugnacious at times but I assure you, his intentions are good and with his guidance, your world can be saved.*

Startled by the voice in her head, she answered, *do you always read people's minds?*

Not always, but this mission requires it.

I see, she said, nodding her head. *Listen, I understand the pain he's carrying is enormous and how he bears it is beyond my comprehension; it would drive me insane. However, his snide remarks and accusations are getting on my nerves. He needs to trust me and I know retaliating against him will only worsen the situation, but regardless of how he feels, my only concern is this planet and the people who live on it. Now, if it means putting up with his rudeness, I will, but after this is over, I'm going to kick-box him into the next century.*

After the mission is complete, he answered, *I will help you.*

A wide smile covered Rina's face as she shook her head in silent laughter.

I commend you for understanding his emotional state and not lashing back, he said. *Be patient, my lady. You will see his greatness soon.*

Yeah…if I don't maim him first.

She was reaching her wit's end and Kalin would eventually feel the full brunt of her frustration.

Shiro's voice caught his attention: "…all the time. Say, how come your laser blast didn't dissolve the bug like the Oridians?"

"Because of its size," said Kalin.

"This is so cool," said Rina, examining the beast.

She was standing between the mouth and claw when the large pincer began sliding along the dirt, pushing her towards its open mouth.

"Whoa!" she said.

Marante aimed his Barra, but she waved for him to stop. "Wait! I don't want bug snot all over me."

She leaned back on the claw and jumped up, stepping onto an eye of the creature, then flipped backwards over the pincer. Before she landed on her feet, several laser blasts hit the insect and it exploded, releasing chunks of gelatinous muck.

Rina was drenched in red blood. Thick pieces of brownish-red meat oozed down her body. Slimy green entrails draped across her head and shoulders. Marante rushed to her.

"My lady," he said, ready to help but not wanting to touch her. "Are you all right?"

She stared straight ahead with a blank look on her face, stuttering indecipherable words. She slowly raised her hands dripping with yellow guano.

"I...I...need a shower."

Marante sensed a flood of hatred rise up in Rina and he wished he had brought a satchel of Sarvin Crystals.

"I was free," she angrily said to Marante, trembling. "Why didn't you wait?"

"I did not shoot, my lady," he said, pointing. "Kalin did."

Kalin was staring at Rina when suddenly he broke into a full-blown belly laugh, leaning against the cave wall, holding his stomach. Rina's nostrils flared as she watched him. Marante sensed her anger had risen to an almost uncontrollable level. He stepped back and noticed a plate-sized clump of moist red flesh clinging to the front of her shirt. Marante turned to Kalin.

She could have been hurt.

You saw it was molting; its shell was pliable. No harm done.

~ 135 ~

Your impudence was not called for. She will not tolerate this behavior.

I can take any woman anytime, Kalin replied, chuckling.

Not this one.

She hopped onto a wide flat boulder in front of Kalin, standing eye level to him. Kalin stood straight and cleared his throat. His vain attempts to stifle his laughter increased her anger. A small pool of blood and mire was forming at her feet, and a strong hideous odor made Marante's stomach lurch.

Kalin pinched his nose. "You stink."

"Why?" she demanded coldly.

"Because I had to kill it, buttercup," he said, releasing his nose. "Fess up, squirt, or this is just the beginning."

Rina took the wad of meat off her shirt and rammed it into Kalin's face with both hands, slamming him against the wall.

"I've already fessed up, you stupid prump," she said, mashing in the sarcous. "How's it feel to be smothered in bug snot?"

Kalin grabbed her wrists and shoved her away, making her stumble back, but she kept her stance on the rock. He began spitting and peeling off slimy chunks of flesh.

"You little—"

Before he could finish his sentence, Rina's foot kicked his jaw. He was flung around and with a loud grunt, bashed into the wall. He moaned, sliding to his knees, then fell onto all fours, shaking his head, trying to clear his senses. Rina jumped off the boulder and stomped away down the tunnel.

"Uh, my lady," Marante said courteously; he wanted to keep all his teeth. "The lighted tunnel on your left—please, if you may."

She glared back at him and he humbly bowed his head.

This woman is beyond angry, he thought, peeking at her. *She is deadly.*

Rina began trotting at a fast pace. Marante sensed her rage and her attempts to calm down. She veered into the illuminated tunnel, out of sight.

Marante sneered at Kalin. "She should have hit you harder."

"She's starting to piss me off," Kalin said, rubbing his jaw as he stood up. He wiped his face with his white sleeve. "Did I get it all?"

"I am not telling you," said Marante as he turned away.

Rina's voice echoed through the tunnel. "Ugh, guys…you're not going to believe this."

CHAPTER 14
Shiro

Shiro was watching Kalin straighten the Barra on his shoulder. He stood at over six feet tall with neck-length black hair so thick it resembled fur. Except for his long-sleeved white shirt, everything he wore was the color black. His short open vest edged a wide belt surrounding a trim waist. Thick sinews filled his skin-tight pants and the cuffed pirate boots made him appear tough and rugged.

Why can't I look like that? thought Shiro.

His glasses sat bent and crooked on his nose. One lens was shattered, making it hard to see out of his left eye. Cornea implants would have corrected his vision but he hated doctors, which meant his overbite had never gotten fixed, either.

"She's crazy," said Kalin. His face glistened pink with moisture from the scorpion blood.

"You got guts," said Shiro, noticing the red bruise on his jaw. *It has to hurt.* "I've seen her beat guys to the floor. They couldn't walk for days."

"Let's go," said Kalin.

They began jogging down the tunnel.

"How could that skinny squirt beat up a guy?" asked Kalin. "She's a twirp."

"The twirp's been taking self-defense lessons since the age of three," said Shiro, trying to keep up the pace. Kalin had a long stride. "She's a master of judo and kick-boxing. I wouldn't mess with her."

"Yeah, well, she can't break me."

Shiro laughed aloud. "She already did. With one kick."

Kalin's brow furrowed and Shiro worried about being punched. A hit from Kalin would deck him and he'd fall in the dirt. He cringed at the thought. Bacteria was his downfall, something nearly impossible to tolerate until the meds. Wherever he touched dirt, he'd feel invisible bugs crawling on his skin and he would literally scratch until he bled. Why he became a geophysicist was a question he had asked himself every time he did fieldwork. He'd decided a long time ago that his OCD would not hinder his love of geology, so thanks to the Young family, Dr. Rand, long sleeves and pants, he learned to cope.

However, down here, the dives onto the dirt and the quaking had him covered in dust; his hands were filthy, but the crawly sensation on his skin was bearable. When was the last time he'd taken his meds? He checked his watch. Twenty-one hours ago? *Impossible*. He'd skipped a dose, yet he was relatively calm. Perhaps the experience here in the core was good. Maybe the will to survive was overpowering the psychological stressors. He couldn't think of any other reason for the symptoms to lessen. It was strange.

"I can take Rina," said Kalin. "She's nothing compared to a Bulguan. They're part woman, part animal and they eat men."

"How nice," said Shiro. "Thank you for that delightful image."

"Rina's easy. She'll break soon."

Kalin was smart, but stupid when it came to Rina. She was special. Shiro's condition had chased away good people, bothering them to the point of not wanting to hang with him anymore, but not Rina. Although she teased him at times, she was always there for him. Rina was the best friend he'd ever had.

"She's not lying, Kalin," he said. "In the sub, she stopped a detonation that would've killed most of the people above. Rina would do anything to save this world. Even die for it."

Kalin grabbed his arm and pulled him to a stop. "Are you hiding something?"

Kalin's green eyes were staring straight into his, searching for any kind of deception.

"No," said Shiro and he yanked his arm back. He would not be intimidated. "And neither is she."

"I understand she's your friend," said Kalin, "but I can't help but feel she's lying and I need to know why."

"What if she honestly doesn't know why we were brought here? What if only Vorkis knows why? I mean, Rina doesn't lie to people and I can't see her starting now."

"Captain," said Marante, tapping several orbs on the scanner as he approached them.

"What?" asked Kalin.

"The scanner is operative for the moment. The tunnel where Rina went is correct. Another tunnel from there will take us to the Command Center."

"It's about time you fixed it," said Kalin. "Let's go before it breaks again."

Marante scowled at him. Their relationship was similar to his and Rina's; attack when you can but don't hurt. The men running beside him were very human, though one of them didn't look it. When Shiro had awakened in the sub, he didn't think he would end up in the core of Earth with two aliens from different worlds. Marante was the scientist and the cool one. His black oval eyes shined like liquid pools of oil and since they'd met, he'd noticed Marante's small rounded nose had altered in size and color several times, possibly reflecting his emotions. It was impolite to laugh at him, but it really was a humorous oddity.

Kalin on the other hand, had all the brawn and energy of a fearless hero, yet inside he was a powder keg ready to burst. The anxiety Kalin lived with had to be overwhelming.

It must be killing him, just as it does me.

The thought brought back the memory of waking up in a bed of grass, the sounds of his parents' screams, the heat of the fiery plane as he listened to them die. Then he shoved it away, along with the horror, focusing again on the men beside him. On the left was a paper-thin alien with a pumpkin-sized head who could be Captain Kirk's best friend. On the right was a tall muscular hero whom any woman would give her left arm to have. And in the middle, there he was—a fat bucktoothed geek with broken glasses and a pasta belly.

It just not fair, he thought.

They turned left down the passageway and he squinted at the glaring light from the large bright opening at the end of the tunnel. Upon reaching the entrance, they stood at the threshold of a seemingly endless cavern. In front of them beyond the fine white sand, dense tropical foliage led to a narrow beach where a crystal-clear blue ocean went on as far as the eye could see. In the distance over the calm water, a patch of low dark clouds was slowly moving across. *It's raining inside the core!* Shiro stared in awe. *This cavern has its own weather system!* From up above, synthetic sunlight bathed the whole area creating a living functioning environment.

"There must be an enormous amount of condensed phosphorous in the ceiling," he said, staring up. "The glow is diffusing the visual height of this cavern. I can't see how high up it goes."

"Over two miles," said Marante, studying the scanner, "and the phosphorous ranges from six hundred to almost a thousand feet thick."

"Wow," said Shiro. "No wonder the insects survived."

"There she is," said Kalin, pointing.

Rina was standing waist-deep in the ocean, scrubbing herself clean. The men walked across the soft sand and joined her. She sloshed out of the water. Kalin squatted and washed his face.

"I think we're in Jurassic Park," she said, pointing to a large tarantula-type spider weaving a web around an entrance to another tunnel. The bug was the size of a house.

"Good heavens!" said Marante. "More pheladons?"

"Yeah," said Kalin, standing up. "Quit being so chicken."

"I will stop when you grow up," Marante retorted.

"You cleaned up nicely," said Shiro, grinning at Rina. He had to jab her. "Even the dung smell is gone."

Rina's red T-shirt clung to her torso, revealing her shapely form.

"Still don't believe in bras?" he added.

"This has not been a good day," she said, tilting her head to the side and squeezing the water from her hair, "and I'm going to kick your butt if you start with me."

"Tell that to the guys whose mouths are gaping," he said, nodding his head to Kalin and Marante. Their gazes were glued to her. She stood in front of the two with her hands on her hips, dripping water.

"I'm not in the mood for hormonal idiocy," she said. "The first man who makes a comment is going to die. Understand?"

They agreed, clearing their throats as they turned away at the same time.

"Good," she said. "Now, which way out of here?"

"The scanner has failed again," said Marante, frustrated. "From the last reading, the pheladon is blocking our needed passageway."

A high-pitched screech came from inside the webbed tunnel. A gigantic creature, half spider and half scorpion burst through the web. It leapt into the air towards the spider who quickly jumped away. The insects faced each other moving in a circle, their claws raised high, their salivating fangs spread apart. The four slowly began walking backwards towards the tunnel they'd exited, keeping their stare on the beasts.

"What's the big one called?" asked Kalin. "The front half of it looks like a scorpion."

"Yeah, it's a Mastigoproctus Giganteus," said Rina. "A whip scorpion, commonly known as a Vinegaroon. The strong smell is acetic acid, something we Earth-humans call vinegar, hence the name. A year ago, I was setting up seismic sensors in the desert and one of the insects sprayed a cut on my finger. The thing attacked me and I had to beat it with a shovel six times to kill it. They're relentless. I had the taste of vinegar in my mouth for days. That one has yellow ringlets on its hind legs. It's a new species."

"Of course it's a new species," said Shiro. Sometimes she was so smart she was dumb. "Look at the size of it. We need to leave."

As they reached their tunnel, the sounds of pounding footsteps came from within.

"Hide!" Shiro whispered fiercely.

They ducked behind a thick patch of leafy bushes just outside the entrance. Another enormous spider came dashing out and raced towards the fighting insects.

~ 143 ~

"Where did it come from?" Shiro asked, peering back into their cave. "We were just in there."

"It probably sensed its mate was in trouble," said Rina, her attention fixed on the creatures. "This is amazing."

Shiro couldn't believe she was doing it again. Four years ago at Mt. St. Helens, she insisted they get closer. They'd missed the pyroclastic cloud by seconds because Rina wanted to video tape the event. She did this type of thing all the time. Now, here they were watching giant insects battling and again, the scientist in her was taking over.

"We're not staying here, Rina," he demanded. "We need to go."

"Back into the tunnel," said Kalin.

"Wait," said Rina, stepping out from behind the bushes, entranced by the spectacle. "The Vinegaroon is winning."

One massive claw of the Vinegaroon grabbed the leg of the male spider and tossed him into the air. The spider hit the ground with a loud boom and bounced towards them. The three men leapt away, but Rina didn't make it in time. A spider leg bashed her chest and she went airborne, landing in the sand fifty feet away and moaning. The monstrous spider had crushed the bushes that once hid them. The creature lay on its back, screeching and kicking fiercely as it tried to upright itself.

Kalin shoved his Barra into Shiro's arms and hurried off. He slid along the wall face, steering clear of the flailing legs.

I wish I had Kalin's courage; thought Shiro, *even Rina's would do*. Then he felt Marante's hand on his shoulder, as if comforting him. *Could he have sensed my sadness?*

"See," whispered Marante, "he has her."

Kalin slung Rina's body over his shoulder. Her wet hair flopped forward over her head and she started yelling. Kalin shushed her and pointed. She spread the hair apart and immediately quieted at the sight of the insect. The writhing creature had moved further from the wall, making it easier for them to pass. Kalin rushed back to them and sat her on the earthen floor.

"Thanks," she said, pushing back her drenched locks. "So you do care?"

"Actually, no," said Kalin, looking down at her. "I need to know your connection to Vorkis."

"So much for heroes." She brushed the sand from her legs. "I guess it's just not in you."

Kalin was about to say something when Marante broke in.

"Are you all right, my lady?"

Shiro was glad Marante stopped the ensuing argument. The whole thing was ridiculous.

"Yes, I'm fine," she said.

"Can you walk?"

"No, Rina, can you run?" said Shiro.

She nodded and Marante helped her to stand.

"Do we have to go back in there?" Shiro asked nervously. "What if it has babies?"

"If we go back the same way we came in, we may get lost," said Marante.

"I don't think we have a choice," said Rina, glancing at the warring beasts blocking the other tunnel.

"We'll have to find another way to the Command Center," said Kalin. "Let's go."

A gut-piercing screech came from behind. The Vinegaroon had torn off four of the female's eight legs. She wobbled to and fro; fountains of black blood spurted from the open sockets. The male spider shrieked, arched its legs back and with a single push, leapt onto its feet. It made a head-on attack. The Vinegaroon hissed and sprayed a clear liquid into the spider's face before jumping in the air. The spider crashed into the rock wall. It staggered on weakened legs, rubbing its face into the dirt, trying to remove the acid.

Although two hundred feet away, the strong odor burned Shiro's sinuses while tears streamed down his face. He cupped his hands over his mouth and nose, hoping to filter out the caustic fumes while keeping a close watch on the beasts. The Vinegaroon pounced onto the back of the spider and it hit the ground hard causing a strong earth tremor; its legs spread straight out under the weight. Shiro nearly lost his footing trying to keep his eyes on the insects. The spider shrieked in agony as the Vinegaroon's huge claws ripped into its thorax and pulled out its entrails. Then the giant insect buried its face into the body of the spider, eating it alive.

"We have to go now!" said Shiro.

The Vinegaroon lifted its head out of the dead spider and stood on its hind legs. Chunks of slivered meat and yellow viscous dangled from its mouth. A loud shrill permeated the air and they covered their ears in searing pain. It turned its head and hissed at the four standing by the tunnel entrance. They fled down the passageway.

CHAPTER 15
Bauman

Brazil: Amazon Basin

Carved into the mountain eons ago, the Blythen temple was hidden beneath a blanket of trees and brush known as the Brazilian rainforest. No sunlight had ever touched the cold damp tunnel leading to the sanctuary. In this once sacred place, ancient people offered human sacrifices to a horrific thirty-foot tall statue, which stood on a platform behind the rectangular floor outline of the long-departed altar. On both the ceiling and walls, thick twining roots had weaved their way between the huge stone blocks, filling the sanctuary with tangled vines and offshoots; a welcome haven for venomous snakes and insects. For two thousand years, the jungle claimed this place as its own, until the return of man. Now all that remained of the living forest were the covered piles of damp ashes against the walls.

The local Cichinta natives called the area "Tierra de Muerto," or "Land of the Dead," a place cursed by the gods. One year ago, six of their best hunters had gone into the jungle searching for a missing boy. Their mutilated bodies along with that of the child, were found floating in the river with the words "Do Not Return" carved into their chests, backs, arms, and legs. Since then, no one had ventured into this territory, except those who belonged to the New Continuum.

A few mangled bodies are a small price to pay for obscurity, thought Bauman, donning a maroon-colored zippered jacket and black pants; a new dress code he'd implemented.

He was sitting at his desk on the platform where the altar once stood, elevated above everyone, an appropriate position for someone who was about to be deified. Before him and six steps down was his tactical unit consisting of ten men whose stations formed a giant oval in front of him. Their one-piece black uniforms had an assortment of Velcro pockets with the *NC* logo in bright yellow just below the left shoulder. *New Continuum*. He was proud of the name he'd chosen. He was also proud of the men he'd handpicked. They were the best and just a small fraction of the army he'd created.

This new base had state-of-the-art technology, compliments of the United States government. As Secretary of Defense, it was all too easy. High-tech computers and equipment filled the tables where his men busily talked into their headsets, keeping tight control of the operation. Missile and Aircraft Detecting Systems, Thermal Imaging of the ground and air, Sound Sensors able to pick up a man's whisper from ten miles away, were just a few of the many defenses he'd incorporated. Standing double-high behind his team were eight, seven-foot wide LED screens displaying real-time satellite imagery. It was the most efficient covert operation he'd ever seen. Nothing was out of place. *Perfect military order*. A long sigh of contentment loosened his muscles.

He lifted his black knee boots onto the brown granite desk and leaned back. Three of the screens switched from satellite views to numerous bank accounts throughout the world.

This is too good to be true, thought Bauman, smiling.

His fingers tapped the desk next to a red button he couldn't wait to use. The white phone rang. *Finally*. He pressed the speaker button. From a secured bunker in North Dakota in which Bauman had oversaw the construction; a massive face filled four screens. Hans Steinmann had a striking resemblance to the famous Alfred Hitchcock, with his bulbous cheeks and drooping lips; however, this sixty-nine-year-old was ruthless and unafraid to kill anyone who got in his way. The poisonous maggot lived behind security guards and lawyers, a cowardly recluse who refused to confront the public.

"I hate failure!" Hans said, his second chin wiggling like Jell-O. "I can and will replace you if need be."

Bauman swung his feet off the desk. "It was just a minor set-back." Hans had the patience of a starving tiger. Bauman adjusted the wide black belt surrounding his hefty waist and said, "You need to chill, Hans. Nothing can stop us."

He heard Hans's fist hit the table; the big man's whole face shook like an earthquake.

"I swear, Ted, if you fail again, the trench will be your grave."

Bauman wished he could punch the rimless glasses off Hans's face. He was a six-hundred-pound sack-of-snot who swore he was a descendant of Napoleon, despite the fact he was half-German. This man was born into money, millions just handed to him. Steinmann Conglomerate was at the top of the Fortune 100 companies, and he had his greedy fingers into everything from pencils to NASA. He was the richest man in the world, yet he craved more. The only reason Bauman had accepted his bribe was because three hundred fifty million dollars was hard to resist. Another six hundred fifty million was waiting when the plan succeeded.

"The mission is moving forward as planned," Bauman said calmly, imagining how refreshing it would be to chop off Hans's fat limbs with a chainsaw. "Everyone that could have divulged our secret is dead. Relax, buddy; the world will be yours soon."

Hans leaned back in his custom-made electric wheelchair. Bauman recalled the day he'd ordered his men to install an extremely wide metal sliding door, because Hans's wouldn't fit through otherwise.

"Make sure you get it right this time," said Hans. "If this works, all the money and power will be ours, and you will be my right-hand man."

"Thank you," said Bauman, forcing himself to sound civil. Hans never told the truth. "How are my men treating you? Is the bunker comfortable?"

"Your men are excellent," said Hans. "The security is impeccable. We all feel safe."

"Good. Is the High Council there with you? I'd like to give them my regards."

"Yes," said Hans, "all twenty of us are here anxiously awaiting our moment of victory. Gentlemen, say hello to General Bauman."

The camera backed up. Offering their greetings were eight

distinguished men sitting along a black granite table. Behind Hans six bodyguards and five lawyers stood like hardened cement. Everyone from the High Council was present.

"Perfect," said Bauman. "Now here's my hello."

He mashed the red button on his desk and heard the metal exit door slam shut. Several fiery explosions ripped through the room. Chairs and bodies flew across the screen. Burning rafters crashed down onto the table and floor. The cries of dying men satisfied Bauman.

Phase III is complete, he thought.

He heard pounding and shouts. The camera swerved to the right. Three screaming men were desperately beating on the metal door, their clothes torn and smoldering. Bauman pushed the button again and another explosion tore their bodies apart. Burning limbs shot through the yellow flames like missiles. Then all quieted down, leaving only the soft rustling sounds of burning wood and flesh.

The camera scanned the room and stopped at the table. Bauman leaned forward, staring curiously at the charred fingers grabbing the edge of the toppled wheelchair. The picture zoomed in.

Yes! he thought, delighted.

Hans's shattered glasses were dangling off his left ear. Blackish-red skin was peeling off the right side of his head. He was alive.

"You can't have the money," he said in a weak voice, his breathing shallow and erratic.

Bauman laughed aloud, eyeing the other screens where the increasing bank totals were already into the billions.

"When I hit the button it automatically emptied your accounts into mine. I hacked into your system ages ago." He grinned. "Goodbye, Hans."

He pressed the button one more time and the wheelchair exploded. The picture turned snowy.

Bauman sat back, content.

"Excellent work, gentlemen," he said. His heart was racing; everything belonged to him…except the world, and that was next. He took a deep breath and forced himself to calm down; control was essential. "Is the dive proceeding as planned?"

Rick and Joe got off their seats and rushed to stand at attention behind him.

"The *X-38* will be ready at 0600 hours, sir," said Rick.

Bauman swiveled in his seat and gazed up at Rick. Even though his lanky physique made him appear weak, Rick was a real soldier who took pride in his work. He was invaluable for his loyalty and his intricate knowledge of computers. The new brainwashing techniques were outstanding, something he'd never thought possible. No extreme torture was necessary—just a large amount of the new drug Prenasic along with several weeks of shock treatment. Of course, new memories had to be implanted, but he didn't mind being a father to sons who would do anything he asked.

What more could a parent want?

"In four hours we will rule," he said, checking his wristwatch. "Very good, son." He turned to Joe. "And what's the state of the Mariana?"

Joe's wife and two girls had been murdered by terrorists who'd infiltrated the base at Guantanamo Bay. He'd been left bitter and alone, an easy target for Bauman's treatment. Unfortunately, Joe was losing the respect he'd once had. His mind was rejecting the new ideologies. Bauman was concerned.

"The trench is continuing to widen at a steady pace," he said, failing for the second time in two hours to address Bauman as "Sir."

Bauman vaulted out of his seat and punched Joe square in the face, making him stumble back. "You will not forget to address me in the proper way!" he yelled. "Do you understand, soldier?"

Immediately Joe regained his composure and saluted him with blood pouring out of his nose. "Yes, sir! Sorry, sir!"

"Go clean yourself," scoffed Bauman as he sat down.

"Yes, sir."

Joe did an about-face and left the sanctuary. Bauman straightened his dark red sleeves and looked up at Rick.

"This is between you and me, son," he signaled Rick to come closer.

Rick leaned down and Bauman whispered in his ear.

"Joe is showing signs of treason and I need you to shadow him. Can you do this for your father?"

"Yes, of course, sir. I would do anything for you."

Maybe having kids isn't so bad, thought Bauman. *Better yet, make your own when they're grown up.*

"Thank you, son," he said. "Now fire up the chopper and get us to the airfield. We have to be airborne within the next two hours."

Rick stood straight and shouted, "Yes, sir!" Then left to join the others below.

Bauman rested back, admiring his self-accomplished world. Thanks to Rina's ingenuity, the elite "Jordy" program had made it all possible. The last time he tracked her she was heading to the bottom of the Mariana with a minimal supply of oxygen. He clasped his hands behind his head, satisfied he was the richest man in the world.

All he had to do now was set off the biggest bomb the world has ever known.

CHAPTER 16
Rina

"Is there anything else we have to run from?" asked Shiro, panting and bent forward with his hands resting on his thighs. "This is killing me."

"Maybe," said Rina. *He's so out of shape.*

A gut-piercing scream came from a side tunnel.

"Zorcon," said Marante quietly.

Kalin signaled them to shush.

"No more running," said Shiro.

"Quiet," whispered Rina.

They followed Kalin into the side tunnel. The screaming turned into desperate cries of agony. The passageway opened to a wide cavern with another exit tunnel at the far end. Two Zorcons were standing off to the left with terrified expressions, watching another comrade jump about recklessly, holding his head.

The sick one rushed to them and stood in front of Kalin, clutching his throat and gasping for air; his red eyes bulging out in horror. White foam gurgled from his mouth, then he collapsed to the ground, violently convulsing. His eyes turned black and he stopped breathing. Something in Rina's gut told her to run.

"What the heck is that?" asked Shiro, pointing.

The tail end of a tiny creature was struggling to back out of the Zorcon's ear. A thick coating of blanched blood concealed its shape. It fell onto the hard dirt and whined. Blobs of grey matter and crushed organs spilled onto the earthen floor and over its body. From out of nowhere, a shrill resonated through the cavern. Rina covered her ears to the shattering sound, feeling as if her joints had been loosened. Almost instantly, hundreds of red bulbs burst open spraying down black liquid.

Not again, she thought, keeping her head bowed, hoping not to get the warm sap on her face.

Little Oridians, no bigger than a small beetle with long claws and miniature spikes, ran on all fours down the steep walls and into the unrestricted ear canal of the dead Zorcon. They scampered in and out of his eyes, nose, and ears, visibly crawling under his skin, which began to shrivel as they devoured him. Rina's stomach wrenched and she cupped her hand over her mouth. One baby emerged at the entranceway of the canal covered in pinkish goo. It squealed and darted off towards a Zorcon who nervously blasted the animal with his Barra.

Near the opposite tunnel, an adult Oridian stepped out from the wall face, a red crest of softened flab on its head. The monster raised its long arms in the air and roared, its lips quivering in anger. With one push of its legs, it leapt in front of the nervous Zorcon and punched its claw into his torso. The Zorcon groaned, his eyes rolled white, and he slumped forward onto the beast. The creature lifted him high in the air then slammed him onto the ground. The crunching sounds of breaking bones sent chills up Rina's spine.

The other Zorcon stumbled back, frightened and trembling. Kalin aimed his Barra and fired. The Oridian faded away into yellow dust. Rina's mouth dropped open in shock as she stared up the fifty-foot-high rock walls. Thousands of red eggs crammed the stone.

"We're in a nest," she said.

Just then, the cavern filled with the popping sounds of ovules splitting open. The squeaks of the baby Oridians crawling out of the eggs sounded like flocks of newborn birds, but these were carnivores, flesh-eating monsters. They had to get out of there.

Shiro sneezed.

The hatchlings turned to them. An eerie silence settled in. The tiny gray bodies began glimmering with moisture. A deep growl came from behind. Rina swung around. Two more hunched Oridians were glaring at them. They appeared to be younger in age, their crests not fully formed though they stood over seven feet tall. The four began backing away towards the opposite tunnel. A slightly audible shriek came from a nearby baby. One adult clicked its tongue a few times then made a trilling sound. The baby raced down the wall towards the group and like a swarm of killer bees, the rest joined in on the charge.

"Run!" yelled Kalin.

They dashed into the tunnel with the Zorcon close behind. The babies were agile, zipping up and down the walls at an incredible speed. On the tunnel ceiling, hundreds of red eggs cracked open as they passed beneath.

"How are we going to kill these things!" said Shiro.

The Zorcon screamed. He'd fallen on the floor. Rina grinded her sneakers in the dirt to stop but Kalin grabbed her arm.

"He needs our help," she said.

"He'll eat you for lunch," said Kalin. "Now let's go!"

He pulled Rina to running again and she peeked back. A moving gray mound was wavering over the Zorcon. Within moments, the hatchlings scattered. Nothing was left of the Zorcon, not even bones.

"They're catching up!" yelled Shiro.

Kalin pulled Rina in front of him. He flipped his Barra over his shoulder and blindly started shooting. Ahead of them, outlined shapes of Oridians were forming on the tunnel walls. Marante began shooting the ones who were materializing. The four twisted and turned, ducked and jumped over giant talons grabbing for them just missing the dagger-like teeth voraciously snapping. Roars rumbled through the tunnel. The pounding gallops of adult Oridians was clearly heard and closing in.

"Faster!" shouted Kalin.

Rina couldn't believe what she was seeing. Kalin was running backwards and keeping up with their speed, blasting the oncoming animals. With her attention to the rear, she barreled into Shiro who had stopped.

"Whoa!" said Shiro and Marante in unison as they struggled to keep their balance.

She pulled Shiro back and noticed the cliff. It was at least a one-hundred-foot drop down into a river.

"What now?" asked Shiro.

"It's over we go!" shouted Kalin, who was coming at them full speed with his arms spread eagle.

He rammed into them and they tumbled off the cliff, screaming as they plunged into the fast-moving river. Rina went in feet-first and sank into the warm water. She swam her way to the top and looked around. It was hard to see; the undercurrent was strong and pulling her away. The others were nowhere in sight. Up above, the adult Oridians were hunched over the edge of the cliff, whooping and yelping as their babies jumped off. Hundreds of tiny splashes began dotting the swirling water.

She felt something crawling on top of her head. It jumped every time she reached for it. Desperate, she smacked her head several times hoping to squash it, but the baby was quick and leapt away each time, getting closer to the right side of her head. Drowning it was her last hope, so she slipped under the water. She covered her ear with one hand and began combing her fingers through her floating long black hair, trying to snatch the small animal that kept skirting her grip. She came up for air where she bobbed anxiously, waiting to feel its location. A tiny movement revealed it was sitting just above her earlobe. She screamed and gulped in water as it scurried towards her ear canal.

Something gripped the top of her head and plucked the creature off. It was Kalin. He crushed it bare-handed.

"Let's go," he said, "and keep up."

She nodded nervously, shaking from the horrendous ordeal. Then she swam like never before, still feeling the creature in her hair; knowing more were in the water. To stop herself from panicking, she reasoned because of their lighter weight, they'd been carried away by the current.

That'll work, she thought.

She followed Kalin through a large archway where brown river rock lined both sides of the riverbank. Off to the right, Marante and Shiro were waiting. Marante helped her out of the water.

"Thank you both," she said, glancing at Kalin who turned away to fiddle with his Barra.

He's so obstinate.

"You're welcome," said Marante. "Are you well, my lady?"

Marante was a true gentleman, a suave intellect whose kind and gentle ways extolled his human attributes. Although he was strange looking, his compassion was real. Why he was hanging with Kalin was questionable. Though Rina was grateful Kalin had saved her life, he was still Marante's opposite, a rough loud-mouthed gorilla.

"How could those runts turn into those big mother lizards?" asked Shiro.

"Drat, the scanner has malfunctioned again," said Marante, tapping an orb. "The creatures will undergo several stages of metamorphosis before reaching adulthood. And according to the previous readings, the younglings visual perception is equivalent to ours."

Rina wished she had more time to study the remarkable creatures. *Does instinct control them? Or is there intelligence? Are they warm-blooded?*

"There's another tunnel," said Kalin, pointing to an opening at the far end of the chamber alongside the flowing river.

"Therein lies our escape route," said Marante. "We must hurry."

The sounds of tapping feet echoed through the cavern. The babies were now in the chamber and racing towards them. Thousands more were crawling on the ceiling above, smothering the rock, ready to drop down.

"Run!" she yelled.

They sped toward the exit tunnel. Rina's lungs were at the point of igniting and she could only imagine how Shiro felt. Marante was pulling him along, helping him to keep up the speed. They ran into a dark chamber where they could barely see. Their dyspnea echoed in the heavy air. The strong odors of mold and feces made it almost unbreathable. She noticed the babies had stopped their advance just outside the cavern, hissing and tapping the cobblestone but not entering the chamber.

"Hold it," she shouted, pulling Shiro's arm.

They all skidded to a halt. Trying to catch her breath, she blinked several times, adjusting her vision to the cold emptiness surrounding her. It was a vast oval chamber at least one hundred feet high and a good quarter of a mile long. In the distance was another exit tunnel.

"Why aren't the babies coming in?" she asked.

"Fear has seized them," said Marante, his gaze going around the chamber. "We are not alone."

Rina studied the stone ceiling above them. There was something odd about the rock; it glistened with dampness but there were no audible trickles of water. Just then, two glowing white eyes appeared pinched tight in unmistakable anger. Two more became visible next to them, then two more. Before she knew it, hundreds of eyes manifested in the rock face filling the chamber with light.

Oridians.

"We're going to die," said Shiro.

"Let's slowly head for the exit tunnel," said Kalin. "Nice and easy. No quick moves. Marante, level four and take the front; keep Rina and Shiro between us."

"Aye, sir," said Marante, adjusting a holo on his Barra.

They began taking small steps forward. Marante led while Kalin brought up the rear, walking backwards and pushing Rina against Shiro. Kalin slid out a white handle from the inside of his black fold boot. He held it downward, out of view. Marante lifted from his waist pouch a silver pistol the size of a flare gun.

This is going to be bad, thought Rina.

She had always considered herself a fairly brave person but being eaten alive was something beyond her comprehension. These creatures were the stuff of nightmares and for the first time in her life, she felt fear.

Stay close and tight, Marante said in her mind.

A high-pitched whirring sound similar to a missile, was honing in on their location. Rina looked up and saw the shadowy shape of an

Oridian dropping down. She grabbed Kalin's vest and yanked him away. The three-toed feet of the animal pounded the ground, shaking the earthen floor. It stood over nine feet tall with massive muscle and sharp teeth. It lifted its head and roared, vibrating her bones. Just then, a barrage of booming sounds filled the cavern. They were surrounded by salivating creatures whose only focus was to eat them. The monsters charged and the shooting began.

The beasts attacked from all sides. The Barras of the two men sent out streams of blue light that tore through the oncoming swarm. The silver pistol in Marante's other hand shot out fiery balls of orange light. Each globule expanded to encase six to eight animals before exploding, ripping the beasts apart. Kalin's white handle was now a blade the size of a gladiator sword that sparked as it sliced into the creatures. Chopped heads and appendages were flying in all directions. Black blood and greenish bowels were sousing them like rain. The speed and movements of the men told her they'd done this before.

One Oridian grabbed her arm and she screamed, ready to kick it when Kalin swung his blade around and severed the hand. The monster shrieked and Marante blasted it with his Barra. She nervously shook the claw from her arm and hugged Shiro's back. He was hyperventilating. She turned him around. He was soaked in dark slime and his breathing was so fast she was sure he'd faint at any moment. If he were to fall, it would be his death. Getting on her tippy-toes she wrapped her arms around his neck and whispered into his ear.

"We're going to make it through this. Look at the way these guys are fighting. They're pros. Hang in there. Remember, you go, I go."

She released her grip but stayed close enough to grab him if he fell. His cramped worried eyes told her he was desperately trying not to lose it. She took his hands and cupped them over his mouth, hoping it was enough to slow down his breathing. A cool stiff breeze of fresh air howled through the cavern, then all was silent. The roars and growls had stopped. Rina's gaze slowly went around the chamber. They were standing in an empty circle surrounded by massacred animals, a bloodbath of disemboweled Oridians. Her whole body was drenched in black snot.

"It's not my fault," said Kalin, stepping away from her. His tan skin was barely noticeable beneath the black gunk.

"I know," she said, pinching her nose. "How come they didn't disintegrate?"

"We lowered our weapons output to conserve energy," said Marante. His facial color now blended with his eyes. He put his hand on Shiro's shoulder. "It is an awful sight, isn't it?"

"I'll say," said Shiro, wiping the muck off his face. "It's gross."

"You're all right with this?" asked Rina in surprise. "How come you're not hysterical from the filth?"

"I'm fine," he said. "I don't know how, but I'm okay."

"You can't be okay," she said. "You should be screaming like a girl."

"Hey," he said, perturbed. "You're not the only one with guts, missy. I—"

Heavy growls and snarls began echoing again. Glowing white eyes started reappearing on the ceiling and walls. Another attack was coming.

"Our weapons need more time to recharge," said Marante, hoisting his guns ready to fire. "Any suggestions?"

"I have an idea," said Kalin. He touched a blue button on the side on his Barra and a door slid open. "I'm not sure if we'll survive this but it's better than being eaten alive." He looked at Rina. "Though they'd probably vomit you out. I'm sure they don't like rotten meat."

Rina pretended not to hear him; her patience was wearing thin and it took all her strength not to break his nose. Several orbs lit up the small compartment of the Barra. Kalin touched a yellow orb and a miniature holo rose up showing the schematics of the Barra. She stared in wonder, wishing she knew how to work the weapon. One shot was all she needed to take out his b—

Such vile thoughts, my lady, said Marante in her mind.

She glanced at him and couldn't help a smile. *There's only one way to stop a tyrant—release the dogs of war.*

Marante chuckled. *Perhaps something less radical would suffice, though I do enjoy William Shakespeare.*

"I'm setting it to overload," said Kalin. "We need to get at least seven hundred feet away."

"What kind of blast are we talking about?" asked Rina.

They were surrounded by rock that could easily cave in. The door shut and Kalin laid the weapon on the ground. A red light was blinking on the Barra.

"A big one," he said. "Now go!"

The four bolted for the passageway.

"I hate running!" yelled Shiro.

"Shut up and run faster!" shouted Rina.

As they entered the far tunnel, a thunderous explosion sent dirt and rocks tumbling from every side. A cloud of dust whooshed through the passageway, hurling their bodies in the air.

CHAPTER 17
Justin

Justin was sure the hammering pain in his head had cemented his eyelids shut. Wherever he was, it was warm, stuffy, and stank like dead clams. His conscious mind began to spin swirling his senses.

Oxygen, he thought. *I need air.*

As he inhaled a deep breath, bubbles of thin plastic fluttered inside his nostrils and he immediately turned his head so as not to suffocate. He forced his eyes open. It was dark. Nothing was visible. His left shoulder was throbbing.

The bullet, he thought. *I must have blacked out after I got hit.*

He was lying partly on his right side with his arm jammed beneath him and his back resting against something soft. With every breath, the plastic heaved in and out. An icy cold ran through him.

I'm in a body bag.

The loud roars of outboard engines became clearer. He was on a fast-moving boat and whoever was out there thought he was dead. Something heavy was lying on top of him. There was a wicked bounce and whatever lay on him pounced down hard, nearly crushing his left shoulder. He quelled a scream, trembling to the fiery pain. As he calmed, he recalled the dreadful events that brought him here.

Bauman was going to kill over two thirds of the world's population, including all of its leaders. A wave of horror enveloped Justin as he recalled his last memory. He was of lying on the floor and helplessly watching everyone's heads jolt back from the bullets going through their foreheads. His stomach churned to the grisly flashback. The vision would haunt him forever.

Rina! Panic engulfed him as he remembered Bauman's words: "The dead bodies of her and Shiro are at the bottom of the Mariana Trench." His spirit collapsed and he wanted to wail in agony.

My baby is dead!

Vivid memories of her playing and laughing as a child kept racing through his mind and he couldn't stop whimpering. Her long black hair and bright aqua-blue eyes made her beautiful. He'd raised her to be compassionate, caring, a fighter for justice—and it got her killed. More tears streamed out, his aching heart swallowing the blame. She'd seen through Bauman and fearlessly confronted him. She had more courage than an army of soldiers and yet at times he'd doubted her judgment, passing it off as punitive hostility.

What kind of a father was I?

He did everything possible to raise her right, always guiding her in the right direction. His thoughts went to Shiro and how much he loved him as a son. Shiro must have been frightened as they neared their demise but Rina was there to console him. The death of his two children would not go unnoticed. They were murdered along with his office staff and who knows how many others. Justin's bones and muscles tightened to an upsurge of hatred. Bauman's betrayal had to be exposed or millions would die, and killing his henchmen on this boat may be unavoidable.

Bauman will not win this.

He only hoped he still had his keychain with Mary's knife in his left pocket. Bauman would have taken his cell phone. His right arm was wedged tight beneath his side which meant his injured left arm would have to reach into his pocket. It was throbbing like a drumbeat. The slightest stirring may alert anyone within view, but there was no choice.

His face scrunched in pain as he bent his left elbow and slid his hand into his black pants pocket. A warm trickle of blood flowed from the wound and down his white shirt. He sighed in relief when his fingers touched the pocketknife between the many keys. Cautiously, he began pulling the key ring out, keeping his motions slow and precise. The giant wad jammed up on the rim of his pocket. He tugged several times with no success.

If I had just listened to Rina and lightened the load. This is going to hurt.

With his hand clutching the heap, he yanked hard and the keys popped out. A horrendous pain shot through him like a thousand knives tearing into his skin. His whole body shook with each breath as he waited for the torment to subside. He fiddled through the key chain until he found the small knife and slid the blade out.

A four-inch incision would be a start.

In front of his chest, he pushed the knife through the black plastic and began slicing upward. After cutting two inches, the slit flared open and a glob of dark reddish-tan gelatin plopped onto his shirt. The mangled blonde hair told him it was Barbara. The back of her head was blown out. He turned away from the foul stench and vomited his food.

Poor Barbara, he thought, weeping silently.

She was innocent and yet Bauman shot her without hesitation. There was a heavy bounce and more grey matter spilled through. He had to get out of there. With the next bounce, he stiffened his body and shoved Barbara's corpse off him. After recovering from the pain, he noticed a ray of light shining through. With the tip of his knife, he quietly continued slicing until he could see out. He was in a cuddy cabin and hopefully alone. Another vicious bounce sent a glob of blood and brain from his chest onto his chin.

In a panic, he desperately tore his way out of the bag, not caring who was in the room. With the upper half of his body free, he quickly sat up taking several breaths. The odor of gasoline satiated the air. He covered his mouth as he coughed to the burning sensation in his throat. The light tan ceiling was only inches away, so he looked down. He was sitting on a stack of body bags. Barbara's sack was to his right, wedged between a bench and another body. Mortified, he began ripping at the remaining plastic with the knife, kicking his legs, anxious to get off the mountain of death. Another wicked bump and he was thrown backward where he recklessly rolled, banging his injured shoulder and landing on his right side with a thud. A shooting pain gripped his body and he felt himself losing consciousness.

Not now, Justin. Hold on.

He focused straight ahead, determined to freeze the twirling images and relax his tense muscles. To his surprise it worked. He was facing a smooth almond-colored wall and lying on an ocean-blue padded seat. It was soft and he struggled to sit up leaning on the wall behind him. The body bags took up the end of the long bench, and his stretched legs almost touched them. If others were in the cabin with him, they would have revealed themselves by now.

There was another bench seat across from him. Sitting within the almond walls above the benches were twelve round portholes covered with blue curtains. He peeked out the curtain next to him. The sun was bright and it was a calm day; however, judging from the size of the water crests, the ship was hauling butt. They were in a hurry to get somewhere. The teak exit door was behind him to the left and up two steps.

A muscle near his pierced shoulder spasmed and he flinched. Black coagulated blood filled the wound and a small stream of red was draining out. The bullet was lodged deep inside. His shirt was soaked with blood, grey matter, and vomit; the smell was sickening. Nauseated again, he hurried and slipped it off, tossing it aside. To his right, a small compartment sat within the sidewall. He unlatched the lock and slid the door open. Inside were four neatly folded green camouflage shirts and he took one out.

The military is always efficient, he thought.

The big shirt was clean and all he needed. With his knife, he slashed off a sleeve and rolled it up, pressing it into the wound and feeling the lump of the embedded bullet. He tore off the other sleeve and wrapped it around his shoulder creating a pressure bandage. With the remaining shirt he constructed a splint, then he slumped back to relax. A deep pain burrowed through his chest. It wasn't the bullet.

Rina. He closed his eyes and exhaled, trying to blink away the tears.

Too many lives are at stake; there's no time to mourn.

He pulled his knees up to his chest and swung his legs off the seat. A twine of colored wires were leading into the compartment beneath the bench across from him. He had to check it out.

Standing should be easy; staying on his feet would be difficult. The dizziness and the moving vessel were a bad combination. He cautiously rose to his feet and pressed his back against the wall, using it as a support to glide along sideways and not fall down. Upon passing the stairs, he counted ten body bags on the bench. His heart ached as he remembered the faces of his friends. He reached the bench and lifted the seat. Six five-gallon gas cans stood side by side wired to each other. The same colored wires ran beneath the other bench he'd just come off. The ship was rigged to explode.

Great, thought Justin. *How much time do I have?*

The door leading out was shut. He kneeled on the second step and with his right hand cracked open the door about an inch. He could see the helm of the ship. No one was there.

He strained to stand and after two dizzying steps, he slipped on the damp floor and hit the main deck face first. Lying on his stomach, he felt warm blood running from his nose. Angry now, he sat up and swiped at the blood pouring down his chin. He shook his head in disgust and pinched the nape of his nose.

I'm such an idiot.

He gazed around the boat. It had an inboard engine and was at least thirty-five feet long. The main console sat beneath an extended roof, which protected him from the weather and sun. The name "Boston Whaler" was engrained on the backrest of the Captain's vinyl seat.

Nothing but the best, he thought.

The detonator had to be near the helm. He grabbed onto the stair railing and pulled himself to his feet. Over the dashboard, a streamlined glass-domed window gave a full view of the empty bow and the barren ocean. A sudden rush of loneliness came upon him. If he failed, he would die alone and no one would know what happened to him. Rina and Shiro's deaths would have meant nothing.

There's no way Bauman's winning this.

He settled into the captain's seat. The console consisted of the ship's silver steering wheel, speedometer, compass, and several flip switches for the accessories like bilge pumps and bait wells. A short chain dangled from the inserted key. Lining the top and sides of the white console was stainless steel railing. A small blue box was attached to the base of the steering wheel that was moving on its own.

Autopilot, he thought.

The vertical silver gearshift controlling the speed was almost all the way up; the speedometer said the ship was doing over seventy knots. He leaned to the side and looked underneath. A timer was attached to four gray blocks of C-4. The LED read three minutes.

"Crap! " he said aloud.

He quickly slid to the floor and laid down, ignoring the pain in his shoulder, studying the set-up through tear filled eyes. Many times he'd used C-4 when doing field work in geology. This detonator was a military standard issue, the same kind he used on geological sites.

There was no reason to use an expensive one, he thought. *Everyone was supposed to be dead.*

He had to leave the countdown intact. If they were reading it, he didn't want them to know anyone was alive. After setting the timer on his wristwatch to match the readout, he disconnected the red and blue wires to the detonator, leaving the green and white wires alone. The countdown meter was still active.

The engines and the remote device had to be shut down simultaneously. He got to his knees and followed the wires leading out from the bomb. They were taped inside the console wall and ran along the floor then up into the captain's cooler bench. His watch read two minutes. He flipped up the seat cushion. Colorful wires looped in and out of the cup-sized remote mechanism wedged between two blocks of styrofoam.

He carefully lifted it out, shut the seat cover, and set the unit on the bench. When he stood, a wave of dizziness almost made him fall and he clutched the railing for support.

I've got to keep it together.

Standing sideways between the console and bench seat, he

clamped his right hand around the gear-shift, then looped two fingers into the chain dangling from the inserted key. Engine shut off was critical. Wobbling on his right leg, he slowly lifted his left foot until it reached the top of the seat. He pressed his black shoe against the remote control unit, pushing it into the backrest, holding it in place.

So far, so good.

Carefully slipping his arm out of the splint, he leaned over his bent leg, stretched his left arm, and gripped the green and white wires that needed to be torn from the remote. The pain was creating more tears and it was going to get worse.

One minute. I can do this, he thought; his left fingers tingled, straining to hold the wires.

Thirty seconds. His arm quivered as he pulled the damaged muscles in his shoulder.

Ten seconds. Sweat rolled down his face. His arm began trembling.

Two seconds. Now!

He tore out the wires, slammed the throttle down, and yanked the key out. The engines rumbled to a halt and the ship jolted forward. The bow sank beneath the water sending a big wave splashing over. Justin bashed into the console and grabbed the railing above the wheel to keep himself from flying off the vessel. The boat teetered with the thrashing waves then settled in the calm seas.

The pain in his shoulder was excruciating. The pressure bandage was soaked in blood. He tossed the shredded wires on the deck and slipped his arm back into the splint. Whether or not Bauman knew he'd escaped, he didn't know.

I'll find out when I hear a missile coming.

He leaned on the wheel, exhausted. A beeping sound came from his wristwatch. At OSRI, he had set it to chime every thirty minutes to remind him of the President's speech.

The nukes.

There was less than four hours to evacuate over eight million people. Looking out over the bow, land was barely visible.

I have to try!

His hand turned the key and the engines roared to life. He pushed the gear shift all the way up, spun the wheel around, and headed back to land at full speed.

CHAPTER 18
Kalin

"Am I alive?" asked Shiro.

"No," said Kalin, rising to his feet. Shiro was lying flat on his back on the riverbank. "You're dead."

Rina's head popped up from under a mound of dirt. "Did we kill the babies?"

"Yeah," said Kalin, helping Marante stand. "Let's clean up in the river."

"Are you sure there aren't any babies in there?" asked Rina.

"I am not sensing any life forms," said Marante.

"Good," said Shiro, and he dove into the water.

Kalin walked in up to his boot cuffs keeping an eye on Rina, who was swimming about.

There's something in her I can't place, he said to Marante in his mind. *I know she's lying.*

You must believe me when I say she is telling the truth, but alas, there is a place deep in her mind my telepathy cannot reach.

Ha! So I was right, thought Kalin with a smile.

A low whirring sound came from down the tunnel.

"What is that?" asked Kalin.

Shiro splashed out of the river as if being chased. "Is it another monster? Do we have to run again?"

"It is plausible," said Marante, standing drenched next to Kalin. "You really must adjust your thoughts about running."

"I hate running," said Shiro.

"Shh, listen," said Rina beside him as she squeezed the water from her long hair. "It sounds like purring."

Kalin slipped the white handle from his boot. He held it up in the air and watched Rina's eyes open wide as the branches weaved out, forming the silver blade.

"It's a Norin Blade," he said quietly, hoping to intimidate her. "It'll start cutting three inches from your skin."

"Can I hold it?" she asked, mesmerized at the sight.

"No," he said in disappointment. "You can't be trusted. Marante, ready your Barra."

Rina glared at him with vicious eyes.

A little more and she'll break, he thought.

A little more and you may not have the items needed for procreation, said Marante.

What's that supposed to mean?

Keep up your antagonizing and you will see. He could hear Marante's laughter.

"I think the purrs are getting louder," said Rina.

"Great," said Shiro, his voice echoing. "It's probably more running."

"Shh!" they said together at him.

The four began creeping along the wall. The tunnel expanded to a wide cavern with a straight cliff on their left. They tiptoed to the edge and peeked down. At the bottom of the crevasse, two train-size millipedes were entwined and softly purring. Their brown bodies hosted hundreds of legs, ten to each of their many segments. The larger insect on top was pulsing.

"Wow," said Shiro. "They're doing it."

"That's gross," said Rina, turning around.

"What's wrong?" asked Kalin. "Never had sex before?"

"That's none of your business."

"It might do you some good," he said. The Norin blade liquefied back into its handle and he stuffed it back into his boot.

"Shut up, jerk," she said.

"Now you're getting nasty."

Kalin twisted her arm behind her back and wrapped his other arm around her waist.

"What are you not telling me?" he asked, wrenching her arm a little harder.

"Stop!" she said. "You're hurting me."

"Tell me the truth," he said, sniffing her hair. *She even smells good.*

"I am telling the truth," she said, squirming. "I'm an Earth-human for Pete's sake. I didn't know people existed outside my world until five hours ago."

He let her go and pushed her away.

"You're a real psycho," she said, rubbing her arm. "I'll bet the only women you can get are brainless morons who can't read."

Marante busted out laughing. "She already knows you."

"Rina, look at this," said Shiro, his attention still on the mating creatures. "They're beginning to separate."

"At least they're real women," said Kalin, "not the kind that muscle up to you. Ilya is more of a woman than you'll ever be."

"Can she count to ten?"

Kalin glared at her. Truth is, a Tàtress didn't have the mental capacity to assimilate mathematics, something with the brains inability. But Ilya was kind and gentle, and Kalin was glad to have her as a companion. She'd eased his pain many nights and although it was customary for Saleran males to have only one wife, as King he would change that, making her one of his many wives. Rina on the other hand was mouthy, obnoxious and despite the fact he had never hit a woman, one slap would make him very happy. He felt Marante's stare.

I will not allow that, he said in Kalin's mind. *No more bickering.*

Leave me alone, Kalin said, annoyed at Marante's intrusion.

Shiro waved at them to come. "You have got to see this."

The three joined Shiro at the edge of the cliff. The writhing male millipede suddenly detached from its female partner. Black legs wriggled against its tan-colored underside. As it rolled onto its back, a twelve-foot bright red penis disjoined, ejaculating sperm. A thick spurt flew up into the air. Rina, Kalin, and Marante jumped away. Shiro got splattered.

His hair and clothes were drenched in gray sperm. He raised his trembling hands. Rina doubled over laughing.

"This is not funny," said Shiro. "I'm…I'm going to throw up." He bent forward and made several dry heaves.

She covered her mouth, attempting to stop. "I'm sorry," she said, her voice a higher pitch, "but it's only sperm. It's not infected."

"Okay," he said, "want some?"

He swung a wad of semen at her. Rina quickly moved away and the jelly-like substance splashed onto the rock wall behind her, sticking to it like glue.

She stuck her tongue out at him. "I'm going to tell everyone you got spermed by a bug."

"I will kill you," said Shiro through gritted teeth. "I'm still nauseous and I don't need your jokes."

"You are mine," she said with a strange accent, "to torture as I please."

Kalin smiled and shook his head. "You both are too much. Shiro, I have something to help you with that."

He reached inside his vest pocket and removed a Sarvin pouch. After dropping a few orange crystals on Shiro's head, he watched them twinkle down his body.

"They're called Sarvin Crystals," he said, happy to see Rina's mouth drop open. "They remove dirt and heal cuts."

"You mean you deliberately let me stand there covered in scorpion blood?" said Rina.

Kalin chuckled. "Yep. I figured you needed a good humbling."

Rina lunged for him but Marante stretched out his long arm and stopped her. "Calm down, my lady," he said, struggling to hold her. "We must remain level-headed to save your world. Kalin, apologize to her."

"No way," he said. "Remember, sweetheart, I always win." He went into a full-blown belly laugh.

A sticky sludge hit Kalin in the face. He began coughing and choking on the slime he inadvertently swallowed. Rina was standing stiff, sneering at him with sperm dripping from her hand. The rock face behind her was clean. He dropped to all fours and puked.

"Can your Sarvin Crystals remove your stomach contents?" she said.

Kalin jumped to his feet and rushed towards her. "You little—"

Marante blocked his way. "That was well deserved." He snatched the bag from Kalin's hand and poured a few crystals on his head.

Kalin closed his eyes, anxious for them to finish so he could throw her off the cliff. His patience was gone.

But Vorkis is still free, said Marante, *so you must hold on*.

"I won't forget this, twirp," he said, spitting the words through clenched teeth.

"Good," she said. "Now you know how it feels to be totally grossed."

She stepped onto a small boulder in front of him, then gripped his black vest pulling him close. He couldn't believe her audacity.

This girl has absolutely no fear of me.

"I'm sorry, Kalin," she said, her voice soft and surprisingly caring. "What you swallowed was horrible and it's making me sick."

He was shocked by her apology. Her crème-colored skin had to be soft as silk and the thick black lashes surrounding her aqua-blue eyes seemed to make them glow. She was truly a natural beauty. He sighed, disappointed he couldn't hit her.

"I wouldn't worry too much," said Shiro, staring at the regurgitated food. "It's there on the floor."

Rising above the partially ingested pile was the jellied clump of gray sperm. Kalin took the sack from Marante's hand and gulped down a bunch of the orange crystals. Popping sensations ran all the way into his stomach. From down the passageway they heard a boom, then a clang followed by a low hum.

"That was the sound of Xeon Diffusers," said Marante, addressing Rina and Shiro. "They are the machines dredging this core."

"Let's go," said Kalin. He couldn't let this beauty overtake him. "The sooner we get this mission done, the better."

He hurried away from the crowd, irritated he let a twirpy woman get to him.

Look beyond her stubbornness, said Marante in Kalin's mind. *You are just as pig-headed.*

You didn't swallow that crap.

No, but you were not covered in insect viscera either, replied Marante.

I don't want to talk about this anymore, said Kalin.

Rina suddenly appeared beside him. "You were wrong not to help me, Kalin," she said. "I need an apology."

Kalin stopped walking and focused on her eyes. She meant every word.

"Okay," he said, eager to shut her up. "I'm sorry for not using the Sarvins on you but if you ever do anything like that again, I'll hit you so hard you'll be seeing triple the rest of your life. Got it?"

"Marante's right," she said, smirking. "We have to stop fighting if we're going to save this world."

"It's about time you smartened up," he said.

"Excuse me, but you started it," she said. "Listen, it's obvious I don't like you and you don't like me, so let's be mature and just move on."

"Fine," he said, picking up his pace. *Just one slap.* "Now shut it."

She was still there. "I'll change the subject." Her voice was lighter now, not so tough.

"Don't you ever shut up?" he asked, aggravated she'd ignored his last comment.

"No," she said. "How are we going to become friends if we don't talk?"

"I don't want to be your friend," Kalin said in frustration.

"You really aren't used to women like me, are you?"

Her roguish smile peeved him some more.

"No. A woman is supposed to be quiet and submissive, not stubborn and annoying."

"Ah, yes," she said. "Brainless morons who can't count to ten."

Kalin was ready to slam her with an insult when she continued,

"But I guess everyone has his own taste. One day I'm going to find a man whose brain is not in his pants."

Shiro cleared his throat, waving his hand. "Over here, piglet. You met one over seven years ago."

"You don't count, sperm boy."

"Quit calling me sperm boy, hemorrhoid."

Kalin listened to the two discuss Rina's man type. They argued like a real brother and sister, calling each other names and using put-downs. Kalin felt remorse. He never fought with his brothers, even common wrestling amongst siblings was considered hostile, a factor he blatantly resisted as a child, thereby receiving many punishments. Living in the House of Altor was confining and the Laws of Ethilia were oppressing. He'd gotten to a point where insanity would've overtaken him if he hadn't left. All he wanted was a normal life but being of Saleran royal blood, it couldn't happen.

"I'm done talking to you, shmohawk," said Rina. "Kalin, is Vorkis' physique similar to yours?"

"Yes, but I got to say this," said Kalin, "you don't respect Shiro very much, do you?"

She tilted her head and gazed at him oddly. "That's the way we are. If he didn't fight with me, something would be wrong." She glanced back at Shiro. "Right?"

"Yeah," said Shiro. "It's the way we get along. I'm always right and she's always wrong."

"In your dreams," she said, then turned to Kalin. "I don't mean to step out of line, but it seems to me the battle between you and Vorkis will end with one of you dead, so why take the chance if your race depends on you for survival?"

Wrong question. The steam of rage rose up into his nostrils. "I am so tired of people not understanding. Do you have any idea what it's like to watch your family die?"

"Yes," she said. "My mother and I were in a country called Chile when an 8.5 earthquake occurred. The stone shack we were in collapsed. The local natives freed us, but she died in my arms."

"Are you an only child?" asked Kalin.

"Yes, I was adopted."

"So they're not your real parents."

"No, they're not," she answered, perturbed, "but I still love them. Get real, Kalin, your reasoning is stupid."

He clamped his hands around her upper arms and lifted her off the floor. Instead of seeing fear, her body went rigid, her eyes filled with determination.

"Picture this, Princess," he said. "Your father is lying on the floor rotting. Your little sister is in your arms screaming in agony as her body parts fall off in your hands. Imagine standing on the balcony of your home and listening to millions of people crying as a flesh-eating virus kills every person on the planet, leaving only you alive." He pulled her closer, nose-to-nose. "Until you've done that, don't tell me not to avenge their deaths."

Her eyes crinkled in pity and he backed her away, slowly putting her down. She had an enormous amount of compassion, more than what he had.

"I'm sorry for what happened," she said, "and I understand how that could change a person's thinking. But Kalin," she added, gently holding his arm, "their memories, their lives, live in you. If you die, you'll be killing them again. Don't risk that. Don't let Vorkis win."

"Didn't you hear what I just said?" he yelled. He yanked his arm away. "Are you stupid like everyone else?"

"If everyone is saying the same thing," she said calmly, "we can't all be wrong."

"You are wrong! Vorkis is going to die at any cost. This conversation is over," and he stormed away.

"What if it comes down to Vorkis or Earth, Kalin?" she said loudly. Her voice echoed in his ears. "Would you kill millions more because of Vorkis?"

Kalin refused to acknowledge her. How dare a primitive Earth-human question him? Their vile history proved their race knew nothing of justice.

"Kalin, wait!" yelled Marante. Grudgingly he turned around. "What?"

Marante approached him, busily studying the miniature holos on the scanner. Rina and Shiro followed.

"Since the beginning, I had configured the scanner to find the source of the REM signal and thus Vorkis' Command Center," said Marante. "When we met Rina and Shiro, the scanner lost its primary function because its signal was being disrupted by something more powerful. I temporarily reconfigured the unit for Pril." He showed Kalin the holo. "You were correct. The source of—"

Got her! thought Kalin.

He ran back to Rina, clenched her upper arms and slammed her against the rock wall. Her head wobbled deliriously.

"Where's Vorkis?" he screamed. In an outrage, he bashed her body against the wall again. "Where is he?" he shouted in her face.

"Ow! What?" she said, shaking her head. "Are you crazy?"

"He gave you Pril to throw us off his trail." He squeezed her arms tighter. "Where is he?"

"What are you talking about?" she said, squirming to free herself. "Let me go! You're hurting me!"

"Kalin!" demanded Marante. "It is enough!"

"She's working for him and she dies here."

He clamped one hand around her neck cutting off her airway and then pulled the Norin Blade from his boot. He held it up to her face and he watched her eyes widen in horror as the branches wove into a twelve-inch knife.

Shiro latched onto Kalin's arm, wrestling to free Rina. "I won't let you hurt her. "

Two white beams of light shot out of Kalin's eyes and hit Shiro in the chest, sending him airborne and crashing into the far wall.

"You must stop, Kalin!" said Marante. "There is more."

"What more could there be?" he said, tightening his grip on her neck. She was turning blue. "Anyone working for him is going to die."

"I'm-not-working-for-him," squeaked Rina.

"She is not an Earth-human," said Marante. "There is no record of her life-form in our database."

"What?" asked Kalin.

"Let her go!" yelled Shiro, who was getting to his feet.

Kalin momentarily stared at Rina and then released her. She fell to the floor gasping for air, clutching her throat. Shiro ran to her and helped her to sit.

"You're just like Vorkis," said Shiro, looking up at him. "Are you going to kill us too?"

"Explain, Marante," said Kalin, ignoring Shiro's comment.

Marante squatted beside Rina. "My lady, you are carrying Pril but I cannot pinpoint its location. Do you have anything in your pockets or perhaps some form of jewelry?"

Rina's mouth gaped and she looked down at her chest. Her hand tightened around something beneath her red T-shirt.

"The necklace?" said Shiro.

She pulled out a large black pendant dangling on a jewel-encrusted chain. Kalin's breath caught in his chest. The Pril was the size of a flattened egg.

"Where did you get that?" asked Marante.

"My mother was a volcanologist and found this after an eruption."

"That is the purest and largest piece of Pril ever discovered," said Marante, studying the scanner. "May I touch it?"

"Yes," she said, "but I can't take it off; it's a promise."

"You have my word I will not take it from you," said Marante.

She nodded at him. He held the stone in his hand and immediately began adjusting the scanner.

"What exactly is Pril?" asked Shiro.

"Throughout history legend told of stones with enormous power," said Marante. "One day it was accidentally discovered by a ship of younglings who decided to illegally use an asteroid field for target practice. They blasted an asteroid and the force of the explosion incinerated them and the star system they were in. Up until the present, only grains of Pril have been found. I never thought I would ever see a piece this size."

"What makes you think I'm not an Earth-human?" asked Rina.

"You have internal organs that are inexplicable," said Marante. "Do you have any recollection of your home world?"

Rina's inward emotions told Kalin she really was innocent.

"No," she said, confused. "I...I only know Earth."

"I knew it," said Shiro. "She's probably British too."

"Knock it off," said Rina. "This is serious." She turned to Marante. "The scanner has got to be broken."

"The scanner was working normally up till when you were found, then it began to function intermittently. It could not handle the enormous signal coming from such a large piece of Pril. However, I have made the final adjustments and now the unit is operating perfectly."

"It has to be wrong," she said. "I have to be human...an Earth-human." Her bottom lip was quivering.

Kalin saw her disillusionment and sensed her frustration. Distraught, he leaned back on the wall holding his forehead. For the first time in his life, he almost murdered an innocent person because he let an evil man dominate his thoughts.

Is Shiro right? Am I just like Vorkis?

The thought made him nauseous. He had to be better than Vorkis. Clear thinking and control were imperative if victory was his goal. Now, however, due to his own stupidity, he had to suck in his pride and apologize to the most annoying back-talking brat he'd ever met.

Life sucks, he thought.

"It explains a lot of things, Rina," said Shiro. "Like why your IQ is off the scale, and sometimes I swear you can read my mind. Who knew all this time I've been hanging with *ET*. I think it's great."

"I...I guess it's okay," she said, uncertainty in her voice. "It does explain a lot of things. But why they didn't tell me? I was told my real parents died in a plane crash. How could they lie to me?"

"Earth-humans harbor a mortal fear of the unknown," said

Marante. "What do you think they would have done to a child from another planet? I dare not think about it. And perhaps it was their space craft that crashed, therefore not a lie."

"You're not alone," said Kalin, gently placing his hand on her shoulder. "You're an alien on this world, but not beyond its barriers."

Shiro pushed his hand off. "Don't touch her," he demanded.

Shiro's angry stare told him he meant it and even though he was an easy take, Kalin decided to respect his wishes. After all, he'd messed up big time with Rina.

"I'm sorry, Shiro, for hurting you," said Kalin, "and I'm sorry, Rina, for not trusting you and being a total jerk."

"Apology accepted," said Shiro, grinning. "Now, what the heck came out of your eyes?"

"They're called Xevniors," answered Kalin, "an energy ray only Saleran men possess and the reason why I'm the only one who can defeat Vorkis."

Kalin noted Rina's growing acceptance of her newly discovered heritage, her mind thinking, reasoning on the situation. She was a strong, decisive individual willing to acknowledge change. A true scientist.

While helping her to stand, Shiro asked her, "Do you think your real parents were aliens and Justin and Mary adopted you?"

She gazed at him momentarily, then answered, "No, I think my mom, Mary, was the alien. My father hardly ever spoke to me about astronomy, but I've always felt there was something different about my mom. Even though she was a volcanologist, she had a special love for the cosmos. And remember the look in her eyes when she told us the space stories? It was as if she'd been there and I wonder now if they were real experiences."

"I wouldn't doubt it," said Shiro.

She turned to Kalin and put her hands on her hips. "Are you through being a jerk?"

The twirp was going to nail him. "Yes," he glanced away, the shame was overwhelming. *There has to be a way out of this.* "Can we move on now?"

"Absolutely not," she said. "I need an apology from you. On your knees, Kalin of Salera."

"I will not get on my knees, squirt, forget it."

"You've insulted me, covered me in scorpion gunk, accused me of working for your enemy, almost knifed me and, oh, let's not forget nearly breaking my arm and choking me to death. I think those things demand a humble apology, don't you?"

Kalin turned away, rolling his eyes. This was payback. Marante was nodding his head.

You must comply, said Marante.

I really miss Ilya, he said in his mind.

There was no choice; he had to do it. He slowly faced her again and went down on one knee at a time. It was by far the most humiliating, agonizing, torturous situation he'd ever gotten himself into. And the smirk on her face made it worse.

"I'm sorry for everything," he said. "I should've trusted you."

With a coy smile, she stroked his right cheek. Her hand was warm and soft, her eyes gentle and caring. Without warning, her fist bashed his left jaw. His head spun to the right and he almost lost his balance, catching himself with both hands on the ground. He pushed himself back up to his knees and glared at her.

"Apology accepted," she said grinning.

Kalin leapt to his feet, pointing his finger in her face. "I wouldn't have hit you."

"You deserved it," she said, smacking his hand away, "so suck it up and quit being a baby."

He heard Marante chuckle.

"What kind of stories did your mother tell?" asked Marante.

"She was so cool," said Shiro. "We would climb this big tree and—"

"Wait!" she said, clutching Shiro's arm, her eyes scrunched in worry. "The box."

"Oh crap," said Shiro.

Rina grabbed Kalin's vest with both hands. "I have to get to my house in Colorado now, this moment, or it's all over."

"Why?" asked Kalin, gently removing her desperate grip, watching the anxiety grow on her face.

"My mother had given me a big stone box and in it was more Pril. She had to know what it was because I had to swear to keep it hidden and never leave the cover open. If Vorkis finds it, we're done. The chunk of Pril is bigger than a basketball."

Kalin felt the hairs on his arms straighten. "Are you sure it's Pril?"

"Yes," she said. "My mom said it was the same ore as the pendant."

Kalin turned to Marante. "If this planet implodes, the energy released would cause a black hole big enough to devour this quadrant of the galaxy."

Just then, the air rumbled and the tunnel violently shook. Rina stumbled into Shiro's arms and they fell backwards onto the ground. The earthen floor beneath Kalin cracked open, and he and Marante screamed as they plummeted down a dark crevasse.

CHAPTER 19
Rina

Rina was on all fours peering into the dark abyss. She felt her life fading away along with the sounds of Kalin's and Marante's screams. Two of the bravest men she'd ever met, her friends, were gone. They'd risked everything to save Earth, even their lives. Waves of doubt rippled through her soul.

How are we going to save the world without them? We're not familiar with the machinery or the weapons, and which way is the Command Center? Can we actually stop the implosion?

"We have to go," said Shiro. "I think I hear people coming."

She cocked her head and listened, trying to stifle her emotions. Trotting footsteps were coming their way. Shiro helped her to stand; her whole body was trembling. She inhaled a deep breath and forced her legs to stiffen. Keeping her thoughts centered on Earth was essential and no matter how hard, failure would be unforgivable.

"Let's go," she said.

When they turned, four Zorcons were pointing their Barras at them. They raised their hands in surrender.

"You will come with us," said the closest Zorcon, his stare glued to her necklace.

He pointed with his Barra and they started down the passageway with two Zorcons in front of them and two behind. She glanced back at the fissure. A ten-foot rift had swallowed Kalin and Marante. Shiro squeezed her hand. She had to relax so she could think straight.

She hadn't slept in more than forty-eight hours; exhaustion was taking its toll and it was difficult to concentrate. Shiro cleared his throat. He was surveying their surroundings, planning something. Throughout this whole experience, he'd gotten stronger in character. Even the filth didn't seem to bother him. They turned into a short tunnel and walked to the end. The rock face slid open, revealing the bright white interior of an elevator and they entered.

"Level Three," said the Zorcon.

It was then she realized Zorcons sounded like *Cylons* from the old *Battlestar Galactica* series.

Rina's stomach twisted at the sight of the creatures. Their clear skin evinced all movement, even pulsing veins. They were true monsters. She didn't sense any motion and was surprised when the elevator doors reopened. A Barra nudged her back and she stepped out onto a steel grated platform with twining stairs leading down.

"Go," said the Zorcon.

Gray smoke and dust marred the visibility of the cavern. Two huge machines, resembling giant robots on rolling tracks, were using laser beams to dredge into the stone.

Xeon Diffusers, she thought.

Hundreds of Zorcons were busily working. On the other side of the cavern, a wide river was rushing through. They reached the bottom floor and approached a strange black domed vehicle resembling an SUV shaped like a Volkswagen. The Zorcon touched a maroon pad on the side of the craft. The black metal turned into yellow static, then evaporated into an eight-foot-wide opening. The inside of the vehicle was beige with plush cushions.

"Get in," said the Zorcon.

Rina and Shiro entered the vehicle and sat. The four Zorcons took the seat in front of them. One of them tapped a white pad above the opening next to Rina's head and the door reappeared. The vehicle lifted and drove off. It was a soft ride similar to a hovercraft. Shiro elbowed her side.

"You go, I go, doesn't work for me," he whispered.

"No speaking!" said a Zorcon.

What's he up to?

The vehicle slowed and she shifted her weight; they were turning. Shiro leaned back and rested his arm behind her.

"So tell me," he said, addressing the guards, "why do you obey the biggest jack-ass in the universe?"

He quickly hit the white pad above the door next to her head. The portal appeared and he pushed her out of the moving vehicle. She hit the ground rolling and bashed into the rock wall. Bruised and aching, she lifted her head and saw the craft stop.

"Go, Rina!" yelled Shiro.

She stood up, ready to dash back to help him, but the vehicle sped off, leaving three Zorcons running towards her. She ran away as fast as she could, swerving into different tunnels and finally finding an outcrop large enough for her to hide behind. The Zorcons raced by her and she sighed in relief.

They had Shiro. She remembered Kalin telling her they would have her for lunch. *Are they cannibals?* She had to find him.

This part of the core was barely lit. Water droplets were echoing throughout the tunnel. *Are there more scorpions? I hope not.* She began feeling her way through the darkness, hoping nothing would bite her. The faraway sounds of digging machines were getting louder. She needed a gun and that would be the place to get one.

A deep voice resonated through the tunnel. "I know you can hear me, Rina."

She stopped dead in her tracks.

"My name is Vorkis and I have your friend, Shiro. If you do not allow yourself to be found, my servants, the Zorcons, will eat him alive. You have three minutes."

They are cannibals!

Panic overwhelmed Rina. Frantic, she looked around trying to recall the way back to the main tunnel. *Follow the machines!* Shiro's terrifying death was her only thought. She had to give in.

"I'm here!" she yelled, hearing her voice echo in the tunnel. "Come, I'm here! Find me!"

She stumbled through the darkness, sloshing her way through the puddles and falling several times, cutting herself on the jagged rocks. Her tear-filled eyes made it hard to focus. Her rapid breathing was echoing in her head. Desperation engulfed every emotion. Shiro couldn't die. Nothing else mattered.

"I'm lost! Don't hurt him! Find me!"

In the distance, a hazy amber light was barely visible. She began running towards the area when out of nowhere, someone tackled her. It was Kalin.

"Let me go!" she shouted.

"Shiro's as good as dead." He turned her around and held her upper arms tight. "Vorkis will never let him survive."

She wriggled free. "You don't know that! I have to save him!"

She started to run again but Kalin pulled her back.

"It is too late, my lady," said Marante.

Gurgling screams, ripping flesh, and cracking bones resonated through the tunnel. Rina felt the loud snap of fear inside her and she screamed in horror. Kalin wrapped her in his arms and pressed the side of her head against his chest, covering her other ear with his hand. Her body twitched violently as the morbid sounds continued. Suddenly, the agonizing cries stopped. Only the sound of grinding stone was heard. Her leg muscles gave way and Kalin caught her. He flipped her body over his shoulder and ran.

A cold numbness had penetrated all her senses. Unable to move, her arms dangled, bouncing to the stomps. Her mind was blank, her emotions void. Guilt and emptiness were all that remained. All strength had been devoured in a second's time. Kalin sat her softly on a boulder.

"Everything's lost," she said, whimpering. "Shiro's gone."

Kalin was on his knees in front of her. She gazed into his green eyes as he tenderly moved the hair straddled across her face. *It's his fault.* He was the one who had stopped her. *I could have saved him.* She angrily slapped his hand away and stood up, ready to kick him in the head. He jumped to his feet, grabbed her arm and swung her around, holding her from behind with her hands crossed over her chest.

"He would be alive if it weren't for you!" she shouted, using all her strength to squirm free. His grip was tight.

"Shiro was dead the moment he met Vorkis," said Kalin. "He

would have made you watch him die."

Her heart was screaming for the pain to go away. He released her and she turned around, pounding her fists on his chest.

"No!" she said, crying. "You're wrong! I could have saved him!"

"Look at what he did to his own people," he said, calmly. "He's pure evil, Rina, and I'm living proof."

"I know…it was my fault," she wept, "my fault…I was lost…." She fell to her knees.

"I'm so sorry," he said softly, kneeling beside her.

"I couldn't find my way back," she stuttered, her body trembling.

"Kalin is correct," said Marante, squatting next to her. "Vorkis would have forced you to watch Shiro die, and then he would have taken your Pril. That is something we must never allow."

Her best friend had died horribly because of a stupid rock.

"I don't want this thing!"

She went to rip off the necklace, but Kalin gently caressed both her hands.

"As long as you have it, Shiro didn't die in vain."

She whimpered, "What kind of animals would do that?"

"These Zorcons are traitors to their own world," said Marante. "They refused to obey their own laws when it came to consuming human flesh and were banished from their society." His voice softened. "My lady, Shiro gave his life for this world. We should honor him by saving it."

Rina took several deep breaths to calm herself. Her father always knew what to say, but he wasn't here. Shiro was dead and there was nothing she could do. It was the Zorcon's fault, and she would make sure they were wiped out from the universe.

"That was their last meal," she said, standing up and wiping the tears away. "They're going to pay."

Just then, a Zorcon jumped out from an alcove, pointing a Barra at them.

"You will come with me," he said.

Rina snatched the Barra from Marante's hand.

"Eat this," she said.

Three laser shots hit the Zorcon. The creature slammed into the wall and slid to the ground. Smoldering holes opened his chest cavity. Rina stared with a seething hate, wanting so much to kill it again. She shook the weapon hard, wondering why the creature's body was still there.

"What's wrong with this thing?" she said. "I thought it was set to disintegrate."

"I reset it so it could regenerate faster," said Marante.

Kalin gently pried the Barra from her fingers.

"This isn't over," she said.

She ran to the dead body and began kicking it, using all her might to maim the corpse. Kalin's arms wrapped around her and lifted her away.

"He's dead," he said. "You killed him. That's enough."

"It's not enough!" she screamed. "I want him dead again, and again. They're all going to die!"

She wiggled her way out of his arms and launched herself again at the dead body, stomping on the dead carcass.

"Shiro's death will only be of value if you save the lives of the people above," said Marante, standing beside her. "Mutilating a corpse will not avenge his death. Please, my lady…," he put his hand on her shoulder, "do not let hate overcome you. It will be your downfall."

She stopped the assault, trembling and unable to speak while tears continued to flood her face. Marante squeezed her shoulder and almost instantly, the grief and hate lessened to a controllable level. Her breathing returned to normal.

His powers are amazing.

"You were the one who helped Shiro make it through this, weren't you?" she said, gazing at him.

"Yes," said Marante, "it is a gift. Your people need you."

"According to our calculations," said Kalin, "your world has approximately three hours before implosion. We have to finish this."

She removed Marante's hand from her shoulder. "Sometimes vengeance is good, especially when it comes to slaughtering worthless animals."

"Not all Zorcons are worthless animals, my lady," said Marante. "Those who live on their world are law-abiding citizens and only eat animal flesh. They are not all evil."

"Hey," said Kalin. "She's talking about the ones here and I agree with her. These Zorcons need to be slaughtered just like Vorkis."

Rina's breath caught in her chest when she heard Kalin's words, *Just like Vorkis. Am I just like Kalin filled with vengeful hatred? Can I allow the hatred to overtake me like it has Kalin?* At the moment, the emotion was too strong to let go, too powerful to ignore, but eventually she would have to deal with it. For now, these Zorcons were dead meat and there was nothing she could do about it.

"Do not listen to him, my lady," said Marante. "Hate is controlling Kalin; you must be better than that. You must concentrate on saving your world. Shiro would have wanted it that way. His kindness and warm heart is what saved you and you must do the same for those above."

Rina sighed. Shiro saved her and she had to do the same for Earth. Hunting Zorcons would have to wait.

"Just what are you saying?" asked Kalin. "Am I such a bad person?"

"When it comes to your family and the lives of your people, yes," said Marante, "as I have told you several times."

Rina watched Kalin shaking his head, angered at Marante's words. The look in his eyes revealed the hate controlling him, his unreasonable determination...*his weakness.*

How many lives would it take to satisfy my vengeance? More than she could count. *Do I really want to turn into Kalin? Would I become like Vorkis, cold and inhuman?* Both men were set on killing, one for justice, which eventually may lead to genocide, and one who killed to gain power, a sure sign of insanity. The options weren't good.

"There's no choice in the matter," said Kalin. "Slaughtering innocent people is something that shouldn't go unpunished. I—"

Rina gripped Kalin's arm. "Wait a minute," she interrupted; the conversation was turning nasty. "I thought you guys were dead. How did you survive the fall?"

"We landed in another river," said Marante.

Only then did she notice both men were soaked.

"We'll finish this conversation later," Kalin said adamantly to Marante, who calmly nodded.

Kalin pulled out his satchel of Sarvin Crystals and dropped a few on her head. She watched them sparkle down her body, healing the cuts and bruises and even mending her torn clothes.

"Thank you," she said.

From down the tunnel, the sounds of heavy equipment grew louder.

"I'm taking out those machines," she said.

"We have to get Vorkis first," said Kalin.

"Kalin," she said softly, "I know what you mean now. I understand the power of hatred. The emotion is so strong it's almost impossible to suppress. But as much as I despise Zorcons, I have to think of the people above. They're relying on me to save them and I have to put my feelings aside." She moved closer to him. "What happened to you is way worse than what happened to me and you need to fight it with all you've got, for your family and your people. Don't give them up for Vorkis."

Kalin turned away, not listening as usual. His race might die because of him and he refused to see it. He was only thinking of himself.

How selfish, she thought.

"Okay, fine," she said sternly. "Go ahead and kill off your race. Be like Vorkis and finish what he started. Salera will go down in history as being left in the hands of the biggest loser in the galaxy."

Kalin sneered at her with the meanest face she'd ever seen. He was visibly shaking with clenched fists and his brow was furrowed so tight every crease was bright red.

"Stop living for yourself," she said, refusing to cower, angered he didn't care. "There's more at stake here than you."

Without warning, someone grabbed her neck and yanked her back while shooting at Kalin and Marante who dove away.

CHAPTER 20
Kalin, Rina

Kalin helplessly watched Rina's face redden to Vurro's hand squeezing her neck. A Barra pressed her right temple.

"Show yourself, coward!" shouted Vurro, his muzzle drooling white foam. "Or the female dies!"

How did he make a two-week trip in seventy-two hours? asked Marante in Kalin's mind.

"Vurro, how did you get here so fast?" yelled Kalin.

"Do not alter the subject!" he shouted, his lips quivering over pointed razor-sharp teeth. "Show yourself!"

"Let her go and I'll let you live," said Kalin. "Hurt her, and you're dead."

Vurro stood silent; his nearly black skin amplified the glow of yellow eyes.

He has been working with Vorkis for close to five years, said Marante.

Kalin sensed his friend's telepathy digging into Vurro's mind.

He assisted in the plan to annihilate all Salerans, said Marante.

Vurro's elongated maw widened into a nefarious smile. "A glorious moment I will never forget," he said as dangling strings of saliva jiggled in the air.

Kalin's need to take him out was beginning to overpower him.

Marante clasped his arm. *His only thought is to kill the Prince of Salera. Do not give in to his pleasure.*

Kalin nodded and set his Barra for stun.

"Show yourself!" yelled Vurro. He pushed the Barra hard against Rina's temple and her head jerked to the side.

"Don't, Kalin!" she shouted, digging her nails into Vurro's hand. "He's a maggot!"

Vurro squeezed her neck harder, his rigid claws cutting into her skin. A bluish tinge began tinting her lips. She put her hand over her fist and elbowed Vurro's stomach. He stumbled away in pain. She jumped and sliced a kick in mid-air, her foot collided with his head. His body swung around and bashed face-first into the wall. Rina stood over the unconscious form rubbing the front of her neck when a blue beam hit her in the back. She lurched forward and fell helplessly onto Vurro.

"No!" cried Kalin, leaping to his feet.

A volley of laser blasts whizzed past him and he ducked down for cover. Several Zorcons were hiding behind another outcrop.

"I have to get her," he said, firing at anything that moved.

A low buzzing sound preceded a green transport beam that spread over Rina and Vurro. Their bodies lifted and flew towards the Zorcons. Within moments, Rina and Vurro were teleported away with the Zorcons. Vorkis' laughter resonated through the tunnels.

"You're a fool, Kalin," he said. "I have the Pril. Come. I am waiting."

Kalin picked up a rock and angrily threw it at the wall. It bore through the black stone with a puff of smoke. He turned to Marante. "We have to find her."

"We must stop the planet implosion," said Marante, "or there will be no one to save."

"You go for the Xeons." Kalin picked up Vurro's Barra and tossed it to Marante. "I'm going for Rina."

"Done," said Marante, and they ran their separate ways.

***

Rina

Voices echoed in Rina's head as cold fingers tapped her face. She opened her eyes slowly and saw a smiling man in his forties.

"How are you?" he asked.

"Fine," she said as the man helped her to sit. Her head was pounding and her stomach hurt.

"Where am I?" she asked.

"You're in an underground jail. Creatures from outer space called Zorcons brought you here ten minutes ago. My name is Vinny," he added.

"You're not in a good place," said a voice behind her, "I'm Lisa."

Rina turned to see a young girl with short black hair and stringy black bangs sitting over her pure white skin. Dark eye make-up surrounded her brown eyes; the classic Goth look. The cavern smelled of mold. Rina counted fifteen people in scraggly filthy clothes. Some were huddled on their knees praying while others were visibly crying. Lisa sat beside Rina.

"There's a blast hole in your shirt," said Lisa. "What's your name?"

"Rina," she said, reaching around and feeling the opening near the small of her back. "I remember being shot but there's no pain or flesh wound."

"They healed you," said Vinny, scratching his head through his salt and pepper hair. Layers of brown dirt covered his skin. "They always heal the ones they want to save for later."

"Yeah," said Lisa, brushing off her torn jeans. "We're the Zorcons' meal ticket."

"You could show a little more compassion," Vinny said, irritated.

Rina could tell this was not the first time Lisa had annoyed him.

"Hey," Lisa said firmly, "she has a right to know how she's going to die."

"You need to control—"

"It's okay," said Rina, placing her hand on Vinny's arm. "I've had several run-ins and—" she reached for her necklace. It was gone. "Crap! I have to get out of here."

"We all want to get out," Lisa said, sarcastically. "What makes you so special?"

"My pendant contains a stone of pure energy and Vorkis is going to use it to kill millions."

"You gave him Pril?" said Lisa, rising to her feet. "You idiot!

Why did you bring it down here?"

Rina now knew why Vinny disliked Lisa.

"I was kidnapped and didn't know what it was until a short time ago. Stop being so presumptuous; ask before you cast judgment."

"Whatever. Now we're all dead for sure."

"Don't mind her," said Vinny. "Her mouth gets in the way of her brain."

"Stuff it," the girl muttered.

Vinny pointed to an exit. "The only way out is blocked by an invisible shield. We've tried everything to break through and failed."

"Take me to it," said Rina.

"Are you a scientist?" asked Vinny.

"Yes," answered Rina. "Now please help me."

Every muscle was aching as Vinny helped Rina ease off the stone bed. She nearly fell from dizziness, but he caught her.

"Careful," he said. "They healed your wound but your body is still weak. You need to rest."

"No time," she said, forcing her unsteady legs to straighten, "or Lisa wins."

"Now that's an awful thought," said Vinny.

Lisa rolled her eyes.

Vinny helped her to the exit where she stood in front of the shield. She glided her fingers over the clear wall and though it twinkled to her touch, it was solid and strong.

"It must be a REM shield," she said softly. She turned to the crowd. "How did all of you get down here?"

"We were transported like in *Star Trek*," said Lisa, standing behind them. "I was walking home from school in broad daylight when the next thing I knew I was looking at the scariest monsters I'd ever seen."

"I was driving on the Long Island Expressway in New York at three a.m. when the Zorcons took me," said Vinny. "Every one of us was transported here to be food for the Zorcons. One of them told me they even have some of us in safe keeping for when they leave."

"Yep," said Lisa, "stashed away in a fridge like meat in a butcher shop."

Vinny shook his head in disgust. "Two months ago there were twelve hundred of us and now we're all that's left. I heard two of them saying they were leaving the planet soon."

"Yes, they are," said Rina. She flattened her cheek against the shield trying to peek into the sidewalls of the exit.

Suddenly, the transparent face of a Zorcon appeared in front of her. Rina gasped and stepped back, startled at the hideous animal who slowly stood upright. Two Zorcons with Barras were standing behind him.

"I am Master Taru, Captain of the Guard."

"And the ugliest thing this side of the universe," she said.

Vinny put his hand on her shoulder as if to say, "Don't." She moved closer to the shield. Taru's wide grin revealed white serrated teeth glistening against the blood-red background of his mouth. His glowing red eyes were pressed into an evil glare.

"You will make a fine meal," he grinned.

"Let down this shield and we'll see who gets who, coward."

"You were the one with the plump male," said Taru, still smiling. "He was delicious. I especially enjoyed his eyes."

An irrepressible hatred instantly engulfed Rina. With clenched fists, she lifted her face and roared with all her might. An onslaught of heated air scorched her throat as her lungs threatened to collapse. Desperate to contain the agony Shiro must have felt, her eyes flooded with bitter tears while her heart cried out in agony. No one could bring Shiro back. He'd died the most horrible death anyone could suffer. It was over.

This monster killed him. Now it's his turn to die.

Left with a ravaged heart and trembling with depleted lungs, she caught her breath and pounded her fists on the shield so hard a booming sound shook the walls of the cavern. Frightened, Taru stumbled back into the two guards, who raised him to his feet.

"You'd better hope I never get out of here!" she shouted, her voice raspy from inflamed vocal cords. "I'm going to rip you to shreds!"

Taru vaulted back to the shield and snarled, moving in on Rina's face. She leaned closer to him, unafraid, carefully studying his bones, watching them move in their joints, picking which ones to break first. Nose-to-nose with him through the shield and repulsed by his putrid breath, she refused to cower. He snapped his teeth several times, growling and hissing but she held her ground, glaring into his hideous eyes.

"Take this one to dining room three," he said.

"No!" bellowed a voice from down the tunnel.

Taru immediately bowed to a blue lizard guy.

"Yes, Lord Vurro," answered Taru.

Vurro walked towards them, his massive chest and arms billowing with ripples of muscle. His long snout, similar to a lizard, exposed shark-like teeth. Protruding from beneath his snug, tan-colored pants, his ten-toed feet pounded the earthen floor, expanding and contracting like water-filled balloons, pulverizing the dirt beneath, creating small clouds of dust with each step. Two wide bands of brown leather crisscrossed a broad grainy blue-skinned chest filled with swollen white pustules that looked ready to pop. As he stood in front of Taru, he glanced at Rina.

This creature enjoys intimidation, she thought.

"The female is to be taken to Vorkis," said Vurro. "His Highness is waiting."

"Yes, my lord, we will obey," said Taru, bowing again.

Taru waved his hand over the wall beside the shield and it disappeared. Rina dashed out and slammed Taru into the rock wall. She dug her nails into his face and tore whatever she could. He pushed her away and she went reeling back into him. Her knee rammed his groin and he crumbled to the floor clutching himself, gasping for air. She pounced on him punching hard, determined to avenge Shiro's death. His white blood was sprinkling everywhere. Taru was screaming for her to be removed. Something bashed the back of her head and everything went black.

CHAPTER 21
Kalin

Kalin inched his way through the dark tunnels of the complex. On the ceiling, the Vitra Crystals were scarce and few. Just like the kings of old who created moats around their castles, Vorkis formed a moat of darkness around his Command Center.

The penetrating odors of mold and earth weighed on his lungs. Outlines of cragged boulders were vaguely visible in the thick darkness. The tinkling sounds of dripping water surrounded him, which explained the mud he was walking through. A loud snap came from behind. He swung his Barra around ready for a fight, but nothing was visible.

Easy, Kalin, your mind is playing tricks on you.

Yet something didn't feel right. He slowly backed away, keeping his finger on the trigger of the Barra, his keen eyes probing the passageway. *Nothing. Okay, I am losing it.* He made a u-turn and was about to continue on but stopped.

It's quieter.

The sounds of the drips were only in front of him, none from behind. He carefully turned around, keeping a tight grip on his Barra. The tunnel was pitch black, darker than what lay before him, and a rank odor of decay was now present. From the corner of his left eye, he saw it. A slight movement. He kept his stare straight, not moving his head, keeping his peripheral vision fixed on the long thin object. It twitched. Several more came into focus.

Ten feet in front of him, six red eyes appeared resembling fiery meteors. Below them were large chelicerae, two moving plates with attached white fangs covering the beast's mouth. Something hard hit Kalin's chest and he went flying landing face first in the mud. His Barra flew the opposite way. A giant claw latched onto his legs and lifted him in the air upside down.

Kalin screamed to the knifing pain, bending upwards as he tried to loosen the pincer. The insect raised him near the ceiling as if examining its latest meal. Kalin let himself hang, his arms swinging above his head; he had to conserve his energy and wait for the right time to bash the thing. Jagged black bristles dotted the creature's ebony body. Four pairs of thorny appendages led into an elongated shell attached to a flattened thorax. Numerous spikes and barbs embedded the wide pedipalps, long arms ending with two colossal claws. The yellow ringlets on the hind legs told him it was the same monster from the tropical cavern.

The Vinegaroon.

The beast lurched Kalin to its mouth, dangling him in front of stringy crimson saliva stretched between its sharp fangs.

It's trying to torture me, thought Kalin.

Stretched across its cavernous maw were crinkled veins of mustard-colored entrails.

Remnants of the spiders.

A strong acrid odor began burning his eyes. He turned just in time to see the other claw coming at him.

"Eat this," he said.

He punched the claw with all his might and it zoomed into one of the arachnid's eyes. The Vinegaroon screeched, dropping him on his side in the mud. He started to stand when pain darted up both legs, almost sending him to the floor. The creature had backed away, writhing against the wall, squealing to its recent wound.

That's all I need. A pissed off man-eating bug.

Kalin's calf muscles felt like they'd been torn off his bones. Thankfully, no skin was broken. An eerie stillness had settled the air. He stiffened when he realized the monster was silently watching him. Its other five eyes were working just fine. In one swift motion, it scrunched to the floor and pushed up, leaping in the air towards him. He dove away, rolling on the dirt to his feet. The beast shrilled and Kalin bolted down the tunnel with the Vinegaroon in a full charge and getting closer. Without his Barra, he was helpless.

He swerved left into another tunnel, hoping it was smaller but instead it was bigger. There was a yellow light at the end, and it was getting hotter, the air was thicker, heavier. The light changed into an orange glow and he dashed towards it. Without warning, the ground beneath him ended. He skidded to a stop, teetering at the edge of a cliff, wavering about, trying not to fall into a fast-moving river of boiling lava.

His pounding heart reminded him how much he hated surprises, and he stepped back. The river was at least two hundred feet across, and the tunnel continued on the other side. There was no way he could jump it unless he got a running start. The cavern was at least three hundred feet high. Clicking sounds came from behind.

It's blocking the exit on purpose.

He needed something for defense. Indigo-colored stones lay scattered across the earthen floor. *They'll have to do.* The damaged eye of the monster had turned white. Kalin picked up a rock the size of a melon and bounced it in his hand, letting the beast know he wasn't going down without a fight. He moved to his right; a clear shot into a good eye was imperative. Kalin flung the stone.

The creature lifted its claw to block the attack but the rock bore through its shell. It shrilled in pain, bashing its other claw on the ground several times. Kalin covered his ears to the piercing sound that jarred his organs. The beast opened its mouth and shot out a wad of black spit. Kalin leapt away sideways, banging his head on the wall and almost losing consciousness. The saliva hit the dirt ten feet from him, hissing and smoking, melting a two-foot hole into the brown soil.

Acid.

His eyes instantly burned as if on fire, watering to the pungent gas that blurred his vision. Kalin dragged himself up to a sitting position. The bump on the side of his head was growing.

Through streaming tears, he could see the insect watching him. To rub his eyes would give away his weakness, so he kept still. There was nowhere to go. The acid saliva was blinding him. His eyes had swollen into slits.

I won't die this way.

Slyly, he began moving both hands through the dirt, searching. The point of a huge rock lay beside his right hand. He wrapped his fingers around it and pulled, nothing happened. It was part of a slab beneath him, so he dug his fingers into the soil around the jagged stone, slicing his skin open. His thoughts went to Saleran-humans and how highly they considered their perfection. Never growing old, living their lives on Salera to the fullest, always believing their immortality would save them from anything. They were wrong. The tiniest of all creatures stole their lives. *But am I any better?* Before his people died, he took life for granted, accepting the toughest missions from the Federation no matter how dangerous they were, playing with death and never thinking twice of those who loved him.

Women were a pleasurable hobby, nothing more. He deliberately chose words that would lure them, hoping they would believe his lies and figuring they would get over him, but did they?

Can a person really forget love, any kind of real love? Could I ever forget my family and the love I have for little Disa? Never.

The pain in his heart would always be there. A harsh emptiness overcame him as he thought of the many women who'd fallen in love with him and whom he'd blatantly tossed aside.

Then there was Rina. Her words sounded in his head: "…kill off your race…finish what Vorkis started…there's more at stake here than you." Her words ground inside his chest, ripping at his very soul. If it weren't for Vurro, he probably would have choked her. But the twirp had something he didn't have. She was ready to kill every Zorcon in sight but stopped herself, thinking about how her actions would affect others.

How did she do that? Could I do it?

His family's horrifying demise, especially Disa's, was too difficult to overcome. His only hope was the regeneration of his race and this was always a soothing thought. However, after months of picturing ways of how to kill Vorkis, it would be hard to quell the hate and rage. A sharp sting in his finger made him flinch.

Peeping through slivered eyes, he realized his fingers were bleeding bad. It hurt, but not compared to what he had to do. Tightening his muscles, he gripped the pinnacle of the stone and squeezed. Warm blood streamed down the hard rock. A loud crack echoed as the piece snapped free. He scurried to his feet, leaning on the wall for support. Every muscle hurt. His lungs burned. The view through his puffed eyes was getting smaller; soon they would swell completely shut. The monster was creeping towards him with its claws low and outstretched, ready to snatch him, so he bounced the stone in his hand. The beast halted its advance.

From across the river of lava he heard the hum of an Avec. The black vehicle drove in from the opposite tunnel and stopped at the other cliff. The dome evaporated and six Zorcons stood with their Barras pointed at the insect. They weren't aware of his presence or else he would have been the target. Instead, they blasted the Vinegaroon, who screeched and leapt wildly about.

This is my chance.

Kalin's bloody fingers felt their way along the rock face. He had to reach the back of the cavern to get good distance.

If I don't make it, at least I'll go my way.

He counted his footsteps. It wasn't too long ago when he temporarily lost his sight, a result of seeing his family die. The three weeks were agonizing and if it weren't for Marante, he would've killed himself.

He remembered Marante's words: "If you take your life, you will have accomplished Vorkis' desire."

Vorkis.

The name alone made his gut ache. He could feel his hand squeezing Vorkis' neck; the sensation was so real. His vision was improving with distance from the acid and the tears were slowing. The creature was on the far side of the cavern, hissing and shrieking at the Zorcons who kept a volley of steady laser fire on the insect. Finally, he had reached the needed distance of about sixty feet. He took a deep breath and bolted for the river.

If the Vinegaroon spotted him, it was over. One leap from the monster and he would be dead. He could see spits of lava shooting up from the river which made the jump more lethal.

Get hit by one of those and I'm done. A chance I have to take.

He had to time himself so his leap would be at the very edge of the cliff, giving himself more lift.

One— two—"three!" he shouted and pushed off the cliff's edge with all the strength in his legs.

"Aah!" he cried out as his body lifted into the air.

His arms and legs flailed as the momentum carried him over the boiling lava. He hit the dirt and rolled to the far wall. The shooting had ceased. The Zorcons were staring at him.

"Surprised, huh?" he said aloud, happy he'd survived the jump. His swollen eyes were almost normal. "You got worse problems than me." He nudged his chin towards the beast.

The Vinegaroon was already in the air over the river. It pounced on the Avec sending it crashing to the ground. The screaming Zorcons were helpless against the giant insect, which was throwing them one-by-one against the wall. Morbid sounds of shattering bones filled the cavern. The Zorcon bodies lay crumpled on the floor. The creature scurried to them and began their disembowelment.

Kalin quietly crawled to the Avec. Its engine was still humming. The weight of the monster had not disabled it. He quietly climbed into the vehicle and sat in the gray cushioned seat. The metal dome of the vehicle didn't reappear. According to the open holo in front of him, it had been damaged from the spider attack. He pressed a yellow button and the vessel silently rose in the air. Avecs were amazing machines, able to climb walls and hover on ceilings while keeping its passengers stable and secure. Protruding from the white dashboard was the steel vertical maneuvering stick. Above this, lay three recessed orbs. To his right was the accelerator, a silver T-shaped lever. With a Zorcon Avec hooked into the Command Center, he could find Vorkis. He just had to get away alive.

To fly over the river would alert the beast, and to make an about-face would do the same. The only choice was to slowly back his way down the tunnel and hope the insect didn't notice.

Here goes nothing, he said to himself, and carefully inched the accelerator stick towards him. *Nice and easy.*

The vehicle began its reverse out of the cavern. Not banging the walls would be a challenge. He kept checking the creature which was busy with its recent kill. This tunnel wasn't dark and there was a glowing red light at the far end. Whatever the light was, it was the reason the Zorcons had come to destroy the monster. Vorkis was near. He could feel it. Finally, he lost sight of the beast. He waved his hand over an orb and a holo of the insect appeared. It was still eating, and he was fifty yards from it.

Good. Now to find a place to turn around.

The tunnel was narrow but the ceiling was a good forty feet high. A shriek echoed. The Vinegaroon was running towards him at full speed.

"Crap!" he said and pulled back the shifter into full reverse.

The vehicle lurched with a bounce then sped backwards down the tunnel, zigzagging and hitting the rock walls, sending sparks into the air. Driving in reverse was not his forte; he could never keep the vehicle straight. The creature was closing in. A claw clipped the nose of the Avec. It skidded on the ground and continued its backtrack.

Kalin jerked the control stick sideways and the Avec flipped upside down, racing down the passageway. The monster screeched, skidding to a halt. It was what Kalin needed. He drove the vehicle up towards the ceiling and flipped it right side up as he came down. Finally, he was driving front forward. In the holo, all he saw was the legs of the beast. It was in the air and ready to pounce. He rammed the accelerator all the way up.

The insect landed ten feet from the Avec. A glob of acid spit splashed the wall next to him and he swerved away, hearing it hiss into the stone. He weaved through the tunnel, scraping the walls, attempting to avoid the caustic missiles whose sprinkles were boring holes into the Avec's metal. There wasn't much time. The red light at the end of the tunnel was ahead. He waved his hand through the holo and smiled. It was a Zorcon multi-level feeding lounge with forty Zorcons inside.

Perfect.

The Avec bashed through the doors, throwing tables and Zorcons into the air. Its engines whined to a stop, but the vehicle continued sliding on the floor until it crashed into the far wall.

Kalin hustled to stand on the seat. Dread overcame him at the sight of the Lurivin, a fifty-foot-diameter glowing sphere hovering inches above the shiny black metal floor. The giant ball pulsated with a deep eerie hum. Inside was the latest in food preservation using Teridin, a clear gel now bright red due to the hundreds of Earth-human body parts floating within. Legs, arms, and faces frozen with fear made him sick. Someone coughed.

At least thirty Zorcons were standing in front of the Lurivin, their tables filled with food. Shocked at his presence, their mouths were covered with fresh blood and their cheeks were engorged with raw human meat. The familiar clicking sounds came from the shattered entrance. The Vinegaroon's red eyes were glued on the Zorcons. Kalin grinned.

"Lunch time!" he yelled.

The creature leapt into the air. The Zorcons scattered. The monster's landing shook the room, forcing the Zorcons to stumble and fall. The insect quickly gathered them together with its legs then used its massive claws to grab several at a time by their necks, throwing them against the wall to their deaths.

Kalin leisurely hopped out of the Avec and walked up the stairs to the exit. The Vinegaroon screeched at him and he turned, saluting it. His attacker had become his hero. Next to the exit were shelves lined with Barras. He watched the Vinegaroon tear into a screaming Zorcon. The monster seemed to enjoy the sound; maybe that's why it hadn't killed him sooner. Kalin took a Barra off the rack.

"Sorry, but I can't let you hunt me again," he said.

He blasted the Lurivin and it burst, releasing a torrent of Teridin and body parts into the room. The giant wave slammed the Vinegaroon into the far wall. Its shrieks became gurgles as the decayed matter smothered the insect and the remaining Zorcons.

Kalin nodded and slipped the Barra onto his shoulder then headed out the door. The lit hallway was white and clean, a refreshing change from the dingy tunnels. He heard the screech of the Vinegaroon again and took off running down the passageway.

CHAPTER 22

Kalin, Marante

The sound of the Vinegaroon faded as Kalin ran through the corridors of the complex. He came upon a hallway where the floor was gray Hitan, a metal harder than diamond. Hundreds of NBs embedded the rock walls and ceiling. The droll humming of electronics was a sure sign he was nearing the Command Center.

Up ahead was a crossway and he stopped, peeking around the corner. Four Zorcons were standing at attention before two oversized sliding doors. *The Command Center.* The hallways were empty. Why didn't Vorkis have troops protecting his main hub? The anxiety of the kill was getting stronger by the moment. The bitter taste of death rolled across his tongue.

Approaching the guards, Taru's face had several deep scratches and there was a black patch over his left eye. He was about to enter the Command Center when Vurro called to Taru. The big pimple was strutting as if he owned the world. Kalin listened in on their conversation.

"How soon?" asked Vurro.

"It is completed, my lord," answered Taru.

"I hope this new toy will satisfy Vorkis. The Rajans actually believed they could use it on me," he scoffed. "Fools. I took great pleasure in destroying their capital city."

"It is magnificent, my lord."

A voice came over the Comlink attached to Vurro's brown belt. "Lord Vurro, the infiltrator is in Sector Four. What are your orders?"

"Do nothing," commanded Vurro. "I am on my way. Taru, inform Lord Vorkis I will capture a specimen for him."

"Yes, my lord." Taru bowed then entered the Command Center.

Vurro began walking towards Kalin who quickly crouched down. He had to find a place to hide. Frantic, he tiptoed away at a fast pace and entered the first door that opened; a small fully stocked munitions room. Up against the walls, every type of handheld weapon filled the open racks from Barras to Cratons, small silver balls able to blow up almost anything. The door began sliding open. Someone was coming in.

Kalin rushed to the darkened corner at the far left and squeezed himself between two racks. Through the shelves and above the tops of small canisters, he could see it was Vurro. Kalin wanted so much to tear off his head.

Vurro stood at the entrance eyeing the shelves when he raised his snout and sniffed the air. His lips quivered over serrated teeth. The Setrellan-human's keen sense of smell had detected him. Vurro leaned forward and looked to his left. Kalin held his breath trying to flatten himself more against the wall. He could feel sweat streaming down his face. If he was discovered now, it was over. Vorkis would surely make a run for it and it would be months before Kalin could locate Vorkis again.

Vurro shifted his head from side-to-side, sniffing the air, trying to pinpoint the smell. He looked to his left again and growled. Kalin positioned his finger on the trigger of his Barra, ready to shoot, when he noticed across from him, sitting on a shelf was his Barra from the *Quasar*, the one he'd lost with the Vinegaroon. Vurro spit a green wad of phlegm at the weapon and it stuck. The stench was so nauseating Kalin wanted to vomit. He recalled the many fights with Setrellan-humans because of their spit and the many times he had to throw out his clothes because of the irremovable odor. Vurro chuckled then stepped up to the front rack, slid two strapped Barras on each of his shoulders and left the room.

Kalin's muscles relaxed and he sighed in relief. The smell was worse than a rotting body and he needed to get out of there. For starters, the Grid Room was where the power was apportioned for the complex and where he could do the most damage. It had to be near the Command Center. He slid out of the cramped space and hurried to the doors that slid open. The gust of clean air was refreshing.

Slinking back to the crossway he peeked around again; the guards were still there. He quietly snapped a tiny piece of stone off the rock wall and flicked it down the corridor. It flew a hundred feet passed the soldiers before skidding on the floor. The Zorcons immediately swung their Barras toward the sound. Kalin dashed across the hallway unnoticed.

He leaned on the wall to catch his breath. Rina's words echoed again in his mind: "…there's more at stake here than you." An uneasy feeling began creeping in. *What about my people?* They were already dead and even if he found someone to bear his children, they would be only half Saleran at most.

That'll work for now, he thought. This was not the time for soul-searching.

Thanks to his Saleran blood, the cuts on his hands were almost healed. He wondered how Rina was doing. Vorkis' sadistic mating habits had butchered many women. The gentleman side of him said he should save her first, but he was too close to the kill. His main mission was almost complete. Rina was smart, brave, and he doubted any man could ever get his way with her. She would have to wait.

He set his Barra to vaporize. His Comlink blinked. Earth had less than two hours. The ground beneath him trembled. A cloud of dust flittered down from the ceiling. Gazing up and around the tunnel, the implosion was imminent unless Marante could shut down the Xeons.

The humming sound was louder farther down the hallway, so he quietly headed toward it. A short distance from him the metal floor stopped, and a dirt floor layered with footprints led to the right. He inched his way to the edge of the wall and squatted, then took a quick peek. The tunnel was long and barely lit. At the very end, two Zorcons with their glowing red eyes stood in front of a door surrounded by blue light.

Found it.

Kalin laid on his stomach and body-crawled on the dirt. The darkness was a good cover.

Vorkis may have numbers in Zorcons, but none with brains.

He picked up a tiny stone and tossed it their way. They turned in his direction, aiming their Barras. Two shots evaporated the Zorcons into yellow dust. Kalin hustled to his feet and flipped the Barra onto his shoulder.

Inside the Grid Room, hundreds of data panels lit up the twenty-by-twenty-foot room. Three different-sized podiums with several orbs were ready for use. At the largest podium, he tapped a blue orb and watched a holo rise up. He waved his hand through the holo, making his adjustments. Kalin left the room with a wide grin, content Vorkis' world would soon be destroyed.

***

Marante

Along a three-hundred-foot high wall, four Xeon Diffusers stood beside each other in a row. Marante was crouched in a corner sixty feet from the first Xeon. The clamor of metal gears was gut-piercing and he could barely think straight.

According to the holo emanating from his scanner, five Zorcons were atop each seventy-foot-tall apparatus, busily monitoring their sections of the core from a glass-enclosed Command Bridge. Marante gulped as he stared at the monstrous machine.

The bridge was sitting on top of broad barreling shoulders, rounding into weighty arms that ended with giant metal claws. Thick plates of black steel formed their distended chests then narrowed into thin waists able to spin in any direction. Below this, wide metal girders, simulating hips, were attached to two enormous pistons enabling the Xeons to raise or lower. Earth digging rolling tracks inched the Xeons forward.

Marante's scanner confirmed the primitive machines were stolen from Ritan III, a young civilization two thousand years behind in technology, and one the Federation ignored. Similar to Earth, the Ritan-humans were oblivious to the Federation's existence. Their space program limited them to their own star system of twelve planets, using the ancient technology of cryogenics to travel. He couldn't help but wonder, would Vorkis' plan have been revealed sooner if the Federation had accepted the Ritan-humans into their organization? It was something to consider when time was less demanding. Marante studied the Xeon nearest him on the scanner. To collect the Pril, Vorkis had made his own modifications.

Jutting out from the machine's chest were twelve robotic catheters equipped with high-powered lasers and scanners whose wide cone-like beams were scurrying along the wall. The golden lights changed to red, and blue laser beams blasted holes in the hard stone.

It found Pril, thought Marante.

From the same breastplate, six silver flexible hoses sprouted, wiggling like worms into the blown-out pockets and vacuuming the Pril into a small white sack at the base of the tubes. The bucket claws were in constant motion removing fallen stones and dirt from the work area, allowing a clear pathway. Despite crusted layers of dried soil, huge dents, and corroding rust, the Xeons, though mechanically crude, were accomplishing the task with little difficulty.

A thin sheen of sweat covered Marante's head and face. The Xeons resembled gigantic beasts with bulky claws and tentacles. Two years ago, Kalin had insisted he watch an old Earth-human movie called *Alien*. He had seen hundreds of different life forms from all over the galaxies, but never before had any creature been depicted with such horror and suspense. It had given him nightmares for weeks. Of course, Kalin laughed at him each time he jumped frightened in his seat. Marante swore revenge. Ever since, certain places and things revived the memory of the *"Alien."* He hoped he wouldn't have those nightmares again.

Marante rechecked his scanner. Vorkis would need six full sacks to equal one ounce of Pril but with two ounces of the ore already in his possession, it would not be long before the third was gathered. The excavation was tedious and time-consuming, and although he had Rina's necklace, his greed would compel him to mine all he could before leaving the planet.

The Xeon closest to him had three Zorcons on the ground keeping guard. They wore Athers, special earplugs that muted all sounds except for voices. He wished he had a pair. At the bottom rear of the unit, he would attach his scanner to the green Hesion Box, break the code, and program the Xeon to self-destruct, thus avoiding any outward tampering with the unit itself. The force of the blast should ignite the other machines, thus ending the dredging.

Without warning, the cold barrel of a Barra pressed against the side of his head. The wicked laugh told him it was Vurro.

CHAPTER 23
Rina, Kalin

A hard slap on the face and Rina awoke to a dark-haired man with slate-blue eyes. A thick goatee surrounded his thin lips and aside from the furry eyebrows, he was somewhat attractive.

"Who are you?" she asked softly.

"Vorkis," he said, stiffening up. "What's your name?"

"Rina." She was lying on a table unable to move her arms and legs or even turn her head. "Why are you destroying my world?" Her head hurt so bad she wondered if she was slurring her speech.

"What is your species called?" he asked.

"Answer my question first," she said. *Does his breath stink because he eats humans like Zorcons?*

"I am not a patient man," he said. "Tell me or someone you know will die."

"You killed my best friend," she said.

"Earth-humans attach themselves to unimportant things. You are not one of them."

"At least I didn't slaughter my friends and family. You're a worthless piece of crap who doesn't deserve to live."

His top lip twitched several times. "Be careful, Rina, I've—"

A Zorcon cleared his throat. "My lord, please excuse the interruption, but I have the information you requested." He handed him a scanner.

"According to the Earth-human records," Vorkis said, reading, "your father is alive." He faced the Zorcon. "Locate him."

"As you wish, Your Highness," answered the Zorcon, who bowed and walked out of her vision.

Vorkis tossed the scanner aside and rested his hands on the table. His gaze went up and down her body giving her the creeps.

"I'm curious about you," he said. "I'm not familiar with your species so I'll ask you again, what are you? And where did you get the Pril?"

"I'm Earth-human," she said. "My mother found the rock after a volcano erupted."

His stare told her he wasn't buying it.

"Very well," he said.

To her astonishment, he pulled her up to a sitting position as if nothing held her down. The table she was on was completely lit and possibly made of glass. The faint sounds of jabber came from a distance. Against the walls of the cavernous room, she counted twenty terminals with Zorcons monitoring holograms. Vorkis sniffed her hair and she jerked away, grossed by his touch.

"I'm amazed at your resemblance to a Saleran female," he said. "You even smell like them."

"You're sick," she replied. She noticed he was wearing her necklace. "I want that back. It belongs to me."

"It was yours. Now it's mine."

"Why do you hate so much? Are you a coward?" She'd probably get it for that one.

He grabbed the hair atop her head and yanked her head back. She gasped, trying to loosen his painful grip.

"To kill gives one power," he said, spittle sprinkling her face. "After exterminating the fools on Salera, I have become the most powerful being in the galaxy and no one can take that from me. Not even Kalin."

He pushed her head away hard, letting go of her hair, and she almost fell on her side. She rubbed her head, glad to feel the clump of hair was still there.

"Come," he said. "I'll show you what real power is."

He slid her legs off the table and lifted her to her feet. Her gaze went up his towering physique; he was Kalin's height and just as broad. She wondered if Kalin could really beat him. He nodded to his left.

Twenty feet away, Marante stood on a raised round platform

where a white transparent beam of light encapsulated him. A gash opened the side of his head and blue fluorescent blood was streaming out. His nose was black and his clothes were shredded.

They dragged him.

"Tell me who you are and you will save him," said Vorkis.

There was a cough and Rina noticed Taru at a podium not far from them.

"You animal!" she screamed and vaulted for him.

"No!" cried out Taru, cowering away.

Vorkis pulled her back.

"I will say this much," he said, laughing as she fought him. "I've never heard of a woman overpowering a Zorcon. I am impressed."

Marante groaned. He was pale and weak. She had to do something.

Stall for time, my lady, said Marante in her mind.

She turned around and faced Vorkis. "Why don't you let me at him again? I can give you a real good show."

"You intrigue me, Rina," he replied, "and I love the offer but alas, he is my Captain of the Guard and I need him."

His gaze focused on her eyes, sending a cold shiver through her bones. Kalin was right; Vorkis was pure evil. He swung her around to face Marante. This time his hands clamped her upper arms tight, holding her in place.

"Marante is in a Telvor Beam," he said. "It's a gift from a friend. You've met him already, General Vurro. This magnificent creation dissolves brain cells, a very slow and excruciating process. There are five levels. With each level, suffering increases. At level five the brain liquefies."

Her heart thumped harder with each second. She couldn't panic. She had to buy more time. "You're demented."

"Thank you." She could hear his smile. "Now it's my turn to play."

The beam surrounding Marante began fluttering, and his face scrunched in pain as streams of light attacked his cranium.

"Stop it!" said Rina.

"Tell me who you are," said Vorkis.

"How can I tell you something I don't know?" she said anxiously.

"Level two!" shouted Vorkis.

The pulses quickened and Marante clenched his teeth. Desperate to make them stop, Rina squirmed to free herself, but Vorkis squeezed her arms so tight she was sure her bones would snap. Her knees gave way from the pain, but he held her up.

"The longer you take, the more damage you inflict," said Vorkis. "Now, tell me who you are."

"I don't know!" she cried.

"Level four!" yelled Vorkis.

"No!" shouted Rina.

The streams of light changed into pulsing white halos. Marante's face was drawn and pinched tight, contorting with every wave, his thin body twitching with each contraction.

"All right!" she said. "Release him and I'll tell you!"

"Excellent," said Vorkis.

He signaled Taru and the beam shut off. Marante slumped forward and fell off the lowering platform, hitting the floor with a thud.

"Let's see how well you handle the Telvor," said Vorkis. He gripped a wad of hair on the top of her head and dragged her body to the platform, her legs sliding on the floor. She dug her nails in his hand while pushing with her legs trying to ease the pain. He clutched her arm and flung her body onto the platform. Instantly, the white beam encased her, straightening her out and stiffening her muscles. She was unable to move. It felt like a vice. Breathing was difficult. The platform raised her to a foot above Vorkis.

"Now tell me who you are," said Vorkis, crossing his arms over his chest.

Rina eyed Marante lying on the floor. *At least he's out of the Telvor*. Vorkis was attempting to read her mind again. Somehow when she was told she wasn't an Earth-human, her mind began doing amazing things, and she hoped it would continue.

"My mother and I are from a planet called Verlea," she said. "We came to Earth when I was a baby."

"Verlea?" he mused. "What sector?"

"Sector?" asked Rina. "I have no idea. All I know is Verlea was destroyed by a comet. My mother and I were the only survivors, but she died three years ago."

Rina hoped the story was believable because she still had a hard time believing it herself.

"And the stone?" he asked.

"Six months before my mother died, she was on assignment studying an active volcano. She found the black stone at the base of the mountain and put it in the pendant. That's everything. Now let us go!"

Vorkis nodded then suddenly stepped onto the platform, startling her, and moved himself into the beam.

"The Telvor is programmed for your bio-readings," he said. "Only you are affected."

His hands slipped around her waist and he lifted her to his eye level. She still couldn't move. He pulled her close, nose-to-nose, sniffing her skin and hair.

"I must say I didn't realize how much I missed the scent of a Saleran woman," he said.

"Don't you dare, I'll—"

He kissed her hard. Warm blood filled the inside of her bottom lip as his teeth dug into her skin. He pulled away slowly, leaving a string of bloodied saliva between their lips. Angered and repulsed, she spit it at him.

Vorkis signaled Taru and the platform lowered. After wiping away the red spit, he backhanded her face. The brunt force sent her sliding across the floor and into the rock wall. For a moment, she was incoherent, her mind wavering in and out of consciousness. She moaned and rolled onto her right side, facing the lab. Taru's frightened voice jostled her awake.

"My lord! The Oridians are rampant throughout the complex!"

Angry roars and laser fire sounded outside the lab.

"How could that be?" Vorkis demanded, glancing down at his Neth Blocker. The red light was off. "What the—" He tapped the unit.

"Your NBs are dead," said someone out of sight.

Vorkis quickly spun around. Rina smiled. Kalin was just inside the entrance, his Barra pointed at Vorkis. Seven Oridians entered the room from behind him. Gathering her senses, Rina checked the NB on her shirt; it was on.

"They can't see me," said Kalin, "but they can see you."

A large female stood on her haunches and whooped. The Oridians began hobbling towards Vorkis, their bodies moist with hunger. Vorkis swiftly pulled Marante off the floor and pinned him in a headlock, clutching his forehead with his other hand. The creatures halted their movement, looking at each other as if confused.

Vorkis just went invisible because of Marante's NB, thought Rina.

Taru and the other Zorcons were trembling in a corner when the animals growled and began racing towards them. The Zorcons ran out of the lab screaming with the Oridians in pursuit.

"I can snap his neck," said Vorkis. "Back off, Kalin. I'm leaving."

Rina jumped to her feet and charged, barreling her body into Vorkis. He tumbled to the floor with Marante. Kalin fired and hit Vorkis in the chest. His body bashed into the rock wall where it bounced off and hit the floor with a thud.

"Did you kill him?" asked Rina, staring and wondering if it was over.

"No," said Kalin, pulling Marante away. "Not yet."

He knelt on one knee and gently tapped his friend's cheek.

"It is about time," said Marante.

"You need to stop the dredging," Kalin told his friend. "The planet has one hour left. Take, Rina, she'll help you. I've got Vorkis."

"I will not allow your death," said Marante as Kalin helped him to his feet.

"Please, Marante," said Rina, tears forming in her eyes. "I need you to save Earth."

"Let us go, my lady," he said. He turned to Kalin. "Do not die."

"Down the hall and to the left," said Kalin. "Now go!"

Marante and Rina rushed out of the lab.

***

Kalin

In a dark corner of the cavern, Kalin saw the moving shadow of something large.

CHAPTER 24

Bauman, Justin

"How much time?" asked Bauman.

Rick answered, "Fifty-four minutes, twelve seconds, sir."

Right on schedule, thought Bauman, who hung up the phone.

They were flying at thirty-eight thousand feet. He gazed around his private stateroom. The DD-10 jet was the most luxurious on the market, however, in order to make his kind of flying machine, its guts had to be literally torn out and thrown away. Hans Steinmann had made everything exactly to his specifications. Every window and inner wall was bulletproof, inside and out; even the controls in the cockpit were designed to withstand close-range bullets. The jet incorporated satellite observation and control, stealth capabilities, and a Global Positioning System that could pinpoint an ant from space. It was entirely self-reliant, not requiring ground control nor a runway. This was his secondary base away from the Blythen Temple and the perfect place to watch the world die.

Bauman ran his fingers along the edge of the high-gloss cherry-colored desk, feeling the thick coating of polyurethane. The knotty-pine wood was inlaid with numerous wood knots of assorted shapes and sizes, and only he knew which one activated his hidden Command Center. He tapped the knot directly beside the red phone, his connection to the soon-to-be ex-president. In front of him on the desk, a rectangular door slid open and a small black control panel rose up, displaying three rows of nameless colored buttons and four vertical slide controls. Hans Steinmann was the only other person who knew how to work the system and he'd been eliminated.

He pressed the blue button in the middle of the top row and the mirrored wall in front of the desk slid open. Six LED displays with quadruple screens revealed the inside of the jet. Beyond the lounge with its ten white swivel seats set in front of oversized portholes, the

OPC (Operations Center) was where eight of his homemade sons were manning the four terminals on each side of the walkway. The cockpit lay beyond this and the two pilots were busily maintaining the flight. A red star flashed in the upper righthand corner over Joe's image.

There's one more thing I need to take care of.

Word had spread there was a spy within the New Continuum. For an infiltrator to be effective they had to be close, upper level, someone who could be in a position to stop them, and only one person questioned his efforts. Joe. Rick had traced two of Joe's hidden emails to an unknown accomplice named "Big Bear", and both mentioned he'd soon clip the eagle. When they deciphered the message, it was concluded the eagle was Bauman. He focused on Joe.

It's time.

He stood up, straightened his maroon jacket, and walked out of the room. The thick gray carpet in the lounge stopped at the OPC where black rubber padded the floor. He took his place behind Joe.

"Did Justin's boat detonate?"

"Yes," Joe answered. "It's gone. I still think killing the doctor was not necessary. Brainwashing would have been more useful."

He knows!

Bauman immediately gripped Joe's head with both hands and spun his neck until it snapped. The soldier's limp body slid off the chair and to the floor. Bauman felt the stares.

"Bag the traitor and throw him below."

Two crewmen quickly rose out of their seats. "Aye, sir!"

As they dragged Joe away, Bauman stood behind Rick. The young man began sweating.

Excellent.

***

Justin

Indialantic, Florida

Just beyond the beach where Justin needed to land, the five-story

OSRI building stood in stark contrast against the gray skyline. The water had receded and although the beach had been cleaned, the town was still in shambles. Construction equipment was in full force; *they started to rebuild.* He sighed; grateful the small town would be beautiful again. Only a few figures dotted the white beach, folks most likely waiting for the debris to be removed so they could move on with their lives.

The town of Indialantic had only six policemen and that was all they needed because the crime rate was low. Hopefully, the officers would be far enough away to give him enough time to reach OSRI. He held the shifter in place as the vessel zoomed forward. A gentleman in a black bathing suit was standing on the beach, waving his arms and yelling. Justin couldn't understand his words. He waved for him to move, but the man stood there jumping and shouting, then dove out of the way as the ship rammed onto the sandy beach. Justin nearly flew over the console again.

"Are you nuts?" said the man, running towards him. "You could have killed yourself."

At least six sunbathers were approaching. There was no time to answer. Justin jumped out of the craft and ran towards the street. He could hear the people talking about the blood on his shirt. It didn't matter; thousands would die if he couldn't contact the President. A woman screamed.

They found the bodies.

The lights in the OSRI building were out. Bauman probably sent everyone home. He dashed into the empty parking lot as the police sirens wailed. The main doors were locked. He pulled out his keys and fiddled through the collection, his hands were badly shaking and he nearly dropped them. After finding the key he flung the door open and raced to the receptionist's desk. The phone was dead. Standard operations said if no one was going to be in the building for a lengthy time, all phones were shut off at the telephone company. His only chance was the computers. If he could restart the generators, the wifi would work and he could text message his friend, Admiral Payton.

Justin bolted down the hallway and into the room marked "Danger: High Voltage." He was exhausted and grateful most Florida homes and businesses did not have basements. The two generators were sitting side by side in a room with special venting. Starting them would be easy. Slowing down the police would be much harder.

His shoulder was still oozing blood. The screeching of tires told him the police were in the parking lot. He flipped several switches and pushed up the main power lever. The generators clicked several times then hummed. The lights came on, and the front doors slammed open. The police had entered the building.

He ran out of the room and struggled up the stairs to the third floor. Each step brought more light-headedness. If he could reach the MCC he could isolate himself in there with the security doors. It would hold him long enough to contact his friend, Admiral Payton, who was at the Peace Conference. Justin rounded another corner and was about to pass the first lab door when he stopped abruptly. Three policemen were inside the lab armed with rifles. They were searching for him.

Half the fleet came, he thought to himself, *with the other half probably on their way. And why not? A crazy man drives his boat onto the beach and ten dead bodies are discovered. The worst murder in this town's history. Great, Justin, planned real well.*

The lab had two entrances. The hallway to the MCC was just beyond the second door around the corner. He checked his wristwatch; there was less than one hour to evacuate the Peace Conference and five states. Knowing Payton's emergency plan, the Peace Conference could be emptied in fifteen minutes but the people living on the New Madrid fault would be in dire jeopardy, and he hoped the Admiral could get the message out quickly.

Going on all fours would keep him out of sight from the police, but his shoulder was the problem. He got to his knees and nearly fell when he put pressure on his left arm.

This is no time to be a wimp, he thought. *Suck it up.*

The floor was carpeted, *thank goodness*, and he softly inched his way past the first open door without incident. He saw them checking under tables, inside closets, and even looking outside the windows to see if he'd crawled out onto the ledge. Sweat was streaming down his face and he wondered if it was from sheer terror or from the excruciating pain in his shoulder. At the second door, an officer was standing in the entrance with his back to the hallway.

Oh, crap, he thought. *If they catch me now, it's over.*

He was so close he could smell the officer's cologne. Slowly he started crossing the doorway. His injured arm was trembling and sweat drops were hitting the floor. There was a loud cough above him. Justin froze and held his breath. The policeman leaned back and looked down the hallway in the opposite direction of Justin, then casually returned his attention to the lab. Justin swiftly crawled around the corner and stood up, resting against the beige wall, trying to regain his strength. His watch read twenty-five minutes.

He finally reached the MCC. The red button to lock the doors was on the lower level at the main terminal, Rina's computer. He scurried down the carpeted steps and bashed the button. The security doors slammed shut with a boom. The cops now knew where he was. It was only a matter of time before they either blew up the entry or shut off the generators. Right now, they were pounding on the doors. Time was running out. He sat at the computer and began typing. Although the sweat was stinging his eyes, his fingers flew across the keyboard. When he stopped, he'd made so many typing errors he couldn't read his own words.

Slow down, Justin, you can do this.

He deleted the message and started another one. Loud gunshots dented the metal doors and he nearly jumped out of his skin. He faced the computer.

This will have to do. He hit "Enter." *Waiting is the worst.*

Twenty minutes remained. He resent the message just in case the first one didn't go through. The ring Mary had given him was sitting beside the keyboard and he quickly slipped it on. The voice of an officer using a bullhorn told him to give up; he was surrounded. Justin flicked on the hallway cameras. On the middle wall screen, he could see two policemen heading downstairs to the generators. He stood up in a panic. He had to stop them, but how? Just then, the computer beeped.

The words appeared, "If you're Dr. Young, prove it."

Justin plopped in his seat and typed. "I sent you a gift of pickles and ice cream. Payton, hurry, the cops are ready to break in so answer me quick." He sent it out.

The police were almost to the generators. A message beep sounded.

"I'm not with those idiots at the Peace Conference, I'm in Maine. The bombs are a go."

Justin sat shocked, running the many amiable conversations through his mind, wondering how he'd missed this. His friend of twenty years was working with Bauman the whole time. He typed back, "Why?"

"Less problems and the pay is better. Sorry, Justin. Goodbye."

Suddenly the lights and power went off. The security doors slid open and four officers rushed in, ready to shoot. Justin swiveled around and raised his hands in the air, trembling to the anger inside him, knowing he'd failed.

CHAPTER 25
Kalin, Rina

Kalin stood at a podium meticulously running his fingers through the holo as he made the final adjustments to the REM. He watched the left rock wall form jagged stakes. Vorkis was unconscious on the floor, and he was surprised he was still breathing. The kicks and punches had been exhilarating and his heart leapt at what was to come.

He dragged Vorkis by the arm and flung him against the wall, watching a bloodied stake break through his right shoulder. Killing him now was not his intent, mutilating torture was first. Kalin straightened the limp body and rammed the remaining stakes through his arms and legs, impaling Vorkis on the wall.

He stepped back and leaned against a podium across from him, gazing at the red blood soaking Vorkis' gray tunic and black pants. It had been a long time since he'd felt this good. Vorkis blinked his eyes open. Kalin lifted the Norin Blade from his boot.

"It's me and you," he said, twirling the glowing blade in his hand. "What do you think I should do to the man who killed my family and people?"

"I would let him go and fight him to the death," said Vorkis in a weak voice.

Kalin nodded. "I could do that. Or I could slice him up and laugh while he bleeds to death."

Holding up the fully erect Blade, Kalin lunged at Vorkis' face and pointed the tip of the blade at his left eye. Vorkis groaned as the searing heat began singeing his eyelashes.

"How about I cut out your heart and let you watch it stop pumping?" Kalin smiled. "Now that's a great idea."

He rammed the Norin Blade into the stone next to Vorkis' neck. The hard rock exploded into fine black dust. Vorkis cringed in pain as the blade sizzled through his skin, cauterizing the veins in his neck.

Kalin stepped back, coughed up a wad of phlegm and spit it in his face.

Vorkis' roared as he squirmed to free himself. "I will kill you!"

Kalin smiled. *More.* When he yanked out the Norin Blade, he noticed Rina's Pril pendant around Vorkis' neck. He ripped it off and held it up.

"This belongs to a friend of mine," he said, before stuffing it in his pocket.

Deep growls came from behind. Vorkis' eyes opened wide. Three Oridians were standing twenty feet from them. Kalin stepped to the side, allowing the Oridians a full view of Vorkis. The creatures hobbled toward him, hissing and snarling, their mouths drooling, their bodies moist.

Vorkis shouted nervously, "What do you want? I can't undo what's been done."

"I want your life," said Kalin, backing to the door. "Nothing else."

"We can rule this galaxy together. You are my cousin, my family. Don't do this."

"You were never a part of us!" yelled Kalin. "You slaughtered your own people like animals." The Oridians were almost to Vorkis. "Now you're going to die like one and I'm going to watch."

A loud rumble came from all directions and the cavern shook. Rocks and debris tumbled from the ceiling. Two giant pillars of black stone came crashing up through the floor near the wall, throwing tables in the air. Kalin and the Oridians fell onto the roiling floor. Sparks and mini-explosions blasted through each wall terminal. Kalin latched onto a leg of the secured Bio-Table just as the flat glass burst into flying shards. He huddled on the floor and curled his body, wrapping his arms around his head.

Suddenly, it stopped. Everything was still. Ten of the twelve lab stations were ablaze. The two spires of black stone were tilted against the rock wall. Vorkis was sitting on the floor, pulling a spike from his thigh. Kalin jumped to his feet, ready to fight, when the three Oridians leapt onto Vorkis. His screams echoed throughout the complex. Another violent quake shook the ground, forcing the ceiling to crumble and fall. Kalin leapt away and rolled into the hallway just as huge stones and rocks tumbled down, blocking the entrance to the cavern. The ground settled to a mild continual tremor.

There isn't much time, he thought, gazing about. *I hope Rina and Marante work this out or it's over.*

He heard the muffled cries of a man being torn apart. A wide smile came to his face. Justice was being served.

***

Rina

As Rina and Marante hurried down the tunnel, wails of death sent chills up Rina's spine. Marante stumbled and Rina grabbed him before he hit the ground. He was surprisingly light in weight. She stood him up and leaned him against the wall.

"You stay here," she said. "I'll stop the dredging."

"You are not familiar with the sys—"

The ground shook hard, the rumble deafening. The two staggered out of the way of the stones and boulders falling from above. From down the tunnel, a river of lava broke through the ceiling.

"We must hurry!" said Marante.

Rina wrapped Marante's arm around her shoulder. "Let's go!"

They reached the unguarded doors of the Command Center when the quaking stopped.

"This place is going to go at any moment," she said, looking about.

"It seems the Oridians had a glorious day," said Marante.

Several Barras, puddles of white blood, and severed Zorcon body parts littered the gray Hitan floor. The sight of the shredded carnage made her sick. She counted fourteen small mounds of brown dirt. Numerous blast holes pitted the black rock. A dead Oridian lay beside the entrance.

Hundreds of NBs embedded the walls and ceiling, all with their red lights off. Around the oval cavern, dark blue consoles containing colorful orbs took up the space. In the center of the room was a flat round table sitting on a platform with orbs along its edge.

Marante went to the center table. He waved his hand over a blue orb and a huge hologram rose up from the middle of the table, displaying the inside of the trench and the underground complex. The view was three-dimensional and in full color. He waved his hand over another orb and rows of data appeared. With one hand, six of his fingers began tapping specific equations within the holo, changing their values. The last set of numbers blinked white then vanished.

"The instability of the planet's electromagnetic field is interfering with holo function," he said. "However, I have shut down the Xeon Diffusers. I have also contacted the *Quasar* and several teams are on their way down with terra emulation modules called Deltrons. Unfortunately, the planet will implode in less than forty minutes. That may not be enough time to assemble the Deltrons. I am going to authorize a teleport of you to the *Quasar*."

"No," Rina said firmly. "I'm not leaving until the planet is safe."

"My lady," said Marante, turning to her, "you must go. I cannot allow your sacrifice—"

She interrupted. "I know how much you care but this is my life and my world, and I will not leave until I know it's safe."

Marante's eyes scrunched into black slits. "You are as stubborn as Kalin," he said, then faced the holo again.

A deafening roar resonated; the chamber shook violently. She grabbed Marante and pulled him beneath the table. Massive boulders fell from above, pounding the floor and rolling. Explosions and black smoke filled the cavern. In front and to their right, part of the wall gave way, crumbling to the floor. The quaking slowed to a steady tremble.

Marante peeked out. "It is safe, come."

Rina stared in awe, watching Marante lift himself out from the crunched position. His legs bent not only at the knee but also at mid-thigh and mid-calf. He had four joints on each leg, not including his hips.

Why didn't I notice this before? thought Rina.

His hand reached down for her. "Come, my lady."

She took his hand and he lifted her. "I also have two more joints in each arm," he said, spreading his arms out sideways and bending them inward, forming a perfect square.

"You are the coolest dude," she said, wondering what else an x-ray would reveal.

His eyes scanned the room. "I will check on the Deltrons' progress. If the implosion occurs before the units are assembled, we will also lose the lives of our people who are assembling them."

When Rina turned around, she gasped. The whole back half of the cavern had caved in. Only the table remained in the center, and the entrance behind her was still open. The constant quiver beneath her feet told her the implosion was sooner than thirty minutes away.

"There are Earth-humans in a jail down here that need saving," she said.

"Yes, I see," said Marante, studying the holo. "Unfortunately, we lack the time to save them all. The implosion has moved up; only fifteen minutes remain. Some will have to be expended. I will order your teleport."

"No way," said Rina. "They go now."

"Why are you being so stubborn?" asked Marante, his voice up an octave. "With this barely functioning equipment, only three can teleport at a time. Not all will survive. I cannot and will not allow your death."

"Marante," she said, caringly, "these people didn't ask for this. They've suffered enough just being down here and watching their friends die. I could never live with myself if I allowed their sacrifice. They get teleported. Do it now."

"Do not order me," he said. "You are not my captain."

She was about to retort when five Oridians entered the Command Center. The hunched beasts grunted, gazing about.

"We've got company," said Rina, watching the animals sniff the air.

Marante glanced at the Oridians. "They cannot see us. I must concentrate." He returned to the holo.

"They're looking right at us," said Rina, not taking her eyes off the creatures. "I think we need to worry."

The monsters were nearing. She could smell their dung-like odor.

"It may seem they are alert to our presence but they are not," said Marante, keeping his attention on the holo. "Pay no mind to them."

"You said the electromagnetic field of the planet was interfering with the holo. Could it be interfering with our NBs?"

Marante quickly waved his hand through the holo. "Oh, dear," he said, touching his bloody head. "The NBs are not blocking the scent of blood. We have a problem."

"Yeah," said Rina. "Five of them. I have a bleeding cut on my lip."

"I must separate from you," said Marante. "More of my blood is exposed."

He slipped off his black tunic and wrapped it around his head.

"I'll handle this, " she said, "you stop the implosion or we're all dead."

Marante nodded and reseated. Lying on the floor fifteen feet away was a Barra. She laid on her stomach and started belly crawling towards the gun. The beasts were nearing Marante when they stopped and smelled the air again.

Their eyes focused on the Barra lying just out of her reach. She pulled up the hem of her red T-shirt and pressed it to the slit on her lip. The metal floor against the skin of her stomach was cold and she stifled a loud shiver. The ape-like animals were unknowingly closing in, so she scrunched up her body into a ball.

Work fast, Marante, she thought, hoping he was reading her mind.

The largest of the Oridians stood two inches from her face and she almost barfed. The stench of feces was overpowering. Four black toes on each foot hosted claw-like nails six to eight inches long, and each was tapping the floor. Thick callous soles padded the monster's feet. Their gray leathery skin was composed of thousands of minute scales.

They're reptiles, she thought. *I wish I had time to study this thing.*

Shiro was right. She was a scientist no matter what the danger. The animal before her made several whooping sounds, startling her. She swore her heart stopped pumping. The other beasts gathered behind the big one.

The Oridian stepped back and lowered its head to the floor, moving its elongated jaw closer. The creature's eyes seemed to be riveted on hers. It snarled with quivering lips above long sharp terrifying teeth. The monster sniffed the ground near her face, then raised its head and was ready to lower it down on hers when a shrill came from outside the cavern. The beast swiftly cocked its head towards the entrance. Blobs of warm thick saliva dripped on her face and hair, sliding down her cheek toward her mouth. Vomit rose into her throat.

"Get away from her," said Marante, standing with a Barra. His NB was on the table. The Oridians roared and charged. Marante fired several shots and the animals burst into clouds of yellow dust. He placed the Barra on the table and continued his adjustments of the holo.

Rina got on her hands and knees, spitting. "This is gross," she said, swiping at the sticky saliva. Her hands slipped to a rough tremor and she almost banged her face on the floor.

"Nine Earth-humans have been teleported," said Marante, "but you must be next, my lady. Implosion will occur in two minutes; you must teleport now or die."

"Show me how to work the holo and you go," she said, standing up. "I'll stay and make sure they all get teleported."

"I cannot believe this!" he said angrily. "You are acting like Kalin with no sensibility. I will not leave you here to die." He focused on the holo. "Three more have teleported. One minute. Unless a miracle happens, we are not making it out alive."

"Marante," she said softly, "I don't want you to die with me. You're brilliant and this universe will suffer without you. Please, I'm begging, teleport yourself now."

"I can be stubborn too," he said, "and it will be a cold day under the suns when I will leave a lady to die. No, I will stay and do not think you can change my mind. As Earth-humans say, give it up."

"You are so pig-headed!" she said. *I need another angle.* "Do you think we'll feel any pain? I wonder if your life flashes across your mind before you die?"

Marante was shaking his head as if disgusted. "No, we will not feel any pain, and yes, your life flashes across your mind. Must you be so pessimistic? You really have no fear of death, do you?"

"I'm not afraid of dying. My only regret is not being able to say goodbye to my father."

"I see," said Marante. "My only regret is that you are here with me. I wish you were safe somewhere else."

The ground went into violent convulsions. Marante tumbled off the seat and rolled beneath the table. Rina stumbled to the floor and Marante pulled her to him.

"The end has begun, my lady!" he shouted over the loud roar.

Rina felt tears flooding her eyes; she missed her father already. Marante wrapped both his long arms around her and squeezed. Visions of pale sandy beaches with sparkling white-leaved palm trees and serene blue oceans filled her mind. Dominating the teal opaque sky, three giant silver-gray planets with multi-colored rings rotated on their axes; one was as large as Jupiter.

What is this place? she asked herself.

It is my home world, Chaslea, answered Marante in her mind. *I thought you would like to see it.*

A giant boulder slammed on the ground in front of them and they screamed, jerking back. Another crashed on top of it, cracking the two in half. From the sidewall, a fissure the size of a car began spiking towards them.

Good-bye, my lady, said Marante, *I am sorry I could not protect you.*

He hugged her again, and she felt his large hand gently press her head against his chest.

CHAPTER 26
Rina, Kalin

The quaking ceased. The fissure stopped abruptly. Not even a slight tremor was felt. All was quiet. Rina slowly crawled out from beneath the table. Her muscles hurt from the stress when she noticed the holo was still on. Marante got to his feet and went to the table.

"Six of the twelve Deltrons have been completed, and have already replicated thirty percent of the missing core. Apparently, Tolba, the Chaslean left in charge of the *Quasar*, had ordered them preassembled long before I contacted him. All of the Earth-human prisoners are aboard the *Quasar*. Wait…something else is happening. There is an Earth-human submersible inside the crevasse that leads to the planet's REM tunnel and—oh dear." He stopped talking for a moment then continued. "It seems a countdown with less than two minutes remaining has been activated in the vessel. Its eruption will not only ignite three hundred fifty nuclear weapons inside the REM crevasse, but also will ignite one hundred fifty of the same bombs within the mid-section of a large continent. Are they trying to destroy the planet?"

"It's General Bauman!" said Rina, staring at the visual display of an *X-38* in the trench. "He's going to use nuclear weapons as a catalyst to create devastating earthquakes, leaving only a minimal amount of Earth-humans that he can rule. Can you stop the countdown?"

"The magnetic fields of the Deltrons are affecting the holo." Wavering lines distorted the picture. "I may not have enough time."

"Please, Marante," said Rina, putting her hand on his shoulder. The anxiety was making her nauseous. "They're so innocent. Millions are going to die, including my father. Please, try."

"If I alter the attributes incorrectly, it can ignite the vessel. Let me concentrate."

She moved away. *Will Bauman win?* She started pacing back and forth, holding her head in her hands. The seconds seemed like eons and sweat began soaking her red T-shirt.

"Forty seconds," he said.

Her breathing sped up; she knew now what Shiro felt like when he was near hyperventilating.

"Twenty seconds."

"Don't count," she demanded. "It's making me crazy."

"I have good news," he said. "The countdown has been cancelled, the vessel has been shut down, and the Deltrons are working at an amazing pace." He smiled at her. "Your world is saved, my lady."

The thrill of exhilaration rushed through Rina and she leapt into his arms.

"You did it!" she shouted.

She squeezed him tight and he moaned. Bones and joints formed hills along his cream-colored shoulders that led to a narrow neck. His bulging head was enormous and she wondered how his thin neck managed the weight. Down his back, the shape of each vertebra protruded from under his skin. It was creeping her out.

"Yes, yes," said Marante, trying to loosen her grip.

She was more than happy to let him go.

"I'm sorry," she said, noting his black nose which meant he was in pain. "I didn't mean to hurt you. I got excited."

"I understand," said Marante. "I know you would never intentionally hurt me. And no, my telepathy is not always active, I have full control of it."

She pointed her finger at him perturbed. "You need to stop reading my mind."

He smiled wide. "I will stop when you learn how to. Telepathy is something common amongst the human species. I am sure you can do it if you try."

"Maybe I can," she said grinning, "and when I do, I'm not telling you. I'm just going to read your mind until I find something to blackmail you with."

"Perhaps," he chuckled, "but alas, I am not the one who likes to sleep naked on the beach."

Rina gasped. "I can't believe it! Not even Shiro knows that. I only did it once and I wasn't totally naked, and no one was around. This is so unfair."

"Your secret is safe with me," said Marante, "unless you play dirty, then all promises are off."

Rina let off a loud laugh, enjoying his good sport. She hugged him again. "You are so great."

This time he wrapped his arms around her tight. Marante was caring and respectful, more so than men on Earth. She was tempted to kiss him on the mouth but stopped. *That might be a bit much*, so she gently kissed his cheek. His nose instantly turned a bright pink and she stepped back.

"I'm sorry if I offended you," she said, staring at his golf ball-size nose.

"Chaslean-humans are very…passionate in different areas of our bodies," he said, smiling. "You will learn this with time."

"Yes, I will," she smiled, needing to change the subject. "Now tell me, what exactly are Deltrons?"

"They are machines that emit solid energy crystals, which after time alter themselves to become the rock surrounding them, an invaluable Saleran creation. We have used them in the cores of larger worlds with great success."

"Oh good," she said, feeling stupid. This new technology was way beyond her.

Someone cleared his throat behind them.

"Kalin!" said Rina, ecstatic to see him alive. She dashed to him and they hugged.

"Did you fight Vorkis?" she asked, running her fingers through his thick black hair. No bruises, bumps, or any signs of a battle were evident.

"I let the Oridians take care of him," he said. "They do such a nice job. Oh yeah, I found this hiding in the corner of the lab."

Rina couldn't believe her eyes, Shiro was standing at the

entrance. Tears immediately formed.

He grinned with his crooked teeth. "Vorkis killed another earth guy in my place. He said he might need me for later. He knocked me out and left me in the corner of the lab."

A blue-black bruise spotted his left jaw. She squeezed him tight, crying, never wanting to let him go.

"It's nice to be loved," he said, holding her.

She released him and punched his arm. "I can't believe you pushed me out of the car!" She swiped at her tears. "You were supposed to save both of us, not just me. Do you know the agony I've had to endure?"

"Sorry," he said, rubbing his arm, "but I couldn't let you die."

She got up in his face. "Don't you ever, ever do that again! Do you understand me?"

"Is Verlea the name of your home world?" asked Marante, slipping on his black tunic.

"What?" she asked, confused.

Marante had the knack of changing a conversation quickly. Rina stared as Kalin piled a bunch of Sarvin Crystals on Marante's head. The ragged tears in Marante's tunic mended and the cloth filled in all the crevices on his body until no protruding bones were visible.

That's amazing, she thought.

"Is Verlea the name of your planet?" he asked again.

"Maybe," she said, sending evil glares at Shiro, "but I don't know for sure. I'll have to ask my dad when we get up top." She hugged Shiro again. "I'm still upset at what you did, but I'll never forget what you gave up for me, and I'm so glad my best friend is alive. By the way, did you know Bauman sent another sub and Marante shut it down?"

"For real?" he said happily.

"Yep," she said, cuddling his arm.

"Listen," said Shiro to Kalin and Marante, "we can't thank you guys enough for what you've both done."

Rina walked to Kalin and took his hands. They were large and callused. Not those of a prince. Chivalry was once common among men of Earth. *Was Saleran society like that? How many more heroes are there in the universe?*

"Thank you, Kalin, for everything," she said. "I was out of line back there and I'm sorry."

"It's okay," he said, sprinkling Sarvins on her head. "You were almost right. I'm not a loser."

"No, you're not," she agreed.

"But now it's over, so let's talk about you and me, sweetheart."

Oh great, she thought. *I've already hinted how much I hate being called superficial names, yet he still does it.*

His wanting gaze made her uncomfortable. Kalin was handsome and strong but she wasn't ready for a relationship, or whatever he would call a relationship; somehow myriads of women popped into her mind. He wasn't the type for just one. Besides, she'd just found out she wasn't an Earth-human. There was too much to learn and a heap of questions needed answers. He tenderly cupped her face; his hands were warm and caressing.

"Even when you were dirty," he said, "you were beautiful."

He leaned down to kiss her and she reactively grabbed his hands, pulling them off. She smiled and stepped away. He tilted his head and looked at her strangely.

"I just saved your world," he said, "Not even a kiss?"

"You and Marante saved my world and we couldn't have done it without you. I want to thank you both from the bottom of my heart. I will be eternally grateful for what you've done, and I will never forget it."

She refused to be another addition to his list of women. Kalin glared at her. He'd read her mind. Shiro slapped Marante's shoulder.

"You're the man, my man," said Shiro.

"Ouch," said Marante. "I have done nothing."

"Yes, you have," said Kalin. "You put your shirt back on."

"What did you say?" asked Marante.

"You need to keep those nasty bones under your shirt," said

Kalin.

"I will not allow you to insult my race, you—you unappreciative, arrogant, self-absorbed—"

"Yeah, yeah," said Kalin, smirking and waving him off.

Rina chuckled, "You guys are great."

Just then, a holo rose up from the center table. An alien resembling Marante appeared.

"Captain, do you read me?"

Kalin joined Marante and Shiro at the holo. This was her chance to study the dead Oridian near the entrance. She walked to the creature and squatted to examine it. The animal's eyes and maw were wide open, and it was laying stiff like a dead bird with its head and legs bent back.

"Yes, Tolba," said Kalin. "What's the progress of the Deltrons?"

"They are near completion, sir, and we have the Earth-human prisoners aboard. They are in stasis and are being revitalized."

"Good work, Tolba. Get another team down here to extract this equipment. We don't need marauders invading this world for these Saleran creations."

"Aye, sir."

"Kalin," said Rina in a strained voice. She couldn't breathe.

Vorkis had a knife to her throat. Taru was standing next to him with a Barra pointed at them. Rina felt Vorkis' warm blood saturating her clothes. She forced her eyes to the side; several hefty streams of blood were running down his face.

"She's mine," said Vorkis.

The next thing she saw was a flash of light.

***

Kalin

Kalin was momentarily stunned. *What—* "Tolba, what's the destination of that teleport?"

"Vorkis' ship, sir."

"Disable his hyperdrive!" he shouted.

"I cannot comply. His REM has been modified and—sir!" Suddenly, screams and loud booms sounded in the background. "We are under attack! The REM shield has been disabled. Teleporter beams have been activated throughout—"

The communication went dead, leaving only static.

CHAPTER 27
Kalin, Marante

An unnerving cold ran through Kalin. Three thousand people aboard the *Quasar* were in jeopardy and Vorkis had Rina.

"Use my emergency teleport to the *Quasar* and from there beam me aboard Vorkis' ship," said Kalin. "On the *Eloquin*, I can save Rina and stop the attack on the *Quasar*."

Marante was silent. Kalin sensed his reluctance.

"There's no choice in the matter," he said. "Vorkis will use anyone to get me. We have to do this now or Rina and everyone aboard the *Quasar* is dead."

Marante sighed loudly, nodding his head. "You were correct all along, Kalin, and I apologize. Vorkis' insanity must be stopped. I just do not want to lose my best friend."

Marante was finally understanding.

"You won't," answered Kalin, hoping he was right. "Use whatever means necessary to defend the ship," he said, handing his Comlink to Marante, "and don't let Vorkis use his hyperdrive."

"Aye, sir," said Marante, attaching the Comlink to his upper sleeve. He placed his hand on Kalin's shoulder. "Be careful, my friend, and bring her back alive."

Marante tapped the Comlink six times then vanished in a flash of light. Kalin readied himself, holding his Barra, anxious to fire. A battle with Zorcons was imminent. Many times Marante had proven he could keep his cool under severe stress, and this time was no different. Two minutes had passed.

What's happening up there?

***

Marante

"Status," asked Marante, sitting in the captain's chair on the bridge.

The two Chaslean-human crewmen, Hapnu and Advon, were to his right, busily monitoring the activity on Vorkis' ship. Tolba was to his left next to Oxil, another Chaslean-human, and both were working on holos, managing the emergencies throughout the vessel. Each station displayed numerous holos and it took months of study on Salera to learn how to merge and manipulate several holos at once. They were the best.

The bond between Salerans and Chasleans was sealed centuries ago. The evil society of Vassons had tricked both civilizations into believing the other was preparing for war. Kalin and Marante saved each other's lives and people, forming an eternal bond of friendship between both races, something unheard of in the five thousand years of recorded Saleran history. How grateful he was to have a brother such as Kalin.

"The *Eloquin's* shields are absorbing the blasts of our Monto Lasers," said Tolba. "Two hundred Zorcons have boarded. Security walls have been activated in the hallways but the Zorcons are implementing Vion Blasters. The shields will not hold very long." He glanced at Marante. "Sir, this is the first time we have encountered anyone with technology equal to ours."

"With all the diversified species in the universe, I am sure this will not be our last," said Marante. "Our first priority is to get the Captain aboard Vorkis' ship. We must find a way through his shield."

"The new Edia Beam is small enough to penetrate Vorkis' shields," said Tolba, studying a holo, "but it must be exact. I am surprised Vorkis has not altered his shield for this latest Saleran science."

"He was forced to leave Salera is a hurry and may not have been able to steal it," said Marante. "Position the Captain closest to Rina yet guarded for his immediate safety."

"Aye, sir."

Marante tapped an orb on his armrest and a holo swirled up from the floor in front of him. He had to find out why the REM shield had failed. Ilya walked in and stood next to Marante. She was wearing a light blue sequined two-piece skirt and top that barely hid any flesh. From the corner of his eye, he could see her creamy smooth stomach and the shape of her enhanced breasts.

Her sweet perfume masked her unnatural ways. Although the males in her race did not lack Henual Cells, the projected ten-year study to help the females during puberty was cancelled because the women enjoyed their ghastly behavior with animals. Tàtresses made him sick and he hoped she wouldn't touch him.

"Zorcons are all over the place," she said, putting her hand on his shoulder. "I've come prepared." She held up a hand Barra. "Can I be of help?"

"The Trinon Crystals of the REM are almost depleted," said Marante, concentrating on the grid in the holo. "Someone deliberately used a high-energy power source to drain them. They will have to be restored. Tolba, start the emergency reparation. Who was the last person at the system?"

"Don't bother," said Ilya.

Marante felt the cold nozzle of the Barra press into the skin on his head. Immediately, Tolba and the other crewmen sprang out of their seats.

"Stop!" she said, gripping the Barra with both hands. "I'll shoot him! Back off!"

Marante raised his hand and they halted. The holo switched off.

"You two," she said, pointing to Hapnu and Advon, "get over by Tolba."

The men were staring at Marante, waiting for a signal. He dared not allow Vorkis another victory by killing anyone on this vessel; besides, he had to find out the details of Ilya's mission. He nodded his head and the crewmen joined Tolba.

"Why?" he asked.

Waves of visions flashed through Marante's mind; she was allowing him access. His stomach ached with nausea.

"He loves no one but himself," said Marante. "You are just

another pawn."

"He loves me!" said Ilya, her lips squeezed together in contempt. "Everyone I touch loves me! I'm the best he's ever had."

Marante faced her, peering straight into the nozzle of the Barra. He sensed a strong determination in her. It was not passion or recklessness; it was something deeper, something…*no!*

"You gave birth to Vorkis' child?" asked Marante, shocked a Saleran conceived an offspring outside its species.

Ilya smiled proudly. "Yes, and our daughter is just fine."

"How?" asked Marante. "Your kind is not compatible with a Saleran."

"Poor Marante," said Ilya, sliding the nozzle along his cheek. She leaned down close to him, nose-to-nose. "How about a big kiss?" she said, deliberately blowing her putrid breath in his face.

Stupid Kalin. "Do it," he said. "I will enjoy what I can, then toss you aside like the others."

"Your mind games won't work on me," she said, annoyed. "I'm smarter than you, because not only have I been helping Vorkis for months, we also discovered another use for teleporters."

"I see," he said. "The implantation of a pre-altered embryo at the moment of molecular reconstruction."

"You got that right, fat head," she said, smirking. "Our baby has grown at a tremendous rate and is smarter than you. Vylla is loyal to me and her father. She's the heiress to the Saleran throne and I will be the Queen Mother."

"Your child is a mutation," said Marante. "She will not survive long enough to enjoy life. That experiment has been tried on off-worlds and the creatures lived for no more than six months before their bodies began to decompose."

"My baby will live!" she said, nervously pointing the Barra. "Vorkis promised, and he would never fail me."

Marante was silent. Ilya was convinced their plan would work.

"I can't wait to see the color of your blood; I love florescent blue. Now get out of the captain's chair. I don't want the seat dirtied when

I blow your head off."

"No," said Marante.

Tolba, can you hear me? he said in his mind.

Yes, sir, answered Tolba.

Lurch the ship.

Ilya stepped away and held the Barra straight out with both hands. "Move it!" she said.

The *Quasar* jerked hard and Ilya stumbled. A laser shot whizzed past Marante's head and he vaulted from his seat. He wrestled the Barra from Ilya then twisted her arms behind her back, surprised at her strength. Hapnu and Advon rushed over and held her in place.

Outraged and humiliated, she roared while squirming to free herself, rustling her blonde hair and tearing the seams of her short skirt with wild kicks. White foam drooled from her mouth. Her skin reddened to almost a light purplish color, and her blue eyes were now bloodshot.

Perhaps more than Henual Cells are absorbed, thought Marante.

She truly was acting like an animal. A cantankerous look covered her face. Her desire to kill him had taken over.

"Nothing you do will matter," she said between heavy breaths. "The *Quasar* is ours. You've lost."

"We will never lose to the likes of you," he said. "Tolba, teleport the Captain when ready."

"Aye, sir," said Tolba, grinning. "Teleporting now."

Two Chaslean guards dressed in red uniforms entered the bridge. One guard pointed a Menzor Light at Ilya and she stiffened inside the pink beam encasing her. Hapnu and Advon released her. The other guard removed a Binon Strap from his black belt and touched it to Ilya's wrists. Immediately, the glowing orange band clamped tight.

"I hate you!" she screamed.

"That is very acceptable," said Marante, reseating himself in the captain's chair. The holo rose up again and he began his adjustments. "At least I cannot be easily fooled."

The guard pressed another button on the Menzor and she lifted off the floor. She was ready for transport.

"Put her in Brig A3," said Marante. "She is to have no visitors."

"You won't win!" she shouted, still fighting to free herself as they glided her away. "He'll come for me!"

Her voice faded as the doors to the Lift slid shut.

"Sir," said Tolba, "what chance does the Captain have on Vorkis' ship alone? He is severely outnumbered."

"He has a fifteen percent chance of survival," he said. "That is more than he has faced on other missions, and his hatred will give him strength."

Marante sensed the others, though worried, had accepted his reasoning. He just wished he could do the same.

CHAPTER 28
Bauman

"Who did this?" screamed Bauman.

"I don't know, sir," Rick answered. "All systems on the sub have shut down. Nothing is registering."

Bauman was shaking with anger. He felt the eyes of his men. His face was probably pink and puffed so he slowed his breathing, trying to relax. He was their Commander and Chief and it was essential to stay in complete control.

"We can still win this," he said, straightening the sleeves of his maroon-colored tunic, proud of the new uniforms. "Detonate the New Madrid. At least we'll be rid of the idiots who rule the world."

"Aye, sir," said Rick. He flipped up a gray cover on the ebony panel and pressed the red button.

Nothing happened. He pressed it again. No detonation.

"What's going on here?" said Bauman, leaning over Rick and pushing the button.

"Those nukes have been shut down also," said Rick. "Sir, there's a phone call coming from Admiral Payton Williams."

Bauman picked up the receiver next to the screen. "What the heck is going on, Payton?"

"Justin is still alive," said Payton. "He must have found a way to stop the nukes."

Bauman roared so hard it felt like every vein in his neck had exploded. He started banging the receiver on the table. Rick jumped out of his seat.

How could the plan have failed? It was perfect.

For over nine years, every problem, every angle, every situation conceived had been dealt with, so what happened? All conspirators were eliminated.

"How could he still be alive?" shouted Bauman into the receiver.

"I don't know," said Payton, "but you need to get it under control. We're at the final phase and we don't need you breaking equipment. There's always Javelin One. Remember, all self-destruct codes have been deleted."

The computer beeped and he looked at Rick who was standing beside him and studying the screen. Bauman signaled him to sit back down.

"Sir, Telstar VIII is picking up what I think is laser fire in space," said Rick, typing. "There's some kind of battle going on."

"Laser fire?" The satellite picture showed short beams of light exploding. "Something's come up," he said to Payton. "I'll call you later." He hung up the phone and leaned over Rick, focusing on the monitor. "Follow a beam and magnify at impact."

The white beam exploded and in the residue was a clear picture of docking bay doors.

"Freeze it," said Bauman.

The two men studied the image.

Bauman chuckled, "Talk about breaks."

"Sir, is that what I think it is?" asked Rick.

"Yes, it is," said Bauman. "We can use this to our advantage. Get me Frank Bollen on the horn."

Rick swiveled in his seat. "Sir, I would never contradict you in any way, but these are real creatures from another world. Shouldn't we investigate? They may come after us."

"Nonsense," answered Bauman, glancing down at Rick's buzzed blonde hair, which looked like short fine bristles. "The existence of alien life has been known for over two centuries. Look at them." He pointed to the frozen scene. "They're in a battle. They're not interested in us. Get Bollen now."

"Yes, General, sir!" said Rick, turning around.

"I'll take the call in my office," said Bauman.

"Yes, sir!"

Bauman walked to the rear of the jet and into his private stateroom, shutting the door. He sat at his computer and began typing

~ 258 ~

an article for the papers. It included the photos of the laser blasts in space and the docking bay doors.

Everyone's attention will be on this, including the military.

If his original plan was discovered, he could say Payton and he had unraveled a secret plot by aliens whose intentions was to terminate most of the Earth's civilization and enslave the rest. The upper administration would have to buy it; the proof was there. This would clear them of any charges of treason.

They would also have the story of Justin Young, an unstable man whose missing daughter's diary exposed his irrational psychotic episodes. Of course, a fake diary would have to be planted in Justin's house and he would have to be blamed for the deaths at OSRI, including the untimely disappearance of Rina and Shiro, whose bodies were never found.

Then there would be the truth from the Secretary of Defense, General Theodore Bauman and Admiral Payton Williams, both devoted high-ranking officers who had proven their loyalty for a total of over eighty years, receiving medals and honors, many directly from several presidents of the United States.

Yes, it's starting to feel better all the time.

To disgrace Justin in front of the whole world would be a victory. To kill Justin himself and make it look like a suicide would be even better. A warm sensation soothed his body when he thought of his hands crimped around Justin's neck. Of course, this all would be initiated if Javelin One failed which it wouldn't. Not even the President could stop Javelin One. A wide grin crossed his face. His phone rang.

A deep computer-generated voice said, "Bollen."

"We have a problem," said Bauman.

Frank Bollen, whoever he really was, could hack into any agency worldwide and get away with it. He was the best of the best. His work was pricey but worth it. Once, on a mission, Bauman accidentally overheard a conversation between an Isis deterrent and Bollen, who was refusing the work offered. He smirked at the thought of Bollen having scruples. The man was a spook, wanted in seventeen countries for treason. He was a master of disguise and illusion, the perfect ghost.

Unfortunately, certain aspects of his agenda had to be revealed to Bollen, who showed no interest at all—he just didn't care. Bollen was the one who'd set up the transfer of funds from Hans Steinmann's accounts to his. Thus, it was decided a long time ago, Bollen would have to be terminated. He knew too much.

"Am I to assume your plan didn't work?" asked Bollen.

"It's just a bump. I'm going to send you an article with a picture I need inserted into the Associated Press files. I want this on the front page of every paper in America. I need the world's attention centered on it."

"It'll cost ten mil," said Bollen. "Transfer it to my account now and you'll have it within the next thirty minutes."

"Done," said Bauman, typing the transfer. "Just get it right."

"Have I ever failed you?"

A dial tone sounded. Bauman sighed in relief. *There's always a way out.* He picked up the phone and hit a key.

"Initiate Javelin One," said Bauman.

"Aye, sir," said Rick.

His obedience is admirable.

Bauman tapped a button and the wall before him slid open. He hooked into Rick's monitor and watched it on screen. The words "NC" for a better world…contrasted brightly against a picture of Earth.

The display changed to an orbiting satellite. It carried twenty-four nuclear missiles.

All I need is four.

CHAPTER 29
Rina

"Welcome aboard, Rina," said Vorkis.

She was on the floor coughing, trying to regain her breath from Vorkis choking her. A Zorcon was pouring Sarvin Crystals on his head.

"This ship was named for my sister, *Eloquin*," said Vorkis, looking down at her. His voice was soothing, almost pacifying. "She was my first victim. It's a reminder of how easily I can overtake people."

Rina was sitting on the floor and using her hand to block out the strong light as she looked up at him.

"Why am I not surprised?" she said sarcastically. "You make it a habit to kill family."

Vorkis laughed aloud, glaring at her with vindictive eyes. She crawled out of the bright light shining down from above and studied her surroundings. They were in a dark round room and everything was the color black, except for a giant white circle on the floor, where Vorkis was standing under the light. She could barely see the five Zorcons in the shadows. A set of sliding doors was off to her right.

This place is special, thought Rina. She stood to her feet. *Some kind of sacred room, a sanctum of sorts.*

Vorkis was motionless, allowing the orange Sarvins to heal him. The Oridians must have seriously injured him for the crystals to take this long. *Is the chemical compound of Sarvins plant-based?* She sighed. Being a scientist in a new environment is hard when you're always fighting for your life.

A strong smell of rotten meat permeated the air and she wondered if the whole ship stank. Another Zorcon stepped out of the blackness and up to the circle. Her nail scratches were still on Taru's face and a black patch covered his left eye. White blood spotted his gray uniform.

Why didn't Vorkis allow Taru to use the Sarvins? Probably because he'd let a girl get the best of him. Good. He'd deliberately tormented her with Shiro's fake death and the thought of how he ate people was sickening. *This guy has got to go.*

"Easy," said Vorkis. "It is the Zorcon way."

His words rustled her nerves. *Am I becoming like Kalin, so bent on revenge I can't see that Zorcons are just another type of animal?* Taru licked his lips at her. *Nope, he needs to die.*

"Aren't you curious about where you are?" asked Vorkis.

He raised his arms sideways and two Zorcons wearing purple uniforms scurried out of the darkness and began undressing him. She hadn't seen those two in the shadows and wondered how many more were hidden. Vorkis cleared his throat and grinned. They were removing his gray pants. Rina quickly spun around, embarrassed.

"Is there a problem, my dear?" asked Vorkis. "Have you never seen a naked man?"

"I have no desire to see you," she said. Celibacy came with a price.

"We can save it for later," said Vorkis. She heard the swish of the doors open and shut. "You can look now," he said.

He was dressed Ninja style. His black shirt and pants were loose. Attached to his ebony sash was a small gray case, a twelve-inch knife, and a long curved sword similar to a samurai. His crooked smile told her he was proud of his appearance.

"What are you supposed to be?" she asked.

He bowed. "I am an Uru Master. I steal the life of my enemy. I hear him beg, then I take his life slowly and with pain. This is the way of Uru. This is my way."

"You're nuts," she said.

He pulled the knife from his belt and walked towards her, swinging it by his side. With each step he took, she moved back farther until she was against the wall, frantically looking for a place to run. There was none. In the darkness, he hovered over her like a giant; his blue eyes glowed white as he put the knife to her face. She didn't move; she couldn't move. This guy was a cold-blooded killer. She was a foot away from the man who was ready to exterminate the whole Earth-human race. Would a kick in the groin level him? She doubted it. With that getup, he'd expect it.

He grabbed the back of her head, crimping a clump of hair. A dim light clicked on above them. She tried to push him away but froze when he started gliding the flat side of the knife along her cheek. The smooth metal was icy cold. Pressing the tip just below her left eye he leaned close to her face, nose to nose. His breath stank and something told her he wanted a scream; he wanted her fear. If he tried to kill her now, she wouldn't go down without causing him some kind of pain.

She stood firm, staring straight into his eyes, refusing to blink. His thin lips slid into a nefarious smile and he let go of her. He reached over her forehead and plucked out a single hair; she refused to give him the pleasure of a flinch. Holding the knife vertically, he ran the hair along the edge of the blade. It split in two.

"When I'm done with you, I will cut you like this strand of hair," he said.

"Not if I can help it," said another voice.

Vorkis swiftly turned around and a laser blast caught him in the shoulder.

"Kalin!" shouted Rina.

Without answering her, he dove onto the deck and rolled, firing several more shots killing the guards. All the lights came on. Taru was cowering near the wall mumbling and pleading for his life. Vorkis seized her from behind and held the knife to her throat.

"If you shoot," said Vorkis, "she dies with me."

"Blow him away!" she said.

The knife dug deeper and she felt the warmth of her own blood trickle down her neck.

"Let her go," said Kalin. "It's me you want. Fight me to the death, Vorkis. Winner takes Rina and Salera."

The blade eased a little.

"An interesting proposition, cousin."

"Isn't this why you teleported to your cheap replica of an Uru Temple?" said Kalin, keeping his aim on Vorkis.

"Your familiarity with Uru is surprising. I suppose your rebellious attitude toward Saleran laws led to this knowledge, which proves you were never a real Saleran. You should be happy I ended such useless lives. You and I could rule this galaxy together. The offer still stands. What say you, cousin?"

Every vein in Kalin's neck bubbled to a deep purple color. Beads of sweat saturated his face and hands, his body was quivering to the hatred inside him. He was doing all he could not to shoot.

"Never," said Kalin through clenched teeth. "Let's get this on."

"So be it. To the death."

He slipped the knife into his sash and shoved Rina away. She fell to the floor; lightheaded, she sat up and pressed her hand over her bleeding cut.

"Don't do this, Kalin," she said, fighting a wave of nausea. "Think of your family."

A gush of blood spurted from between her fingers. Faintness whooshed through her head. The creep had nicked an artery.

"Taru!" shouted Vorkis, "the female."

He removed the flat gray case from his black sash and tossed it to Taru who caught it.

"Yes, Your Highness."

Taru opened the case and sprinkled the crystals on her head. As the cut healed, she watched him attach the small box to his gray belt. Taru pulled her up to standing and put a Barra to her left temple.

"Shoot him, Kalin," said Rina, tilting her head as Taru pushed the weapon harder into her skin. "Shoot him and your problems will be over."

"Maybe," he said, laying down the Barra. "But this would be more satisfying." He took off his black vest.

What is it with guys? thought Rina. *A woman would have shot him.*

The two men stood in the center circle. Vorkis closed his eyes and raised his clenched hands over his head, then lowered them into a praying position in front of his face. Kalin's eyes were riveted on his enemy. Vorkis winked at Rina and threw her a kiss. His hands were so fast she didn't see him grab the twelve-inch knife and fling it at Kalin. It burrowed into his shoulder and he staggered back.

"Now we are even," said Vorkis.

The tip of the knife was jutting out of Kalin's back; it had gone clear through. He gritted his teeth while slowly sliding out the blade. His shoulder was bleeding profusely. He inhaled a deep breath and stashed the knife in his black belt.

"Thanks," he said. "I needed it."

Vorkis frowned in obvious disappointment. He whipped out his silver sword and roared, charging Kalin. The swing of the blade was fast and Kalin leapt away just in time. Sparks burst from the weapon as it hit the metal deck. Kalin rolled to his feet and kicked the sword out of Vorkis' hands. Vorkis lunged at Kalin and they tumbled to the floor wrestling.

Vorkis scratched and ripped with his nails, tearing at Kalin's clothes. He dug his teeth into Kalin several times, gnawing like an animal. Kalin's clothes were shredded in several places and he was bleeding from his nose and lips. Vorkis never let up. He worked fast and hard, bombarding Kalin with his fists, nails, teeth—whatever he could use to maim him. It was the most sadistic fighting she'd ever seen.

Kalin managed to punch Vorkis in the face. He jerked away far enough for Kalin to shove him off with his feet. Not a second later, Vorkis lunged for him again. Kalin swung his leg and got Vorkis in the head, making him stumble away.

I have to do something, thought Rina. *I must have telepathy like everyone else.* She shut her eyes and concentrated. *Marante....*

The snap of Kalin's leg and his scream brought her back to reality. She went to help him but Taru yanked her back. He pressed the gun so hard against the side of her head, she was sure it would crack her skull.

"I have not forgotten the injuries you gave me," said Taru. "I will enjoy killing you."

Blood was pouring from Vorkis' nose. He picked up the sword, walked to Kalin and raised the weapon high in the air.

"Now you will die," he said.

Kalin whipped the knife from his belt and plunged it deep into Vorkis' stomach. His mouth gaped and he hunched forward, dropping the sword. He clamped both hands on the hilt and fell back against the wall.

"You're dead," said Kalin, struggling to stand on his one good leg.

"And you will join me," said Vorkis, pulling the knife from his stomach.

Thick white beams of light exploded from Vorkis' eyes, striking Kalin in the chest. His body went airborne and bashed into the far wall, then bounced on the floor. He lay squirming, his face squeezed in pain. Vorkis slid to the floor, cupping his wound and keeping the beams of light on Kalin. With one hand, Taru opened the gray case on his belt and scooped up a handful of Sarvins. He threw them in the air at Vorkis and they landed scattered on top of him. The orange crystals twinkled near the open cut.

"You see, my dear," said Vorkis, catching his breath, the beams unrelenting, "long ago, Salerans rejected their gift of Xevniors and, with time, it eventually dwindled within the race. Only I realized the value of this magnificent force and rekindled its power. With all the water in his system gone, he will die and I will win."

Kalin was turning paler with every moment. His flesh was literally shriveling. He was dying. Panic had set in.

Rina went into a panic. *I need to do something...anything.* Taru was her best target.

She elbowed him in the stomach and yanked the Barra from his hand. Before he fell, she lifted the Sarvin case from his belt and tossed it to Kalin, who was lying still, facing the opposite wall. Vorkis stopped his Xevniors and leapt to his feet. She fired and hit his newly mended shoulder. His body flipped around and he crumpled to the deck, delirious. Six Zorcons rushed into the room and surrounded Vorkis, pointing their Barras at her. She kept her aim at whatever she could see of Vorkis and moved away from Taru, who was getting to his feet.

"You can't block him entirely," she said aloud, knowing it wouldn't be a good shot.

"You will not win this," said Taru. "You are on His Majesty's vessel. Where do you think you can go?"

She hated his robotic voice, but he was right. There was nowhere to go. He licked his lips again.

That's it, she said to herself. *I'm done.*

She fired at the Zorcon standing in front of Vorkis, then turned and blasted Taru. His head exploded, spraying blood and chunks of grey matter throughout the room. A laser beam cut into Rina's stomach, slamming her against the wall. She lay on the floor, barely able to breathe when she heard Kalin's voice.

"Hold on, Rina! Don't let go!"

His words sounded like faint echoes. Her eyes opened slightly and she saw him on his feet. The pain was unbearable; she wanted to die. An unnatural cold set into her bones. The world was fogging up and Kalin seemed so far away, almost like a dream. She saw heavy white beams shoot out of Kalin's eyes. His Xevniors lifted the guards and threw them across the room. Vorkis sat up, horrified; the beam got him straight in the face.

Go, Kalin.

"I'm coming, Rina," shouted Kalin, keeping the beams on Vorkis as he shuffled sideways to her.

The hole in her stomach was almost the size of her hand and she couldn't move. Her body was numbing; she couldn't feel her hands and feet. Vorkis twitched and convulsed to the life-sucking beams. Six more Zorcons rushed into the room. Kalin's Xevniors sent them crashing into the wall. Vorkis wasn't moving. She watched Kalin snatch up Vorkis' knife and stuff it in his belt as he ran to her.

"I got you," he said, gently lifting her.

Memories of her childhood raced through her mind. Mary was there; Justin was crying. She saw the doors slide open and five more Zorcons dashed in with Barras. A bright light flashed.

Rina could barely open her eyes. Shiro and Marante were standing beside her bed facing Kalin, who was on the other side. Kalin was gently stroking her hair.

"You'll be okay," he said softly. "We're on my ship the *Quasar*. Just lie still and let the doctor take care of you."

She didn't see a doctor but there was an amber light, similar to a scan was running along her body. The pain in her stomach was lessening. The hole was closing up.

"Are the Deltrons active?" asked Kalin, stripping off his shredded white shirt.

"Yes," said Marante, who grasped her hand. *I heard you, my lady,* he said in her mind, *and was able to lock onto your position.*

She squeezed his hand.

"The core of the planet is stabilizing," continued Marante. "What about Vorkis?"

"He's alive," said Kalin, putting on a clean shirt.

"You did not kill him?" Marante handed him a black sheath for the knife.

"It was either him or Rina and I couldn't let her die. Did you deactivate his hyperdrive?"

"Temporarily, yes."

Kalin slipped Vorkis' knife into the sleeve. "I need to go back."

"At the moment, the teleporter is inoperative."

"I have to get Vorkis now before he tries to run."

"I must inform you of our situation, Captain," said Marante. "A saboteur damaged the REM and teleporter, which are now under repair. Over two hundred Zorcons teleported aboard but we managed to create Montroth Fields to encapsulate them. They are all in custody."

"Who was the saboteur?" asked Kalin.

Marante frowned. "It was Ilya, Kalin. Ilya was the traitor."

Kalin froze, staring at him in disbelief. "What?"

Marante nudged his head. Ilya was standing behind him with two Chaslean security guards on either side of her.

"Ilya?" said Kalin.

"You were nothing but a toy, and not a very pleasant one," she said defiantly. "Vorkis loves me. He'll save me. He won't leave me with scum like you."

"I thought we had something special," said Kalin. "I can't believe you did this," shaking his head in disappointment. "Why?"

"You're useless," she said. "I need a man with power and brains. You think way too much of yourself, and on a scale of one to ten, you're below one."

"Can this one count passed ten?" asked Rina, hoping the snide comment would prick her.

"My lady," said Marante, helping Rina to sit up on the edge of the bed.

Kalin turned to her and smiled, holding her face with his warm hands.

"I would be dead if you hadn't thrown me the crystals. Thank you."

"You gave up killing Vorkis to save me," she said. "I know how much that meant to you. Thank you, Kalin."

She wrapped her arms around him, hugging him tight. He kissed her cheek then gently pushed her away and reached in his pants pocket.

"This belongs to you," he said.

He pulled out her necklace and slipped it over her head.

"I thought I'd lost this forever," she said, gazing at the Pril in her hand. "Thank you so much."

"This is so sickening," said Ilya.

Rina peeked over Kalin's shoulder. "Who's the bimbo?"

"This is Ilya," said Kalin, clearing his throat with a smile. "Ilya,

Rina. Ilya's going to be handed over to the Federation for crimes against Salera and Earth. I doubt if she'll live another year. The death sentence will be quick and painless."

"I hate you so much," said Ilya, approaching him. "I can't believe I actually slept with you."

"Yeah," said Kalin, "and I've had a lot better."

Ilya kicked Kalin in the groin and he buckled forward with a grunting sound. The guards immediately restrained her.

"I'd rather die than be with you another day!" shouted Ilya.

Rina jumped off the bed and took a stand between Ilya and Kalin.

"Let her go," she said.

Marante was pouring Sarvins on Kalin who was on his knees, moaning. Kalin waved to the guards and they released Ilya.

The Tàtress stood eight inches taller than Rina with the slender figure of a top model. Her short golden hair neatly circled her doll-like face, but her beauty ended there. She had the heart of a T-Rex.

"So this is what you've lowered yourself to?" said Ilya. "A short, unsophisticated, dumb-looking blackhead?" She leaned down to Rina in a curtsy, placing her hands on her knees and talking with puffy lips as if to a child. "What's the little worm going to do? Hit me?"

"You got that right, slut," said Rina.

She laid a left hook on Ilya's nose, sending her sliding across the floor and bashing into the wall.

"Save your freaking me-attitude for someone who cares," said Rina. "I can whip you anytime, anyplace, whore."

"Do something, Kalin," pleaded Ilya, disheveled and crying. She swiped at her upper lip. "She broke my nose! I'm bleeding!"

The area surrounding her eyes began bruising. Streams of blood flowed from her crooked nose.

"Captain," said Tolba over Kalin's Comlink.

"Yes, what is it?" said Kalin, who was on his feet and grinning wide.

Tolba's voice was barely audible over Ilya's sobs.

"Take Ilya to the brig," said Kalin, chuckling. "Monitor her but don't heal her just yet. Keep her that way for twelve hours. She's to have no contact with anyone. Teleport her meals."

Ilya wailed in agony. The guards dragged her out of the room.

Kalin tapped his Comlink, still smiling. "Repeat, Tolba."

"Vorkis has teleported to the planet's surface. He has a hostage and is threatening to kill the Earth-human scientist if his demands are not met."

Rina gripped Kalin's arm as if her heart had stopped pumping. "Who does he have?" she asked.

"He is in a place called Colorado," said Tolba. "The hostage is an Earth-human named Justin Young."

CHAPTER 30
Rina, Justin

Rina cupped her hands over her face and started bawling. Justin was in the hands of a vicious murderer. Her chest hurt and she was trembling so badly it was hard to speak between the erratic breaths.

"He's my father," she said. "He'll kill him."

Shiro put his arm around her shoulder and squeezed her tight. "Hey, your father's a smart man and I'm sure he's trying to figure out how to escape. Besides, Rina, these people saved our whole planet; they can save your father too. Right, Captain?"

"Absolutely," said Kalin. "Don't worry, Rina, we'll get him. Tolba, what are his demands?"

"He wants the Earth-human female to teleport down. After he acquires the Pril, he will release them. If she is not on the planet within fifteen minutes, he will start dismembering the Earth-human. Sir, the teleporter is not fully functional."

"How do I get down there?" she asked, swiping the tears off her face.

"You're not going down there," said Kalin.

"Have you lost your mind! Did you hear what he said? My father's life is at stake. I have to go."

Marante was at a terminal working a holo. "Teleporting will be risky," he said. He swiveled in his seat. "My lady, the captain is correct. Vorkis will kill you and your father once he has the Pril. It is too dangerous." A beep came from the holo. Marante swung around and tapped another orb. "Vorkis wishes to speak with Rina."

She began to walk to Marante when Kalin grabbed her arm.

"You're not going," he said.

She angrily yanked her arm away. "He's my father. There's no choice."

"I won't authorize a teleport," he said.

Frustrated, she gripped the lapels of his shirt and pulled him down to her face. "I swear on my mother's grave I'll make you pay if anything happens to my dad."

"Speak, Rina," said Marante. "Vorkis can hear you."

Kalin removed her hands and shook his head no. She opened her mouth to speak, but he shushed her by putting two fingers on her lips. She pushed his hand away and said in his mind, *back off!*

"Only I know where the Pril is, Vorkis," she said aloud, glaring at Kalin. "My father knows nothing."

"Come to me, Rina," said Vorkis, "and you will spare his life. If Kalin teleports with you, I will cut your father into small pieces."

"You hurt him and you'll get nothing."

"Agreed," he answered. "I am waiting."

"The transmission has been terminated," said Marante. "Is this concerning the large piece you mentioned before?"

"Yes," she said. "He must have read my mind."

"No," said Shiro. "He read my mind."

Everyone turned to him.

Shiro hung his head low as he spoke. "When I was being interrogated I remembered the larger piece. I never divulged anything but he must have read my mind. I'm sorry, Rina. This is all my fault."

She patted his shoulder. "Vorkis has powerful telepathy, it's not your fault. Knock it off, Kalin."

He was still shaking his head no. An ugly yet satisfying vision appeared in her mind: Kalin bald. Tearing out the hair on his head may humble him.

"I can't let you do this," said Shiro, clutching her upper arms tight. "Let me go. Tell me where the Pril is and I'll give it to him."

Shiro was the best friend anyone could have. He was brave, caring, and willing to die for her again.

"No," she said, gazing at his worried expression. "I almost didn't survive your death. Besides, Vorkis wants me, and I can't take chances with my father's life." She looked at Marante. "How do I get down there?"

Kalin cleared his throat. Marante stared at him, waiting for an answer.

"Kalin," said Rina, "you're frustrating me again. You know I can't let my father die at the hands of that animal, so why are you doing this?"

"Because I can't let you die," said Kalin, "and that's why I'm going with you."

"No way!" she said, raising her hands. "My father's dead if you come."

"Either I go with you or you don't go at all." He pressed a Comlink to the inner part of her left sleeve. "This is how it'll work. You'll teleport first. I'll be three minutes behind you and wearing a modified Neth Blocker that Marante will create and Vorkis can't detect. I'll teleport the same way we breached his REM in the core. He'll never know I came."

"Wait," said Shiro, "why can't you just teleport Justin out of there?"

"Because Vorkis is sure to detect its energy signature and possibly kill Justin before we can teleport him," said Marante, studying the holo. "Besides, the last teleport of Kalin and Rina nearly crashed the system, which right now, is working at minimum capacity. We can only teleport one at a time."

"Kalin," said Rina sternly, "you're risking my father's life and I can't have it. I go alone."

"Hear me out," said Kalin. "He knows I'm going to come; he's not stupid. He wants me dead and I'm sure there's a trap waiting. I've dealt with men like this before; it's just another type of game."

She sensed his confidence but was still leery about his plan. "Are you certain he won't detect you?"

"Positive. Vorkis doesn't have the latest Saleran technology, but I do. Here, take this."

He handed her Vorkis' knife in the sheath. Rina slid the weapon out of its holder. An eerie feeling of death crept over her.

"He almost slit my throat with this."

"Yeah," said Kalin, "and you may have to do the same to him."

A shiver ran through her. "I'm not a killer. I can hit people, but to take a life is different."

"You blew away Taru," Kalin reminded her. "Pretend it's him." He turned to Marante. "Put a tracker on his ship."

"Aye, Captain."

"Taru was different, Kalin," she said, concerned. "He tortured people before he ate them alive. He needed to die. I don't know if I can do this."

"Even if you can't kill him, it's going to be your only protection." He gently touched her cheek. "Are you ready for this?"

"I guess," she stared at the blade. *Could I kill Vorkis and live with that forever?* The planet and all life had been almost obliterated. Earth-humans were being fed to Zorcons. And for two agonizing hours, she thought Shiro was dead. Suddenly, the knife felt good.

"Where are they, Marante?" asked Kalin.

"They are on a mountain."

"It's my house in Colorado," she said. She stuffed the sheath into her brown belt.

"My lady," said Marante, "you must block Vorkis' telepathy or he will know Kalin is with you. I will instill this method in your mind on how to do this."

"Thanks, Marante. It'll be very helpful. Now, let's do this."

"Over here," said Kalin, pointing to a blue circular light on the white floor. "Step onto it, gorgeous."

"Was this always here?" she asked, surprised she hadn't seen it before. The ocean-blue color was beautiful.

"No," said Marante. "We can place teleporter pads anywhere on the ship or planet. Oh," he added, "and they come in different colors."

"Okay," she said, grinning at Shiro, who was smiling back; he too was enjoying the new science. As she passed Kalin, she said, "I hate those ridiculous girly nouns, so can it."

"Make me," he said with a smirk. "And just to let you know, doll, if you were another woman, you wouldn't be standing on that teleporter pad."

"This had better work, Kalin," she said, glaring at him as she stood in the center of the blue pad. "And I mean it with the names."

Kalin winked and threw her a kiss. She rolled her eyes.

"The Trinons are fluctuating," said Marante. "The teleport will not be to the precise location, but I will get you close."

There was a flash of light and she was standing in a wooded hillside, just outside the town of Ouray in the Rocky Mountains.

***

Justin

Each step creaked as they walked upstairs to the attic. The last thing he recalled was being in the police car when a bright light flashed and he was in his Colorado home, standing in his living room and facing this angry man who was threatening his life. Although the man looked pale and weak, Justin knew he meant every word he said. The laser blast that set the couch on fire had done the trick.

"Walk faster," the man said.

"You could at least tell me your name. I'd like to know who's going to kill me."

"Vorkis," he answered. "Now move it!"

He poked the gun in his back.

"What did you say the rock was called?"

"Pril."

The solid redwood door at the top of the stairs hadn't been opened in three years. After Mary died, Shiro had brought her clothes and all her packed boxes to the attic and shut the door. Neither he, nor Rina and Shiro had the strength to go up there.

Justin turned the handle and shoved the door open; the hinges squeaked from age. On the opposite ends of the long room, dusty rays of sunlight beaconed through the windows. Racks of clothes and unmarked boxes lined the walls. The smell of mothballs reminded Justin that Mary had been a packrat; she never threw anything out.

Vorkis pushed him into the room and he fell to the floor. When he flipped around, he was peering into the barrel of the strange gun.

"Find it or die."

CHAPTER 31
Kalin

"Where are we?" asked Kalin, kneeling beside Rina who was hunkered down and peeking between some green leafy bushes.

"We're seven miles from my house," she said. "I couldn't leave because I had to wait for you. For all I know, my dad could be dead already."

"I doubt it," said Kalin. "Vorkis needs him alive for you to tell him where the Pril is. Why did you wait for me? You could have gone alone."

"Because I need you to kill Vorkis."

She finally understands, thought Kalin.

"Are you sure he didn't detect your presence?" she asked.

"Positive. No one in the galaxy can match Marante when it comes to REMs and teleporters. Where's your house?"

Rina pointed to the left. "Near the top of that mountain over there."

Patches of rock and tall trees littered the mountainside.

"We need a truck," said Rina.

"A what?" He couldn't see her house.

"Let's go," she said, pulling his arm. "We'll find one in town. Follow me."

Their trek down the hillside was a battle against dense bushes, and Rina's deliberate quick release of the low-hanging branches.

She's still trying to get me back. He dared not bring it up; he deserved every bit of torture from the way he'd treated her.

"What is this place?" asked Kalin, stopping another limb from whacking his face.

"It's the town of Ouray," said Rina. "We're going to enter it through the alley between those two buildings. But we have to be careful. The sheriff doesn't like me."

"Why not?" asked Kalin, hearing the whoosh of a branch just missing his head.

"His son, Wayne, is a pervert and uses his father's position to do what he wants," she said. "I broke his nose twice for being an idiot."

"Somehow I'm not surprised," said Kalin. Rina would punch first and never ask questions.

"Eight hundred people live here year-round," she said. "Although the sheriff is a jerk when it comes to his son, he's managed to keep the town virtually crime free, except for me, which they could never prove."

"Of course," he said, smirking. Rina was a handful and he imagined how easy it was for her to dupe the officials. She was bright, intelligent, and her curvaceous body was mouth-watering. *A definite beauty.* "Go on."

"Wayne's a braggart and a big-time liar," she said. "Every so often he spreads stories about me and him, so every so often I do something nasty like poison his drink to make all his hair fall out."

"All his hair?" asked Kalin.

"Yep, every last strand," she said proudly, "from the top of his head all the way to his toes. The chemical mixture was simple, and it took three months before new growth appeared."

"And why did you do this?" asked Kalin.

"He broke into my house, stole my favorite ring, and gave it to his girlfriend. His fingerprints were all over my bedroom. His father did nothing, so I took care of it. I told him next time all his protruding parts will shrivel and break off. I think he's afraid of me now because he doesn't talk to me anymore."

"I'd be scared too."

"We'll need a four-by-four."

"A what?" he asked, feeling uneasy. Earth-human technology was primitive and dangerous.

"You'll see," she said coyly.

He cringed at the thought of possible pain and was relieved a case of Sarvins was attached to his black belt. Her telepathy was developing and he wondered if she was reading his mind. A wave of fear spread through him.

Would she actually do it? This is going to freak me out.

They entered the alley between two brick buildings where a tantalizing smell began making him hungry. Although he longed for the food, some Earth-human habits were repulsive, especially the one where they ate butchered animals. He recalled ten years ago when visiting the planet for a vacation, an Earth-human female named Marlene introduced him to a hamburger. One bite and he was hooked, scoffing the thing down so fast she didn't have time to tell him it consisted of beef from a deceased cow. The thought of what he'd eaten made him vomit fivesix times. However, when he'd returned to the *Quasar*, he replicated the sandwich using a vegetable base, omitting the slaughtered meat. Since then, he's eaten hundreds of them. His stomach growled.

"Quiet, Kalin," she said. "It's an Italian restaurant, not a burger joint."

Kalin stopped dead in his tracks. *She read my mind.*

"And don't worry," she said glancing back at him. "I'll let you keep one testicle. Everything else has to go."

Aggravated at her suggestion he said, "That's it, I'm blocking your telepathy."

"You're a hero, Kalin, and a good one. But you need to concentrate on my father and not on me."

I'm not blocking your telepathy because we need to stay connected, but don't read my mind. That's an order.

Make me.

Rina, there are things in there I don't want you seeing.

She stopped walking. *Good point. I don't want to see them either.*

They'd finally reached the end of the alley and when they stepped out, it was like entering a storybook town. Tall majestic trees draped the main road where numerous terrain vehicles parked inward on both sides of the street. Dozens of people were strolling along the sidewalks enjoying the quaint shops.

"Over there." She pointed with a menacing grin. "That red Titan four-by-four will do just fine."

"That actually works?" said Kalin, having qualms over its safety. "It has wheels."

"Let's go."

Several tourists were suspiciously eyeing them and no wonder; Kalin was shouldering his Barra and Rina was carrying a twelve-inch knife in a black sheath. An older man with tinsel hair was staring.

"What are you people?" he asked.

"Rockers," said Rina, drawling her words. "Wanna' join our group, Pop?"

"Not for all the money in the world," he answered, giving them the once over before turning away.

The truck door was unlocked and she entered on the side with, *a steering wheel?* thought Kalin. *This is getting worse by the moment.*

"Hurry up, get in."

"You can't be serious," he said, sliding into the seat. "We're going to die in this." He wanted to beat Marante for not getting them closer to the house.

She reached under the dashboard. "I have to hot wire this thing."

The smell of gasoline told him it was a combustion engine. An electric shock to the steering wheel should do the trick. He tapped the center of the wheel and the engine started.

"What was that?" she asked.

"I rapped it," he said casually, hoping it impressed her.

Rina had the perfect smile.

"Sometimes you come in handy."

In between them and jutting out from the humped floor was a tall black metal stick, and next to it was another smaller one. Kalin tried to snuggle into the cushioned seat. It was uncomfortable and didn't form to his physique. A man with blue spiked hair came running out of a store. He was scrawny with barely any muscle, wearing tan shorts and a green shirt.

Any girl could beat this guy up, thought Kalin.

"Stop!" he shouted, waving his arms frantically.

Rina shifted the tall lever and the truck reversed onto the main road. Ramming the lever forward the vehicle popped into gear, screeching the tires and leaving a trail of smoke. She swerved down the road, avoiding other vehicles that blared their horns as they passed. There were three pedals on the floor, and she was simultaneously pressing the outer two.

Manually shifting the gears? thought Kalin. *Wonderful. I'm back in the Stone Age.*

She turned onto a dirt road just outside the town and raced alongside a fast-moving stream filled with smooth rocks.

I can hear my eulogy, thought Kalin, gripping the safety handle next to the windshield. *He was the last of his race and killed by a crazy woman driver.*

"Won't the sheriff come after us?" asked Kalin, squeezing the grab handle as the truck's two side wheels lifted off the ground rounding a corner.

"Yeah," said Rina calmly, "eventually. The goofy looking guy was Wayne, and this is his truck. But don't worry, there are only three cops in town and with that many tourists, they'll be too busy to come after us. Besides, he knows I'll return it."

"Sounds like you've done this before," he said, hoping the truck wouldn't flip over from all the swerving to avoid the dips in the dirt road.

"Yep," she said proudly. "Wayne is a low-life and I love sticking him hard. It's just my way."

"Great," said Kalin. "I'm with a psycho chick."

In the distance, an old battered covered wooden bridge caught his attention. Gaping holes breached its sunken roof and weathered walls. Blocking the entrance were splintered boards and three orange cones. They were headed straight for them.

"You're not going over that, right?" he asked, squirming in his seat.

She laughed. "It's only a hundred twenty years old and besides, it's a shortcut."

"You can't do that!" he yelled, and they crashed through the barrier.

Pieces of wood went flying everywhere. Rotten trusses squealed against the weight of the vehicle. The planks rattled and bent. The high-pitched sounds of snapping wood and popping nails smothered his terrified scream.

"You're killing me!"

Kalin sighed in relief when the wheels touched solid ground. Looking back, he watched the bridge fold inward, collapsing into the stream. Just then, the vehicle skidded to a halt, spitting pebbles and dirt and slamming him into the dashboard chest first.

"Do you want me dead?" he demanded, feeling the bruise on his chest.

"Hang on," she said, moving the small shifter up until it clicked into place.

She just ignored me, he thought.

"This transmission was special ordered," she said, "built like the old ones. Only this type of four-wheeler can make it up the mountain."

"Am I going to die?" asked Kalin, irritated. "Because I want to live a little longer."

Rina chuckled, "No, you're not going to die. But it is going to hurt."

"Great," he said, "more pain."

She moved the taller lever into the marked second gear and mashed the pedals. The truck lurched then zoomed down the gravel road. Kalin glanced out the rear window. In their wake was a thick cloud of brown dust.

He gazed at her and realized Rina was special. Most women would have crumbled in the presence of monstrous spiders, scorpions, and man-eating Zorcons, but she refused to let her emotions get the best of her. The two times he'd sensed real fear were understandable. The first was when she tried to save Shiro from the Zorcons, and the second was when Vorkis had her father. This woman had been through dire circumstances even some men couldn't handle, yet she managed to keep it together. Her thinking was clear and focused, her aqua-blue eyes riveted on the path before her; she was determined to speed up the mountain at any cost.

"It's going to get a little rough," she said.

Before he could answer, she made a sharp left and headed straight up the mountainside. The uneven pasture bounced him all over the seat. Boulders of all sizes jetted from the brown soil and grass. He saw the giant rock just before the front wheels hit and the vehicle went airborne. Rina screamed with joy as her body rose off the seat. Kalin bashed his head on the ceiling and yelled a flurry of vulgar words. His grasp on the handle saved him from landing on her lap.

"Slow down!" he said, trying to steady himself. "It's best we get there alive."

"What's wrong, wimp, can't take it?"

He touched the growing bump on his head. "Do you always drive like this?"

"You're on my turf now, buddy, so suck it up," she said, swerving to avoid a fallen tree.

Kalin smiled and scoffed, "You are one scary chick."

"Thank you," she said, grinning.

Rina rammed her foot on the center pedal and the truck ground to a stop. Kalin's head banged the windshield and he shouted more obscenities. Before them was a ten-foot high concrete wall covered in deep green vines.

"You're nuts!" he said, rubbing another bump on his head.

"Sorry," she said. "My house is on the other side of this wall. I go alone from here."

Kalin tapped his Comlink. "Marante." He had to catch his breath. "What's the status on Vorkis and Rina's father?"

"Justin is unharmed," said Marante. "I must inform you of the self-destruction of Vorkis' ship. We had just disarmed the vessel when it exploded. Unfortunately, before this, the Zorcons surrounded the entire planet with a Neuron Field. Scanners, teleporters and all weapons on the *Quasar* will not function within the field."

"That sounds bad," said Rina.

"It is," said Kalin.

Rina unbuckled a strap from around her shoulder and waist. "I'm going in."

"What was that you just released?" he asked, disturbed. "Was that a restraining device?"

"Oops," she said, getting out of the truck and holding the door open. "Sorry," she smiled, "I guess I forgot to tell you about the seat belts."

"Why you little—"

"Rina!" called Vorkis.

She was startled by his voice, but then turned to him. "Kalin, go to the far corner of this wall by the lake. Wait there and we'll come to you. I'm going through the outer gate over there." She pointed to two brick pillars with a black doublewide wrought iron gate.

"Don't take any chances," said Kalin. "Get your father and run for it."

"Thanks," she said. She winked at him and bolted for the gate.

Kalin climbed out of the window and onto the top of the truck. He cautiously peeked through the vines. Rina was already jogging up the long driveway. The brown house was three levels and constructed of thick dark timbers. Bulky wooden porches surrounded each floor and off to the side, an enormous tree sat near the end of the cement boundary wall. In the distance was a beautiful serene lake.

Rina stood on the ground in front of the porch steps. "Vorkis! I'm here. Release my father and I'll give you the Pril."

The double doors to the house were flung open and there stood Vorkis with a Barra to Justin's head. Kalin quietly got off the vehicle and dashed to the iron gate. The pavement sloped downward so he belly-crawled across the driveway, out of sight. The concrete blockade was at least three feet thick and he wondered if intruders were common in the area. Upon reaching the other side, he rolled to his feet and traipsed along the barrier until it ended. A five-foot opening separated the diagonal corner where another wall ran parallel to the lake. Rusted hinges gave evidence of a long-gone metal gate. On the ground encasing the corners were several huge stones. The lake was two hundred feet away. The large tree had a thick trunk wider than the vehicle Titan. Long branches heavy with green leaves shadowed a wooden table with benches. Kalin sensed them approaching and flattened himself against the thick wall, listening to their conversation.

"Why did you slaughter your people?" asked Rina.

"My intention was to enslave them," said Vorkis, "but my plan failed and instead my creation mutated beautifully, accomplishing more than I expected."

"You're sick," said Rina.

"Power is all that matters, my dear," answered Vorkis. "Without it, you are nobody."

"We're here," she said, standing next to Kalin. "Let my father go."

"Give me the Pril and you both will live," said Vorkis.

Kalin's back was against the wall with the side of his face pressing the cool cement, aware of Rina's every move. She turned in Kalin's direction and squatted, not looking at him. She lifted one of the large stones and Kalin saw a silver wire attached to it. On the return side of the wall, below the last hinge, a door ground open.

"My mother told me to hide this and never let anyone see it," she said. "It's been here for years."

She slid out a square box big enough to fit Marante's head. Assorted shells were inlaid into the black shiny case. She placed the box in front of her, out of Kalin's view. The lid squeaked opened and it was the first time ever Kalin heard Vorkis gasp.

CHAPTER 32
Kalin

Kalin heard the thwack of a Barra and a body thump the ground. "Dad!" cried Rina.

She ran out of Kalin's sight and he readied his Barra. Vorkis squatted to pick up the box, and then stopped. His stare slowly went up from Kalin's black boots to the nozzle of the Barra.

"Back off," said Kalin, shutting the box with his boot. He stepped out from behind the wall, keeping the Barra hoisted to his shoulder, his aim steady.

Vorkis eased up to his feet with his hands in the air, still dressed in Uru. Rina was helping Justin.

"You surprised me again, cousin," said Vorkis. "I was unaware of your Xevniors."

"You always did presume too much," said Kalin, noticing a small Hapton on Vorkis' wrist.

The round device resembled an Earth-human wristwatch and allowed remote access to certain programs on vessels. Three red lights were blinking on its face.

"You detonated your own ship? You killed all your men."

"Of course I did," said Vorkis. "Did you expect anything less?"

Vorkis' kick to Kalin's stomach was so fast and strong, the Barra flew out of his hands and he crashed against the cement wall, crumbling the concrete. Kalin immediately ignited his Xevniors, lifting Vorkis in the air and bashing him on the ground, belly down. Without hesitating, Kalin jumped to his feet and kicked him in the ribs flipping him onto his back, then knelt beside him and clamped his hands around his neck.

"This is for Disa," he said, squeezing hard and relighting his Xevniors.

Vorkis desperately flailed his arms, trying to reach him. Kalin kept himself at arm's distance, tightening his grip. Without warning, a laser blast tore into Kalin's stomach. His body flew into the air and slammed into the wall, then slid down to sitting on the ground. His head wobbled as he placed his hand over the large bloody hole.

"No!" shouted Rina and she began running to Kalin.

"Die, Saleran filth!" yelled Vurro, who fired again.

Justin pulled her back and a pair of white beams shot out from his eyes. They hit the blue pulse of the Barra and exploded. Kalin blinked several times, not believing what he'd just seen.

"You? But—" said Rina.

Vorkis was getting to his feet. Kalin stiffened up and reactivated his Xevniors. Vorkis crumpled to the ground in pain.

"You will die!" shouted Vurro. Two more laser blasts headed for Kalin.

Justin dove towards Kalin with outstretched arms. Instantly, a clear purple shield surrounded them. The laser beams struck the energy barricade and dispersed into white twinkles. Justin landed on the ground next to him. Although Kalin's Xevniors were passing through the shield, he halted them, too weak to continue. His bloodied hand slipped to his side and he closed his eyes. Vivid memories of Salera and his family raced through his mind and for the first time since their deaths, he wanted to live. Salera deserved to be teeming with life, with children, with families, with the glory she once had. He finally understood what everyone had been trying to tell him.

Someone touched his hand and he opened his eyes.

"Hang on," said Justin on one knee. "You'll be all right."

He held Kalin's wrist and pointed his left palm at Rina. A yellow beam shot out and raised her off the grass, pulling her towards them.

"Woooo!" said Rina.

She slid through the shield and stopped abruptly next to Justin and Kalin. Justin tapped the small gray case on Kalin's belt. Rina smiled.

"How did you know about Sarvins?" she asked, surprised.

"I read his mind," he said. "Stay here."

Justin stepped outside the shield, Kalin staring after him in awe. This was the strongest being he'd ever met. Rina knelt beside him and removed the case from his belt. Kalin gazed into her beautiful eyes as she poured the orange crystals on his head.

"You were right," he said in a weak voice. His vision was fading. "You were right all along." Each breath was becoming shallower.

"You're a good guy, Kalin," she said, touching his cheek. Tears lined her dark lashes. "A real hero I'm proud to call my friend. Now don't talk." She placed her fingers over his mouth. "I know what you're feeling; I've been there. Save your strength and let the crystals do their job."

"You can't have the Pril," Justin said to Vorkis.

Vurro was going to shoot again when Vorkis raised his hand and he stopped, lowering the Barra.

"Who are you?" asked Vorkis.

"I'll tell you this only once," said Justin. His right fist was beginning to glow. "Leave this world and never return."

Kalin struggled to his feet. "This is my fight," he said aloud, keeping a fixed glare on Vorkis. Despite feeling weak, he straightened up, ready to take him on.

"Infidels!" shouted Vurro, who fired again.

Justin raised his glowing fist and caught the blue beam in his hand. He raised his other palm and swung his arm back, yanking the Barra out of Vurro's hands and flinging it back towards Rina. A lavender beam from Justin's hand formed a transparent sphere around Vurro. He was yelling and banging on the bubble as it rose higher into the atmosphere, lifting him out of sight.

He turned to Kalin. "He's all yours, son."

"Excellent," said Vorkis. "Let us fight again and this time I will show you who is to be King of Sal—"

Before Vorkis could finish his words, Kalin's Xevniors sent Vorkis flying back into the giant tree. Kalin leapt in the air and flipped, slipping the Norin blade from his boot and ramming it into Vorkis' leg as he landed. Vorkis screamed in pain and kicked Kalin in the face, making him tumble away.

"Now I will kill you with your own weapon," stated Vorkis, sliding the knife out of his leg.

Kalin jumped to his feet and held out his upturned palm. The Norin blade flew out of Vorkis' hand and straight back to Kalin where he caught it. Startled by the loss of the weapon, Vorkis didn't catch sight of Kalin's leap in the air towards him. He pounced on Vorkis' chest and began repeatedly punching his face until he heard bones cracking. Vorkis grabbed Kalin's fist with his right hand and flung him off. Kalin rolled to his feet and lunged at Vorkis again, who was struggling to stand when suddenly, Vorkis blasted his Xevniors at Rina.

Kalin skidded to a stop as he saw the beams hit Rina in the chest, throwing her back into the cement wall. The wide beams shrunk to a pinpoint on the Pril in her necklace then reversed direction and went crashing back into Vorkis' eyes. He screamed and collapsed back, holding his face. Rina's body slid to the floor, leaving a blood trail on the wall.

"No!" cried Kalin, rushing to her.

"I got her," said Justin, who was already holding her in his arms. "Finish this, son."

Kalin trembled with fiery hatred. Although Vorkis was on his back and near convulsing, it was no relief for Kalin. Only his death would suffice. But then Kalin noticed the change. All the hair on Vorkis' head and face was gone, burned off, leaving charred, smoldering skin. His eyes were completely black, the lids seared and crisp. The left side of his face was drooping, morphing his cindered eye. On the right side, his lips had burned off, revealing black rotted teeth. Blood streaked out of his nose from the several lesions splitting it open. His once cream-colored skin was a slimy crimson and peeling away. Nothing was left of his Saleran characteristics. Vorkis now looked like the monster he truly was. Justice had finally begun and this time he would end it. Vorkis staggered to his feet. His enemy had no more to give.

"You can never defeat me," said Vorkis, and he pressed his thumb onto his left forearm. Teleporter beams ignited.

Kalin dove for the nearby Barra and rolled, shooting into the beam. Vorkis doubled over holding his stomach, then was gone in a flash of light.

"Marante!" he said. "What's the destination of that teleport?"

There was silence. Kalin stood up, panting.

Marante answered, "Apparently, Vorkis had an Ensit implant and altered a short-range scan to bounce him through the Neuron Field. That form of teleporting is dangerous and in his weakened state, there is a very strong possibility he did not survive. However, we detected the signature of a space pod leaving orbit at warp speed but unfortunately, there is no way to track it. I am sorry, my friend, he is gone."

Kalin roared until his lungs burned. He slumped to his knees trembling and holding his stomach that seemed to be on fire. A hand touched his shoulder.

"He definitely was hurt," said a voice from behind, "I think you got him."

Kalin turned to see Rina and Justin. He jumped to his feet and hugged her tight, lifting her off the ground.

"I'm so glad you're alive," he said.

"Yeah, but I can't breathe," she said, straining. "Ease up."

"Sorry," he said and let her down. "I just wish I knew if he was dead."

"I sensed he was in tremendous physical pain," said Justin. "You definitely hit him and with the deformation he incurred from the Pril, I doubt he survived."

Kalin sighed. His enemy may still be out there. Rina took his hand.

"Are you okay?" she asked.

He looked down at the most beautiful face he'd ever seen and smiled.

"I can't worry about him anymore," said Kalin. He touched

Rina's cheek. "There are more important things in life."

He cupped her face and kissed her on the lips. She struggled to get free then stopped.

There's no way I'm letting her get out of this.

"You have a great kiss," said Kalin, trying not to tremble from the hormonal excitement. *Why is my body reacting like this?* He took a deep breath and turned to Justin.

"What exactly can Pril do?" he asked, furtively glancing at Rina. Reeling back was not easy.

"What you call Pril can do amazing things. Cellular regeneration is just one of them."

"I thought it was mom," said Rina looking at Justin.

"No, baby girl, it's been me all along," he said. "Mary was the one who insisted on not telling you sooner. She felt your life would be simpler if you believed you were an Earth-human." He lovingly touched her cheek. "We had planned on telling you before you turned twenty-one, but with your mother's death I put it off. Forgive me, sweetheart."

"I guess you did what you thought was best," she said. Then she noticed the blood. "Your shoulder—you're hurt."

"Bauman shot me but thanks to the ring, my wound is healed. I'm okay."

"Good," she said. "Now tell me, where am I from?"

"You're from a planet called Verlea," said Justin, "three hundred galaxies from here."

"Three hundred?" reiterated Kalin.

"Yes, a short trip."

"That's amazing," said Rina. "So all the stories were real."

"Yes, they were," said Justin. "Your Earth-human mother, Mary, wanted you to know your heritage. Your real mother, Eliana, and I chose Earth because of the quality of people, knowing we could easily protect ourselves and meld into their way of life. Our galaxy had several civilizations just aching to get their hands on Verlean technology, so when the planet exploded, we knew we were targets if anyone discovered we had survived. Therefore, Earth and the seclusion of the Rocky Mountains seemed a good place to start anew, but then our guidance system failed.

"You were three months old when we crashed at night not far from here. The ship broke in half, exposing the cockpit. I was thrown from the vessel, but Eliana was badly injured and on the second level with you. She wrapped you in a fireproof blanket and tossed you to me. I ran several hundred feet away and placed you in a safe area then hurried back to save her. Verlean ships were designed to inhibit a mass explosion, vaporizing instead of creating more damage, and Eliana disintegrated along with the ship.

"Mary witnessed the whole event and decided to help you and me. Eventually, I fell in love with her. She insisted she be the one to tell you Verlea's history so if the government ever became suspicious of aliens living amongst us, she wanted them to suspect her, knowing her anatomy would prove otherwise. I didn't want to put her in that kind of danger but she was stubborn. Wayne was the only person who ever suspected anything odd about you, so I used the Rycon to alter his thoughts."

"Rycon?" asked Rina.

"It's the real name of Pril," said Justin, "and I'll teach you how to use it."

"Wayne is the guy with the blue hair, right?" asked Kalin.

"Yes," said Justin. "Rina's punches that threw him twenty feet back are what made him suspicious. No harm was done and he retained all his memories."

"You can actually change thoughts?" asked Kalin. "Even memories?"

"Yes, but I don't like doing it. No one's mind should ever be tampered with."

Kalin gazed up at the sky and wondered if Vorkis was dead.

Shooting into a teleporter beam sometimes worked, sometimes it didn't. He closed his eyes as the aching in his heart began again.

The nightmares are going to haunt me forever.

A hand touched his shoulder. It was Justin.

"I know what it's like to lose your family and your people," said Justin.

"No one could ever feel what I've been through."

"Rina and I are the last of our race," explained Justin. "Three hundred and fifty billion Verlean-humans died because twelve people made the wrong decision. The pain will always be there, Kalin, but with time, it will subside enough to let you live a normal life."

"My little sister died in my arms," said Kalin, wanting the pain in his chest to stop. "Nothing will erase that memory."

"Before my ship vaporized, Eliana shouted she loved me and asked me to care for our baby."

He stopped talking and closed his eyes. Kalin sensed his hurt.

Justin looked at him and continued, "She knew it was her end and there was nothing I could do to save her. I had warned the Verlean Council the planetary shield would fail against an explosive Resdin comet that size; its mass was enormous. They laughed at me and said I was crazy. Three days later, Verlea exploded. There were times I wanted to create a Time Teleporter and kill the Council, but I would have changed history and altered my future, my daughter's future—a worse mistake than theirs. You, on the other hand, are Salera's future and history. You alone have the chance to make your planet better than before, make it more glorious. Enjoy your heritage and the world you were raised on. This is your moment, your time, Kalin. Make the most of it."

Justin's words reminded Kalin of his father, Altor, who many times was reasonable and confident, a man who instilled hope and courage, a true leader.

Can I actually live a normal life? thought Kalin.

Marante was right. Revenge had overtaken him. He was willing to let a whole civilization die just to kill one man. *How could I have let myself get this far?* In all his missions with the Federation, not once had he ever considered allowing even one death, never mind the deaths of so many. He was a Saleran, a savior of lives, not a mass murderer. Remorse began to set in.

"I'm sorry, Kalin," said Rina. "I wish there was a way to take your pain away."

He smiled at her, "I'm just glad you're alive. I'm sorry for risking the lives of you and your world. No death is worth him."

Marante's voice came over the Comlink. "Captain, we have a problem."

Kalin inhaled a deep breath, feeling his inner strength return.

"So much for pain and sorrow," he said. "Go."

"Four armed missiles have been launched from an orbiting probe. Their trajectory will take them to a terra lesion zone approximately one thousand miles southeast of you. If they impact, over twenty-five million will die."

CHAPTER 33
Rina

"I am on the Ignis and on my way down to you," said Marante. "Communication with the *Quasar* is inoperative. Due to the primitive technology of the missiles, the Neuron Field will have no effect on them. There is a huge gathering of sorts at the intended target. We must stop the missiles."

"Can we listen in on the gathering?" asked Justin aloud.

"Who is this?" asked Marante.

"I'm Rina's father, Justin."

"Pleasure to meet you, sir. I am connecting the broadcast."

"…and this day will be remembered forever as the day that every nation on this planet willingly gathered together to peacefully unite this world."

Clapping hands and loud cheers were audible.

"It's the Peace Conference," said Justin as he glanced at Rina. "Every national official is there. It's got to be Bauman. His original plan failed and now he's going after all the leaders of every country. Can you detonate the missiles in the sky, Marante?"

"I'm afraid not, sir. The Neuron Field will neutralize our weapons."

"How about remotely adjusting their guidance systems?" said Rina.

"The Neuron Field will prevent that too," said Kalin. "All our weapons are useless. We're going to have to think of another way."

The Ignis, thought Rina. *A ship.*

"How big are your docking bays?" she asked.

"What's that got to do with this?" asked Kalin.

"Just answer the question; how big are your docking bays?"

"Big enough to hold a few Earth buildings. How is—"

She cut him off, "Marante, are the missiles on a single line trajectory?"

"Yes," he answered.

"Wait a minute," said Kalin, furrowing his brow in thought. "Are you thinking what I'm thinking?"

"Your REM was powerful enough to create a planet tunnel into the core, which means it can take an enormous amount of pressure and heat," said Rina. "Can it handle the explosions of four nuclear bombs?"

"Maybe," said Kalin.

Using her telepathy, Rina could see his thoughts racing.

"You are both out of your minds," said Marante. "There is an eighty percent probability we will not survive."

"It's the only plan we've got," said Kalin. He winked at Rina and made that flirtatious smile.

"Marante, what's their ETA?"

"Five minutes, captain."

"What's your ETA?"

From out of nowhere, a door began lowering behind them. No other sign of a vessel was visible. The light was almost blinding. Atop the ramp, Rina saw the silhouette of Marante's angular frame.

"Good," said Kalin, grabbing Rina's hand. "Let's go."

"Wait," she said, lifting the box of Rycon.

"Kalin," said Justin, "we're talking about four, fifty-kiloton nuclear missiles the size of small buildings. Are you sure the docking bays can handle their sizes?"

Kalin tapped his Comlink and an enormous silver sphere appeared above the house. Its circumference took in their whole field of vision, shadowing the mountaintop and mirroring its surroundings.

Justin's stare went up the giant craft. "That'll do," he said. It vanished again except for the ramp.

"What about Vurro?" asked Rina, clutching the box.

"Vurro's in a low orbit around the planet," said Justin. "The Rycon Sphere will keep him alive until we pick him up."

"Let's go," said Kalin. "There isn't much time."

"Quickly!" said Marante, waving them in.

As they ascended towards Marante, Rina watched her father's worried expression change into wonderment as he gazed at the Chaslean-human.

"Pleasure to meet you, Marante," said Justin, shaking his hand.

"The pleasure is all mine, sir," said Marante. "We must hurry."

Kalin held Rina's hand as they ran down the blue-carpeted hallways. A light scent of gardenias perfumed the air. On the ceiling and walls were murals of colorful Novas, Pulsars, and every type of astro phenomenon.

This is beautiful, she thought, and wondered if the décor of the *Quasar* was similar. The brief stay in the Med Lab hadn't allowed her time to examine her surroundings.

"The Ignis is your premium class star cruiser," said Kalin. "It's small compared to the *Quasar*, but it's a tough little ship."

Small, thought Rina. *Holy cow.*

In the semi-lit bridge, everything was shiny black except for the colorful orbs on the control console. They dotted the area like sparkling gems.

Holo orbs, she thought.

Hovering in front of the console were three white cushions. Kalin sat on the middle one and Marante took the seat to his left. The cushions instantly grew and molded to their bodies, creating armrests and high backs. The lights dimmed.

Kalin tapped a yellow orb. A gold liquid gathered in the center of the giant wall facing them, then burst into an array of colored lights. A twenty-by-thirty-foot three-dimensional picture formed, displaying her house and grounds. No fluctuations or any discolorations were present; it was as if she could reach out and touch her favorite tree. Marante was manipulating a holo. The technology was incredible. Her father had an ear-to-ear grin.

The screen split in two. On one side were the missiles; the other half showed her house shrinking in size as they rose into the atmosphere. They must have been traveling at a tremendous speed but there was no physical stress from the G-forces. The engines were barely audible. If it weren't for the screen, she would have never known they were airborne.

"Impact in less than ninety seconds," said Marante, studying a holo.

Kalin waved his hand over another orb and a holo revealed the trajectory of the missiles. She leaned on the back of his chair looking over his shoulder, watching him move his fingers through the holo, touching wisps of numbers. She felt the slight turn of the ship. He had adjusted their course.

The holos have to be biochemical-reactive, she thought, *possibly epicritic. Wow.*

"If the REM does not react in time," said Marante, "we will be incinerated."

"Have you ever done this before?" she asked.

"No," said Kalin, focused on the screen. "If this works, it'll go down in the books as the Rina Crunch. We're coming up on the missiles."

"I have merged docking bays six and seven," said Marante, working his holo. "The REM will automatically shield the area after the missiles enter and before the doors close. Purging of radioactive materials will commence immediately after detonation. Captain, it is possible the Neuron Field may interfere with the ship's REM."

"I know," said Kalin. "Either way, this is going to hurt."

Rina glanced over at Marante's holo, which showed the inside of a long wide-open room. He wasn't kidding about the size; three Empire State buildings could fit.

"Ten seconds to impact," said Marante.

"Sound off," said Kalin. "Justin, belt yourself in."

Justin took the box of Rycon from Rina. "I'll hold it," he said, and sat on the cushion to the right of Kalin.

Kalin pulled Rina on his lap and wrapped his arms around her. The armrests snuggled them in place.

"Are these chairs safe?" she asked. Floating things never made her feel safe.

"Of course," he said. "They're designed to keep you secure in the event of a crash."

"Great. Now ease up on your grip. It's too tight."

Kalin rested his chin on her shoulder, rubbing her cheek with his.

"What's wrong?" he said, smiling and squeezing harder. "Never had a guy caress you before?"

He was doing it again. Aggravating her to the point where she wanted to bust his lip. "You are such a jer—"

"Three-two—" said Marante.

With a deafening boom, the ship jolted back and everyone screamed. Jagged sparks flew across the recessed orbs. The vessel rumbled with the wild shock waves. The liquid screen went flying into the air in all directions. Panels burst from the sidewalls setting off mini fires. Automatic extinguishers clicked on, snuffing out the flames. Kalin tapped a yellow orb and it exploded, sending shards of glass into the palm of his hand.

This is it, Rina thought, *we're dead.*

Then all was quiet. The floating gold liquid swished back to the wall, forming a picture of the docking bay where dark smoke blocked the view. She heard the faint whisper of exhaust fans removing the heavy smoke from the bridge.

"Did we do it?" asked Rina, coughing, "or are we all going to die from radiation poisoning in three months?"

"The REM shield initiated two millionths of a second before the weapons detonated," said Marante. "Decontamination is in progress. It worked."

Rina stood up and shouted, "Yes!"

She jumped back into Kalin's lap and started kissing his face with joy.

"We did it!" she said, looking into his green eyes. "You did it." She wrapped her arms around him and squeezed.

"Rina," he said softly. "As much as I'm enjoying this, remember the 'I'm only a man' part?'"

She gasped and scurried off his lap. "Sorry," she said. "I got excited."

"So did I," he said, trying to steady his breathing. "You really are a hot babe," he added, swiping cold sweat off his brow with the back of his injured hand.

"You're hurt," she said, taking his hand and examining the pieces of glass jutting out from his bleeding cuts. "We need more Sarvins. I used the last ones on you."

"I'm all right," he said. "I've had worse."

Justin approached them and touched Kalin's arm. The wounds on his hand began to heal. The pieces of glass pushed out of his skin and clinked as they hit the floor. Rina stared in awe.

"Sarvins would take at least a minute to heal these deep cuts," said Kalin, rubbing his palm. "These wounds have completely healed within seconds. I can only imagine what else Rycon can do."

"Its capabilities are far greater than what you or Marante can imagine," said Justin. "Your science doesn't even come close to what Rycon can do. It's like nothing you've ever seen before."

CHAPTER 34
Bauman

One man to rule them all, thought Bauman, *and my private army will see to it.*

Snuggling into his plush leather chair, he smiled at the man reflected in the wall mirror. He would soon be the most powerful person on Earth with an arsenal befitting a small country. He stood and checked himself in the mirror. Aside from his slight paunch, the maroon tunic and black pants made him appear strong and fit. He adjusted his wide ebony belt and straightened his sidearm.

Ready.

He walked down the long hallway past the crew's quarters and the mess hall and when he reached the lounge, he stopped. His gaze went beyond the OPC and all the way into the cockpit. The ten men were performing perfectly and considering the minor setback, everything was going well.

"Sir!" said Rick, his voice up a notch. "Two G-5 Eagle jets are demanding we head for Area 51 in Nevada. What are your orders?"

"What?" asked Bauman, shocked. *How in the world did they find us?*

He furtively glanced between the portholes. The two jets were flying on both sides of them in escort formation.

Not me!

He hurried to the OPC and pressed a speaker button above Rick's head.

"This is General Theodore Bauman, Secretary of Defense. To whom am I speaking?"

"Captain Brian Daniels, sir. Our orders are to escort you to Area 51. Do you comply?"

"No!" said Bauman. "We do not comply! Our mission is of absolute secrecy, and you're blowing it to pieces. Return to your base!

That's an order!"

There was silence. *Are they onto us?* It didn't matter; it ended here.

"Our orders come directly from President Larson, sir," said Daniels. "We are to escort you to Area 51. Do you comply?"

Bauman refused to answer. He was aware of the procedure; they had to ask him three times for compliance and if the response was negative or mute, they'd use physical force. He turned to Rick.

"Launch Streamer Jaunt."

"Aye, sir."

The hum of doors opening beneath the aircraft was heard. Bauman watched the monitor. A thin gray gun barrel with a steel skeletal covering lowered, a green light was blinking. Two thumping sounds vibrated the floor. Nebulous yellow balls burst from below the jet laterally and hit the Eagles broadside. Sparks and bolts of electricity engulfed the vessels, then faded away in streaks of light.

Bauman went to the lounge area and sat in a chair, observing the two jets struggle in the air. Nothing would save them, not even their ejection seats. Rina's virus was the best. The aircrafts swayed side-to-side, their engines sputtering to the many attempts by the pilots to ignite them. Slowly the noses of the jets slid earthward and they started their descent. Their speed increased as they plummeted towards the water below, spinning wildly. The high-pitched whirring sounds decreased with distance from the DD-10, until the two crafts crashed into the Caribbean Sea. He rested back concerned. Rick had initiated the jamming frequencies of this DD-10, yet no alarm sounded a breach.

Was it sabotage? Did Larson know about Blythen? The Mariana?

"Sir!" said Rick, frantically typing. "The missiles have vanished!"

"What!" Bauman jumped out of his seat and dashed to Rick's side.

"Four nuclear missiles just don't disappear," he said, looking over Rick's shoulder.

The jet went dark; all power had turned off. Bauman heard the whine of the engines shutting down. Alarms and red emergency lights blinked on throughout the craft. Bauman grabbed a ceiling handle as the jet listed to one side. They were going down. The lights and power came back on and the engines roared again.

"Our course has changed, sir," said Rick. "We're heading for Area 51."

This is mutiny! Desperate to stop them, Bauman drew his pistol and stormed into the cockpit with the gun hidden behind him.

"I did not give an order to change course!"

Both pilots were startled.

"The jet is being controlled, sir," said the pilot. "We can't maneuver."

"Liar!" yelled Bauman. "You're working for them."

He swung the gun out from behind and fired into the pilot's face. Blood and brains splattered the instrument panel. Bauman aimed the gun at the co-pilot.

"Turn this jet around now!" he demanded.

"Sir!" shouted Rick from the OPC. "We have President Larson on the com. He says it's urgent."

"You've got until the end of my conversation with Larson to adjust our course," said Bauman, "or it's over for you."

"Yes, sir!" said the frightened man, who started pressing buttons and flipping switches.

Bauman stuffed the gun into his holster and returned to the OPC. Rick moved to the next station and Bauman sat, pushing away the thin strands of tousled hair that had fallen across his brow. He nodded to Rick. Payton appeared dressed in his blue Naval uniform. His silver hair was thick and wavy, almost bushy in appearance, as were his wild eyebrows.

"It's over, Ted," said Payton. "They got us."

Two men grabbed Payton's arms and yanked him from his seat. President Albert Larson took his place, a perfectly groomed African-American who should have never made the Presidency. Larson knew nothing of how to run a country, how to enforce the laws, and especially how to reel the power he commanded. Why, he'd even appointed spics and chinks to his cabinet, saying a variety of different backgrounds would enlighten the decision-making process.

"We've received a report from Intel and it's been confirmed," said Larson. "You, the Admiral, and your men are facing serious charges of murder and treason. Why did you kill those men in the jets? They were acting on my orders."

"I didn't, sir," said Bauman. "There's a logical explanation and it wasn't us." *This is going to be easy.* "We are not traitors and I can prove everything."

"How is that possible?" asked Larson. "We saw what you did, Ted. You're not the only one with a satellite uplink. According to this"—he skimmed through the pages in his hand, his reading glasses perched on the tip of his wide nose—"you and Payton collaborated with Hans Steinmann to create over four hundred nuclear missiles, thus breaking all the laws of the Nuclear Arms Agreement. You hired Frank Bollen, the most notorious criminal of the century, to steal the plans for you and, thanks to your emails, he's been arrested. Your days are over, General. You are hereby stripped of all command. Ten more fighters are on their way to escort you to Area 51. First sign of resistance and they'll shoot you down."

Bauman stared at Larson wanting to maim him. The thought of a man whose ancestors were slaves holding the highest office in the world was all he could take. His face flushed with anger, his fists tightening to the rage inside him.

"Nobody strips me of my command," said Bauman, leaning into the monitor, "you lame, weak-minded nigger. You and your kind deserve to die. Only the white man has rights to this planet. My New Continuum has thousands of members. You can never stop us."

"We already have," said Larson. The connection was terminated.

"Hello, idiot."

Bauman quickly straightened up, startled by the familiar voice. Rina was standing in the lounge.

Is my mind playing tricks on me?

His men were on their feet, gaping at her. *They're seeing her too.* She was still wearing the same jean shorts and red T-shirt.

"You're not real," he said, staring with curiosity. "You're dead at the bottom of the Mariana Trench."

"Guys usually tell me I'm beautiful," she said, laughing. "You're the first fat oaf to say I look dead. How does it feel to lose, jerk?"

Bauman shook his head. *This can't be real.* He eyed the men standing around him. *One of them is pulling this trick. They'll have to be eliminated.*

"Your men didn't do this, Bauman," she said, "so leave them alone."

His breath stopped in his chest. *She read my mind!*

"Your private Command Center back there has a nice log of everything you've done through the years," she said, "including the names of all the people you've killed to cover up your plan. I sent the file to President Larson. The world knows what you did, Bauman. It's over."

Bauman quickly drew his gun and fired pointblank into Rina's chest. The bullet passed through her creating circling waves of white, then lodged into the far wall.

"You really are brainless," she said. "I'm a hologram, and yes, I'm very much alive. Get over it, idiot; you lost."

The aliens, he thought with a sudden pervasive sense of failure. Only they could have saved her, and their technology was assuredly too advanced for him. However, he was a general in this man's Army and no one would ever take him down. He stiffened up and glared into her eyes. There was one last chance and distraction was the key.

"All weapons on this jet have been disabled," she said. "Don't even think of using the Keldin Pulse again."

He raised his clenched fists and roared at the top of his lungs until his chest sank in from the lack of air. Rick and the other men vaulted from their seats and ran into the lounge. Bauman picked up the keyboard across from Rick's station and bashed it through the monitor causing smoke and sparks to shoot out. He shouted obscenities as he punched and kicked anything within reach, slicing his knuckles. Out of options he leaned on Rick's chair, heaving from exhaustion, succumbing to defeat. The flames behind him had subsided, leaving burnt smoldering equipment.

"The President is anxious to arrest you so we're going to help him," she said. "The lights at the Peace Conference will momentarily go dark and when they come back on, you and the hood will be standing on the main stage in front of twelve thousand people dressed only in your underwear and socks. The MPs and the Secret Service will be all over you like white on rice. How's that for a grand ending?"

The holograms of Justin and Shiro appeared standing next to Rina.

"And if you're not wearing underwear, so be it," said Shiro, grinning wide, "commando makes for better comedy."

Bauman was speechless. All those who could've stopped him, did, and for the first time in his life there was nothing he could do. It was over. However, he would not be humiliated. He took the gun from his holster and raised it to his temple, closing his eyes.

"After your attempt to shoot me," said Rina, "all guns were disabled. Suicide is too easy an out for a murderer like you."

He opened his eyes in distress and pulled the trigger. An empty click sounded.

"And one more thing…," said Justin.

The last thing Bauman saw was Justin's fist heading for his face.

CHAPTER 35
Rina

It was a calm light-jacket day, the air crisp and clean. Rina was sitting atop the hillside overlooking the City of Light. Except for the hundreds of dried-up trees within and around the city, Salera was beautiful. The pink-purple sky with its three suns reflected the brilliant rainbow colors of the odd-shaped buildings, sparkling as if covered with diamonds. Light purple-colored grass and dazzling flowers ranging from plate-size to cup-size covered the mountainside in an array of colors.

This place must have been awesome in its heyday, she thought.

She glanced back at the Krystal Palace, an enormous white structure rivaling any castle on Earth. Even from the distance of two miles, it was clearly the center of authority on Salera. Its height was well over two thousand feet with twenty turrets rising into the clouds. Kalin refused to enter the palace and wouldn't allow anyone entrance either. He said for now he wanted the palace and its grounds to remain as they were.

His pain is so deep, she thought, *and expected.*

He'd ordered another ship, smaller than the Ignis to be docked on the surface as their living quarters, a sphere-shaped vessel called the Ristan. At half a mile wide, it resembled a small opal-colored moon hovering just above the grass. Everyone respected Kalin's wishes, including Rina, even though it gnawed at her not to see the inside of the palace. It was magnificent.

Her thoughts returned to Earth. The news said the planet had been stable for over six weeks. She wondered how the Oridians were dealing with the new devices they couldn't reach because of the REM shields.

Shiro was lying on the grass next to her with his hands clasped behind his head. Nearby, an immense tree whose breadth was close to the size of a mansion, stood lifeless with layers of white bark peeling off, its leaves long gone from the hefty branches.

"Let me get this straight," said Shiro. "What you're saying is that on Earth, your dad couldn't find the ore he needed to create the perfect Seismic Depth Locator, so instead, he used the Rycon to alter a metal close enough to its properties and thus was able to invent the SDL. But why stop there? He could've kept going with even more super inventions."

"Because Earth-humans need to progress at their own rate," she said, "and not be handed powerful devices that could be used to destroy life."

"So why didn't he heal himself after Bauman shot him?"

"He was slowly healing, it's his natural ability, but the ring would have made it happen sooner and he wasn't wearing it at the time."

"Hey, look at that." He pointed up. A fireball shot across the sky.

A meteor? she thought. *Or is it Dad?*

Justin was ecstatic when Kalin gave him the Ignis. This was the happiest she'd ever seen him, and it was hard to keep him out of the ship. He said the vessel needed a major upgrade, which kept him busy. On rare occasions, he actually left the ship to spend time with her. Marante never left his side, always studying, constantly amazed at the new sciences he was learning.

Seven days ago, life was simple; now it was full of wonders. Justin said her Verlean chemistry was beginning to assert itself. Her senses were becoming keener, sharper, and this she liked.

Footsteps came from behind. It was Kalin. He plopped down beside her. Although he was the most pig-headed man she'd ever met, he was definitely a looker. He was resting on his side facing her with one leg bent inward, the other stretched out straight. Not wanting him to know she was checking him out, she shifted her eyes without turning her head.

Kalin was a physically perfect man with thick beautiful black hair down to his shoulders, radiant green eyes, bulging muscles aching to be touched and a gorgeous smile to make any woman melt.

Why don't I have feelings for him? Am I abnormal? He saved Earth and millions of people, so what's wrong with me?

It had to be the tons of women. The thought of living with a man who couldn't stay focused was something she could not accept. Kalin was a womanizer and there was no way she'd hook up with a guy like him. He ran his fingers through his black hair.

"So what gives, gorgeous?" he said.

She hated the mindless nametags. They were more proof of his womanizing.

"Whatever happened," she said, "I didn't do it."

He laughed aloud. "So you admit you may have started something."

"Yeah," she said, chuckling. "It's my way."

He scooted closer and an uneasy feeling shot through her. His scent was light and airy, sort of like the famous Veltar Cologne on Earth. His green eyes contained splashes of light brown making them...*absolutely beautiful.*

"We have to talk about us," he said.

"Yeah, okay," said Shiro, standing up and not bothering to brush off his khaki pants, a definite sign his OCD had diminished. "I'll see you guys later."

"You're leaving?" she asked, trying not to reveal her desperation. "You don't have to go. Whatever Kalin has to say, you can hear."

"Ugh...no thanks," he said, his eyes on Kalin.

She quickly turned to Kalin, who immediately stopped shaking his head and smiled at her. He was trying to get her alone—again. His many attempts to corner her in private had failed with her many excuses. She was trying to avoid the discussion of their being a twosome, but alas, it had to happen. Truth was, her life was too busy to get involved and besides, becoming the latest addition to Kalin's list of used women was out of the question.

"Fine," she said, not taking her eyes off Kalin. "I'll see you later, Shiro. Absolutely no way, Kalin."

"You don't know what I was going to say," he said, annoyed.

~ 313 ~

"Stop being so presumptuous."

"Okay," she said, folding her arms across her chest. "Speak."

"I was wondering, Ms. Know-it-all, if you would accompany me to a formal ball we're going to have on the *Quasar*?"

That wasn't what she'd expected. She felt stupid and the smirk on his face made it worse. He was enjoying her downfall.

"Is this what all the fuss was about?" she said. "A date? Why did you make it sound so serious?"

"It is serious," he said. "It's my coronation as King of Salera and I can't imagine going with anyone but you."

She couldn't help a smile. "So it's not really an official date, it's more like an escort, right?"

Kalin sighed and looked away. There was something he wasn't telling her. She wondered if her empathic abilities were strong enough to delve into Kalin's emotions. He was looking the other way and she needed his attention on her.

"Kalin," she said, "are you all right?"

"Yeah," he said, turning to her. "I'm fine."

This was it. She focused on his eyes and stopped abruptly, almost jolting back. *He has strong feelings for me!* Immediately, she turned away, embarrassed by what she'd discovered. Two fingers on her chin shifted her face towards him.

"I guess it's all out in the open now," he said. "It's more than an escort, Rina. I want it to be an official date, and not the only one."

"Kalin," she said, hoping her words wouldn't hurt too much. "I…you…there are too many women in your life. It goes against everything I believe in. I'll go with you to the ball, but it ends there. I'm sorry."

Kalin's eyes turned into menacing slits. "I knew you'd be stubborn. Look, it took a long time but I learned my lesson. You're the only girl I'll ever trust and I'd be happy with only you. Use your empathic powers again, search inside me; you'll see I'm telling the truth."

She hesitated. Back on the *Quasar* when he'd confronted Ilya, she had sensed his feelings for the bimbo. He was hurt by what she'd done, but not badly.

Because I wanted you then, he said in her mind.

"Quit reading my mind," she said, irritated.

"Sorry, I'm a little desperate. I'll stop for now."

Kalin was staring at her with eyes of want, but with a womanizer there was always doubt.

"Okay," she said. "I will search your mind, but if I find even the slightest suspicion, I'm going to beat you up."

"Go for it."

His calm demeanor made her uncomfortable. She unwillingly got to her knees, sat back on her calves, then cupped her hands around his face, glaring into his eyes. He didn't flinch. Colorful waves of truth and honesty flowed through his soul like soft glowing wisps of air. Warmth and caring filled his thoughts, thoughts that centered on her—and only her. She pulled away upset with what she'd found. He wasn't lying.

"So, how about it, Rina?"

"It'll never work," she said, searching for another excuse. "I…it…your Queen has to be able to have your kids. I can't." She let out a heavy sigh, happy she remembered.

A voice came from behind. "We need to talk."

It was her dad and by the way he was strutting, it couldn't be good. He signaled for her to slide over so he could sit between them.

"What are you up to?" she asked, moving aside.

"It's time you both knew the truth," said Justin.

He pulled a black flat shiny scanner from his jeans pocket and tapped the miniature yellow orb. A three-dimensional holo of Rina rose up. Scrolling data was beside her form.

"Perfect," he said with a wide grin.

Rina leaned close to him. "What kind of scanner is that?"

"It's a Bruet Scanner," said Kalin. "It's named after the Saleran who invented it. When it's used on this planet, it automatically hooks into the main frame of the Great Hall of Knowledge, which in turn amplifies its power. A normal scanner will decipher what Earth-humans call DNA but a Bruet Scanner will go further, breaking down the DNA all the way to when conception took place."

Justin corrected him. "This was a Bruet Scanner, now it's Verlean. Everything in the Great Hall was downloaded into it."

"Wow!" said Kalin, eyeing the device. "I want one."

"I already gave one to Marante, but I'll make one for you too."

"Thanks," said Kalin. "So why are you scanning Rina?"

The holo shifted to a minute gland deep within Rina's cerebellum. Shiro and Marante sat on the grass in front of them with big smiles on their faces.

This is really bad, she thought. Her stomach twisted into knots.

"I'll start at the beginning," said Justin. "Verlean-humans are just like Saleran-humans; we can't procreate outside our kind. As the head of the Research Department on Verlea, I began testing the secretions of over two thousand glands found in Verlean men and women. The female Alitary Gland was always thought to control passion and was so minute in mass, it had been overlooked in our studies. The hormone it secretes is called Proxium and does indeed contain the secrets to genetic reproduction. All the tests confirmed a slight increase in the output would allow female Verleans to procreate with any human race. Unfortunately, our test subjects were women older in age and we didn't get the results we wanted. Although a few Verlean women were able to reproduce outside our species, they bore children who couldn't, hence Saleran-humans."

Kalin instantly sat up straight. "What? Are you saying Salerans are descendants of Verleans?"

Rina felt as if her bottom jaw had hit the ground.

"Yes," said Justin, shifting his stare at Rina. "When the experiment failed, we decided to genetically alter a Verlean embryo within one week of conception. It was a complete success. Proxium levels in the patient would not increase until she passed the age of twenty-one, which is why I had to wait to tell you, Rina. I had to make sure it worked."

"Me?" said Rina, perturbed at the thought. "You experimented on me? Your only child?"

"I would never hurt my baby girl. DNA alteration is a simple procedure with no harm to the patient. The lives of Verlean-humans were becoming stagnant. Our society was falling into listlessness and the joy of living was slowly dwindling. Because of this, the High Council approved the procedure. Eliana, your Verlean mother, insisted her daughter be the first Verlean with this gift." He slid his finger through the holo.

"According to this, your Proxium is at its highest level and will remain there. You can now revive the Saleran and Verlean races."

Kalin's mouth went from an open gape to a wide smile. He jumped to his feet and shouted, "Yes!"

"Wait!" said Rina, raising her hand to stop him from jumping up and down. "Back up! Dad, are you saying I can have Saleran kids?"

"Yes, and true Salerans, right down to the DNA. You see, you have two wombs; one will carry our race and the other can carry the race of any known human. And your body will determine the gender, a trait we preserved from our Verlean chemistry."

"That's impossible," she said.

"Sweetheart," said Justin, "this is Verlean science and yes, it's possible. You're living proof."

"So how could she create a Verlean male without male chromosomes?" asked Shiro.

"When her Alitary gland was altered, we redesigned her future Verlean womb giving it the ability to create its own Verlean male DNA. Theoretically, the two should work together. Once her human womb conceives, her Verlean womb will also."

"Hold it! Are you saying every time I get pregnant I'm going to have twins?"

"Possibly, but we won't know for sure until it happens," said Justin. "You're a new species of Verlean, be proud of it, and I'm happy to say this is something you'll genetically pass on. Your children, male and female, will be able to multiply with any human.

However, our original Verlean females were only able to conceive every ten years, but only time will tell if this is the same for you."

Rina held her face, exasperated. "This is a nightmare."

"Your Verlean race will be rejuvenated too," said Shiro. "You can't pass that up."

"One Verlean and one Saleran," said Kalin, "sounds good to me."

Rina let her breath out in one whoosh and closed her eyes, trying to relax. Bringing back life to an empty planet was not in her future plans, yet it would be a sin to ignore it. Then there was the exciting reality of bringing back her race of Verleans. The regeneration of two species should be a privilege, *but it doesn't feel like one.* She gazed at the City of Light and imagined what it would look like filled with all sorts of humans living everyday life.

"It was beautiful," said Marante, his voice low in solemn respect, "the most beautiful city I had ever seen in my travels. Do you see this lifeless tree next to us?" he pointed, "and those about the city? They are Gebin Trees and were once filled with red, yellow, and blue leaves the size of what Earth-humans call Volkswagen Beetles. They are a special type of plant that thrives on Exomones, a scent secreted into the air when humans are content. Salera was such a peaceful world. There was no unhappiness here. For over five thousand years, the Gebin Trees flourished on Salera's joy until the unthinkable happened. Now they are asleep, waiting for life to return."

She sensed Marante's inner sadness. *Can I give up the rest of my life for Salera? For Verlea?* This real Kalin was mature, responsible and a definite hero, the kind you don't give up. He was talking to Marante, smiling and laughing, just beaming with joy. The whole idea was overwhelming, and she struggled to slow down her breathing. Her dad wrapped his arm around her shoulder, pulling her close and squeezing her tight.

"Relax, baby girl," he said. "No one is going to try to talk you into staying here except Kalin. However," he glanced at Kalin, "we know this is your choice, your life, and no one can demand that from you. Whatever you decide, I'll back you up one hundred percent. Take time to think about it. It's an important decision that only you can make."

"It's such a huge responsibility," she said, hearing her voice crack. "I'd...I'd have to give up my whole life and...."

"Wait," said Kalin, who quickly sat down beside her.

He pushed the hair away from her face and gently slid his fingers across her cheek.

His touch was warm and...*forever with him? How? I'd kill him.*

"Hear me out," he said. "I know we've had our differences in the past but there isn't anything that can't be resolved if we both work together. We're intelligent people, Rina, we know better."

Did he just actually make sense?

He continued, "And I also know the scientist in you is very much alive. It would be wrong on my part to hinder your love of learning, so I've just decided a tour of the galaxies is in order. After we're married, we'll take the *Quasar* and go wherever you want. You'll see astonishing things, meet hundreds of intelligent life forms that are so different, you'll wonder how they're alive at all. Ever been to a...what do Earth-humans call it...a...black hole?"

Her jaw hit the ground again.

"We can enter them," he said, "and yes, there are peaceful life forms living within these dark places. You'll be amazed at what they look like, but I'm not going to tell you; I'm going to show you. The point is, I will not suppress your love of knowledge. There's so much for you to see and if learning makes you happy, I'm good."

"A black hole?" said Shiro. "Holy cow."

Kalin smiled his perfect smile. He was content with his plans and she had to admit, his plans were good. Learning the technology on the Quasar alone would keep her busy for years but...*marriage?*

"Kalin, I'm not ready for marriage...I don't...I'm—" The right words weren't coming out and she felt stupid. Nothing in life had prepared her for this. She couldn't let it happen, so she stiffened up and crossed her arms over her chest. "Don't take this wrong, Kalin, but your careless ways with women is not going to work for me. What if we do hook up and you decide you want more? I can't and won't be the good little wife while you traipse around with other women. You'll land up dead and I'll be the one responsible for killing off the Saleran race."

"Is that what you're worried about?" he asked. "You searched my heart and the only woman you found in there was you. I can't even think of anyone else, never mind want to be with them. To me, all those other women don't exist anymore. No one can or will ever take your place. I'm yours forever."

"Wow," said Shiro. "Those are good words. I need to write this down." He whipped out a pen and pad from his pocket and started scribbling.

Uncertainty was still pounding inside her as she gazed into Kalin's eyes. Her probing revealed he was telling the truth, but it was hard to accept. *Could a womanizer actually fall in love and mean it?* His heart was telling her it was.

Kalin took her hand. "Stay with me, Rina. Be my wife. We'll think about kids later. Right now, I just want you."

"Hold on, Kalin," said Shiro. "You can't expect her to just jump into your arms, she's not in love with you. Rina has always been her own person, and this has to be done slowly. If you want her, you're going to have to work for her. Marriage will have to wait. End of story."

"Hear, hear," said Marante. "You are right, my friend. Patience, Kalin, and you will win her love."

Shiro had said exactly what she wanted to say and she wondered if he was empathic. Kalin was thinking hard, eyeing the two. She sensed his discontent. This was probably the first time he'd ever had to work for a woman's love.

"Love has to be mutual for a marriage to work," said Justin. "Rina needs time and you're going to give it to her if you want her as your wife."

"Is this how you feel?" asked Kalin.

"Yes," she said, grateful he was complying and not being

argumentative. "I'm willing to give you a chance and I say that with a crowbar in my hand. Don't blow it by wanting other women or it's over, and I'll know if you do."

Kalin glared at her. He was not happy.

"I can't believe that after all we've been through you still don't trust me. I trust you with all my heart, but what choice do I have? If I don't agree, I'll lose you forever and...," his voice softened, "I can't do that. It would kill me. So, yes, I'll agree with your decision even though it's upsetting."

"And furthermore," she said, "no sex before marriage."

Kalin's eyes opened wide. "What?" He jumped to his feet. "You're kidding, right?"

Kalin, said Justin. *I disconnected Rina from this telepathy because I want only you to hear this. Abstinence from sex before marriage is Verlean, a ruling inbred into all its citizens, male and female, to prevent unwanted diseases and the blatant misuse of another. It has worked for thousands of years, keeping our society clean and strong, and I'm grateful she can't change it. You'll just have to deal with it. I'm bringing her back in now."*

"You don't understand," said Kalin, his breathing sped up. "I've been having sex for over four hundred years and now you want me to just stop?"

"There are simple medications to assist you, my friend," said Marante, "and none will cause you any harm."

"Great," said Kalin, flustered by the comment as he plopped back down on the ground.

"What kind of medications?" asked Rina.

"There are hundreds of natural pharmaceuticals designed right here on Salera to lessen the sex drive at different levels," said Marante." He put his hand on Kalin's shoulder. "You will be fine, Prince Kalin, and your reward will be the repopulation of your world with the woman who will love you forever. A small price to pay for such happiness."

Kalin was still upset, but at least now he was breathing normally.

Marante always worked miracles.

"I don't like it," said Kalin, "but what choice do I have?" He turned to Rina. "You win. We'll do it your way."

"No one claimed it was going to be easy," said Justin, "but like Marante said, think of the future. It'll all be worth it."

Kalin asked in an aggrieved tone, "Is kissing allowed?"

"Absolutely," said Justin. "Just keep your pheromones in check. The saliva of a Verlean female is very powerful and one heavy kiss can send a man to his knees. I don't want my daughter to beat you up again, because she will."

Rina couldn't help a loud chuckle.

Kalin glared at her. "Can I be alone with Rina? We need to talk."

The men agreed and got to their feet. Marante tapped his Comlink and with a flash of light, the three teleported away. Kalin stood up and pulled her to standing. He held her waist and lifted her off the ground.

"I suppose you think you're in control now," he said.

"I've always been in control."

She threw her arms around him and kissed him hard. After a few seconds, he pushed her away, almost dropping her. He fell backward flat on his back, gasping for air.

"You okay?" she asked, pleased with the outcome, trying not to smile.

He waved his hand, signaling her to wait for his response. A cold sweat was dripping down the sides of his puffy red face.

Maybe I went too far, she thought, leaning down to examine him.

He quickly swung his body up to sit, frightening her, and she fell back on her rump.

"You just remember," he said between breaths, "I'm King and you'll do as I say. Just because I'm madly in love with you and you have the body of a goddess doesn't mean I'm going to let you rule."

"You're going to be the best King ever, but don't think I'm going to be at your beck and call, buddy. I won't be a slave to any man."

"With your right hook, how could any man survive making you a slave?"

They both laughed and rose to their feet. Kalin gently took hold of her face and kissed her. Tingles began swirling up her torso as he wrapped his arms around her. Warm sensations seemed to excite every gland in her body.

Does his saliva have power like mine?

She couldn't be sure but whatever it was, it was physical and he was causing it. He slowly ended their kiss.

"I'm so glad it's you," he said, holding her face, his lips quivering. Tears began forming in his eyes. "I'll be faithful, Rina Young. I promise."

"Yeah," she agreed. The effect of his kiss was still lingering, but *what the heck, it was great.* "I guess Salera's storm has been conquered."

He nodded in agreement then hugged her tight.

"I'm still a little concerned about the possibility of Vorkis being alive," he said, caressing her tight and stroking her hair, "but I will never allow him to control me again. I'll live my life my way and without him in it."

"Brave words spoken by a true hero. I strongly doubt he made it."

She levitated herself off the ground and wrapped her arms around his neck.

"You can levitate?" asked Kalin, looking down at her feet.

"Yeah, it's something I discovered yesterday; so how about another kiss without the aphrodisiac?"

"Anything you say. You rule."

As they embraced, giant red, yellow, and blue buds began sprouting on the branches of the nearby Gebin Tree.

~The End~